Interplanetary
Odysseys

THE COLLECTED SCIENCE FICTION & FANTASY
OF STANLEY G. WEINBAUM: VOLUME 1

Interplanetary
Odysseys

Classic Tales of Interplanetary Adventure
Including: *A Martian Odyssey*, its Sequel *Valley of
Dreams*, the Complete "Ham" Hammond Series
and Others

Stanley G. Weinbaum

LEONAUR

*Interplanetary Odysseys: Classic Tales of Interplanetary Adventure
Including: A Martian Odyssey, its Sequel Valley of Dreams,
the Complete "Ham" Hammond Series and Others*
by Stanley G. Weinbaum

FIRST EDITION

Published by Leonaur Ltd

Material original to this edition and this editorial selection
copyright © 2006 Leonaur Ltd

ISBN (10 digit): 1-84677-070-X (hardcover)
ISBN (13 digit): 978-1-84677-070-8 (hardcover)

ISBN (10 digit): 1-84677-060-2 (softcover)
ISBN (13 digit): 978-1-84677-060-9 (softcover)

http://www.leonaur.com

Publisher's Notes

In the interests of authenticity, the spellings, grammar and place names
used by the author have been retained.

The views expressed in this book are not necessarily
those of the publisher.

Contents

A Martian Odyssey

Jarvis stretched himself as luxuriously as he could in the cramped general quarters of the *Ares*.

'Air you can breathe,' he exulted. 'It feels as thick as soup after the thin stuff out there!' He nodded at the Martian landscape stretching flat and desolate in the light of the nearer moon, beyond the glass of the port.

The other three stared at him sympathetically—Putz, the engineer, Leroy, the biologist, and Harrison, the astronomer and captain of the expedition. Dick Jarvis was chemist of the famous crew, the *Ares* expedition, first human beings to set foot on the mysterious neighbor of the earth, the planet Mars. This, of course, was in the old days, less than twenty years after the mad American Doheny perfected the atomic blast at the cost of his life, and only a decade after the equally mad Cardoza rode on it to the moon. They were true pioneers, these four of the *Ares*. Except for a half-dozen moon expeditions and the ill-fated de Lancey flight aimed at the seductive orb of Venus, they were the first men to feel other gravity than earth's, and certainly the first successful crew to leave the earth-moon system. And they deserved that success when one considers the difficulties and discomforts—the months spent in acclimatization chambers back on earth, learning to breathe the air as tenuous as that of Mars, the challenging of the void in the tiny rocket driven by the cranky reaction motors of the twenty-first century, and mostly the facing of an absolutely unknown world.

Jarvis stretched and fingered the raw and peeling tip of his frost-bitten nose. He sighed again contentedly.

'Well,' exploded Harrison abruptly, 'are we going to hear what happened? You set out all shipshape in an auxiliary rocket, we don't get a peep for ten days, and finally Putz here picks you out of a lunatic ant-heap with a freak ostrich as your pal! Spill it, man!'

'Speel?' queried Leroy perplexedly. 'Speel what?'

'He means *'spiel'*,' explained Putz soberly. 'It iss to tell.'

Jarvis met Harrison's amused glance without the shadow of a smile. 'That's right, Karl,' he said in grave agreement with Putz. '*Ich spiel es!*' He grunted comfortably and began.

'According to orders,' he said, 'I watched Karl here take off toward the North, and then I got into my flying sweat-box and headed south. You'll remember, Cap—we had orders not to land, but just scout about for points of interest. I set the two cameras clicking and buzzed along, riding pretty high—about two thousand feet—for a couple of reasons. First, it gave the cameras a greater field, and second, the under-jets travel so far in this half-vacuum they call air here that they stir up dust if you move low.'

'We know all that from Putz,' grunted Harrison. 'I wish you'd saved the films, though. They'd have paid the cost of this junket; remember how the public mobbed the first moon pictures?'

'The films are safe,' retorted Jarvis. 'Well,' he resumed, 'as I said, I buzzed along at a pretty good clip; just as we figured, the wings haven't much lift in this air at less than a hundred miles per hour, and even then I had to use the under-jets.

'So, with the speed and the altitude and the blurring caused by the under-jets, the seeing wasn't any too good. I could see enough, though, to distinguish that what I sailed over was just more of this gray plain that we'd been examining the whole week since our landing—same blobby growths and the same eternal carpet of crawling little plant-animals, or biopods, as Leroy calls them. So I sailed along, calling back my position every hour as instructed, and not knowing whether you heard me.'

'I did!' snapped Harrison.

'A hundred and fifty miles south,' continued Jarvis imperturbably, 'the surface changed to a sort of low plateau, nothing but desert and orange-tinted sand. I figured that we were right in our guess, then, and this gray plain we dropped on was really the Mare Cimmerium which would make my orange desert the region called Xanthus. If I were right, I ought to hit another gray plain, the Mare Chronium in another couple of hundred miles, and then another orange desert, Thyle I or II. And so I did.'

'Putz verified our position a week and a half ago!' grumbled the captain. 'Let's get to the point.'

'Coming!' remarked Jarvis. 'Twenty miles into Thyle—believe it or not—I crossed a canal!'

'Putz photographed a hundred! Let's hear something new!'

'And did he also see a city?'

'Twenty of 'em, if you call those heaps of mud cities!'

'Well,' observed Jarvis, 'from here on I'll be telling a few things Putz didn't see!' He rubbed his tingling nose, and continued. 'I knew that I had sixteen hours of daylight at this season, so eight hours— eight hundred miles—from here, I decided to turn back. I was still over Thyle, whether I or II I'm not sure, not more than twenty-five miles into it. And right there, Putz's pet motor quit!'

'Quit? How?' Putz was solicitous.

'The atomic blast got weak. I started losing altitude right away, and suddenly there I was with a thump right in the middle of Thyle! Smashed my nose on the window, too!' He rubbed the injured member ruefully.

'Did you maybe try vashing der combustion chamber mit acid sulphuric?' inquired Putz. 'Sometimes der lead giffs a secondary radiation–'

'Naw!' said Jarvis disgustedly. 'I wouldn't try that, of course—not more than ten times! Besides, the bump flattened the landing gear and busted off the under-jets. Suppose I got the thing working— what then? Ten miles with the blast coming right out of the bottom and I'd have melted the floor from under me!' He rubbed his nose again. 'Lucky for me a pound only weighs seven ounces here, or I'd have been mashed flat!'

'I could have fixed!' Ejaculated the engineer. 'I bet it vas not serious.'

'Probably not,' agreed Jarvis sarcastically. 'Only it wouldn't fly. Nothing serious, but I had the choice of waiting to be picked up or trying to walk back—eight hundred miles, and perhaps twenty days before we had to leave! Forty miles a day! Well,' he concluded, 'I chose to walk. Just as much chance of being picked up, and it kept me busy.'

'We'd have found you,' said Harrison.

'No doubt. Anyway, I rigged up a harness from some seat straps, and put the water tank on my back, took a cartridge belt and re-volver, and some iron rations, and started out.'

'Water tank!' exclaimed the little biologist, Leroy. 'She weigh one-quarter ton!'

'Wasn't full. Weighed about two hundred and fifty pounds earth-weight, which is eighty-five here. Then, besides, my own personal two hundred and ten pounds is only seventy on Mars, so, tank and all, I grossed a hundred and fifty-five, or fifty-five pounds less than my everyday earthweight. I figured on that when I undertook the forty-mile daily stroll. Oh—of course I took a thermo-skin sleeping bag for these wintry Martian nights.

'Off I went, bouncing along pretty quickly. Eight hours of daylight meant twenty miles or more. It got tiresome, of course—plugging along over a soft sand desert with nothing to see, not even Leroy's crawling biopods. But an hour or so brought me to the canal—just a dryditch about four hundred feet wide, and straight as a railroad on its own company map.

'There'd been water in it sometime, though. The ditch was covered with what looked like a nice green lawn. Only, as I approached, the lawn moved out of my way!'

'Eh?' said Leroy.

'Yeah, it was a relative of your biopods. I caught one, a little grasslike blade about as long as my finger, with two thin, stemmy legs.'

'He is where?' Leroy was eager.

'He is let go! I had to move, so I plowed along with the walking grass opening in front and closing behind. And then I was out on the orange desert of Thyle again.

'I plugged steadily along, cussing the sand that made going so tiresome, and, incidentally, cussing that cranky motor of yours, Karl. It was just before twilight that I reached the edge of Thyle, and looked down over the gray Mare Chronium. And I knew there was seventy-five miles of *that* to be walked over, and then a couple of hundred miles of that Xanthus desert, and about as much more Mare Cimmerium. Was I pleased? I started cussing you fellows for not picking me up!'

'We were trying, you sap!' said Harrison.

'That didn't help. Well, I figured I might as well use what was left of daylight in getting down the cliff that bounded Thyle. I found an easy place, and down I went. Mare Chronium was just the same sort of place as this—crazy leafless plants and a bunch of crawlers; I gave it a glance and hauled out my sleeping bag. Up to that time, you know, I hadn't seen anything worth worrying about on this half-dead world—nothing dangerous, that is.'

10

'Did you?' queried Harrison.

'*Did* I! You'll hear about it when I come to it. Well, I was just about to turn in when suddenly I heard the wildest sort of shenanigans!'

'Vot iss shenanigans?' inquired Putz.

'He says, '*Je ne sais quoi*',' explained Leroy. 'It is to say, 'I don't know what'.'

'That's right,' agreed Jarvis. 'I didn't know what, so I sneaked over to find out. There was a racket like a flock of crows eating a bunch of canaries—whistles, cackles, caws, trills, and what have you. I rounded a clump of stumps, and there was Tweel!'

'Tweel?' said Harrison, and 'Tweel?' said Leroy and Putz.

'That freak ostrich,' explained the narrator. 'At least, Tweel is as near as I can pronounce it without sputtering. He called it something like 'Trrrweerrll!'.'

'What was he doing?' asked the captain.

'He was being eaten! And squealing, of course, as any one would.'

'Eaten! By what?'

'I found out later. All I could see then was a bunch of black ropy arms tangled around what looked like, as Putz described it to you, an ostrich. I wasn't going to interfere, naturally; if both creatures were dangerous, I'd have one less to worry about.

'But the bird-like thing was putting up a good battle, dealing vicious blows with an eighteen-inch beak, between screeches. And besides, I caught a glimpse or two of what was on the end of those arms!' Jarvis shuddered. 'But the clincher was when I noticed a little black bag or case hung about the neck of the bird-thing! It was intelligent. That or tame, I assumed. Anyway, it clinched my decision. I pulled out my automatic and fired into what I could see of its antagonist.

'There was a flurry of tentacles and a spurt of black corruption, and then the thing, with a disgusting sucking noise, pulled itself and its arms into a hole in the ground. The other let out a series of clacks, staggered around on legs about as thick as golf sticks, and turned suddenly to face me. I held my weapon ready, and the two of us stared at each other.

'The Martian wasn't a bird, really. It wasn't even bird-like, except just at first glance. It had a beak all right, and a few feathery appendages, but the beak wasn't really a beak. It was somewhat flexible; I could see the tip bend slowly from side to side; it was almost like a cross between a beak and a trunk. It had four-toed feet, and four-fingered things—hands, you'd have to call them, and a little roundish body, and a long neck ending in a tiny head—and that beak. It stood an inch or so taller than I, and—well, Putz saw it!'

The engineer nodded. 'Ja! I saw!'

Jarvis continued. 'So—we stared at each other. Finally the creature went into a series of clackings and twitterings and held out its hands toward me, empty. I took that as a gesture of friendship.'

'Perhaps,' suggested Harrison, 'it looked at that nose of yours and thought you were its brother!'

'Huh! You can be funny without talking! Anyway, I put up my gun and said 'Aw, don't mention it,' or something of the sort, and the thing came over and we were pals.

'By that time, the sun was pretty low and I knew that I'd better build a fire or get into my thermo-skin. I decided on the fire. I picked a spot at the base of the Thyle cliff where the rock could reflect a little heat on my back. I started breaking off chunks of this desiccated Martian vegetation, and my companion caught the idea and brought in an armful. I reached for a match, but the Martian fished into his pouch and brought out something that looked like a glowing coal; one touch of it, and the fire was blazing—and you all know what a job we have starting a fire in this atmosphere!

'And that bag of his!' continued the narrator. 'That was a manu-factured article, my friends; press an end and she popped open—press the middle and she sealed so perfectly you couldn't see the line. Better than zippers.

'Well, we stared at the fire for a while and I decided to attempt some sort of communication with the Martian. I pointed at myself and said 'Dick'; he caught the drift immediately, stretched a bony claw at me and repeated 'Tick.' Then I pointed at him, and he gave that whistle I called Tweel; I can't imitate his accent. Things were going smoothly; to emphasize the names, I repeated 'Dick,' and then, pointing at him, 'Tweel.'

'There we stuck! He gave some clacks that sounded negative, and said something like 'P-p-p-root.' And that was just the beginning; I was always 'Tick,' but as for him—part of the time he was 'Tweel,' and part of the time he was 'P-p-p-proot,' and part of the time he was sixteen other noises!

'We just couldn't connect. I tried 'rock,' and I tried 'star,' and 'tree,' and 'fire.' and Lord knows what else, and try as I would, I couldn't get a single word! Nothing was the same for two successive minutes, and if that's a language, I'm an alchemist. Finally I gave it up and called him Tweel, and that seemed to do.

'But Tweel hung on to some of my words. He remembered a couple of them, which I suppose is a great achievement if you're used to a language you have to make up as you go along. But I couldn't get the hang of his talk; either I missed some subtle point or we just didn't *think* alike—and I rather believe the latter view.

'I've other reasons for believing that. After a while I gave up the language business, and tried mathematics. I scratched two plus two equals four on the ground, and demonstrated it with pebbles. Again Tweel caught the idea, and informed me that three plus three equals six. Once more we seemed to be getting somewhere.

'So, knowing that Tweel had at least a grammar school education, I drew a circle for the sun, pointing first at it, and then at the last glow of the sun. Then I sketched in Mercury, and Venus, and Mother Earth, and Mars, and finally, pointing to Mars, I swept my hand around in a sort of inclusive gesture to indicate that Mars was our current environment. I was working up to putting over the idea that my home was on the earth.

'Tweel understood my diagram all right. He poked his beak at it, and with a great deal of trilling and clucking, he added Deimos and Phobos to Mars, and then sketched in the earth's moon!

'Do you see what that proves? It proves that Tweel's race uses telescopes—that they're civilized!'

'Does not!' snapped Harrison. 'The moon is visible from here as a fifth magnitude star. They could see its revolution with the naked eye.'

'The moon, yes!' said Jarvis. 'You've missed my point. Mercury isn't visible! And Tweel knew of Mercury because he placed the Moon at the *third* planet, not the second. If he didn't know Mercury, he'd put the earth second, and Mars third, instead of fourth! See?'

'Humph!' said Harrison.

'Anyway,' proceeded Jarvis, 'I went on with my lesson. Things were going smoothly, and it looked as if I could put the idea over. I pointed at the earth on my diagram, and then at myself, and then, to clinch it, I pointed to myself and then to the earth itself shining bright green almost at the zenith.

'Tweel set up such an excited clacking that I was certain he understood. He jumped up and down, and suddenly he pointed at himself and then at the sky, and then at himself and at the sky again. He pointed at his middle and then at Arcturus, at his head and then at Spica, at his feet and then at half a dozen stars, while I just gaped at him. Then, all of a sudden, he gave a tremendous leap. Man, what a hop! He shot straight up into the starlight, seventy-five feet if an inch! I saw him silhouetted against the sky, saw him turn and come down at me head first, and land smack on his beak like a javelin! There he stuck square in the center of my sun-circle in the sand—a bull's eye!'

'Nuts!' observed the captain. 'Plain nuts!'

'That's what I thought, too! I just stared at him openmouthed while he pulled his head out of the sand and stood up. Then I figured he'd missed my point, and I went through the whole blamed rigmarole again, and it ended the same way, with Tweel on his nose in the middle of my picture!'

'Maybe it's a religious rite,' suggested Harrison.

'Maybe,' said Jarvis dubiously. 'Well, there we were. We could exchange ideas up to a certain point, and then—blooey! Something in us was different, unrelated; I don't doubt that Tweel thought me just as screwy as I thought him. Our minds simply looked at the world from different viewpoints, and perhaps his viewpoint is as true as ours. But—we couldn't get together, that's all. Yet, in spite of all difficulties, I *liked* Tweel, and I have a queer certainty that he liked me.'

'Nuts!' repeated the captain. 'Just daffy!'

'Yeah? Wait and see. A couple of times I've thought that perhaps we—' He paused, and then resumed his narrative. 'Anyway, I finally gave it up, and got into my thermo-skin to sleep. The fire hadn't kept me any too warm, but that damned sleeping bag did. Got stuffy five minutes after I closed myself in. I opened it a little and bingo! Some eighty-below-zero air hit my nose, and that's when I got this pleasant little frostbite to add to the bump I acquired during the crash of my rocket.

'I don't know what Tweel made of my sleeping. He sat around, but when I woke up, he was gone. I'd just crawled out of my bag, though, when I heard some twittering, and there he came, sailing down from that three-story Thyle cliff to alight on his beak beside me. I pointed to myself and toward the north, and he pointed at himself and toward the south, and when I loaded up and started away, he came along.

'Man, how he traveled! A hundred and fifty feet at a jump, sailing through the air stretched out like a spear, and landing on his beak. He seemed surprised at my plodding, but after a few moments he fell in beside me, only every few minutes he'd go into one of his leaps, and stick his nose into the sand a block ahead of me. Then he'd come shooting back at me; it made me nervous at first to see that beak of his coming at me like a spear, but he always ended in the sand at my side.

'So the two of us plugged along across the Mare Chronium. Same sort of place as this—same crazy plants and same little green biopods growing in the sand, or crawling out of your way. We talked—not that we understood each other, you know, but just for company. I sang songs, and I suspected Tweel did too; at least, some of his trillings and twitterings had a subtle sort of rhythm.

'Then, for variety, Tweel would display his smattering of English words. He'd point to an outcropping and say 'rock,' and point to a pebble and say it again; or he'd touch my arm and say 'Tick,' and then repeat it. He seemed terrifically amused that the same word meant the same thing twice in succession, or that the same word could apply to two different objects. It set me wondering if perhaps his language wasn't like the primitive speech of some earth people— you know, Captain, like the Negritoes, for instance, who haven't any generic words. No word for food or water or man—words for good food and bad food, or rainwater and seawater, or strong man and weak man—but no names for general classes. They're too primitive to understand that rain water and seawater are just different aspects of the same thing. But that wasn't the case with Tweel; it was just that we were somehow mysteriously different—our minds were alien to each other. And yet—we *liked* each other!'

'Looney, that's all,' remarked Harrison. 'That's why you two were so fond of each other.'

15

'Well, I like you!' countered Jarvis wickedly. 'Anyway,' he resumed, 'don't get the idea that there was anything screwy about Tweel. In fact, I'm not so sure but that he couldn't teach our highly praised human intelligence a trick or two. Oh, he wasn't an intellectual superman, I guess; but don't overlook the point that he managed to understand a little of my mental workings, and I never even got a glimmering of his.'

'Because he didn't have any!' suggested the captain, while Putz and Leroy blinked attentively.

'You can judge of that when I'm through,' said Jarvis. 'Well, we plugged along across the Mare Chronium all that day, and all the next. Mare Chronium—Sea of Time! Say, I was willing to agree with Schiaparelli's name by the end of that march! Just that gray, endless plain of weird plants, and never a sign of any other life. It was so monotonous that I was even glad to see the desert of Xanthus toward the evening of the second day.

'I was fair worn out, but Tweel seemed as fresh as ever, for all I never saw him drink or eat. I think he could have crossed the Mare Chronium in a couple of hours with those block-long nosedives of his, but he stuck along with me. I offered him some water once or twice; he took the cup from me and sucked the liquid into his beak, and then carefully squirted it all back into the cup and gravely returned it.

'Just as we sighted Xanthus, or the cliffs that bounded it, one of those nasty sand clouds blew along, not as bad as the one we had here, but mean to travel against. I pulled the transparent flap of my thermo-skin bag across my face and managed pretty well, and I noticed that Tweel used some feathery appendages growing like a mustache at the base of his beak to cover his nostrils, and some similar fuzz to shield his eyes.'

'He is a desert creature,' ejaculated the little biologist, Leroy.

'Huh? Why?'

'He drink no water—he is adapt' for sand storm—'

'Proves nothing! There's not enough water to waste anywhere on this desiccated pill called Mars. We'd call all of it desert on earth, you know.' He paused. 'Anyway, after the sand storm blew over, a little wind kept blowing in our faces, not strong enough to stir the sand. But suddenly things came drifting along from the

Xanthus cliffs—small, transparent spheres, for all the world like glass tennis balls! But light—they were almost light enough to float even in this thin air—empty, too; at least, I cracked open a couple and nothing came out but a bad smell. I asked Tweel about them, but all he said was 'No, no, no,' which I took to mean that he knew nothing about them. So they went bouncing by like tumbleweeds, or like soap bubbles, and we plugged on toward Xanthus. Tweel pointed at one of the crystal balls once and said 'rock,' but I was too tired to argue with him. Later I discovered what he meant.

'We came to the bottom of the Xanthus cliffs finally, when there wasn't much daylight left. I decided to sleep on the plateau if possible; anything dangerous, I reasoned, would be more likely to prowl through the vegetation of the Mare Chronium than the sand of Xanthus. Not that I'd seen a single sign of menace, except the rope-armed black thing that had trapped Tweel, and apparently that didn't prowl at all, but lured its victims within reach. It couldn't lure me while I slept, especially as Tweel didn't seem to sleep at all, but simply sat patiently around all night. I wondered how the creature had managed to trap Tweel, but there wasn't any way of asking him. I found that out too, later; it's devilish!

'However, we were ambling around the base of the Xanthus barrier looking for an easy spot to climb. At least, I was! Tweel could have leaped it easily, for the cliffs were lower than Thyle—perhaps sixty feet. I found a place and started up, swearing at the water tank strapped to my back—it didn't bother me except when climbing—and suddenly I heard a sound that I thought I recognized!

'You know how deceptive sounds are in this thin air. A shot sounds like the pop of a cork. But this sound was the drone of a rocket, and sure enough, there went our second auxiliary about ten miles to westward, between me and the sunset!'

'Vas me!' said Putz. 'I hunt for you.'

'Yeah; I knew that, but what good did it do me? I hung on to the cliff and yelled and waved with one hand. Tweel saw it too, and set up a trilling and twittering, leaping to the top of the barrier and then high into the air. And while I watched, the machine droned on into the shadows to the south.

'I scrambled to the top of the cliff. Tweel was still pointing and trilling excitedly, shooting up toward the sky and coming down head-on to stick upside down on his back in the sand. I pointed toward the south, and at myself, and he said, 'Yes—Yes—Yes'; but somehow I gathered that he thought the flying thing was a relative of mine, probably a parent. Perhaps I did his intellect an injustice; I think now that I did.

'I was bitterly disappointed by the failure to attract attention. I pulled out my thermo-skin and crawled into it, as the night chill was already apparent. Tweel stuck his beak into the sand and drew up his legs and arms and looked for all the world like one of those leafless shrubs out there. I think he stayed that way all night.'

'Protective mimicry!' ejaculated Leroy. 'See? He is desert creature!'

'In the morning,' resumed Jarvis, 'we started off again. We hadn't gone a hundred yards into Xanthus when I saw something queer! This is one thing Putz didn't photograph, I'll wager!

'There was a line of little pyramids—tiny ones, not more than six inches high, stretching across Xanthus as far as I could see! Little buildings made of pygmy bricks, they were, hollow inside and truncated, or at least broken at the top and empty. I pointed at them and said 'What?' to Tweel, but he gave some negative twitters to indicate, I suppose, that he didn't know. So off we went, following the row of pyramids because they ran north, and I was going north.

'Man, we trailed that line for hours! After a while, I noticed another queer thing: they were getting larger. Same number of bricks in each one, but the bricks were larger.

'By noon they were shoulder high. I looked into a couple—all just the same, broken at the top and empty. I examined a brick or two as well; they were silica, and old as creation itself!'

'They were weathered—edges rounded. Silica doesn't weather easily even on earth, and in this climate!'

'How old you think?'

'Fifty thousands hundred thousand years. How can I tell? The little ones we saw in the morning were older—perhaps ten times as old. Crumbling. How old would that make *them?* Half a million years? Who knows?' Jarvis paused a moment. 'Well,' he resumed, 'we followed the line. Tweel pointed at them and said 'rock' once or twice, but he'd done that many times before. Besides, he was more or less right about these.

'I tried questioning him. I pointed at a pyramid and asked 'People?' and indicated the two of us. He set up a negative sort of clucking and said, 'No, no, no. No one—one—two. No two—two—four,' meanwhile rubbing his stomach. I just stared at him and he went through the business again. 'No one—one—two. No two—two—four.' I just gaped at him. '

'That proves it!' exclaimed Harrison. 'Nuts!'

'You think so?' queried Jarvis sardonically. 'Well, I figured it out different! 'No one—one—two!' You don't get it, of course, do you?'

'Nope—nor do you!'

'I think I do! Tweel was using the few English words he knew to put over a very complex idea. What, let me ask, does mathematics make you think of?'

'Why—of astronomy. Or—or logic!'

'That's it! 'No one—one—two!' Tweel was telling me that the builders of the pyramids weren't people—or that they weren't intelligent, that they weren't reasoning creatures! Get it?'

'Huh! I'll be damned!'

'You probably will.'

'Why,' put in Leroy, 'he rub his belly?'

'Why? Because, my dear biologist, that's where his brains are! Not in his tiny head—in his middle!'

'*C'est* impossible!'

'Not on Mars, it isn't! This flora and fauna aren't earthly; your biopods prove that!' Jarvis grinned and took up his narrative. 'Anyway, we plugged along across Xanthus and in about the middle of the afternoon, something else queer happened. The pyramids ended.'

'Ended!'

'Yeah; the queer part was that the last one and now they were ten-footers—was capped! See? Whatever built it was still inside; we'd trailed 'em from their half-million-year-old origin to the present.

'Tweel and I noticed it about the same time. I yanked out my automatic (I had a clip of Boland explosive bullets in it) and Tweel, quick as a sleight-of-hand trick, snapped a queer little glass revolver out of his bag. It was much like our weapons, except that the grip was larger to accommodate his four-taloned hand. And we held our weapons ready while we sneaked up along the lines of empty pyramids.

'Tweel saw the movement first. The top tiers of bricks were heaving, shaking, and suddenly slid down the sides with a thin crash. And then—something—something was coming out!

'A long, silvery-gray arm appeared, dragging after it an armored body. Armored, I mean, with scales, silver-gray and dull-shining. The arm heaved the body out of the hole; the beast crashed to the sand.

'It was a nondescript creature—body like a big gray cask, arm and a sort of mouth-hole at one end; stiff, pointed tail at the other—and that's all. No other limbs, no eyes, ears, nose—nothing! The thing dragged itself a few yards, inserted its pointed tail in the sand, pushed itself upright, and just sat.

'Tweel and I watched it for ten minutes before it moved. Then, with a creaking and rustling like—oh, like crumpling stiff paper—its arm moved to the mouth-hole and out came a brick! The arm placed the brick carefully on the ground, and the thing was still again.

'Another ten minutes—another brick. Just one of Nature's brick-layers. I was about to slip away and move on when Tweel pointed at the thing and said 'rock'! I went 'huh?' and he said it again. Then, to the accompaniment of some of his trilling, he said, 'No—no—' and gave two or three whistling breaths.

'Well, I got his meaning, for a wonder! I said, 'No breathe!' and demonstrated the word. Tweel was ecstatic; he said, 'Yes, yes, yes! No, no, no breet!' Then he gave a leap and sailed out to land on his nose about one pace from the monster!

'I was startled, you can imagine! The arm was going up for a brick, and I expected to see Tweel caught and mangled, but—nothing happened! Tweel pounded on the creature, and the arm took the brick and placed it neatly beside the first. Tweel rapped on its body again, and said 'rock,' and I got up nerve enough to take a look myself.

'Tweel was right again. The creature *was* rock, and it didn't breathe!'

'How you know?' snapped Leroy, his black eyes blazing interest.

'Because I'm a chemist. The beast was made of silica! There must have been pure silicon in the sand, and it lived on that. Get it? We, and Tweel, and those plants out there, and even the biopods are *carbon* life; this thing lived by a different set of chemical reactions. It was silicon life!'

'*La vie silicieuse!*' shouted Leroy. 'I have suspect, and now it is proof! I must go see! *Il faut que je—*'

'All right! All right!' said Jarvis. 'You can go see. Anyhow, there the thing was, alive and yet not alive, moving every ten minutes, and then only to remove a brick. Those bricks were its waste matter. See, Frenchy? We're carbon, and our waste is carbon dioxide, and this thing is silicon and *its* waste is silicon dioxide—silica. But silica is a solid, hence the bricks. And it builds itself in, and when it is covered, it moves over to a fresh place to start over. No wonder it creaked! A living creature a half a million years old!'

'How you know how old?' Leroy was frantic.

'We trailed its pyramids from the beginning, didn't we? If this weren't the original pyramid builder, the series would have ended somewhere before we found him, wouldn't it?—ended and started over with the small ones. That's simple enough, isn't it?

'But he reproduces, or tries to. Before the third brick came out, there was a little rustle and out popped a whole stream of those little crystal balls. They're his spores, or seeds—call 'em what you want. They went bouncing by across Xanthus just as they'd bounced by us back in the Mare Chronium. I've a hunch how they work, too—this is for your information, Leroy. I think the crystal shell of silica is no more than protective covering, like an eggshell, and that the active principle is the smell inside. It's some sort of gas that attacks silicon, and if the shell is broken near a supply of that element, some reaction starts that ultimately develops into a beast like that one.'

'You should try!' exclaimed the little Frenchman. 'We must break one to see!'

'Yeah? Well, I did. I smashed a couple against the sand. Would you like to come back in about ten thousand years to see if I planted some pyramid monsters? You'd most likely be able to tell by that time!' Jarvis paused and drew a deep breath. 'Lord! That queer creature Do you picture it? Blind, deaf, nerveless, brainless—just a mechanism, and yet—immortal Bound to go on making bricks, building pyramids, as long as silicon and oxygen exist, and even afterwards it'll just stop. It won't be dead. If the accidents of a million years bring it its food again, there it'll be, ready to run again, while brains and civilizations are part of the past. A queer beast—yet I met a stranger one!'

'If you did, it must have been in your dreams!' growled Harrison.

'You're right!' said Jarvis soberly. 'In a way, you're right. The dream-beast! That's the best name for it—and it's the most fiendish, terrifying creation one could imagine! More dangerous than a lion, more insidious than a snake!'

'Tell me!' begged Leroy. 'I must go see!'

'Not *this* devil!' He paused again. 'Well,' he resumed, 'Tweel and I left the pyramid creature and plowed along through Xanthus. I was tired and a little disheartened by Putz's failure to pick me up, and Tweel's trilling got on my nerves, as did his flying nosedives. So I just strode along without a word, hour after hour across that monotonous desert.

'Toward mid-afternoon we came in sight of a low dark line on the horizon. I knew what it was. It was a canal; I'd crossed it in the rocket and it meant that we were just one-third of the way across Xanthus. Pleasant thought, wasn't it? And still, I was keeping up to schedule.

'We approached the canal slowly; I remembered that this one was bordered by a wide fringe of vegetation and that Mudheap City was on it.

'I was tired, as I said. I kept thinking of a good hot meal, and then from that I jumped to reflections of how nice and home-like even Borneo would seem after this crazy planet, and from that, to thoughts of little old New York, and then to thinking about a girl I know there, Fancy Long. Know her?'

'Vision entertainer,' said Harrison. 'I've tuned her in. Nice blonde—dances and sings on the *Yerba Mate* hour.'

'That's her,' said Jarvis ungrammatically. 'I know her pretty well—just friends, get me?—though she came down to see us off in the *Ares*. Well, I was thinking about her, feeling pretty lonesome, and all the time we were approaching that line of rubbery plants.

'And then—I said, 'What 'n Hell!' and stared. And there she was—Fancy Long, standing plain as day under one of those crackbrained trees, and smiling and waving just the way I remembered her when we left!'

'Now you're nuts, too!' observed the captain.

'Boy, I almost agreed with you! I stared and pinched myself and closed my eyes and then stared again—and every time, there was Fancy Long smiling and waving! Tweel saw something, too; he was trilling and clucking away, but I scarcely heard him. I was bounding toward her over the sand, too amazed even to ask myself questions.

'I wasn't twenty feet from her when Tweel caught me with one of his flying leaps. He grabbed my arm, yelling, 'No—no—no!' in his squeaky voice. I tried to shake him off—he was as light as if he were built of bamboo—but he dug his claws in and yelled. And finally some sort of sanity returned to me and I stopped less than ten feet from her. There she stood, looking as solid as Putz's head!'

'Vot?' said the engineer.

'She smiled and waved, and waved and smiled, and I stood there dumb as Leroy, while Tweel squeaked and chattered. I *knew* it couldn't be real, yet—there she was!

'Finally I said, 'Fancy! Fancy Long!' She just kept on smiling and waving, but looking as real as if I hadn't left her thirty-seven million miles away.

'Tweel had his glass pistol out, pointing it at her. I grabbed his arm, but he tried to push me away. He pointed at her and said, 'No breet! No breet!' and I understood that he meant that the Fancy Long thing wasn't alive.

'Man, my head was whirling!

'Still, it gave me the jitters to see him pointing his weapon at her. I don't know why I stood there watching him take careful aim, but I did. Then he squeezed the handle of his weapon; there was a little puff of steam, and Fancy Long was gone! And in her place was one of those writhing, black rope-armed horrors like the one I'd saved Tweel from!

'The dream-beast! I stood there dizzy, watching it die while Tweel trilled and whistled. Finally he touched my arm, pointed at the twisting thing, and said, 'You one—one—two, he one—one—two.' After he'd repeated it eight or ten times, I got it. Do any of you?'

'Oui,' shrilled Leroy. '*Moi—je le comprends!* He mean you think of something, the beast he know, and you see it! *Un chien*—a hungry dog, he would see the big bone with meat! Or smell it—not?'

'Right!' said Jarvis. 'The dream-beast uses its victim's longings and desires to trap its prey. The bird at nesting season would see its mate, the fox, prowling for its own prey, would see a helpless rabbit!'

'How he do?' queried Leroy.

'How do I know? How does a snake back on earth charm a bird

into its very jaws? And aren't there deep-sea fish that lure their victims into their mouths? Lord!' Jarvis shuddered. 'Do you see how insidious the monster is? We're warned now—but henceforth we can't trust even our eyes. You might see me—I might see one of you—and back of it may be nothing but another of those black horrors!'

'How'd your friend know?' asked the captain abruptly.

'Tweel? I wonder! Perhaps he was thinking of something that couldn't possibly have interested me, and when I started to run, he realized that I saw something different and was warned. Or perhaps the dream-beast can only project a single vision, and Tweel saw what I saw—or nothing. I couldn't ask him. But it's just another proof that his intelligence is equal to ours or greater.'

'He's daffy, I tell you!' said Harrison. 'What makes you think his intellect ranks with the human?'

'Plenty of things! First the pyramid-beast. He hadn't seen one before; he said as much. Yet he recognized it as a dead-alive automaton of silicon.'

'He could have heard of it,' objected Harrison. 'He lives around here, you know.'

'Well how about the language? I couldn't pick up a single idea of his and he learned six or seven words of mine. And do you realize what complex ideas he put over with no more than those six or seven words? The pyramid monster—the dream-beast! In a single phrase he told me that one was a harmless automaton and the other a deadly hypnotist. What about that?'

'Huh!' said the captain.

'*Huh* if you wish! Could you have done it knowing only six words of English? Could you go even further, as Tweel did, and tell me that another creature was of a sort of intelligence so different from ours that understanding was impossible—even more impossible than that between Tweel and me?'

'Eh? What was that?'

'Later. The point I'm making is that Tweel and his race are worthy of our friendship. Somewhere on Mars—and you'll find I'm right—is a civilization and culture equal to ours, and maybe more than equal. And communication is possible between them and us; Tweel proves that. It may take years of patient trial, for their minds are alien, but less alien than the next minds we encountered—if they *are* minds.'

'The next ones? What next ones?'

'The people of the mud cities along the canals.' Jarvis frowned, then resumed his narrative. 'I thought the dream-beast and the silicon-monster were the strangest beings conceivable, but I was wrong. These creatures are still more alien, less understandable than either and far less comprehensible than Tweel, with whom friendship is possible, and even, by patience and concentration, the exchange of ideas.

'Well,' he continued, 'we left the dream-beast dying, dragging itself back into its hole, and we moved toward the canal. There was a carpet of that queer walking-grass scampering out of our way, and when we reached the bank, there was a yellow trickle of water flowing. The mound city I'd noticed from the rocket was a mile or so to the right and I was curious enough to want to take a look at it.

'It had seemed deserted from my previous glimpse of its and if any creatures were lurking in it—well, Tweel and I were both armed. And by the way, that crystal weapon of Tweel's was an interesting device; I took a look at it after the dream-beast episode. It fired a little glass splinter, poisoned, I suppose, and I guess it held at least a hundred of 'em to a load. The propellant was steam—just plain steam!'

'Shteam!' echoed Putz. 'From vot come, shteam?'

'From water, of course! You could see the water through the transparent handle and about a gill of another liquid, thick and yellowish. When Tweel squeezed the handle there was no trigger—a drop of water and a drop of the yellow stuff squirted into the firing chamber, and the water vaporized—*pop!*—like that. It's not so difficult; I think we could develop the same principle. Concentrated sulfuric acid will heat water almost to boiling, and so will quicklime, and there's potassium and sodium—

'Of course, his weapon hadn't the range of mine, but it wasn't so bad in this thin air, and it *did* hold as many shots as a cowboy's gun in a Western movie. It was effective, too, at least against Martian life; I tried it out, aiming at one of the crazy plants, and darned if the plant didn't wither up and fall apart! That's why I think the glass splinters were poisoned.

'Anyway, we trudged along toward the mud-heap city and I began to wonder whether the city builders dug the canals. I pointed to the city and then at the canal, and Tweel said 'No—no—no!' and gestured toward the south. I took it to mean that some other race had created the canal system, perhaps Tweel's people. I don't know; maybe there's still another intelligent race on the planet, or a dozen others. Mars is a queer little world.

'A hundred yards from the city we crossed a sort of road—just a hard-packed mud trail, and then, all of a sudden, along came one of the mound builders!

'Man, talk about fantastic beings! It looked rather like a barrel trotting along on four legs with four other arms or tentacles. It had no head, just body and members and a row of eyes completely around it. The top end of the barrel-body was a diaphragm stretched as tight as a drumhead, and that was all. It was pushing a little coppery cart and tore right past us like the proverbial bat out of Hell. It didn't even notice us, although I thought the eyes on my side shifted a little as it passed.

'A moment later another came along, pushing another empty cart. Same thing—it just scooted past us. Well, I wasn't going to be ignored by a bunch of barrels playing train, so when the third one approached, I planted myself in the way—ready to jump, of course, if the thing didn't stop.

'But it did. It stopped and set up a sort of drumming from the diaphragm on top. And I held out both hands and said, 'We are friends!' And what do you suppose the thing did?'

'Said, 'Pleased to meet you,' I'll bet!' suggested Harrison.

'I couldn't have been more surprised if it had! It drummed on its diaphragm, and then suddenly boomed out, 'We are v-r-r-iends' and gave its pushcart a vicious poke at me! I jumped aside, and away it went while I stared dumbly after it.

'A minute later another one came hurrying along. This one didn't pause, but simply drummed out, 'We are v-r-r-iends!' and scurried by. How did it learn the phrase? Were all of the creatures in some sort of communication with each other? Were they all parts of some central organism? I don't know, though I think Tweel does.

'Anyway, the creatures went sailing past us, every one greeting us with the same statement. It got to be funny; I never thought to find so many friends on this Godforsaken ball! Finally I made a puzzled gesture to Tweel; I guess he understood, for he said, 'One—one—two—yes! Two—two—four—no!' Get it?'

'Sure,' said Harrison. 'It's a Martian nursery rhyme.'

'Yeah! Well, I was getting used to Tweel's symbolism, and I figured it out this way. 'One—one—two—yes!' The creatures were intelligent. 'Two—two—four—no!' Their intelligence was not of our order, but something different and beyond the logic of two and two is four. Maybe I missed his meaning. Perhaps he meant that their minds were of low degree, able to figure out the simple things. 'One—one—two—yes!—but not more difficult things—Two—two—four—no!' But I think from what we saw later that he meant the other.

'After a few moments, the creatures came rushing back—first one, then another. Their pushcarts were full of stones, sand, chunks of rubbery plants, and such rubbish as that. They droned out their friendly greeting, which didn't really sound so friendly, and dashed on. The third one I assumed to be my first acquaintance and I decided to have another chat with him. I stepped into his path again and waited.

'Up he came, booming out his 'We are v-r-r-riends' and stopped. I looked at him; four or five of his eyes looked at me. He tried his password again and gave a shove on his cart, but I stood firm. And then the—the dashed creature reached out one of his arms, and two finger-like nippers tweaked my nose!'

'Haw!' roared Harrison. 'Maybe the things have a sense of beauty!'

'Laugh!' grumbled Jarvis. 'I'd already had a nasty bump and a mean frostbite on that nose. Anyway, I yelled 'Ouch!' and jumped aside and the creature dashed away; but from then on, their greeting was 'We are v-r-r-riends! Ouch!' Queer beasts!

'Tweel and I followed the road squarely up to the nearest mound. The creatures were coming and going, paying us not the slightest attention, fetching their loads of rubbish. The road simply dived into an opening, and slanted down like an old mine, and in and out darted the barrel-people, greeting us with their eternal phrase.

'I looked in; there was a light somewhere below, and I was curious to see it. It didn't look like a flame or torch, you understand, but more like a civilized light, and I thought that I might get some clue as to the creatures' development. So in I went and Tweel tagged along, not without a few trills and twitters, however.

'The light was curious; it sputtered and flared like an old arc light, but came from a single black rod set in the wall of the corridor. It was electric, beyond doubt. The creatures were fairly civilized, apparently.

'Then I saw another light shining on something that glittered and I went on to look at that, but it was only a heap of shiny sand. I turned toward the entrance to leave, and the Devil take me if it wasn't gone!.

'I supposed the corridor had curved, or I'd stepped into a side passage. Anyway, I walked back in that direction I thought we'd come, and all I saw was more dim-lit corridor. The place was a labyrinth! There was nothing but twisting passages running every way, lit by occasional lights, and now and then a creature running by, sometimes with a pushcart, sometimes without.

'Well, I wasn't much worried at first. Tweel and I had only come a few steps from the entrance. But every move we made after that seemed to get us in deeper. Finally I tried following one of the creatures with an empty cart, thinking that he'd be going out for his rubbish, but he ran around aimlessly, into one passage and out another. When he started dashing around a pillar like one of these Japanese waltzing mice, I gave up, dumped my water tank on the floor, and sat down.

'Tweel was as lost as I. I pointed up and he said 'No—no—no!' in a sort of helpless trill. And we couldn't get any help from the natives. They paid no attention at all, except to assure us they were friends—ouch!

'Lord! I don't know how many hours or days we wandered around there! I slept twice from sheer exhaustion; Tweel never seemed to need sleep. We tried following only the upward corridors, but they'd run uphill a ways and then curve downwards. The temperature in that damned ant hill was constant; you couldn't tell night from day and after my first sleep I didn't know whether I'd slept one hour or thirteen, so I couldn't tell from my watch whether it was midnight or noon.

'We saw plenty of strange things. There were machines running in some of the corridors, but they didn't seem to be doing anything—just wheels turning. And several times I saw two barrel-beasts with a little one growing between them, joined to both.'

'Parthenogenesis!' exulted Leroy. 'Parthenogenesis by budding like *les tulipes!*'

'If you say so, Frenchy,' agreed Jarvis. 'The things never noticed us at all, except, as I say, to greet us with 'We are v-r-r-riends! Ouch!'

They seemed to have no homelife of any sort, but just scurried around with their pushcarts, bringing in rubbish. And finally I discovered what they did with it.

'We'd had a little luck with a corridor, one that slanted upwards for a great distance. I was feeling that we ought to be close to the surface when suddenly the passage debouched into a domed chamber, the only one we'd seen. And man!—I felt like dancing when I saw what looked like daylight through a crevice in the roof.

'There was a—a sort of machine in the chamber, just an enormous wheel that turned slowly, and one of the creatures was in the act of dumping his rubbish below it. The wheel ground it with a crunch—sand, stones, plants, all into powder that sifted away somewhere. While we watched, others filed in, repeating the process, and that seemed to be all. No rhyme nor reason to the whole thing—but that's characteristic of this crazy planet. And there was another fact that's almost too bizarre to believe.

'One of the creatures, having dumped his load, pushed his cart aside with a crash and calmly shoved himself under the wheel! I watched him being crushed, too stupefied to make a sound, and a moment later, another followed him! They were perfectly methodical about it, too; one of the cartless creatures took the abandoned pushcart.

'Tweel didn't seem surprised; I pointed out the next suicide to him, and he just gave the most human-like shrug imaginable, as much as to say, 'What can I do about it?' He must have known more or less about these creatures.

'Then I saw something else. There was something beyond the wheel, something shining on a sort of low pedestal. I walked over; there was a little crystal, about the size of an egg, fluorescing to beat Tophet. The light from it stung my hands and face, almost like a static discharge, and then I noticed another funny thing. Remember that wart I had on my left thumb? Look!' Jarvis extended his hand. 'It dried up and fell off—just like that! And my abused nose—say, the pain went out of it like magic! The thing had the property of hard ex-rays or gamma radiations, only more so; it destroyed diseased tissue and left healthy tissue unharmed!

'I was thinking what a present *that'd* be to take back to Mother Earth when a lot of racket interrupted. We dashed back to the other side of the wheel in time to see one of the pushcarts ground up. Some suicide had been careless, it seems.

'Then suddenly the creatures were booming and drumming all around us and their noise was decidedly menacing. A crowd of them advanced toward us; we backed out of what I thought was the passage we'd entered by, and they came rumbling after us, some pushing carts and some not. Crazy brutes! There was a whole chorus of 'We are v-r-r-riends! Ouch!' I didn't like the 'ouch'; it was rather suggestive.

'Tweel had his glass gun out and I dumped my water tank for greater freedom and got mine. We backed up the corridor with the barrel-beasts following—about twenty of them. Queer thing—the ones coming in with loaded carts moved past us inches away without a sign.

'Tweel must have noticed that. Suddenly, he snatched out that glowing coal cigar-lighter of his and touched a cartload of plant limbs. Puff! The whole load was burning—and the crazy beast pushing it went right along without a change of pace. It created some disturbance among our 'v-v-r-riends,' however—and then I noticed the smoke eddying and swirling past us, and sure enough, there was the entrance

'I grabbed Tweel and out we dashed and after us our twenty pursuers. The daylight felt like Heaven, though I saw at first glance that the sun was all but set, and that was bad, since I couldn't live outside my thermo-skin bag in a Martian night—at least, without a fire.

'And things got worse in a hurry. They cornered us in an angle between two mounds, and there we stood. I hadn't fired nor had Tweel; there wasn't any use in irritating the brutes. They stopped a little distance away and began their booming about friendship and ouches.

'Then things got still worse! A barrel-brute came out with a pushcart and they all grabbed into it and came out with handfuls of foot-long copper darts—sharp-looking ones—and all of a sudden one sailed past my ear—zing! And it was shoot or die then.

'We were doing pretty well for a while. We picked off the ones next to the pushcart and managed to keep the darts at a minimum, but suddenly there was a thunderous booming of 'v-v-r-riends' and 'ouches,' and a whole army of 'em came out of their hole.

'Man! We were through and I knew it! Then I realized that Tweel wasn't. He could have leaped the mound behind us as easily as not. He was staying for me!

'Say, I could have cried if there'd been time! I'd liked Tweel from the first, but whether I'd have had gratitude to do what he was doing—suppose I had saved him from the first dream-beast—he'd done as much for me, hadn't he? I grabbed his arm, and said 'Tweel,' and pointed up, and he understood. He said, 'No—no—no, Tick!' and popped away with his glass pistol.

'What could I do? I'd be a goner anyway when the sun set, but I couldn't explain that to him. I said, 'Thanks, Tweel. You're a man!' and felt that I wasn't paying him any compliment at all. A man! There are mighty few men who'd do that.

'So I went 'bang' with my gun and Tweel went 'puff' with his, and the barrels were throwing darts and getting ready to rush us, and booming about being friends. I had given up hope. Then suddenly an angel dropped right down from Heaven in the shape of Putz, with his underjets blasting the barrels into very small pieces!

'Wow! I let out a yell and dashed for the rocket; Putz opened the door and in I went, laughing and crying and shouting! It was a moment or so before I remembered Tweel; I looked around in time to see him rising in one of his nosedives over the mound and away.

'I had a devil of a job arguing Putz into following. By the time we got the rocket aloft, darkness was down; you know how it comes here—like turning off a light. We sailed out over the desert and put down once or twice. I yelled 'Tweel!' and yelled it a hundred times, I guess. We couldn't find him; he could travel like the wind and all I got—or else I imagined it—was a faint trilling and twittering drifting out of the south. He'd gone, and damn it! I wish—I wish he hadn't!'

The four men of the *Ares* were silent—even the sardonic Harrison. At last little Leroy broke the stillness.

'I should like to see,' he murmured.

'Yeah,' said Harrison. 'And the wart-cure. Too bad you missed that; it might be the cancer cure they've been hunting for a century and a half.'

'Oh, that!' muttered Jarvis gloomily. 'That's what started the fight!' He drew a glistening object from his pocket.

'Here it is.'

Valley of Dreams

Captain Harrison of the *Ares* expedition turned away from the little telescope in the bow of the rocket. 'Two weeks more, at the most,' he remarked. 'Mars only retogrades for seventy days in all, relative to the earth, and we've got to be homeward bound during that period, or wait a year and a half for old Mother Earth to go around the sun and catch up with us again. How'd you like to spend a winter here?'

Dick Jarvis, chemist of the party, shivered as he looked up from his notebook. 'I'd just as soon spend it in a liquid air tank!' he averred. 'These eighty-below-zero summer nights are plenty for me.'

'Well,' mused the captain, 'the first successful Martian expedition ought to be home long before then.'

'Successful if we get home,' corrected Jarvis. 'I don't trust these cranky rockets—not since the auxiliary dumped me in the middle of Thyle last week. Walking back from a rocket ride is a new sensation to me.'

'Which reminds me,' returned Harrison, 'that we've got to recover your films. They're important if we're to pull this trip out of the red. Remember how the public mobbed the first moon pictures? Our shots ought to pack 'em to the doors. And the broadcast rights, too; we might show a profit for the Academy.'

'What interests me,' countered Jarvis, 'is a personal profit. A book, for instance; exploration books are always popular. *Martian Deserts*—how's that for a title?'

'Lousy!' grunted the captain. 'Sounds like a cookbook for desserts. You'd have to call it 'Love Life of a Martian,' or something like that.'

Jarvis chuckled. 'Anyway,' he said, 'if we once get back home, I'm going to grab what profit there is, and never, never, get any farther from the earth than a good stratosphere plane'll take me. I've learned to appreciate the planet after plowing over this dried-up pill we're on now.'

'I'll lay you odds you'll be back here year after next,' grinned the Captain. 'You'll want to visit your pal—that trick ostrich.'

'Tweel?' The other's tone sobered. 'I wish I hadn't lost him, at that. He was a good scout. I'd never have survived the dream-beast but for him. And that battle with the pushcart things—I never even had a chance to thank him.'

'A pair of lunatics, you two,' observed Harrison. He squinted through the port at the gray gloom of the Mare Cimmerium. 'There comes the sun.' He paused. 'Listen, Dick—you and Leroy take the other auxiliary rocket and go out and salvage those films.'

Jarvis stared. 'Me and Leroy?' he echoed ungrammatically. 'Why not me and Putz? An engineer would have some chance of getting us there and back if the rocket goes bad on us.'

The captain nodded toward the stern, whence issued at that moment a medley of blows and guttural expletives. 'Putz is going over the insides of the *Ares,*' he announced. 'He'll have his hands full until we leave, because I want every bolt inspected. It's too late for repairs once we cast off.'

'And if Leroy and I crack up? That's our last auxiliary.'

'Pick up another ostrich and walk back,' suggested Harrison gruffly. Then he smiled. 'If you have trouble, we'll hunt you out in the *Ares,*' he finished. 'Those films are important.' He turned. 'Leroy!'

The dapper little biologist appeared, his face questioning.

'You and Jarvis are off to salvage the auxiliary,' the Captain said. 'Everything's ready and you'd better start now. Call back at half-hour intervals; I'll be listening.'

Leroy's eyes glistened. 'Perhaps we land for specimens—no?' He queried.

'Land if you want to. This golf ball seems safe enough.'

'Except for the dream-beast,' muttered Jarvis with a faint shudder. He frowned suddenly. 'Say, as long as we're going that way, suppose I have a look for Tweel's home! He must live off there somewhere, and he's the most important thing we've seen on Mars.'

Harrison hesitated. 'If I thought you could keep out of trouble,' he muttered. 'All right,' he decided. 'Have a look. There's food and water aboard the auxiliary; you can take a couple of days. But keep in touch with me, you saps!'

Jarvis and Leroy went through the airlock out to the gray plain.

The thin air, still scarcely warmed by the rising sun, bit flesh and lung like needles, and they gasped with a sense of suffocation. They dropped to a sitting posture, waiting for their bodies, trained by months in acclimatization chambers back on earth, to accommodate themselves to the tenuous air. Leroy's face, as always, turned a smothered blue, and Jarvis heard his own breath rasping and rattling in his throat. But in five minutes, the discomfort passed; they rose and entered the little auxiliary rocket that rested beside the black hull of the *Ares*.

The under-jets roared out their fiery atomic blast; dirt and bits of shattered biopods spun away in a cloud as the rocket rose. Harrison watched the projectile trail its flaming way into the south, then turned back to his work.

It was four days before he saw the rocket again. Just at evening, as the sun dropped behind the horizon with the suddenness of a candle falling into the sea, the auxiliary flashed out of the southern heavens, easing gently down on the flaming wings of the under-jets. Jarvis and Leroy emerged, passed through the swiftly gathering dusk, and faced him in the light of the *Ares*. He surveyed the two; Jarvis was tattered and scratched, but apparently in better condition than Leroy, whose dapperness was completely lost. The little biologist was pale as the nearer moon that glowed outside; one arm was bandaged in thermo-skin and his clothes hung in veritable rags. But it was his eyes that struck Harrison most strangely; to one who lived these many weary days with the diminutive Frenchman, there was something queer about them. They were frightened, plainly enough, and that was odd, since Leroy was no coward or he'd never have been one of the four chosen by the Academy for the first Martian expedition. But the fear in his eyes was more understandable than that other expression, that queer fixity of gaze like one in a trance, or like a person in an ecstasy. 'Like a chap who's seen Heaven and Hell together,' Harrison expressed it to himself. He was yet to discover how right he was.

He assumed a gruffness as the weary pair sat down. 'You're a fine looking couple!' he growled. 'I should've known better than to let you wander off alone.' He paused. 'Is your arm all right, Leroy? Need any treatment?'

Jarvis answered. 'It's all right—just gashed. No danger of infection here, I guess; Leroy says there aren't any microbes on Mars.'

'Well,' exploded the Captain, 'Let's hear it, then! Your radio reports sounded screwy. 'Escaped from Paradise!'

'Huh!'

'I didn't want to give details on the radio,' said Jarvis soberly. 'You'd have thought we'd gone loony.'

'I think so, anyway.'

'*Moi aussi!*' muttered Leroy. 'I too!'

'Shall I begin at the beginning?' queried the chemist. 'Our early reports were pretty nearly complete.' He stared at Putz, who had come in silently, his face and hands blackened with carbon, and seated himself beside Harrison.

'At the beginning,' the Captain decided.

'Well,' began Jarvis, 'we got started all right, and flew due south along the meridian of the *Ares,* same course I'd followed last week. I was getting used to this narrow horizon, so I didn't feel so much like being cooped under a big bowl, but one does keep overestimating distances. Something four miles away looks eight when you're used to terrestrial curvature, and that makes you guess its size just four times too large. A little hill looks like a mountain until you're almost over it.'

'I know that,' grunted Harrison.

'Yes, but Leroy didn't, and I spent our first couple of hours trying to explain it to him. By the time he understood (if he does yet) we were past Cimmerium and over that Xanthus, desert, and then we crossed the canal with the mud city and the barrel-shaped citizens and the place where Tweel had shot the dream-beast. And nothing would do for Pierre here but that we put down so he could practice his biology on the remains. So we did.

'The thing was still there. No sign of decay; couldn't be, of course, without bacterial forms of life, and Leroy says that Mars is as sterile as an operating table.'

'*Comme le coeur d'une fileuse,*' corrected the little biologist, who was beginning to regain a trace of his usual energy. 'Like an old maid's heart!'

'However,' resumed Jarvis, 'about a hundred of the little gray-green biopods had fastened onto the thing and were growing and branching. Leroy found a stick and knocked 'em off, and each branch broke away and became a biopod crawling around with the others. So he poked around at the creature, while I looked away from it; even dead, that rope-armed devil gave me the creeps. And then came the surprise; the thing was part plant!'

'*C'est vrai!*' confirmed the biologist. 'It's true!'

'It was a big cousin of the biopods,' continued Jarvis. 'Leroy was quite excited; he figures that all Martian life is of that sort—neither plant nor animal. Life here never differentiated, he says; everything has both natures in it, even the barrel-creatures—even Tweel! I think he's right, especially when I recall how Tweel rested, sticking his beak in the ground and staying that way all night. I never saw him eat or drink, either; perhaps his beak was more in the nature of a root, and he got his nourishment that way.'

'Sounds nutty to me,' observed Harrison.

'Well,' continued Jarvis, 'we broke up a few of the other growths and they acted the same way—the pieces crawled around, only much slower than the biopods, and then stuck themselves in the ground. Then Leroy had to catch a sample of the walking grass, and we were ready to leave when a parade of the barrel creatures rushed by with their pushcarts. They hadn't forgotten me, either; they all drummed out, 'We are v-r-r-iends—ouch!' just as they had before. Leroy wanted to shoot one and cut it up, but I remembered the battle Tweel and I had had with them, and vetoed the idea. But he did hit on a possible explanation as to what they did with all the rubbish they gathered.'

'Made mud-pies, I guess,' grunted the captain.

'More or less,' agreed Jarvis. 'They use it for food, Leroy thinks. If they're part vegetable, you see, that's what they'd want—soil with organic remains in it to make it fertile. That's why they ground up sand and biopods and other growths all together. See?'

'Dimly,' countered Harrison. 'How about the suicides?'

'Leroy had a hunch there, too. The suicides jump into the grinder when the mixture has too much sand and gravel; they throw themselves in to adjust the proportions.'

'Rats!' said Harrison disgustedly. 'Why couldn't they bring in some extra branches from outside?'

'Because suicide is easier. You've got to remember that these creatures can't be judged by earthly standards; they probably don't feel pain, and they haven't got what we'd call individuality. Any intelligence they have is the property of the whole community—like an ant-heap. That's it! Ants are willing to die for their ant-hill; so are these creatures.'

'So are men,' observed the captain, 'if it comes to that.'

'Yes, but men aren't exactly eager. It takes some emotion like patriotism to work 'em to the point of dying for their country; these things do it all in the day's work.' He paused.

'Well, we took some pictures of the dream-beast and the barrel-creatures, and then we started along. We sailed over Xanthus, keeping as close to the meridian of the *Ares* as we could, and pretty soon we crossed the trail of the pyramid builder. So we circled back to let Leroy take a look at it, and when we found it, we landed. The thing had completed just two rows of bricks since Tweel and I left it, and there it was, breathing in silicon and breathing out bricks as if it had eternity to do it in—which it has. Leroy wanted to dissect it with a Boland explosive bullet, but I thought that anything that had lived for ten million years was entitled to the respect due to old age, so I talked him out of it. He peeped into the hole on top of it and nearly got beaned by the arm coming up with a brick, and then he chipped off a few pieces of it, which didn't disturb the creature a bit. He found the place I'd chipped, tried to see if there was any sign of healing, and decided he could tell better in two or three thousand years. So we took a few shots of it and sailed on.

'Mid-afternoon we located the wreck of my rocket. Not a thing disturbed; we picked up my films and tried to decide what next. I wanted to find Tweel if possible; I figured from the fact of his pointing south that he lived somewhere near Thyle. We plotted our route and judged that the desert we were in now was Thyle II; Thyle I should be east of us. So, on a hunch, we decided to have a look at Thyle I, and away we buzzed.'

'Der motors?' queried Putz, breaking his long silence.

'For a wonder, we had no trouble, Karl. Your blast worked perfectly. So we hummed along, pretty high to get a wider view, I'd say about fifty thousand feet. Thyle II spread out like an orange carpet, and after a while we came to the gray branch of the Mare Chronium that bounded it. That was narrow; we crossed it in half an hour, and there was Thyle I—same orange-hued desert as its mate. We veered

37

south, toward the Mare Australe, and followed the edge of the desert. And toward sunset we spotted it.'

'Shpotted?' echoed Putz. 'Vot vas shpotted?'

'The desert was spotted—with buildings! Not one of the mud cities of the canals, although a canal went through it. From the map we figured the canal was a continuation of the one Schiaparelli called Ascanius.

'We were probably too high to be visible to any inhabitants of the city, but also too high for a good look at it, even with the glasses. However, it was nearly sunset, anyway, so we didn't plan on dropping in. We circled the place; the canal went out into the Mare Australe, and there, glittering in the south, was the melting polar ice-cap! The canal drained it; we could distinguish the sparkle of water in it. Off to the southeast, just at the edge of the Mare Australe, was a valley—the first irregularity I'd seen on Mars except the cliffs that bounded Xanthus and Thyle II. We flew over the valley-' Jarvis paused suddenly and shuddered; Leroy, whose color had begun to return, seemed to pale. The chemist resumed, 'Well, the valley looked all right—then! Just a gray waste, probably full of crawlers like the others.

'We circled back over the city; say, I want to tell you that place was-well, gigantic! It was colossal; at first I thought the size was due to that illusion I spoke of—you know, the nearness of the horizon—but it wasn't that. We sailed right over it, and you've never seen anything like it!

'But the sun dropped out of sight right then. I knew we were pretty far south—latitude 60—but I didn't know just how much night we'd have.'

Harrison glanced at a Schiaparelli chart. 'About 60—eh?' he said. 'Close to what corresponds to the Antarctic Circle. You'd have about four hours of night at this season. Three months from now you'd have none at all.'

'Three months!' echoed Jarvis, surprised. Then he grinned. 'Right! I forget the seasons here are twice as long as ours. Well, we sailed out into the desert about twenty miles, which put the city below the horizon in case we overslept, and there we spent the night.

'You're right about the length of it. We had about four hours of darkness which left us fairly rested. We ate breakfast, called our location to you, and started over to have a look at the city.

'We sailed toward it from the east and it loomed up ahead of us like a range of mountains. Lord, what a city! Not that New York mightn't have higher buildings, or Chicago cover more ground, but for sheer mass, those structures were in a class by themselves. Gargantuan!

'There was a queer look about the place, though. You know how a terrestrial city sprawls out, a nimbus of suburbs, a ring of residential sections, factory districts, parks, highways, There was none of that here; the city rose out of the desert as abruptly as a cliff. Only a few little sand mounds marked the division, and then the walls of those gigantic structures.

'The architecture was strange, too. There were lots of devices that are impossible back home, such as set-backs in reverse, so that a building with a small base could spread out as it rose. That would be a valuable trick in New York, where land is almost priceless, but to do it, you'd have to transfer Martian gravitation there!

'Well, since you can't very well land a rocket in a city street, we put down right next to the canal side of the city, took our small cameras and revolvers, and started for a gap in the wall of masonry. We weren't ten feet from the rocket when we both saw the explanation for a lot of the queerness.

'The city was in ruin! Abandoned, deserted, dead as Babylon! Or at least, so it looked to us then, with its empty streets which, if they *had* been paved, were now deep under sand.'

'A ruin, eh?' commented Harrison. 'How old?'

'How could we tell?' countered Jarvis. 'The next expedition to this golf ball ought to carry an archeologist—and a philologist, too, as we found out later. But it's a devil of a job to estimate the age of anything here; things weather so slowly that most of the buildings might have been put up yesterday. No rainfall, no earthquakes, no vegetation is here to spread cracks with its roots—nothing. The only aging factors here are the erosion of the wind—and that's negligible in this atmosphere—and the cracks caused by changing temperature. And one other agent—meteorites. They must crash down occasionally on the city, judging from the thinness of the air, and the fact that we've seen four strike ground right here near the *Ares*.'

'Seven,' corrected the captain. 'Three dropped while you were gone.'

'Well, damage by meteorites must be slow, anyway. Big ones would be as rare here as on earth, because big ones get through in spite of the atmosphere, and those buildings could sustain a lot of little ones. My guess at the city's age—and it may be wrong by a big percentage—would be fifteen thousand years. Even that's thousands of years older than any human civilization; fifteen thousand years ago was the Late Stone Age in the history of mankind.

'So Leroy and I crept up to those tremendous buildings feeling like pygmies, sort of awe-struck, and talking in whispers. I tell you, it was ghostly walking down that dead and deserted street, and every time we passed through a shadow, we shivered, and not just because shadows are cold on Mars. We felt like intruders, as if the great race that had built the place might resent our presence even across a hundred and fifty centuries. The place was as quiet as a grave, but we kept imagining things and peeping down the dark lanes between buildings and looking over our shoulders. Most of the structures were windowless, but when we did see an opening in those vast walls, we couldn't look away, expecting to see some horror peering out of it.

'Then we passed an edifice with an open arch; the doors were there, but blocked open by sand. I got up nerve enough to take a look inside, and then, of course, we discovered we'd forgotten to take our flashes. But we eased a few feet into the darkness and the passage debauched into a colossal hall. Far above us a little crack let in a pallid ray of daylight, not nearly enough to light the place; I couldn't even see if the hall rose clear to the distant roof. But I know the place was enormous; I said something to Leroy and a million thin echoes came clipping back to us out of the darkness. And after that, we began to hear other sounds—slithering rustling noises, and whispers, and sounds like suppressed breathing—and something black and silent passed between us and that far-away crevice of light.

'Then we saw three little greenish spots of luminosity in the dusk to our left. We stood staring at them, and suddenly they all shifted at once. Leroy yelled '*Ce sont des yeux!*' and they were! They were eyes! Well, we stood frozen for a moment, while Leroy's yell reverberated back and forth between the distant walls, and the echoes repeated the words in queer, thin voices. There were mumblings and mutterings and whisperings and sounds like strange soft laughter, and then the three-eyed thing moved again. Then we broke for the door!

'We felt better out in the sunlight; we looked at each other sheepishly, but neither of us suggested another look at the buildings inside—though we *did* see the place later, and that was queer, too—but you'll hear about it when I come to it. We just loosened our revolvers and crept on along that ghostly street.

'The street curved and twisted and subdivided. I kept careful note of our directions, since we couldn't risk getting lost in that gigantic maze. Without our thermo-skin bags, night would finish us, even if what lurked in the ruins didn't. By and by, I noticed that we were veering back toward the canal, the buildings ended and there were only a few dozen ragged stone huts which looked as though they might have been built of debris from the city. I was just beginning to feel a bit disappointed at finding no trace of Tweel's people here when we rounded a corner and there he was!

'I yelled 'Tweel!' but he just stared, and then I realized that he wasn't Tweel, but another Martian of his sort. Tweel's feathery appendages were more orange hued and he stood several inches taller than this one. Leroy was sputtering in excitement, and the Martian kept his vicious beak directed at us, so I stepped forward as peace-maker. 'I said 'Tweel?' very questioningly, but there was no result. I tried it a dozen times, and we finally had to give it up; we couldn't connect.

'Leroy and I walked toward the huts, and the Martian followed us. Twice he was joined by others, and each time I tried yelling 'Tweel' at them but they just stared at us. So we ambled on with the three trailing us, and then it suddenly occurred to me that my Martian accent might be at fault. I faced the group and tried trilling it out the way Tweel himself did: 'T-r-r-rweee-r-rl! Like that.

'And that worked! One of them spun his head around a full ninety degrees, and screeched 'T-r-r-rweee-r-rl!' and a moment later, like an arrow from a bow, Tweel came sailing over the nearer huts to land on his beak in front of me!

'Man, we were glad to see each other! Tweel set up a twittering and chirping like a farm in summer and went sailing up and coming down on his beak, and I would have grabbed his hands, only he wouldn't keep still long enough.

'The other Martians and Leroy just stared, and after a while, Tweel stopped bouncing, and there we were. We couldn't talk to each other any more than we could before, so after I'd said 'Tweel' a couple of times and he'd said 'Tick,' we were more or less helpless. However, it was only midmorning, and it seemed important to learn all we could about Tweel and the city, so I suggested that he guide us around the place if he weren't busy. I put over the idea by pointing back at the buildings and then at him and us.

'Well, apparently he wasn't too busy, for he set off with us, leading the way with one of his hundred and fifty-foot nosedives that set Leroy gasping. When we caught up, he said something like 'one, one, two—two, two, four—no, no—yes, yes—rock—no breet!' That didn't seem to mean anything; perhaps he was just letting Leroy know that he could speak English, or perhaps he was merely running over his vocabulary to refresh his memory.

'Anyway, he showed us around. He had a light of sorts in his black pouch, good enough for small rooms, but simply lost in some of the colossal caverns we went through. Nine out of ten buildings meant absolutely nothing to us—just vast empty chambers, full of shadows and rustlings and echoes. I couldn't imagine their use; they didn't seem suitable for living quarters, or even for commercial purposes—trade and so forth; they might have been all right as powerhouses, but what could have been the purpose of a whole city full? And where were the remains of the machinery?

'The place was a mystery. Sometimes Tweel would show us through a hall that would have housed an ocean-liner, and he'd seem to swell with pride—and we couldn't make a damn thing of it! As a display of architectural power, the city was colossal; as anything else it was just nutty!

'But we did see one thing that registered. We came to that same building Leroy and I had entered earlier—the one with the three eyes in it. Well, we were a little shaky about going in there, but Tweel twittered and trilled and kept saying, 'Yes, yes, yes!' so we followed him, staring nervously about for the thing that had watched us. However, that hall was just like the others, full of murmurs and slithering noises and shadowy things slipping away into corners. If the three-eyed creature were still there, it must have slunk away with the others.

'Tweel led us along the wall; his light showed a series of little alcoves, and in the first of these we ran into a puzzling thing—a very weird thing. As the light flashed into the alcove, I saw first just an

empty space, and then, squatting on the floor, I saw—it! A little creature about as big as a large rat, it was, gray and huddled and evidently
startled by our appearance. It had the queerest, most devilish little
face!—pointed ears or horns and satanic eyes that seemed to sparkle
with a sort of fiendish intelligence.

'Tweel saw it, too, and let out a screech of anger, and the creature
rose on two pencil-thin legs and scuttled off with a half-terrified,
half-defiant squeak. It darted past us into the darkness too quickly
even for Tweel, and as it ran, something waved on its body like the
fluttering of a cape. Tweel screeched angrily at it and set up a shrill
hullabaloo that sounded like genuine rage.

'But the thing was gone, and then I noticed the weirdest of imaginable details. Where it had squatted on the floor was—a book! It
had been hunched over a book!

'I took a step forward; sure enough, there was some sort of in-
scription on the pages—wavy white lines like a seismograph record
on black sheets like the material of Tweel's pouch. Tweel fumed and
whistled in wrath, picked up the volume and slammed it into place on
a shelf full of others. Leroy and I stared dumbfounded at each other.

'Had the little thing with the fiendish face been reading? Or was
it simply eating the pages, getting physical nourishment rather than
mental? Or had the whole thing been accidental?

'If the creature were some rat-like pest that destroyed books,
Tweel's rage was understandable, but why should he try to prevent
an intelligent being, even though of an alien race, from *reading*—if
it was reading. I don't know; I did notice that the book was entirely
undamaged, nor did I see a damaged book among any that we handled. But I have an odd hunch that if we knew the secret of the little
cape-clothed imp, we'd know the mystery of the vast abandoned city
and of the decay of Martian culture.

'Well, Tweel quieted down after a while and led us completely
around that tremendous hall. It had been a library, I think; at least,
there were thousands upon thousands of those queer black-paged vol-
umes printed in wavy lines of white. There were pictures, too, in some;
and some of these showed Tweel's people. That's a point, of course; it
indicated that his race built the city and printed the books. I don't
think the greatest philologist on earth will ever translate one line of
those records; they were made by minds too different from ours.

'Tweel could read them, naturally. He twittered off a few lines, and then I took a few of the books, with his permission; he said 'no, no!' to some and 'yes, yes!' to others. Perhaps he kept back the ones his people needed, or perhaps he let me take the ones he thought we'd understand most easily. I don't know; the books are outside there in the rocket.

'Then he held that dim torch of his toward the walls, and they were pictured. Lord, what pictures! They stretched up and up into the blackness of the roof, mysterious and gigantic. I couldn't make much of the first wall; it seemed to be a portrayal of a great assembly of Tweel's people. Perhaps it was meant to symbolize Society or Government. But the next wall was more obvious; it showed creatures at work on a colossal machine of some sort, and that would be Industry or Science. The back wall had corroded away in part, from what we could see, I suspected the scene was meant to portray Art, but it was on the fourth wall that we got a shock that nearly dazed us.

'I think the symbol was Exploration or Discovery. This wall was a little plainer, because the moving beam of daylight from that crack lit up the higher surface and Tweel's torch illuminated the lower. We made out a giant seated figure, one of the beaked Martians like Tweel, but with every limb suggesting heaviness, weariness. The arms dropped inertly on the chair, the thin neck bent and the beak rested on the body, as if the creature could scarcely bear its own weight. And before it was a queer kneeling figure, and at sight of it, Leroy and I almost reeled against each other. It was, apparently, a man!'

'A man!' bellowed Harrison. 'A man you say?'

'I said apparently,' retorted Jarvis. 'The artist had exaggerated the nose almost to the length of Tweel's beak, but the figure had black shoulder-length hair, and instead of the Martian four, there were five fingers on its outstretched hand! It was kneeling as if in worship of the Martian, and on the ground was what looked like a pottery bowl full of some food as an offering. Well! Leroy and I thought we'd gone screwy!'

'And Putz and I think so, too!' roared the captain.

'Maybe we all have,' replied Jarvis, with a faint grin at the pale face of the little Frenchman, who returned it in silence. 'Anyway,' he continued, 'Tweel was squeaking and pointing at the figure, and saying 'Tick! Tick!' so he recognized the resemblance—and never mind any cracks about my nose!' he warned the captain. 'It was Leroy who made the important comment; he looked at the Martian and said 'Thoth! The god Thoth!'

'Oui!' confirmed the biologist. *'Comme l'Egypte!'*

'Yeah,' said Jarvis. 'Like the Egyptian ibis-headed god—the one with the beak. Well, no sooner did Tweel hear the name Thoth than he set up a clamor of twittering and squeaking. He pointed at himself and said 'Thoth! Thoth!' and then waved his arm all around and repeated it. Of course he often did queer things, but we both thought we understood what he meant. He was trying to tell us that his race called themselves Thoth. Do you see what I'm getting at?'

'I see, all right,' said Harrison. 'You think the Martians paid a visit to the earth, and the Egyptians remembered it in their mythology. Well, you're off, then; there wasn't any Egyptian civilization fifteen thousand years ago.'

'Wrong!' grinned Jarvis. 'It's too bad we *haven't* an archeologist with us, but Leroy tells me that there was a stone-age culture in Egypt then, the pre-dynastic civilization.'

'Well, even so, what of it?'

'Plenty! Everything in that picture proves my point. The attitude of the Martian, heavy and weary—that's the unnatural strain of terrestrial gravitation. The name Thoth; Leroy tells me Thoth was the Egyptian god of philosophy and the *inventor of writing!* Get that? They must have picked up the idea from watching the Martian take notes. It's too much for coincidence that Thoth should be beaked and ibis-headed, and that the beaked Martians call themselves Thoth.'

'Well, I'll be hanged! But what about the nose on the Egyptian? Do you mean to tell me that stone-age Egyptians had longer noses than ordinary men?'

'Of course not! It's just that the Martians very naturally cast their paintings in Martianized form. Don't human beings tend to relate everything to themselves? That's why dugongs and manatees started the mermaid myths—sailors thought they saw human features on the beasts. So the Martian artist, drawing either from descriptions or imperfect photographs, naturally exaggerated the size of the human nose to a degree that looked normal to him. Or anyway, that's my theory.'

'Well, it'll do as a theory,' grunted Harrison. 'What I want to hear is why you two got back here looking like a couple of year-before-last bird's nests.'

Jarvis shuddered again, and cast another glance at Leroy. The little biologist was recovering some of his accustomed poise, but he returned the glance with an echo of the chemist's shudder.

'We'll get to that,' resumed the latter. 'Meanwhile I'll stick to Tweel and his people. We spent the better part of three days with them, as you know. I can't give every detail, but I'll summarize the important facts and give our conclusions, which may not be worth an inflated franc. It's hard to judge this dried-up world by earthly standards.

'We took pictures of everything possible; I even tried to photograph that gigantic mural in the library, but unless Tweel's lamp was unusually rich in actinic rays, I don't suppose it'll show. And that's a pity, since it's undoubtedly the most interesting object we've found on Mars, at least from a human viewpoint.

'Tweel was a very courteous host. He took us to all the points of interest—even the new water-works.'

Putz's eyes brightened at the word. 'Vater-vorks?' he echoed. 'For vot?'

'For the canal, naturally. They have to build up a head of water to drive it through; that's obvious.' He looked at the captain. 'You told me yourself that to drive water from the polar caps of Mars to the equator was equivalent to forcing it up a twenty-mile hill, because Mars is flattened at the poles and bulges at the equator just like the earth.'

'That's true,' agreed Harrison.

'Well,' resumed Jarvis, 'this city was one of the relay stations to boost the flow. Their power plant was the only one of the giant buildings that seemed to serve any useful purpose, and that was worth seeing. I wish you'd seen it, Karl; you'll have to make what you can from our pictures. It's a sunpower plant!'

Harrison and Putz stared. 'Sunpower!' grunted the captain. 'That's primitive!' And the engineer added an emphatic '*Ya!*' of agreement.

'Not as primitive as all that,' corrected Jarvis. 'The sunlight focused on a queer cylinder in the center of a big concave mirror, and they drew an electric current from it. The juice worked the pumps.'

'A thermocouple' ejaculated Putz.

'That sounds reasonable; you can judge by the pictures. But the power plant had some queer things about it. The queerest was that the machinery was tended, not by Tweel's people, but by some of the barrel-shaped creatures like the ones in Xanthus!' He gazed around at the faces of his auditors; there was no comment.

'Get it?' he resumed. At their silence, he proceeded, 'I see you don't. Leroy figured it out, but whether rightly or wrongly, I don't know. He thinks that the barrels and Tweel's race have a reciprocal arrangement like—well, like bees and flowers on earth. The flowers give honey for the bees; the bees carry the pollen for the flowers. See? The barrels tend the works and Tweel's people build the canal system. The Xanthus city must have been a boosting station; that explains the mysterious machines I saw. And Leroy believes further that it isn't an intelligent arrangement—not on the part of the barrels, at least—but that it's been done for so many thousands of generations that it's become instinctive a tropism—just like the actions of ants and bees. The creatures have been bred to it!'

'Nuts!' observed Harrison. 'Let's hear you explain the reason for that big empty city, then.'

'Sure. Tweel's civilization is decadent, that's the reason. It's a dying race, and out of all the millions that must once have lived there, Tweel's couple of hundred companions are the remnant. They're an outpost, left to tend the source of the water at the polar cap; probably there are still a few respectable cities left somewhere on the canal system, most likely near the tropics. It's the last gasp of a race—and a race that reached a higher peak of culture than Man!'

'Huh?' said Harrison. 'Then why are they dying? Lack of water?'

'I don't think so,' responded the chemist. 'If my guess at the city's age is right, fifteen thousand years wouldn't make enough difference in the water supply—nor a hundred thousand for that matter. It's something else, though the water's doubtless a factor.'

'*Das wasser*,' cut in Putz. 'Vere goes dot?'

'Even a chemist knows that!' scoffed Jarvis. 'At least on earth. Here I'm not so sure, but on earth, every time there's a lightning flash, it electrolyzes some water vapor into hydrogen and oxygen, and then the hydrogen escapes into space, because terrestrial gravitation won't hold it permanently. And every time there's an earthquake, some water is lost to the interior. Slow—but damned certain.' He turned to Harrison. 'Right, Cap?'

'Right,' conceded the captain. 'But here, of course—no earth-quakes, no thunderstorms—the loss must be very slow. Then why *is* the race dying?'

'The sunpower plant answers that,' countered Jarvis. 'Lack of fuel! Lack of power! No oil left, no coal left—if Mars ever had a Carbon-iferous Age—and no water-power—just the driblets of energy they can get from the sun. That's why they're dying.'

'With the limitless energy of the atom?' exploded Harrison.

'They don't know about atomic energy. Probably never did. Must have used some other principle in their spaceship.'

'Then,' snapped the captain, 'what makes you rate their intelli-gence above the human? *We've* finally cracked open the atom!'

'Sure we have. We had a clue, didn't we? Radium and uranium. Do you think we'd ever have learned how without those elements? We'd never even have suspected that atomic energy existed!'

'Well? Haven't they—'

'No, they haven't. You've told me yourself that Mars has only 73 percent of the earth's density. Even a chemist can see that that means a lack of heavy metals—no osmium, no uranium, no radium. They didn't have the clue.'

'Even so, that doesn't prove they're more advanced than we are. If they were more advanced, they'd have discovered it anyway.'

'Maybe,' conceded Jarvis. 'I'm not claiming that we don't surpass them in some ways. But in others, they're far ahead of us.'

'In what, for instance?'

'Well—Socially, for one thing.'

'Huh? How do you mean?'

Jarvis glanced in turn at each of the three that faced him. He hesitated. 'I wonder how you chaps will take this,' he muttered. 'Naturally, everybody likes his own system best.' He frowned. 'Look here—on the earth we have three types of society, haven't we? And there's a member of each type right here. Putz lives under a dic-tatorship—an autocracy. Leroy's a citizen of the Sixth Commune in France. Harrison and I are Americans, members of a democra-cy. There you are—autocracy, democracy, communism—the three types of terrestrial societies. Tweel's people have a different system from any of us.'

'Different? What is it?'

'The one no earthly nation has tried. Anarchy!'

'Anarchy!' the captain and Putz burst out together.

'That's right.'

'But—' Harrison was sputtering. 'What do you mean, they're ahead of us? Anarchy! Bah!'

'All right—bah!' retorted Jarvis. 'I'm not saying it would work for us, or for any race of men. But it works for them.'

'But—anarchy!' The captain was indignant.

'Well, when you come right down to it,' argued Jarvis defensively, 'anarchy is the ideal form of government, if it works. Emerson said that the best government was that which governs least, and so did Wendell Phillips, and I think George Washington. And you can't have any form of government which governs less than anarchy, which is no government at all!'

The captain was sputtering. 'But—it's unnatural! Even savage tribes have their chiefs! Even a pack of wolves has its leader!'

'Well,' retorted Jarvis defiantly, 'that only proves that government is a primitive device, doesn't it? With a perfect race you wouldn't need it at all; government is a confession of weakness, isn't it? It's a confession that part of the people won't cooperate with the rest and that you need laws to restrain those individuals which a psychologist calls anti-social. If there were no anti-social persons—criminals and such—you wouldn't need laws or police, would you?'

'But government! You'd need government How about public works—wars—taxes?'

'No wars on Mars, in spite of being named after the War God. No point in wars here; the population is too thin and too scattered, and besides, it takes the help of every single community to keep the canal system functioning. No taxes because apparently all individuals cooperate in building public works. No competition to cause trouble, because anybody can help himself to anything. As I said, with a perfect race government is entirely unnecessary.'

'And do you consider the Martians a perfect race?' asked the captain grimly.

'Not at all! But they've existed so much longer than man that they're evolved, socially at least, to the point where they don't need government. They work together, that's all.' Jarvis paused. 'Queer, isn't it—as if Mother Nature were carrying on two experiments, one at home and one on Mars. On earth it's the trial of an emotional, highly competitive race in a world of plenty; here it's the trial of a quiet, friendly race on a desert, unproductive, and inhospitable world. Everything here makes for cooperation. Why, there isn't even the factor that causes so much trouble at home—sex!'

'Huh?'

'Yeah: Tweel's people reproduce just like the barrels in the mud cities; two individuals grow a third one between them. Another proof of Leroy's theory that Martian life is neither animal nor vegetable. Besides, Tweel was a good enough host to let him poke down his beak and twiddle his feathers, and the examination convinced Leroy.'

'*Oui*,' confirmed the biologist. 'It is true.'

'But anarchy!' grumbled Harrison disgustedly. 'It *would* show up on a dizzy, half-dead pill like Mars!'

'It'll be a good many centuries before you'll have to worry about it on earth,' grinned Jarvis. He resumed his narrative.

'Well, we wandered through that sepulchral city, taking pictures of everything. And then—' Jarvis paused and shuddered, 'then I took a notion to have a look at that valley we'd spotted from the rocket. I don't know why. But when we tried to steer Tweel in that direction, he set up such a squawking and screeching that I thought he'd gone batty.'

'If possible!' Jeered Harrison.

'So we started over there without him; he kept wailing and screaming, 'No—no—no! Tick!' but that made us the more curious. He sailed over our heads and stuck on his beak, and went through a dozen other antics, but we ploughed on, and finally he gave up and trudged disconsolately along with us.

'The valley wasn't more than a mile southeast of the city. Tweel could have covered the distance in twenty jumps, but he lagged and loitered and kept pointing back at the city and wailing 'No—no—no!' Then he'd sail up into the air and zip down on his beak directly in front of us, and we'd have to walk around him. I'd seen him do lots of crazy things before, of course; I was used to them, but it was as plain as print that he didn't want us to see that valley.'

'Why?' queried Harrison.

'You asked why we came back like tramps,' said Jarvis with a faint shudder. 'You'll learn. We plugged along up a low rocky hill that bounded it, and as we neared the top, Tweel said, 'No breet, Tick! No breet!' Well, those were the words he used to describe the silicon monster; they were also the words he had used to tell me that the image of Fancy Long, the one that had almost lured me to the dream-beast, wasn't real. I remembered that, but it meant nothing to me then!

'Right after that, Tweel said, 'You one—one—two, he one—one—two,' and then I began to see. That was the phrase he had used to explain the dream-beast to tell me that what I thought, the creature thought—to tell me how the thing lured its victims by their own desires. So I warned Leroy; it seemed to me that even the dream-beast couldn't be dangerous if we were warned and expecting it. Well, I was wrong!

'As we reached the crest, Tweel spun his head completely around, so his feet were forward but his eyes looked backward, as if he feared to gaze into the valley. Leroy and I stared out over it, just a gray waste like this around us, with the gleam of the south polar cap far beyond its southern rim. That's what it was one second; the next it was—Paradise!'

'What?' exclaimed the captain.

Jarvis turned to Leroy. 'Can you describe it?' he asked.

The biologist waved helpless hands, '*C'est impossible!*' he whispered. '*Il me rend muet!*'

'It strikes me dumb, too,' muttered Jarvis. 'I don't know how to tell it; I'm a chemist, not a poet. Paradise is as good a word as I can think of, and that's not at all right. It was Paradise and Hell in one!'

'Will you talk sense?' growled Harrison.

'As much of it as makes sense. I tell you, one moment we were looking at a gray valley covered with blobby plants, and the next—Lord! You can't imagine that next moment! How would you like to see all your dreams made real? Every desire you'd ever had gratified? Everything you'd ever wanted there for the taking?'

'I'd like it fine!' said the captain.

'You're welcome, then!—not only your noble desires, remember! Every good impulse, yes—but also every nasty little wish, every vicious thought, everything you'd ever desired, good or bad! The dream-beasts are marvelous salesmen, but they lack the moral sense!'

'The dream-beasts?'

'Yes. It was a valley of them. Hundreds, I suppose, maybe thousands. Enough, at any rate, to spread out a complete picture of your desires, even all the forgotten ones that must have been out of the subconscious. A Paradise—of sorts. I saw a dozen Fancy Longs, in every costume I'd ever admired on her, and some I must have imagined. I saw every beautiful woman I've ever known, and all of them pleading for my attention. I saw every lovely place I'd ever wanted to be, all packed queerly into that little valley. And I saw other things.' He shook his head soberly. 'It wasn't all exactly pretty. Lord! How much of the beast is left in us! I suppose if every man alive could have one look at that weird valley, and could see just once what nastiness is hidden in him—well, the world might gain by it. I thanked heaven afterwards that Leroy—and even Tweel—saw their own pictures and not mine!'

Jarvis paused again, then resumed, 'I turned dizzy with a sort of ecstasy. I closed my eyes—and with eyes closed, I still saw the whole thing! That beautiful, evil, devilish panorama was in my mind, not my eyes. That's how those fiends work—through the mind. I knew it was the dream-beasts; I didn't need Tweel's wail of 'No breet!' No breet!' But—*I couldn't keep away!* I knew it was death beckoning, but it was worth it for one moment with the vision.'

'Which particular vision?' asked Harrison dryly.

Jarvis flushed. 'No matter,' he said. 'But beside me I heard Leroy's cry of 'Yvonne! Yvonne!' and I knew he was trapped like myself. I fought for sanity; I kept telling myself to stop, and all the time I was rushing headlong into the snare!

'Then something tripped me. Tweel! He had come leaping from behind; as I crashed down I saw him flash over me straight toward— toward what I'd been running to, with his vicious beak pointed right at her heart!'

'Oh!' nodded the captain. *'Her heart!'*

'Never mind that. When I scrambled up, that particular image was gone, and Tweel was in a twist of black ropey arms, just as when I first saw him. He'd missed a vital point in the beast's anatomy, but was jabbing away desperately with his beak.

'Somehow, the spell had lifted, or partially lifted. I wasn't five feet from Tweel, and it took a terrific struggle, but I managed to raise my revolver and put a Boland shell into the beast. Out came a spurt of horrible black corruption, drenching Tweel and me—and I guess the sickening smell of it helped to destroy the illusion of that valley of beauty. Anyway, we managed to get Leroy away from the devil that had him, and the three of us staggered to the ridge and over. I had presence of mind enough to raise my camera over the crest and take a shot of the valley, but I'll bet it shows nothing but gray waste and writhing horrors. What we saw was with our minds, not our eyes.'

Jarvis paused and shuddered. 'The brute half poisoned Leroy,' he continued. 'We dragged ourselves back to the auxiliary, called you, and did what we could to treat ourselves. Leroy took a long dose of the cognac that we had with us; we didn't dare try anything of Tweel's because his metabolism is so different from ours that what cured him might kill us. But the cognac seemed to work, and so, after I'd done one other thing I wanted to do, we came back here—and that's all.'

'All, is it?' queried Harrison. 'So you've solved all the mysteries of Mars, eh?'

'Not by a damned sight!' retorted Jarvis. 'Plenty of unanswered questions are left.'

'*Ja!*' snapped Putz. 'Der evaporation—dot iss shtopped how?'

'In the canals? I wondered about that, too; in those thousands of miles, and against this low air pressure, you'd think they'd lose a lot. But the answer's simple; they float a skin of oil on the water.'

Putz nodded, but Harrison cut in. 'Here's a puzzler. With only coal and oil—just combustion or electric power—where'd they get the energy to build a planet-wide canal system, thousands and thousands of miles of 'em? Think of the job we had cutting the Panama Canal to sea level, and then answer that!'

'Easy!' grinned Jarvis. 'Martian gravity and Martian air—that's the answer. Figure it out: First, the dirt they dug only weighed a third its earth-weight. Second, a steam engine here expands against ten pounds per square inch less air pressure than on earth. Third, they could build the engine three times as large here with no greater internal weight. And fourth, the whole planet's nearly level. Right, Putz?'

The engineer nodded. '*Ja!* Der shteam-engine—it iss *siebenund-zwanzig*—twenty-seven times so effective here.'

'Well, there, *does* go the last mystery then,' mused Harrison.

'Yeah?' queried Jarvis sardonically. 'You answer these, then. What was the nature of that vast empty city? Why do the Martians need canals, since we never saw them eat or drink? Did they really visit the earth before the dawn of history, and, if not atomic energy, what powered their ship? Since Tweel's race seems to need little or no water, are they merely operating the canals for some higher creature that does? Are there other intelligences on Mars? If not, what was the demon-faced imp we saw with the book? There are a few mysteries for you!'

'I know one or two more!' growled Harrison, glaring suddenly at little Leroy. 'You and your visions! "Yvonne!" eh? Your wife's name is Marie, isn't it?'

The little biologist turned crimson. *'Oui,'* he admitted unhappily. He turned pleading eyes on the captain. 'Please,' he said. 'In Paris *tout le monde*—everybody he think differently of those things—no?' He twisted uncomfortably. 'Please you will not tell Marie, *n'est-ce pas?'*

Harrison chuckled. 'None of my business,' he said. 'One more question, Jarvis. What was the one other thing you did before returning here?'

Jarvis looked diffident. 'Oh—that.' He hesitated. 'Well I sort of felt we owed Tweel a lot, so after some trouble, we coaxed him into the rocket and sailed him out to the wreck of the first one, over on Thyle II. Then,' he finished apologetically, 'I showed him the atomic blast, got it working—and gave it to him!'

'You *what?'* roared the Captain. 'You turned something as powerful as that over to an alien race—maybe some day an enemy race?'

'Yes, I did,' said Jarvis. 'Look here,' he argued defensively. 'This lousy, dried-up pill of a desert called Mars'll never support much human population. The Sahara desert is just as good a field for imperialism, and a lot closer to home. So we'll never find Tweel's race enemies. The only value we'll find here is commercial trade with the Martians. Then why shouldn't I give Tweel a chance for survival? With atomic energy, they can run their canal system a hundred per cent instead of only one out of five, as Putz's observations showed. They can repopulate those ghostly cities; they can resume their arts and industries; they can trade with the nations of the earth—and I'll bet they can teach us a few things,' he paused, 'if they can figure out the atomic blast, and I'll lay odds they can. They're no fools, Tweel and his ostrich-faced Martians!'

Parasite Planet

Luckily for "Ham" Hammond it was mid-winter when the mud-spout came. Mid-winter, that is, in the Venusian sense, which is nothing at all like the conception of the season generally entertained on Earth, except possibly by dwellers in the hotter regions of the Amazon basin, or the Congo.

They, perhaps, might form a vague mental picture of winter on Venus by visualizing their hottest summer days, multiplying the heat, discomfort and unpleasant denizens of the jungle by ten or twelve.

On Venus, as is now well known, the seasons occur alternately in opposite hemispheres, as on the Earth, but with a very important difference. Here, when North America and Europe swelter in summer, it is winter in Australia and Cape Colony and Argentina. It is the northern and southern hemispheres which alternate their seasons.

But on Venus, very strangely, it is the eastern and western hemispheres, because the seasons of Venus depend, not on inclination to the plane of the ecliptic, but on libration. Venus does not rotate, but keeps the same face always toward the Sun, just as the Moon does toward the earth. One face is forever daylight, and the other forever night, and only along the twilight zone, a strip five hundred miles wide, is human habitation possible, a thin ring of territory circling the planet.

Toward the sunlit side it verges into the blasting heat of a desert where only a few Venusian creatures live, and on the night edge the strip ends abruptly in the colossal ice barrier produced by the condensation of the upper winds that sweep endlessly from the rising air of the hot hemisphere to cool and sink and rush back again from the cold one.

The chilling of warm air always produces rain, and at the edge of the darkness the rain freezes to form these great ramparts. What lies beyond, what fantastic forms of life may live in the starless darkness of the frozen face, or whether that region is as dead as the airless Moon—those are mysteries.

But the slow libration, a ponderous wobbling of the planet from side to side, does produce the effect of seasons. On the lands of the twilight zone, first in one hemisphere and then the other, the cloud-hidden Sun seems to rise gradually for fifteen days, then sink for the same period. It never ascends far, and only near the ice barrier does it seem to touch the horizon; for the libration is only seven degrees, but it is sufficient to produce noticeable fifteen-day seasons.

But such seasons! In the winter the temperature drops sometimes to a humid but bearable ninety, but, two weeks later, a hundred and forty is a cool day near the torrid edge of the zone. And always, winter and summer, the intermittent rains drip sullenly down to be absorbed by the spongy soil and given back again as sticky, unpleasant, unhealthy steam.

And that, the vast amount of moisture on Venus, was the greatest surprise of the first human visitors; the clouds had been seen, of course, but the spectroscope denied the presence of water, naturally, since it was analyzing light reflected from the upper cloud surfaces, fifty miles above the planet's face.

That abundance of water has strange consequences. There are no seas or oceans on Venus, if we except the probability of vast, silent, and eternally frozen oceans on the sunless side. On the hot hemisphere evaporation is too rapid, and the rivers that flow out of the ice mountains simply diminish and finally vanish, dried up.

A further consequence is the curiously unstable nature of the land of the twilight zone. Enormous subterranean rivers course invisibly through it, some boiling, some cold as the ice from which they flow. These are the cause of the mud eruptions that make human habitation in the Hotlands such a gamble; a perfectly solid and apparently safe area of soil may be changed suddenly into a boiling sea of mud in which buildings sink and vanish, together, frequently, with their occupants.

There is no way of predicting these catastrophes; only on the rare outcroppings of bed rock is a structure safe, and so all permanent human settlements cluster about the mountains.

Ham Hammond was a trader. He was one of those adventurous individuals who always appear on the frontiers and fringes of habitable regions. Most of these fall into two classes; they are either reckless dare-devils pursuing danger, or outcasts, criminal or otherwise, pursuing either solitude or forgetfulness.

Ham Hammond was neither. He was pursuing no such abstractions, but the good, solid lure of wealth. He was, in fact, trading with the natives for the spore-pods of the Venusian plant *xixtchil*, from which terrestrial chemists would extract trihydroxyl-tertiaryline or triple-T-B-A that was so effective in rejuvenation treatments.

Ham was young and sometimes wondered why rich old men —and women—would pay such tremendous prices for a few more years of virility, especially as the treatments didn't actually increase the span of life, but just produced a sort of temporary and synthetic youth.

Gray hair darkened, wrinkles filled out, bald heads grew fuzzy, and then, in a few years, the rejuvenated person was just as dead as he would have been, anyway. But as long as triple-T-B-A commanded a price about equal to its weight in radium, Ham was willing to take the gamble to obtain it.

He had never really expected the mud-spout. Of course it was an ever-present danger, but when, staring idly through the window of his shack over the writhing and steaming Venusian plain, he had seen the sudden boiling pools erupting all around, it had come as a shocking surprise.

For a moment he was paralyzed; then he sprang into immediate and frantic action. He pulled on his enveloping suit of rubberlike *transkin*; he strapped the great bowls of mudshoes, to his feet; he tied the precious bag of spore-pods to his shoulders, packed some food, and then burst into the open.

The ground was still semisolid, but even as he watched, the black soil boiled out around the metal walls of the shack, the cube tilted a trifle, and then sank deliberately from sight, and the mud sucked and gurgled as it closed gently above the spot.

Ham caught himself. One couldn't stand still in the midst of a mud-spout, even with the bowlike mudshoes as support. Once let the viscous stuff flow over the rim and the luckless victim was trapped; he couldn't raise his foot against the suction, and first slowly, then more quickly, he'd follow the shack.

So Ham started off over the boiling swamp, walking with the peculiar sliding motion he had learned by much practice, never raising the mudshoes above the surface, but sliding them along careful that no mud topped the curving rim.

It was a tiresome motion, but absolutely necessary. He slid along as if on snowshoes, bearing west because that was the direction of the dark side, and if he had to walk to safety, he might as well do it in coolness. The area of swamp was unusually large; he covered at least a mile before he attained a slight rise in the ground, and the mudshoes clumped on solid, or nearly solid, soil.

He was bathed in perspiration, and his transkin suit was hot as a boiler room, but one grows accustomed to that on Venus. He'd have given half his supply of xixtchil pods for the opportunity to open the mask of the suit, to draw a breath of even the steamy and humid Venusian air, but that was impossible; impossible, at least, if he had any inclination to continue living.

One breath of unfiltered air anywhere near the warm edge of the twilight zone was quick and very painful death; Ham would have drawn in uncounted millions of the spores of those fierce Venusian molds, and they'd have sprouted in furry and nauseating masses in his nostrils, his mouth, his lungs, and eventually in his ears and eyes.

Breathing them wasn't even a necessary requirement; once he'd come upon a trader's body with the mold springing from his flesh. The poor fellow had somehow torn a rip in his transkin suit, and that was enough.

The situation made eating and drinking in the open a problem on Venus; one had to wait until a rain had precipitated the spores, when it was safe for half an hour or so. Even then the water must have been recently boiled and the food just removed from its can; otherwise, as had happened to Ham more than once, the food was apt to turn abruptly into a fuzzy mass of molds that grew about as fast as the minute hand moved on a clock. A disgusting sight! A disgusting planet!

That last reflection was induced by Ham's view of the quagmire that had engulfed his shack. The heavier vegetation had gone with it, but already avid and greedy life was emerging, wriggling mud grass and the bulbous fungi called "walking balls." And all around a million little slimy creatures slithered across the mud, eating each other rapaciously, being torn to bits, and each fragment re-forming to a complete creature.

A thousand different species, but all the same in one respect; each of them was all appetite. In common with most Venusian beings, they had a multiplicity of both legs and mouths; in fact some of them were little more than blobs of skin split into dozens of hungry mouths, crawling on a hundred spidery legs.

All life on Venus is more or less parasitic. Even the plants that draw their nourishment directly from soil and air have also the ability to absorb and digest—and, often enough, to trap— animal food. So fierce is the competition on that humid strip of land between the fire and the ice that one who has never seen it must fail even to imagine it.

The animal kingdom wars incessantly on itself and the plant world; the vegetable kingdom retaliates, and frequently outdoes the other in the production of monstrous predatory horrors that one would even hesitate to call plant life. A terrible world!

In the few moments that Ham had paused to look back, ropy creepers had already entangled his legs; transkin was impervious, of course, but he had to cut the things away with his knife, and the black nauseating juices that flowed out of them smeared on his suit and began instantly to grow furry as the molds sprouted. Ham shuddered.

"Hell of a place!" he growled, stooping to remove his mudshoes, which he slung carefully over his back.

He slogged away through the writhing vegetation, automatically dodging the awkward thrusts of the Jack Ketch trees as they cast their nooses hopefully toward his arms and head.

Now and again he passed one from which dangled some trapped creature, usually unrecognizable because the molds had enveloped it in a fuzzy shroud, while the tree itself was placidly absorbing victim and molds alike.

"Horrible place!" Ham muttered, kicking a writhing mass of nameless little vermin from his path.

He mused; his shack had been situated rather nearer the hot edge of the twilight zone; it was a trifle over two hundred and fifty miles to the shadow line, though of course that varied with the libration. But one couldn't approach the line too closely, anyway, because of the fierce, almost inconceivable, storms that raged where the hot upper winds encountered the icy blasts of the night side, giving rise to the birth throes of the ice barrier.

So a hundred and fifty miles due west would be sufficient to bring coolness, to enter a region too temperate for the molds, where he could walk in comparative comfort. And then, not more than fifty miles north, lay the American settlement Erotia, named, obviously, after that troublesome mythical son of Venus, Cupid.

Intervening, of course, were the ranges of the Mountains of Eternity, not those mighty twenty-mile-high peaks whose summits are occasionally glimpsed by Earthly telescopes, and that forever sunder British Venus from the American possessions, but, even at the point he planned to cross, very respectable mountains indeed. He was on the British side now; not that anyone cared. Traders came and went as they pleased.

Well, that meant about two hundred miles. No reason why he couldn't make it; he was armed with both automatic and flame-pistol, and water was no problem, if carefully boiled. Under pressure of necessity, one could even eat Venusian life—but it required hunger and thorough cooking and a sturdy stomach.

It wasn't the taste so much as the appearance, or so he'd been told. He grimaced; beyond doubt he'd be driven to find out for himself, since his canned food couldn't possibly last out the trip. Nothing to worry about, Ham kept telling himself. In fact, plenty to be glad about; the *xixtchil* pods in his pack represented as much wealth as he could have accumulated by ten years of toil back on Earth.

No danger—and yet, men had vanished on Venus, dozens of them. The molds had claimed them, or some fierce unearthly monster, or perhaps one of the many unknown living horrors, both plant and animal.

Ham trudged along, keeping always to the clearings about the Jack Ketch trees, since these vegetable omnivores kept other life beyond the reach of their greedy nooses. Elsewhere progress was impossible, for the Venusian jungle presented such a terrific tangle of writhing and struggling forms that one could move only by cutting the way, step by step, with infinite labor.

Even then there was the danger of Heaven only knew what fanged and venomous creatures whose teeth might pierce the protective membrane of *transkin*, and a crack in that meant death. Even the unpleasant Jack Ketch trees were preferable company, he reflected, as he slapped their questing lariats aside.

Six hours after Ham had started his involuntary journey, it rained. He seized the opportunity, found a place where a recent mudspout had cleared the heavier vegetation away, and prepared to eat. First, however, he scooped up some scummy water, filtered it through the screen attached for that purpose to his canteen, and set about sterilizing it.

Fire was difficult to manage, since dry fuel is rare indeed in the Hotlands of Venus, but Ham tossed a *thermide* tablet into the liquid, and the chemicals boiled the water instantly, escaping themselves as gases. If the water retained a slight ammoniacal taste,—well, that was the least of his discomforts, he mused, as he covered it and set it by to cool.

He uncapped a can of beans, watched a moment to see that no stray molds had remained in the air to infect the food, then opened the visor of his suit and swallowed hastily. Thereafter he drank the blood-warm water and poured carefully what remained into the water pouch within his transkin, where he could suck it through a tube to his mouth without the deadly exposure to the molds.

Ten minutes after he had completed the meal, while he rested and longed for the impossible luxury of a cigarette, the fuzzy coat sprang suddenly to life on the remnants of food in the can.

An hour later, weary and thoroughly soaked in perspiration, Ham found a Friendly tree, so named by the explorer Burlingame because it is one of the few organisms on Venus sluggish enough to permit one to rest in its branches. So Ham climbed it, found the most comfortable position available, and slept as best he could.

It was five hours by his wrist watch before he awoke, and the tendrils and little sucking cups of the Friendly tree were fastened all over his *transkin*. He tore them away very carefully, climbed down, and trudged westward.

It was after the second rain that he met the doughpot, as the creature is called in British and American Venus. In the French strip, it's the *pot á colle*, the "paste pot"; in the Dutch—well, the Dutch are not prudish, and they call the horror just what they think it warrants.

Actually, the doughpot is a nauseous creature. It's a mass of white, doughlike protoplasm, ranging in size from a single cell to as much as twenty tons of mushy filth. It has no fixed form; in fact, it's merely a mass of de Proust cells—in effect, a disembodied, crawling, hungry cancer.

It has no organization and no intelligence, nor even any instinct save hunger. It moves in whatever direction food touches its surfaces; when it touches two edible substances, it quietly divides, with the larger portion invariably attacking the greater supply.

It's invulnerable to bullets; nothing less than the terrific blast of a flame-pistol will kill it, and then only if the blast destroys every individual cell. It travels over the ground absorbing everything, leaving bare black soil where the ubiquitous molds spring up at once—a noisome, nightmarish creature.

Ham sprang aside as the doughpot erupted suddenly from the jungle to his right. It couldn't absorb the transkin, of course, but to be caught in that pasty mess meant quick suffocation. He glared at it disgustedly and was sorely tempted to blast it with his flame-pistol as it slithered past at running speed. He would have, too, but the experienced Venusian frontiersman is very careful with the flame-pistol.

It has to be charged with a diamond, a cheap black one, of course, but still an item to consider. The crystal, when fired, gives up all its energy in one terrific blast that roars out like a lightning stroke for a hundred yards,, incinerating everything in its path.

The thing rolled by with a sucking and gulping sound. Behind it opened the passage it had cleared; creepers, snake vines, Jack Ketch trees—everything had been swept away down to the humid earth itself, where already the molds were springing up on the slime of the doughpot's trail.

The alley led nearly in the direction Ham wanted to travel; he seized the opportunity and strode briskly along, with a wary eye, nevertheless, on the ominous walls of jungle. In ten hours or so the opening would be filled once more with unpleasant life, but for the present it offered a much quicker progress than dodging from one clearing to the next.

It was five miles up the trail, which was already beginning to sprout inconveniently, that he met the native galloping along on his four short legs, his pincer like hands shearing a path for him. Ham stopped for a palaver.

"*Murra,*" he said.

The language of the natives of the equatorial regions of the Hotlands is a queer one. It has, perhaps, two hundred words, but when a trader had learned those two hundred, his knowledge of the tongue is but little greater than the man who knows none at all.

The words are generalized, and each sound has anywhere from a dozen to a hundred meanings. *Murra*, for instance, is a word of greeting; it may mean something much like "hello," or "good morning." It may also convey a challenge—"on guard!" It means beside, "Let's be friends," and also, strangely, "Let's fight this out."

It has, moreover, certain noun senses; it means peace, it means war, it means courage, and, again, fear. A subtle language; it is only very recently that studies of inflection have begun to reveal its nature to human philologists. Yet, after all, perhaps English, with its "to," "too," and "two," its "one," "won," "wan," "wen," "win," "when," and a dozen other similarities, might seem just as strange to Venusian ears, untrained in vowel distinctions.

Moreover, humans can't read the expressions of the broad, flat, three-eyed Venusian faces, which in the nature of things must convey a world of information among the natives themselves.

But this one accepted the intended sense. "*Murra*," he responded, pausing. "*Usk?*" That was among other things, "Who are you?" or "Where did you come from?" or "Where are you bound?"

Ham chose the latter sense. He pointed off into the dim west, then raised his hand in an arc to indicate the mountains. "Erotia," he said. That had but one meaning, at least.

The native considered this in silence. At last he grunted and volunteered some information. He swept his cutting claw in a gesture west along the trail. "*Curky*," he said, and then, "*Murra*." The last was farewell; Ham pressed against the wriggling jungle wall to permit him to pass.

Curky meant, together with twenty other senses, trader. It was the word usually applied to humans, and Ham felt a pleasant anticipation in the prospect of human company. It had been six months since he had heard a human voice other than that on the tiny radio now sunk with his shack.

True enough, five miles along the doughpot's trail Ham emerged suddenly in an area where there had been a recent mud-spout. The vegetation was only waist-high, and across the quarter-mile clearing he saw a structure, a trading hut. But far more pretentious than his own iron-walled cubicle; this one boasted three rooms, an unheard-of luxury in the Hotlands, where every ounce had to be laboriously transported by rocket from one of the settlements. That was expensive, almost prohibitive. Traders took a real gamble, and Ham knew he was lucky to have come out so profitably.

He strode over the still spongy ground. The windows were shaded against the eternal daylight, and the door—the door was locked. This was a violation of the frontier code. One always left doors unlocked; it might mean the salvation of some strayed trader, and not even the most dishonorable would steal from a hut left open for his safety.

Nor would the natives; no creature is as honest as a Venusian native, who never lies and never steals, though he might, after due warning, kill a trader for his trade goods.

Ham stood puzzled. At last he kicked and tramped a clear space before the door, sat down against it, and fell to snapping away the numerous and loathsome little creatures that swarmed over his *transkin*. He waited.

It wasn't half an hour before he saw the trader plowing through the clearing—a short, slim fellow; the *transkin* shaded his face, but Ham could make out large, shadowed eyes. He stood up.

"Hello!" he said jovially. "Thought I'd drop in for a visit. My name's Hamilton Hammond—you guess the nickname!"

The newcomer stopped short, then spoke in a curiously soft and husky voice, with a decidedly English accent. "My guess would be 'Boiled Pork,' I fancy." The tones were cold, unfriendly. "Suppose you step aside and let me in. Good day!"

Ham felt anger and amazement. "The devil!" he snapped. "You're a hospitable sort, aren't you?"

"No. Not at all." The other paused at the door. "You're an American. What are you doing on British soil? Have you a passport?"

"Since when do you need a passport in the Hotlands?"

"Trading, aren't you?" the slim man said sharply. "In other words, poaching. You've no rights here. Get on."

Ham's jaw set stubbornly behind his mask. "Rights or none," he said, "I'm entitled to the consideration of the frontier code. I want a breath of air and a chance to wipe my face, and also a chance to eat. If you open that door I'm coming in after you."

An automatic flashed into view. "Do, and you'll feed the molds."

Ham, like all Venusian traders, was of necessity bold, resourceful, and what is called in the States "hard-boiled." He didn't flinch, but said in apparent yielding:

"All right; but listen, all I want is a chance to eat."

"Wait for a rain," said the other coolly and half turned to unlock the door.

As his eyes shifted, Ham kicked at the revolver; it went spinning against the wall and dropped into the weeds. His opponent snatched for the flame-pistol that still dangled on his hip; Ham caught his wrist in a mighty clutch.

Instantly the other ceased to struggle, while Ham felt a momentary surprise at the skinny feel of the wrist through its transkin covering.

"Look here!" he growled. "I want a chance to eat, and I'm going to get it. Unlock that door!"

He had both wrists now; the fellow seemed curiously delicate. After a moment he nodded, and Ham released one hand. The door opened, and he followed the other in.

Again, unheard-of magnificence. Solid chairs, a sturdy table, even books, carefully preserved, no doubt, by lycopodium against the ravenous molds that sometimes entered Hotland shacks in spite of screen filters and automatic spray. An automatic spray was going now to destroy any spores that might have entered with the opening door.

Ham sat down, keeping an eye on the other, whose flame-pistol he had permitted to remain in its holster. He was confident of his ability to outdraw the slim individual, and besides, who'd risk firing a flame-pistol indoors? It would simply blow out one wall of the building.

So he set about opening his mask, removing food from his pack, wiping his steaming face, while his companion—or opponent — looked on silently. Ham watched the canned meat for a moment; no molds appeared, and he ate.

"Why the devil," he rasped, "don't you open your visor?" At the other's silence, he continued: "Afraid I'll see your face, eh? Well, I'm not interested, I'm no cop."

No reply.

He tried again. "What's your name?"

The cool voice sounded: "Burlingame. Pat Burlingame."

Ham laughed. "Patrick Burlingame is dead, my friend. I knew him." No answer. "And if you don't want to tell your name, at least you needn't insult the memory of a brave man and a great explorer."

"Thank you." The voice was sardonic. "He was my father."

"Another lie. He had no son. He had only a—" Ham paused abruptly; a feeling of consternation swept over him. "Open your visor!" he yelled.

He saw the lips of the other, dim through the transkin, twitch into a sarcastic smile.

"Why not?" said the soft voice, and the mask dropped.

Ham gulped, behind the covering were the delicately modeled features of a girl, with cool gray eyes in a face lovely despite the glistening perspiration on cheeks and forehead.

The man gulped. After all, he was a gentleman despite his profession as one of the fierce, adventurous traders of Venus. He was university-educated—an engineer—and only the lure of quick wealth had brought him to the Hotlands.

"I—I'm sorry," he stammered.

"You brave American poachers!" she sneered. "Are all of you so valiant as to force yourselves on women?"

"But—how could I know? What are you doing in a place like this?"

"There's no reason for me to answer your questions, but"— she gestured toward the room beyond—"I'm classifying Hotland flora and fauna. I'm Patricia Burlingame, biologist."

He perceived now the jar-enclosed specimens of a laboratory in the next chamber. "But a girl alone in the Hotlands! It's— it's reckless!"

"I didn't expect to meet any American poachers," she retorted.

He flushed. "You needn't worry about me. I'm going." He raised his hands to his visor.

Instantly Patricia snatched an automatic from the table drawer. "You're going, indeed, Mr. Hamilton Hammond," she said coolly. "But you're leaving your xixtchil with me. It's crown property; you've stolen it from British territory, and I'm confiscating it."

He stared. "Look here!" he blazed suddenly. "I've risked all I have for that xixtchil. If I lose it I'm ruined—busted. I'm not giving it up!"

"But you are."

He dropped his mask and sat down. "Miss Burlingame," he said, "I don't think you've nerve enough to shoot me, but that's what you'll have to do to get it. Otherwise I'll sit here until you drop of exhaustion."

Her gray eyes bored silently into his blue ones. The gun held steadily on his heart, but spat no bullet. It was a deadlock.

At last the girl said. "You win, poacher." She slapped the gun into her empty holster. "Get out, then."

"Gladly!" he snapped.

He rose, fingered his visor, then dropped it again at a sudden startled scream from the girl. He whirled, suspecting a trick, but she was staring out of the window with wide, apprehensive eyes.

Ham saw the writhing of vegetation and then a vast whitish mass. A doughpot—a monstrous one, bearing steadily toward their shelter. He heard the gentle clunk of impact, and then the window was blotted out by the pasty mess, as the creature, not quite large enough to engulf the building, split into two masses that flowed around and remerged on the other side.

Another cry from Patricia. "Your mask, fool!" she rasped. "Close it!"

"Mask? Why?" Nevertheless, he obeyed automatically.

"Why? That's why! The digestive acids—look!"

She pointed at the walls; indeed, thousands of tiny pinholes of light were appearing. The digestive acids of the monstrosity, powerful enough to attack whatever food chance brought, had corroded the metal; it was porous; the shack was ruined. He gasped as fuzzy molds shot instantly from the remains of his meal, and a red-and-green fur sprouted from the wood of chairs and table.

The two faced each other.

Ham chuckled. "Well," he said, "you're homeless, too. Mine went down in a mudspout."

"Yours would!" Patricia retorted acidly. "You Yankees couldn't think of finding shallow soil, I suppose. Bed rock is just six feet below here, and my place is on pylons."

"Well, you're a cool devil! Anyway, your place might as well be sunk. What are you going to do?"

"Do? Don't concern yourself. I'm quite able to manage."

"How?"

"It's no affair of yours, but I have a rocket call each month."

"You must be a millionaire, then," he commented.

"The Royal Society," she said coldly, "is financing this expedition. The rocket is due—"

She paused; Ham thought she paled a little behind her mask.

"Due when?"

"Why—it just came two days ago. I'd forgotten."

"I see. And you think you'll just stick around for a month waiting for it. Is that it?"

Patricia stared at him defiantly.

"Do you know," he resumed, "what you'd be in a month? It's ten days to summer and look at your shack." He gestured at the walls, where brown and rusty patches were forming; at his motion a piece the size of a saucer tumbled in with a crackle. "In two days this thing will be a caved-in ruin. What'll you do during fifteen days of summer? What'll you do without shelter when the temperature reaches a hundred and fifty—a hundred and sixty' I'll tell you—you'll die."

She said nothing.

"You'll be a fuzzy mass of molds before the rocket returns," Ham said. "And then a pile of clean bones that will go down with the first mudspout."

"Be still!" she blazed.

"Silence won't help. Now I'll tell you what you can do. You can take your pack and your mudshoes and walk along with me. We can make the Cool Country before summer—if you can walk as well as you talk."

"Go with a Yankee poacher? I fancy not!"

"And then," he continued imperturbably, "we can cross comfortably to Erotia, a good American town."

Patricia reached for her emergency pack, slung it over her shoulders. She retrieved a thick bundle of notes, written in aniline ink on transkin, brushed off a few vagrant molds, and slipped it into the pack. She picked up a pair of diminutive mudshoes and turned deliberately to the door.

"So you're coming?" he chuckled.

"I'm going," she retorted coldly, "to the good British town of Venoble. Alone!"

"Venoble!" he gasped. "That's two hundred miles south! And across the Greater Eternities, too!"

Patricia walked silently out of the door and turned west toward the Cool Country. Ham hesitated a moment, then followed. He couldn't permit the girl to attempt that journey alone; since she ignored his presence, he simply trailed a few steps behind her, plodding grimly and angrily along.

For three hours or more they trudged through the endless daylight, dodging the thrusts of the Jack Ketch trees, but mostly following the still fairly open trail of the first doughpot.

Ham was amazed at the agile and lithe grace of the girl, who slipped along the way with the sure skill of a native. Then a memory came to him; she was a native, in a sense. He recalled now that Patrick Burlingame's daughter was the first human child born on Venus, in the colony of Venoble, founded by her father.

Ham remembered the newspaper articles when she had been sent to Earth to be educated, a child of eight; he had been thirteen then. He was twenty-seven now, which made Patricia Burlingame twenty-two.

Not a word passed between them until at last the girl swung about in exasperation.

"Go away," she blazed.

Ham halted. "I'm not bothering you."

"But I don't want a bodyguard. I'm a better Hotlander than you!"

He didn't argue the point. He kept silent, and after a moment she flashed: "I hate you, Yankee! Lord, how I hate you!" She turned and trudged on.

An hour later the mudspout caught them. Without warning, watery muck boiled up around their feet, and the vegetation swayed wildly. Hastily, they strapped on their mudshoes, while the heavier plants sank with sullen gurgles around them. Again Ham marveled at the girl's skill; Patricia slipped away across the unstable surface with a speed he could not match, and he shuffled far behind.

Suddenly he saw her stop. That was dangerous in a mudspout; only an emergency could explain it. He hurried; a hundred feet away he perceived the reason. A strap had broken on her right shoe, and she stood helpless, balancing on her left foot, while the remaining bowl was sinking slowly. Even now black mud slopped over the edge.

She eyed him as he approached. He shuffled to her side; as she saw his intention, she spoke.

"You can't," she said.

Ham bent cautiously, slipping his arms about her knees and shoulders. Her mudshoe was already embedded, but he heaved mightily, driving the rims of his own dangerously close to the surface. With a great sucking gulp, she came free and lay very still in his arms, so as not to unbalance him as he slid again into careful motion over the treacherous surface. She was not heavy, but it was a hairbreadth chance, and the mud flipped and gurgled at the very edge of his shoe-bowls. Even though Venus has slightly less surface gravitation than Earth, a week or so gets one accustomed to it, and the twenty per cent advantage in weight seems to disappear.

A hundred yards brought firm footing. He sat her down and unstrapped their mudshoes.

"Thank you," she said coolly. "That was brave."

"You're welcome," he returned dryly. "I suppose this will end any idea of your traveling alone. Without both mudshoes, the next mudspout will be the last for you. Do we walk together now?"

Her voice chilled. "I can make a substitute shoe from tree skin. Then," she said, "I'll simply wait a day or two for the mud to dry and dig up my lost one."

He laughed and gestured at the acres of mud. "Dig where?" he countered. "You'll be here till summer if you try that."

She yielded. "You win again, Yankee. But only to the Cool Country, then you'll go north and I south."

They trudged on. Patricia was as tireless as Ham himself and vastly more adept in Hotland lore. Though they spoke but little, he never ceased to wonder at the skill she had in picking the quickest route, and she seemed to sense the thrusts of the Jack Ketch trees without looking. But it was when they halted at last, after a rain had given opportunity for a hasty meal, that he had real cause to thank her.

"Sleep?" he suggested, and as she nodded: "There's a Friendly tree."

He moved toward it, the girl behind.

Suddenly she seized his arm. "It's a Pharisee!" she cried, jerking him back.

None too soon! The false Friendly tree had lashed down with a terrible stroke that missed his face by inches. It was no Friendly tree at all, but an imitator, luring prey within reach by its apparent harmlessness, then striking with knife-sharp spikes.

Ham gasped. "What is it? I never saw one of those before."

"A Pharisee! It just looks like a Friendly tree."

She took out her automatic and sent a bullet into the black, pulsing trunk. A dark stream gushed, and the ubiquitous molds sprang into life about the hole. The tree was doomed.

"Thanks," said Ham awkwardly. "I guess you saved my life."

"We're quits now." She gazed levelly at him. "Understand? We're even."

Later they found a true Friendly Tree and slept. Awakening, they trudged on again, and slept again, and so on for three nightless days. No more mudspouts burst about them, but all other horrors of the Hotlands were well in evidence. Doughpots crossed their path, snake vines hissed and struck, the Jack Ketch trees flung their sinister nooses, and a million little crawling things writhed underfoot or dropped upon their suits.

Once they encountered a uniped, that queer, kangaroo like creature that leaps, crashing through the jungle on a single mighty leg, and thrusts out its ten-foot beak to spear its prey.

When Ham missed his first shot, the girl brought it down in midleap to thresh into the avid clutches of the Jack Ketch trees and the merciless molds.

On another occasion, Patricia had both feet caught in a Jack Ketch noose that lay for some unknown cause on the ground. As she stepped within it, the tree jerked her suddenly, to dangle head down a dozen feet in the air, and she hung hopelessly until Ham managed to cut her free. Beyond doubt, either would have died alone on any of several occasions; together they pulled through.

Yet neither relaxed the cool, unfriendly attitude that had become habitual. Ham never addressed the girl unless necessary, and she in the rare instances when they spoke, called him always by no other name, than Yankee poacher. In spite of this, the man found himself sometimes remembering the piquant loveliness of her features, her brown hair and level gray eyes, as he had glimpsed them in brief moments when rain made it safe to open their visors.

At last one day a wind stirred out of the west, bringing with it a breath of coolness that was like the air of heaven to them. It was the underwind, the wind that blew from the frozen half of the planet, that breathed cold from beyond the ice barrier. When Ham experimentally shaved the skin from a writing weed, the molds sprang out more slowly and with encouraging sparseness. They were approaching the Cool Country.

They found a Friendly tree with lightened hearts; another day's trek might bring them to the uplands where one could walk unhooded, in safety from the molds, since these could not sprout in a temperature much below eighty.

Ham woke first. For a while he gazed silently across at the girl, smiling at the way the branches of the tree had encircled her like affectionate arms. They were merely hungry, of course, but it looked like tenderness. His smile turned a little sad as he realized that the Cool Country meant parting, unless he could discourage that insane determination of hers to cross the Greater Eternities.

He sighed, and reached for his pack sling on a branch between them, and suddenly a bellow of rage and astonishment broke from him.

His xixtchil pods! The transkin pouch was slit; they were gone.

Patricia woke startled at his cry. Then, behind her mask, he sensed an ironic, mocking smile.

"My *xixtchil*!" he roared. "Where is it?"

She pointed down. There among the lesser growths was a little mound of molds.

"There," she said coolly. "Down there, poacher."

"You—" He choked with rage.

"Yes, I slit the pouch while you slept. You'll smuggle no stolen wealth from British territory."

Ham was white, speechless. "You damned devil!" he bellowed at last. "That's every cent I had!"

"But stolen," she reminded him pleasantly, swinging her dainty feet.

Rage actually made him tremble. He glared at her; the light struck through the translucent transkin, outlining her body and slim rounded legs in shadow. "I ought to kill you!" he muttered tensely.

His hand twitched, and the girl laughed softly. With a groan of desperation, he slung his pack over his shoulders and dropped to the ground.

"I hope—I hope you die in the mountains," he said grimly, and stalked away toward the west.

A hundred yards distant he heard her voice.

"Yankee! Wait a moment!"

He neither paused nor glanced back, but strode on.

Half an hour later, glancing back from the crest of a rise, Ham perceived that she was following him. He turned and hurried on. The way was upward now, and his strength began to outweigh her speed and skill.

When next he glimpsed her, she was a plodding speck far behind, moving, he imagined, with a weary doggedness. He frowned back at her; it had occurred to him that a mudspout would find her completely helpless, lacking the vitally important mudshoes.

Then he realized that they were beyond the region of mudspouts, here in the foothills of the Mountains of Eternity, and anyway, he decided grimly, he didn't care.

For a while Ham paralleled a river, doubtless an unnamed tributary of the Phlegethon. So far there had been no necessity to cross watercourses, since naturally all streams on Venus flow from the ice barrier across the twilight zone to the hot side, and therefore had coincided with their own direction.

But now, once he attained the tablelands and turned north, he would encounter rivers. They had to be crossed either on logs or, if opportunity offered and the stream was narrow, through the branches of Friendly trees. To set foot in the water was death; fierce fanged creatures haunted the streams.

He had one near catastrophe at the rim of the tableland. It was while he edged through a Jack Ketch clearing; suddenly there was a heave of white corruption, and tree and jungle growth disappeared in the mass of a gigantic doughpot.

He was cornered between the monster and an impenetrable tangle of vegetation, so he did the only thing left to do. He snatched his flame-pistol and sent a terrific, roaring blast into the horror, a blast that incinerated tons of pasty filth and left a few small fragments crawling and feeding on the debris.

The blast also, as it usually does, shattered the barrel of the weapon. He sighed as he set about the forty-minute job of replacing it—no true Hotlander ever delays that—for the blast had cost fifteen good American dollars, ten for the cheap diamond that had exploded, and five for the barrel. Nothing at all when he had had his xixtchil, but a real item now. He sighed again as he discovered that the remaining barrel was his last; he had been forced to economize on everything when he set out.

Ham came at last to the tableland. The fierce and predatory vegetation of the Hotlands grew scarce; he began to encounter true plants, with no power of movement, and the underwind blew cool in his face.

He was in a sort of high valley; to his right were the gray peaks of the Lesser Eternities, beyond which lay Erotia, and to his left, like a mighty glittering rampart, lay the vast slopes of the Greater Range, whose peaks were lost in the clouds fifteen miles above.

He looked at the opening of the rugged Madman's Pass where it separated two colossal peaks; the pass itself was twenty-five thousand feet in height, but the mountains out-topped it by fifty thousand more. One man had crossed that jagged crack on foot—Patrick Burlingame—and that was the way his daughter meant to follow.

Ahead, visible as a curtain of shadow, lay the night edge of the twilight zone, and Ham could see the incessant lightning that flashed forever in this region of endless storms. It was here that the ice barrier crossed the ranges of the Mountains of Eternity, and the cold underwind, thrust up by the mighty range, met the warm upper winds in a struggle that was one continuous storm, such a storm as only Venus could provide. The river Phlegethon had its source somewhere back in there.

Ham surveyed the wildly magnificent panorama. Tomorrow, or rather, after resting, he would turn north. Patricia would turn south, and beyond doubt, would die somewhere on Madman's Pass. For a moment he had a queerly painful sensation, then he frowned bitterly.

Let her die, if she was fool enough to attempt the pass alone just because she was too proud to take a rocket from an American settlement. She deserved it. He didn't care; he was still assuring himself of that as he prepared to sleep, not in a Friendly tree, but in one of the far more friendly specimens of true vegetation and in the luxury of an open visor.

The sound of his name awakened him. He gazed across the tableland to see Patricia just topping the divide, and he felt a moment's wonder at how she had managed to trail him, a difficult feat indeed in a country where the living vegetation writhes instantly back across one's path. Then he recalled the blast of his flame-pistol; the flash and sound would carry for miles, and she must have heard or seen it.

Ham saw her glancing anxiously around.

"Ham!" she shouted again—not Yankee or poacher, but "Ham!"

He kept a sullen silence; again she called. He could see her bronzed and piquant features now; she had dropped her transkin hood. She called again; with a despondent little shrug, she turned south along the divide, and he watched her go in grim silence. When the forest hid her from view, he descended and turned slowly north.

Very slowly; his steps lagged; it was as if he tugged against some invisible elastic bond. He kept seeing her anxious face and hearing in memory the despondent call. She was going to her death, he believed, and after all, despite what she had done to him, he didn't want that. She was too full of life, too confident, too young, and above all, too lovely to die.

True, she was an arrogant, vicious, self-centered devil, cool as crystal, and as unfriendly; but—she had gray eyes and brown hair, and she was courageous. And at last, with a groan of exasperation, he halted his lagging steps, turned, and rushed with almost eager speed into the south.

Trailing the girl was easy here for one trained in the Hotlands. The vegetation was slow to mend itself, here in the Cool Country, and now and again he found imprints of her feet, or broken twigs to mark her path. He found the place where she had crossed the river through tree branches, and he found a place where she had paused to eat.

But he saw that she was gaining on him; her skill and speed outmatched his, and the trail grew steadily older. At last he stopped to rest; the tableland was beginning to curve upward toward the vast Mountains of Eternity, and on rising ground he knew he could overtake her. So he slept for a while in the luxurious comfort of no transkin at all, just the shorts and shirt that one wore beneath. That was safe here; the eternal underwind, blowing always toward the Hotlands, kept drifting mold spores away, and any brought in on the fur of animals died quickly at the first cool breeze. Nor would the true plants of the Cool Country attack his flesh.

He slept five hours. The next "day" of traveling brought another change in the country. The life of the foothills was sparse compared to the table-lands; the vegetation was no longer a jungle, but a forest, an unearthly forest, true, of treelike growths whose boles rose five hundred feet and then spread, not into foliage, but flowery appendages. Only an occasional Jack Ketch tree reminded him of the Hotlands.

Farther on, the forest diminished. Great rock outcroppings appeared, and vast red cliffs with no growths of any kind. Now and then he encountered swarms of the planet's only aerial creatures, the gray, moth like dusters, large as hawks, but so fragile that a blow shattered them. They darted about, alighting at times to seize small squirming things, and tinkling in their curiously bell-like voices. And apparently almost above him, though really thirty miles distant, loomed the Mountains of Eternity, their peaks lost in the clouds that swirled fifteen miles overhead.

Here again it grew difficult to trail since Patricia scrambled often over bare rock. But little by little the signs grew fresher; once again his greater strength began to tell. And then he glimpsed her, at the base of a colossal escarpment split by a narrow, tree-filled canyon.

She was peering first at the mighty precipice, then at the cleft, obviously wondering whether it offered a means of scaling the barrier, or whether it was necessary to circle the obstacle. Like himself, she had discarded her transkin and wore the usual shirt and shorts of the Cool Country, which, after all, is not very cool by terrestrial standards. She looked, he thought, like some lovely forest nymph of the ancient slopes of Pelion.

He hurried as she moved into the canyon. "Pat!" he shouted; it was the first time he had spoken her given name. A hundred feet within the passage he overtook her.

"You!" she gasped. She looked tired; she had been hurrying for hours, but a light of eagerness flashed in her eyes. "I thought you had—I tried to find you."

Ham's face held no responsive light. "Listen here, Pat Burlingame," he said coldly. "You don't deserve any consideration, but I can't see you walking into death. You're a stubborn devil, but you're a woman. I'm taking you to Erotia."

The eagerness vanished. "Indeed, poacher? My father crossed here. I can, too."

"Your father crossed in midsummer, didn't he? And midsummer's today. You can't make Madman's Pass in less than five days, a hundred and twenty hours, and by then it will be nearly winter, and this longitude will be close to the storm line. You're a fool."

She flushed. "The pass is high enough to be in the upper winds. It will be warm."

"Warm! Yes—warm with lightning." He paused; the faint rumble of thunder rolled through the canyon. "Listen to that. In five days that will be right over us." He gestured up at the utterly barren slopes. "Not even Venusian life can get a foothold up there—or do you think you've got brass enough to be a lightning rod? Maybe you're right."

Anger flamed. "Rather the lightning than you!" Patricia snapped, and then as suddenly softened. "I tried to call you back," she said irrelevantly.

"To laugh at me," he retorted bitterly.

"No. To tell you I was sorry, and that—"

"I don't want your apology."

"But I wanted to tell you that—"

"Never mind," he said curtly. "I'm not interested in your repentance. The harm's done." He frowned coldly down on her.

Patricia said meekly: "But I—"

A crashing and gurgling interrupted her, and she screamed as a gigantic doughpot burst into view, a colossus that filled the canyon from wall to wall to a six-foot height as it surged toward them. The horrors were rarer in the Cool Country, but larger, since the abundance of food in the Hotlands kept subdividing them. But this one was a giant, a behemoth, tons and tons of nauseous, ill-smelling corruption heaving up the narrow way. They were cut off.

Ham snatched his flame-pistol, but the girl seized his arm. "No,' no!" she cried. "Too close! It will spatter!"

Patricia was right. Unprotected by transkin, the touch of a fragment of that monstrosity was deadly, and, beyond that, the blast of a flame-pistol would shower bits of it upon them. He grasped her wrist and they fled up the canyon, striving for vantage-way enough to risk a shot. And a dozen feet behind surged the doughpot, traveling blindly in the only direction it could— the way of food.

They gained. Then, abruptly, the canyon, which had been angling southwest, turned sharply south. The light of the eternally eastward

Sun was hidden; they were in a pit of perpetual shadow, and the ground was bare and lifeless rock. And as it reached that point, the doughpot halted; lacking any organization, any will, it could not move when no food gave it direction. It was such a monster as only the life-swarming climate of Venus could harbor; it lived only by endless eating.

The two paused in the shadow.

"Now what?" muttered Ham.

A fair shot at the mass was impossible because of the angle; a blast would destroy only the portion it could reach.

Patricia leaped upward, catching a snaky shrub on the wall, so placed that it received a faint ray of light. She tossed it against the pulsing mass; the whole doughpot lunged forward a foot or two.

"Lure it in," she suggested.

They tried. It was impossible; vegetation was too sparse.

"What will happen to the thing?" asked Ham.

"I saw one stranded on the desert edge of the Hotlands," replied the girl. "It quivered around for a long time, and then the cells attacked one another. It ate itself." She shuddered. "It was—horrible!"

"How long?"

"Oh, forty or fifty hours."

"I won't wait that long," growled Ham. He fumbled in his pack, pulling out his *transkin*.

"What will you do?"

"Put this on and try to blast that mass out of here at close range." He fingered his flame-pistol. "This is my last barrel," he said gloomily, then, more hopefully: "But we have yours."

"The chamber of mine cracked last time I used it, ten or twelve hours ago. But I have plenty of barrels."

"Good enough!" said Ham.

He crept cautiously toward the horrible, pulsating wall of white. He thrust his arm so as to cover the greatest angle, pulled the trigger, and the roar and blazing fire of the blast bellowed echoing through the canyon. Bits of the monster spattered around him, and the thickness of the remainder, lessened by the incineration of tons of filth, was now only three feet.

"The barrel held!" he called triumphantly. It saved much time in recharging.

Five minutes later the weapon crashed again. When the mass of the monstrosity stopped heaving, only a foot and a half of depth remained, but the barrel had been blow to atoms.

"We'll have to use yours," he said, then stared at it in dismay. The barrels of her Enfield-made weapon were far too small for his American pistol stock!

He groaned. "Of all the idiots!" he burst out.

"Idiots!" she flared. "Because you Yankees use trench mortars for your barrels?"

"I meant myself. I should have guessed this." He shrugged. "Well, we have our choice now of waiting here for the doughpot to eat himself, or trying to find some other way out of this trap. And my hunch is that this canyon's blind."

It was probable, Patricia admitted. The narrow cleft was the product of some vast, ancient upheaval that had split the mountain in halves. Since it was not the result of water erosion, it was likely enough that the cleft ended abruptly in an unscalable precipice, but it was possible, too, that somewhere those sheer walls might be surmountable.

"We've time to waste, anyway," she concluded. "We might as well try it. Besides—" She wrinkled her dainty nose distastefully at the doughpot's odor.

Still in his transkin, Ham followed her through the shadowy half dusk. The passage narrowed, then veered west again, but now so high and sheer were the walls that the Sun, slightly south of east, cast no light into it. It was a place of shades like the region of the storm line that divides the twilight zone from the dark hemisphere, not true light, nor yet honest day, but a dim middle state.

Ahead of him Patricia's bronzed limbs showed pale instead of tan, and when she spoke her voice went echoing queerly between the opposing cliffs. A weird place, this chasm, a dusky, unpleasant place.

"I don't like this," said Ham. "The pass is cutting closer and closer to the dark. Do you realize no one knows what's in the dark parts of the Mountains of Eternity?"

Patricia laughed; the sound was ghostly. "What danger could there be? Anyway, we still have our automatics."

"There's no way up here," Ham grumbled. "Let's turn back."

Patricia faced him. "Frightened, Yankee?" Her voice dropped.

"The natives say these mountains are haunted," she went on mockingly. "My father told me he saw queer things in Madman's Pass. Do you know that if there is life on the night side, here is the one place it would impinge on the twilight zone? Here in the Mountains of Eternity?"

She was taunting him; she laughed again. And suddenly her laughter was repeated in a hideous cacophony that hooted out from the sides of the cliffs above them in a horrid medley.

She paled; it was Patricia who was frightened now. They stared apprehensively up at the rock walls where strange shadows flickered and shifted.

"What—what was it?" she whispered. And then: "Ham! Did you see that?"

Ham had seen it. A wild shape had flung itself across the strip of sky, leaping from cliff to cliff far above them. And again came a peal of hooting that sounded like laughter, while shadowy forms moved, fly like, on the sheer walls.

"Let's go back!" she gasped. "Quickly!"

As she turned, a small black object fell and broke with a sullen pop before them. Ham stared at it. A pod, a spore-sac, of some unknown variety. A lazy, dusky cloud drifted over it, and suddenly both of them were choking violently. Ham felt his head spinning in dizziness, and Patricia reeled against him.

"It's—narcotic!" she gasped. "Back!"

But a dozen more plopped around them. The dusty spores whirled in dark eddies, and breathing was a torment. They were being drugged and suffocated at the same time.

Ham had a sudden inspiration. "Mask!" he choked, and pulled his *transkin* over his face.

The filter that kept out the molds of the Hotlands cleared the air of these spores as well; his head cleared. But the girl's covering was somewhere in her pack; she was fumbling for it. Abruptly she sat down, swaying.

"My pack," she murmured. "Take it out with you. Your—your— " She broke into a fit of coughing.

He dragged her under a shallow overhang and ripped her transkin from the pack. "Put it on!" he snapped.

A score of pods were popping.

A figure flitted silently far up on the wall of rock. Ham watched its progress, then aimed his automatic and fired. There was a shrill, rasping scream, answered by a chorus of dissonant ululations, and something as large as a man whirled down to crash not ten feet from him.

The thing was hideous. Ham stared appalled at a creature not unlike a native, three-eyed, two-handed, four-legged, but the hands, though two-fingered like the Hotlanders; were not pincer-like—but white and clawed.

And the face! Not the broad, expressionless face of the others, but a slanting, malevolent, dusky visage with each eye double the size of the natives'. It wasn't dead; it glared hatred and seized a stone, flinging it at him with weak viciousness. Then it died.

Ham didn't know what it was, of course. Actually it was a *triops noctivivans*—the "three-eyed dweller in the dark," the strange, semi-intelligent being that is as yet the only known creature of that fierce remnant still occasionally found in the sunless parts of the Mountains of Eternity. It is perhaps the most vicious creature in the known planets, absolutely unapproachable, and delighting in slaughter.

At the crash of the shot, the shower of pods had ceased, and a chorus of laughing hoots ensued. Ham seized the respite to pull the girl's transkin over her face; she had collapsed with it only half on.

Then a sharp crack sounded, and a stone rebounded to strike his arm. Others pattered around him, whining past, swift as bullets. Black figures flickered in great leaps against the sky, and their fierce laughter sounded mockingly. He fired at one in midair; the cry of pain rasped again, but the creature did not fall.

Stones pelted him. They were all small ones, pebble-sized, but they were flung so fiercely that they hummed in passage, and they tore his flesh through his transkin. He turned Patricia on her face, but she moaned faintly as a missile struck her back. He shielded her with his own body.

The position was intolerable. He must risk a dash back, even though the doughpot blocked the opening. Perhaps, he thought, armored in transkin he could wade through the creature. He knew that was an insane idea; the gluey mass would roll him into itself to suffocate—but it had to be faced. He gathered the girl in his arms and rushed suddenly down the canyon.

Hoots and shrieks and a chorus of mocking laughter echoed around him. Stones struck him everywhere. One glanced from his head, sending him stumbling and staggering against the cliff. But he ran doggedly on; he knew now what drove him. It was the girl he carried; he had to save Patricia Burlingame.

Ham reached the bend. Far up on the west wall glowed cloudy sunlight, and his weird pursuers flung themselves to the dark side. They couldn't stand daylight, and that gave him some assistance; by creeping very close to the eastern wall he was partially shielded.

Ahead was the other bend, blocked by the doughpot. As he neared it, he turned suddenly sick. Three of the creatures were grouped against the mass of white, eating—actually eating!—the corruption. They whirled, hooting, as he came; he shot two of them, as the third leaped for the wall, he dropped that one as well, and it fell with a dull gulping sound into the doughpot.

Again he sickened; the doughpot drew away from it, leaving the thing lying in a hollow like the hole of a giant doughnut. Not even that monstrosity would eat these creatures.★

But the thing's leap had drawn Ham's attention to a twelve-inch ledge. It might be—yes, it was possible that he could traverse that rugged trail and so circle the doughpot. Nearly hopeless, no doubt, to attempt it under the volley of stones, but he must. There was no alternative.

He shifted the girl to free his right arm. He slipped a second clip in his automatic and then fired at random into the flitting shadows above. For a moment the hail of pebbles ceased, and with a convulsive, painful struggle, Ham dragged himself and Patricia to the ledge.

Stones cracked about him once more. Step by step he edged along the way, poised just over the doomed doughpot. Death below and death above! And little by little he rounded the bend; above him both walls glowed in sunlight, and they were safe.

At least, he was safe. The girl might already be dead, he thought frantically, as he slipped and slid through the slime of the dough-

---

★Note: It was not known then that while the night-side life of Venus can eat and digest that of the day side, the reverse is not true. No day-side creature can absorb the dark life because of the presence of various metabolic alcohols, all poisonous.

pot's passage. Out on the day lit slope he tore the mask from her face and gazed on white, marble-cold features.

It was not death, however, but only drugged torpor. An hour later she was conscious, though weak and very badly frightened. Yet almost her first question was for her pack.

"It's here" Ham said. "What's so precious about that pack? Your notes?"

"My notes? Oh, no!" A faint flush covered her features. "It's —I kept trying to tell you—it's your *xixtchil.*"

"What?"

"Yes. I—of course. I didn't throw it to the molds. It's yours by rights, Ham. Lots of British traders go into the American Hotlands. I just slit the pouch and hid the *xixtchil* here in my pack. The molds on the ground were only some twigs I threw there to—to make it look real."

"But—but—why?"

The flush deepened. "I wanted to punish you," Patricia whispered, "for being so—so cold and distant."

"I?" Ham was amazed. "It was you!"

"Perhaps it was, at first. You forced your way into my house, you know. But—after you carried me across the mudspout, Ham —it was different."

Ham gulped. Suddenly he pulled her into his arms. "I'm not going to quarrel about whose fault it was," he said. "But we'll settle one thing immediately. We're going to Erotia, and that's where we'll be married, in a good American church if they've put one up yet, or by a good American justice if they haven't. There's no more talk of Madman's Pass and crossing the Mountains of Eternity. Is that clear?"

She glanced at the vast, looming peaks and shuddered. "Quite clear!" she replied meekly.

The Lotus Eaters

"Whew!" whistled "Ham" Hammond, staring through the right forward observation port. "What a place for a honeymoon!"

"Then you shouldn't have married a biologist," remarked Mrs. Hammond over his shoulder, but he could see her gray eyes dancing in the glass of the port. "Nor an explorer's daughter," she added. For Pat Hammond, until her marriage to Ham a scant four weeks ago, had been Patricia Burlingame, daughter of the great Englishman who had won so much of the twilight zone of Venus for Britain, exactly as Crowly had done for the United States.

"I didn't," observed Ham, "marry a biologist. I married a girl who happened to be interested in biology; that's all. It's one of her few drawbacks."

He cut the blast to the underjets, and the rocket settled down gently on a cushion of flame toward the black landscape below. Slowly, carefully, he dropped the unwieldy mechanism until there was the faintest perceptible jar; then he killed the blast suddenly, the floor beneath them tilted slightly, and a strange silence fell like a blanket after the cessation of the roaring blast.

"We're here," he announced.

"So we are," agreed Pat. "Where's here?"

"It's a point exactly seventy-five miles east of the Barrier opposite Venoble, in the British Cool Country. To the north is, I suppose, the continuation of the Mountains of Eternity, and to the south is Heaven knows what. And this last applies to the east."

"Which is a good technical description of nowhere." Pat laughed. "Let's turn off the lights and look at nowhere."

She did, and in the darkness the ports showed as faintly luminous circles.

"I suggest," she proceeded, "that the Joint Expedition ascend to the dome for a less restricted view. We're here to investigate; let's do a little investigating."

"This joint of the expedition agrees," chuckled Ham.

He grinned in the darkness at the flippancy with which Pat approached the serious business of exploration. Here they were, the Joint Expedition of the Royal Society and the Smithsonian Institute for the Investigation of Conditions on the Dark Side of Venus, to use the full official title.

Of course Ham himself, while technically the American half of the project, was in reality a member only because Pat wouldn't consider anything else; but she was the one to whom the bearded society and institute members addressed their questions, their terms, and their instructions.

And this was no more than fair, for Pat, after all, was the leading authority on Hotland flora and fauna, and, moreover, the first human child born on Venus, while Ham was only an engineer lured originally to the Venusian frontier by a dream of quick wealth in xixtchil trading in the Hotlands.

It was there he had met Patricia Burlingame, and there, after an adventurous journey to the foothills of the Mountains of Eternity, that he had won her. They had been married in Erotia, the American settlement, less than a month ago, and then had come the offer of the expedition to the dark side.

Ham had argued against it. He had wanted a good terrestrial honeymoon in New York or London, but there were difficulties. Primarily there was the astronomical one; Venus was past perigee, and it would be eight long months before its slow swing around the Sun brought it back to a point where a rocket could overtake the Earth.

Eight months in primitive, frontier-built Erotia, or in equally primitive Venoble, if they chose the British settlement, with no amusement save hunting, no radio, no plays, even very few books. And if they must hunt, Pat argued, why not add the thrill and danger of the unknown?

No one knew what life, if any, lurked on the dark side of the planet; very few had even seen it, and those few from rockets speeding over vast mountain ranges or infinite frozen oceans. Here was a chance to explain the mystery, and explore it, expenses paid.

It took a multimillionaire to build and equip a private rocket, but the Royal Society and the Smithsonian Institute, spending government money, were above such considerations. There'd be danger, perhaps, and breath-taking thrills, but—they could be alone.

The last point had won Ham. So they had spent two busy weeks provisioning and equipping the rocket, had ridden high above the ice barrier that bounds the twilight zone, and dashed frantically through the storm line, where the cold Underwind from the sunless side meets the hot Upper Winds that sweep from the desert face of the planet.

For Venus, of course, has no rotation, and hence no alternate days and nights. One face is forever sunlit, and one forever dark, and only the planet's slow libration gives the twilight zone a semblance of seasons. And this twilight zone, the only habitable part of the planet, merges through the Hotlands on one side to the blazing desert, and on the other side ends abruptly in the ice barrier where the Upper Winds yield their moisture to the chilling breaths of the Underwind.

So here they were, crowded into the tiny glass dome above the navigation panel, standing close together on the top rung of the ladder, and with just room in the dome for both their heads. Ham slipped his arm around the girl as they stared at the scene outside.

Away off to the west was the eternal dawn—or sunset, perhaps—where the light glistened on the ice barrier. Like vast columns, the Mountains of Eternity thrust themselves against the light, with their mighty peaks lost in the lower clouds twenty-five miles above. There, a little south, were the ramparts of the Lesser Eternities, bounding American Venus, and between the two ranges were the perpetual lightning of the storm line.

But around them, illuminated dimly by the refraction of the sunlight, was a scene of dark and wild splendor. Everywhere was ice—hills of it, spires, plains, boulders, and cliffs of it, all glowing a pallid green in the trickle of light from beyond the barrier. A world without motion, frozen and sterile, save for the moaning of the Underwind outside, not hindered here as the barrier shielded it from the Cool Country.

"It's—glorious!" Pat murmured.

"Yes," he agreed, "but cold, lifeless, yet menacing. Pat, do you think there is life here?"

"I should judge so. If life can exist on such worlds as Titan and Iapetus, it should exist here. How cold is it?" She glanced at the thermometer outside the dome, its column and figures self-luminous. "Only thirty below zero, Fahrenheit. Life exists on Earth at that temperature."

"Exists, yes. But it couldn't have developed at a temperature below freezing. Life has to be lived in liquid water."

She laughed softly. "You're talking to a biologist, Ham. No; life couldn't have evolved at thirty below zero, but suppose it originated back in the twilight zone and migrated here? Or suppose it was pushed here by the terrific competition of the warmer regions? You know what conditions are in the Hotlands, with the molds and doughpots and Jack Ketch trees, and the millions of little parasitic things, all eating each other."

He considered this. "What sort of life should you expect?"

She chuckled. "Do you want a prediction? Very well. I'd guess, first of all, some sort of vegetation as a base, for animal life can't keep eating itself without some added fuel. It's like the story of the man with the cat farm, who raised rats to feed the cats, and then when he skinned the cats, he fed the bodies to the rats, and then fed more rats to the cats. It sounds good, but it won't work."

"So there ought to be vegetation. Then what?"

"Then? Heaven knows. Presumably the dark side life, if it exists, came originally from the weaker strains of twilight-zone life, but what it might have become—well, I can't guess. Of course, there's the *triops noctivivans* that I discovered in the Mountains of Eternity—"

"You discovered!" He grinned. "You were out as cold as ice when I carried you away from the nest of devils. You never even saw one!"

"I examined the dead one brought into Venoble by the hunters," she returned imperturbably. "And don't forget that the society wanted to name it after me—the *triops Patriciae.*" Involuntarily a shudder shook her at the memory of those satanic creatures that had all but destroyed the two of them. "But I chose the other name—*triops noctivivans,* the three-eyed dweller in the dark."

"Romantic name for a devilish beast!"

"Yes; but what I was getting at is this—that it's probable that triops—or triopses—Say, what is the plural of triops?"

"Trioptes," he grunted. "Latin root."

"Well, it's probable that trioptes, then, are among the creatures to be found here on the night side, and that those fierce devils who attacked us in that shadowed canyon in the Mountains of Eternity are an outpost, creeping into the twilight zone through the dark and sunless passes in the mountains. They can't stand light; you saw that yourself."

"So what?"

Pat laughed at the Americanism. "So this: From their form and structure—six limbs, three eyes, and all—it's plain that the trioptes are related to ordinary native Hotlanders. Therefore I conclude that they're recent arrivals on the dark side; that they didn't evolve here, but were driven here quite lately, geologically speaking. Or geologically isn't quite the word, because geos means earth. *Venusologically* speaking, I should say."

"You shouldn't say. You're substituting a Latin root for a Greek one. What you mean is aphrodisiologically speaking."

She chuckled again. "What I mean, and should have said right away to avoid argument, is palaeontologically speaking, which is better English. Anyway, I mean that trioptes haven't existed on the dark side for more than twenty to fifty thousand Earth years, or maybe less, because what do we know about the speed of evolution on Venus? Perhaps it's faster than on the Earth; maybe a triops could adapt itself to night life in five thousand,"

"I've seen college students adapt themselves to night life in one semester!" He grinned.

She ignored this. "And therefore," she proceeded, "I argue that there must have been life here before triops arrived, since it must have found something to eat when it got here or it couldn't have survived. And since my examination showed that it's partly a carnivorous feeder, there must have been not only life here, but animal life. And that's as far as pure reason can carry the argument."

"So you can't guess what sort of animal life. Intelligent, perhaps?"

"I don't know. It might be. But in spite of the way you Yankees worship intelligence, biologically it's unimportant. It hasn't even much survival value."

"What? How can you say that, Pat? What except human intelligence has given man the supremacy of the Earth—and of Venus, too, for that matter?"

"But has man the supremacy of the Earth? Look here, Ham, here's what I mean about intelligence. A gorilla has a far better brain than a turtle, hasn't it? And yet which is the more successful—the gorilla, which is rare and confined only to a small region in Africa, or the turtle, which is common everywhere from the arctic to the Antarctic? And as for man—well, if you had microscopic eyes, and could see every living thing on the Earth, you'd decide that man was just a rare specimen, and that the planet was really a nematode world—that is, a worm world—because the nematodes far outnumber all the other forms of life put together."

"But that isn't supremacy, Pat."

"I didn't say it was. I merely said that intelligence hasn't much survival value. If it has, why are the insects that have no intelligence, but just instinct, giving the human race such a battle? Men have better brains than corn borers, boll weevils, fruit flies, Japanese beetles, gypsy moths, and all the other pests, and yet they match our intelligence with just one weapon—their enormous fecundity. Do you realize that every time a child is born, until it's balanced by a death, it can be fed in only one way? And that way is by taking the food away from the child's own weight of insects."

"All that sounds reasonable enough, but what's it got to do with intelligence on the dark side of Venus?"

"I don't know," replied Pat, and her voice took on a queer tinge of nervousness. "I just mean—Look at it this way, Ham. A lizard is more intelligent than a fish, but not enough to give it any advantage. Then why did the lizard and its descendants keep on developing intelligence? Why—unless all life tends to become intelligent in time? And if that's true, then there may be intelligence even here—strange, alien, incomprehensible intelligence."

She shivered in the dark against him. "Never mind," she said in suddenly altered tones. "It's probably just fancy. The world out there is so weird, so unearthly—I'm tired, Ham. It's been a long day."

He followed her down into the body of the rocket. As the lights flicked on the strange landscape beyond the ports was blotted out, and he saw only Pat, very lovely in the scanty costume of the Cool Country.

"Tomorrow, then," he said. "We've food for three weeks."

Tomorrow, of course, meant only time and not daylight. They rose to the same darkness that had always blanketed the sunless half of Venus, with the same eternal sunset green on the horizon at the barrier. But Pat was in better humor, and went eagerly about the preparations for their first venture into the open. She brought out the parkas of inch-thick wool sheathed in rubber, and Ham, in his capacity as engineer, carefully inspected the hoods, each with its crown of powerful lamps.

These were primarily for vision, of course, but they had another purpose. It was known that the incredibly fierce trioptes could not face light, and thus, by using all four beams in the helmet, one could move, surrounded by a protective aura. But that did not prevent both of them from including in their equipment two blunt blue automatics and a pair of the terrifically destructive flame pistols. And Pat carried a bag at her belt, into which she proposed to drop specimens of any darkside flora she encountered, and fauna, too, if it proved small and harmless enough.

They grinned at each other through their masks.

"Makes you look fat," observed Ham maliciously, and enjoyed her sniff of annoyance.

She turned, threw open the door, and stamped into the open.

It was different from looking out through a port. Then the scene had some of the unreality and all of the immobility and silence of a picture, but now it was actually around them, and the cold breath and mournful voice of the Underwind proved definitely enough that the world was real. For a moment they stood in the circlet of light from the rocket ports, staring awe-struck at the horizon where the unbelievable peaks of the Greater Eternities towered black against the false sunset.

Nearer, for as far as vision reached through that sunless, moonless, starless region, was a desolate tumbled plain where peaks, minarets, spires, and ridges of ice and stone rose in indescribable and fantastic shapes, carved by the wild artistry of the Underwind.

Ham slipped a padded arm around Pat, and was surprised to feel her shiver. "Cold?" he asked, glancing at the dial thermometer on his wrist. "It's only thirty-six below."

"I'm not cold," replied Pat. "It's the scenery; that's all." She moved away. "I wonder what keeps the place as warm as it is. Without sunlight you'd think—"

"Then you'd be wrong," cut in Ham. "Any engineer knows that gases diffuse. The Upper Winds are going by just five or six miles over our heads, and they naturally carry a lot of heat from the desert beyond the twilight zone. There's some diffusion of the warm air into the cold, and then, besides, as the warm winds cool, they tend to sink. And what's more, the contour of the country has a lot to do with it."

He paused. "Say," he went on reflectively, "I shouldn't be surprised if we found sections near the Eternities where there was a down draft, where the Upper Winds slid right along the slope and gave certain places a fairly bearable climate."

He followed Pat as she poked around the boulders near the edge of the circle of light from the rocket.

"Ha!" she exclaimed. "There it is, Ham! There's our specimen of darkside plant life."

She bent over a gray bulbous mass, "Lichenous or fungoid," she continued. "No leaves, of course; leaves are only useful in sunlight. No chlorophyll for the same reason. A very primitive, very simple plant, and yet—in some ways—not simple at all. Look, Ham—a highly developed circulatory system!"

He leaned closer, and in the dim yellow light from the ports he saw the fine tracery of veins she indicated.

"That," she proceeded, "would indicate a sort of heart and—I wonder!" Abruptly she thrust her dial thermometer against the fleshy mass, held it there a moment, and then peered at it. "Yes! Look how the needle's moved, Ham. It's warm! A warm-blooded plant. And when you think of it, it's only natural, because that's the one sort of plant that could live in a region forever below freezing. Life must be lived in liquid water."

She tugged at the thing, and with a sullen plump it came free, and dark driblets of liquid welled out of the torn root.

"Ugh!" exclaimed Ham. "What a disgusting thing! 'And tore the bleeding mandragore,' eh? Only they were supposed to scream when you uprooted them."

He paused. A low, pulsing, wailing whimper came out of the quivering mass of pulp, and he turned a startled gaze on Pat. "Ugh!" he grunted again. "Disgusting!"

"Disgusting? Why, it's a beautiful organism! It's adapted perfectly to its environment."

"Well, I'm glad I'm an engineer," he growled, watching Pat as she

91

opened the rocket's door and laid the thing on a square of rubber within. "Come on. Let's look around."

Pat closed the door and followed him away from the rocket. Instantly the night folded in around them like a black mist, and it was only by glancing back at the lighted ports that Pat could convince herself that they stood in a real world.

"Should we light our helmet lamps?" asked Ham. "We'd better, I suppose, or risk a fall."

Before either could move farther, a sound struck through the moaning of the Underwind, a wild, fierce, unearthly shrieking like laughter in hell, hoots and howls and mirthless chuckling noises.

"It's triopts!" gasped Pat, forgetting plurals and grammar alike.

She was frightened; ordinarily she was as courageous as Ham, and rather more reckless and daring, but those uncanny shrieks brought back the moments of torment when they had been trapped in the canyon in the Mountains of Eternity. She was badly frightened and fumbled frantically and ineffectually at light switch and revolver.

Just as half a dozen stones hummed fast as bullets around them, and one crashed painfully on Ham's arm, he flicked on his lights. Four beams shot in a long cross on the glittering peaks, and the wild laughter rose in a crescendo of pain. He had a momentary glimpse of shadowy figures flinging themselves from pinnacle and ridge, flitting specter like into the darkness, and then silence.

"O-o-oh!" murmured Pat. "I—was scared, Ham." She huddled against him, then continued more strongly: "But there's proof. *Triops noctivivans* actually is a nightside creature, and those in the mountains are outposts or fragments that've wandered into the sunless chasms."

Far off sounded the hooting laughter. "I wonder," mused Ham, "if that noise of theirs is in the nature of a language."

"Very probably. After all, the Hotland natives are intelligent, and these creatures are a related species. Besides, they throw stones, and they know the use of those smothering pods they showered on us in the canyon—which, by the way, must be the fruit of some nightside plant. The trioptes are doubtless intelligent in a fierce, blood-thirsty, barbaric fashion, but the beasts are so unapproachable that I doubt if human beings ever learn much of their minds or language."

Ham agreed emphatically, the more so as a viciously cast rock suddenly chipped glittering particles from an icy spire a dozen paces away. He twisted his head, sending the beams of his helmet lamps angling over the plain, and a single shrill cachinnation drifted out of the dark.

"Thank Heaven the lights keep 'em fairly out of range," he muttered. "These are pleasant little subjects of his majesty,* aren't they? God save the king if he had many more like 'em!"

But Pat was again engaged in her search for specimens. She had switched on her lamps now, and scrambled agilely in and out among the fantastic monuments of that bizarre plain. Ham followed her, watching as she wrenched up bleeding and whimpering vegetation. She found a dozen varieties, and one little wriggling cigar-shaped creature that she gazed at in perplexity, quite unable to determine whether it was plant, animal, or neither. And at last her specimen bag was completely filled, and they turned back over the plain toward the rocket, whose ports gleamed afar like a row of staring eyes.

But a shock awaited them as they opened the door to enter. Both of them started back at the gust of warm, stuffy, putrid, and unbreathable air that gushed into their faces with an odor of carrion.

"What-----" gasped Ham, and then laughed. "Your mandragore!" He chuckled. "Look at it!"

The plant she had placed within was a mass of decayed corruption. In the warmth of the interior it had decomposed rapidly and completely and was now but a semi liquid heap on the rubber mat. She pulled it through the entrance and flung mat and all away.

They clambered into an interior still reeking, and Ham set a ventilator spinning. The air that came in was cold, of course, but pure with the breath of the Underwind, sterile and dustless from its sweep across five thousand miles of frozen oceans and mountains. He swung the door closed, set a heater going, and dropped his visor to grin at Pat.

"So that's your beautiful organism!" he chuckled.

"It was. It was a beautiful organism, Ham. You can't blame it be-

---

*They were on British territory, being in the latitude of Venoble. The International Congress at Lisle had in 2020 apportioned the dark-side rights by giving to each nation owning Venusian possessions a wedge extending from the twilight zone to a point on the planet directly opposite the Sun in mid-autumn.

cause we exposed it to temperatures it was never supposed to encounter." She sighed and slung her specimen pouch to the table. "I'll have to prepare these at once, I suppose, since they don't keep."

Ham grunted and set about the preparation of a meal, working with the expert touch of a true Hotlander. He glanced at Pat as she bent over her specimens, injecting the bichloride solution.

"Do you suppose," he asked, "that the triops is the highest form of life on the dark side?"

"Beyond doubt," replied Pat. "If any higher form existed, it would long ago have exterminated those fierce devils."

But she was utterly wrong.

Within the span of four days they had exhausted; the possibilities of the tumbled plain around the rocket. Pat had accumulated a variegated group of specimens, and Ham had taken an endless series of observations on temperature, on magnetic variations, on the direction and velocity of the Underwind.

So they moved their base, and the rocket flared into flight southward, toward the region where, presumably, the vast and mysterious Mountains of Eternity towered across the ice barrier into the dusky world of the night side. They flew slowly, throttling the reaction motors to a bare fifty miles an hour, for they were flying through night, depending on the beam of the forward light to warn against looming peaks.

Twice they halted, and each time a day or two sufficed to indicate that the region was similar to that of their first base. The same veined and bulbous plants, the same eternal Underwind, the same laughter from blood-thirsty trioptic throats.

But on the third occasion, there was a difference. They came to rest on a wild and bleak plateau among the foothills of the Greater Eternities. Far away to the westward, half the horizon still glowed green with the false sunset, but the whole span south of the due-west point was black, hidden from view by the vast ramparts of the range that soared twenty-five miles above them into the black heavens. The mountains were invisible, of course, in that region of endless night, but the two in the rocket felt the colossal nearness of those incredible peaks.

And there was another way in which the mighty presence of the Mountains of Eternity affected them. The region was warm—not warm by the standards of the twilight zone, but much warmer than the plain below. Their thermometers showed zero on one side of the rocket, five above on the other. The vast peaks, ascending into the level of the Upper Winds, set up eddies and stray currents that brought warm air down to temper the cold breath of the Underwind.

Ham stared gloomily over the plateau visible in the lights. "I don't like it," he grunted. "I never did like these mountains, not since you made a fool of yourself by trying to cross 'em back in the Cool Country."

"A fool!" echoed Pat. "Who named these mountains? Who crossed them? Who discovered them? My father, that's who!"

"And so you thought you inherited 'em," he retorted, "and that all you had to do was to whistle and they'd lie down and play dead, and Madman's Pass would turn into a park walk. With the result that you'd now be a heap of clean-picked bones in a canyon if I hadn't been around to carry you out of it."

"Oh, you're just a timid Yankee!" she snapped. "I'm going outside to have a look." She pulled on her parka and stepped to the door, and there paused. "Aren't you—aren't you coming, too?" she asked hesitantly.

He grinned. "Sure! I just wanted to hear you ask." He slipped into his own outdoor garb and followed.

There was a difference here. Outwardly the plateau presented the same bleak wilderness of ice and stone that they had found on the plain below. There were wind-eroded pinnacles of the utmost fantasy of form, and the wild landscape that glittered in the beams from their helmet lamps was the same bizarre terrain that they had first encountered.

But the cold was less bitter here; strangely, increasing altitude on this curious planet brought warmth instead of cold, as on the Earth, because it raised one closer to the region of the Upper Winds, and here in the Mountains of Eternity the Underwind howled less persistently, broken into gusts by the mighty peaks.

And the vegetation was less sparse. Everywhere were the veined and bulbous masses, and Ham had to tread carefully lest he repeat the unpleasant experience of stepping on one and hearing its moaning whimper of pain. Pat had no such scruples, insisting that the whimper was but a tropism; that the specimens she pulled up and dissected felt no more pain than an apple that was eaten; and that, anyway, it was a biologist's business to be a biologist.

Somewhere off among the peaks shrilled the mocking laughter of a triops, and in the shifting shadows at the extremities of their beams, Ham imagined more than once that he saw the forms of these demons of the dark. If there they were, however, the light kept them at a safe distance, for no stones hummed past.

Yet it was a queer sensation to walk thus in the center of a moving circle of light; he felt continually as if just beyond the boundary of visibility lurked Heaven only knew what weird and incredible creatures, though reason argued that such monsters couldn't have remained undetected.

Ahead of them their beams glistened on an icy rampart, a bank or cliff that stretched right and left across their course.

Pat gestured suddenly toward it. "Look there!" she exclaimed, holding her light steady. "Caves in the ice—burrows, rather. See?"

He saw—little black openings as large, perhaps, as a manhole cover, a whole row of them at the base of the ice rampart. Something black skittered laughing up the glassy slope and away—a triops. Were these the dens of the beasts? He squinted sharply.

"Something's there!" he muttered to Pat. "Look! Half the openings have something in front of them—or are those just rocks to block the entrance?"

Cautiously, revolvers in hand, they advanced. There was no more motion, but in the growing intensity of the beams, the objects were less and less rocklike, and at last they could make out the veinings and fleshy bulbousness of life.

At least the creatures were a new variety. Now Ham could distinguish a row of eyelike spots, and now a multiplicity of legs beneath them. The things were like inverted bushel baskets, about the size and contour, veined, flabby, and featureless save for a complete circle of eye spots. And now he could even see the semitransparent lids that closed, apparently, to shield the eyes from the pain of their lights.

They were barely a dozen feet from one of the creatures. Pat, after a moment of hesitation, moved directly before the motionless mystery.

"Well!" she said. "Here's a new one, Ham. Hello, old fella!"

An instant later both of them were frozen in utter consternation, completely overwhelmed by bewilderment, amazement, and confusion. Issuing, it seemed, from a membrane at the top of the creature, came a clicking, high-pitched voice.

"Hello, fella!" it said.

There was an appalled silence. Ham held his revolver, but had there been need, he couldn't have used it, nor even remembered it. He was paralyzed; stricken dumb.

But Pat found her voice. "It—isn't real," she said faintly. "It's a tropism. The thing just echoes whatever sounds strike it. Doesn't it, Ham? Doesn't it?"

"I—I—of course!" He was staring at the lidded eyes. "It must be. Listen!" He leaned forward and yelled, "Hello!" directly at the creature. "It'll answer."

It did. "It isn't a tropism," it clicked in shrill but perfect English.

"That's no echo!" gasped Pat. She backed away. "I'm scared," she whimpered, pulling at Ham's arm. "Come away—quick!"

He thrust her behind him. "I'm just a timid Yankee," he grunted, "but I'm going to cross-question this living phonograph until I find out what—or who makes it tick."

"No! No, Ham! I'm scared!"

"It doesn't look dangerous," he observed.

"It isn't dangerous," remarked the thing on the ice.

Ham gulped, and Pat gave a horrified little moan.

"Who—who are you?" he faltered.

There was no answer. The lidded eyes stared steadily at him.

"What are you?" he tried again.

Again no reply.

"How do you know English?" he ventured.

The clicking voice sounded: "I isn't know English."

"Then—uh—then why do you speak English?"

"You speak English," explained the mystery, logically enough.

"I don't mean why. I mean how!"

But Pat had overcome a part of her terrified astonishment, and her quick mind perceived a clue. "Ham," she whispered tensely, "it uses the words we use. It gets the meaning from us!"

"I gets the meaning from you," confirmed the thing ungrammatically.

Light dawned on Ham. "Lord!" he gasped. "Then it's up to us to give it a vocabulary."

"You speak, I speak," suggested the creature.

"Sure! See, Pat? We can say just anything." He paused. "Let's see—When in the course of human events it—"

"Shut up!" snapped Pat. "Yankee! You're on crown territory now. 'To be or not to be; that is the question just—'"

Ham grinned and was silent. When she had exhausted her memory, he took up the task: "Once upon a time there were three bears—"

And so it went. Suddenly the situation struck him as fantastically ridiculous—there was Pat carefully relating the story of Little Red Riding Hood to a humorless monstrosity of the nightside of Venus! The girl cast him a perplexed glance as he roared into a gale of laughter.

"Tell him the one about the traveling man and the farmer's daughter!" he said, choking. "See if you can get a smile from him!"

She joined his laughter. "But it's really a serious matter," she concluded. "Imagine it, Ham! Intelligent life on the dark side! Or are you intelligent?" she asked suddenly of the thing on the ice.

"I am intelligent," it assured her. "I am intelligently intelligent."

"At least you're a marvelous linguist," said the girl. "Did you ever hear of learning English in half an hour, Ham? Think of that!" Apparently her fear of the creature had vanished.

"Well, let's make use of it," suggested Ham. "What's your name, friend?"

There was no reply.

"Of course," put in Pat. "He can't tell us his name until we give it to him in English, and we can't do that because—Oh, well, let's call him Oscar, then. That'll serve."

"Good enough. Oscar, what are you, anyway?"

"Human, I'm a man."

"Eh? I'll be damned if you are!"

"Those are the words you've given me. To me I am a man to you."

"Wait a moment. 'To me I am—' I see, Pat. He means that the only words we have for what he considers himself are words like man and human. Well, what are your people, then?"

"People."

"I mean your race. What race do you belong to?"

"Human."

"Ow!" groaned Ham. "You try, Pat."

"Oscar," said the girl, "you say you're human. Are you a mammal?"

"To me man is a mammal to you."

"Oh, good heavens!" She tried again. "Oscar, how does your race reproduce?"

"I have not the words."

"Are you born?"

The queer face, or faceless body, of the creature changed slightly. Heavier lids dropped over the semitransparent ones that shielded its many eyes; it was almost as if the thing frowned in concentration.

"We are not born," he clicked.

"Then—seeds, spores, parthenogenesis? Or fissure?"

"Spores," shrilled the mystery, "and fissure."

"But-"

She paused, nonplussed. In the momentary silence came the mocking hoot of a triops far to their left, and both turned involuntarily, stared, and recoiled aghast. At the very extremity of their beam one of the laughing demons had seized and was bearing away what was beyond doubt one of the creatures of the caves. And to add to the horror, all the rest squatted in utter indifference before their burrows.

"Oscar!" Pat screamed. "They got one of you!"

She broke off suddenly at the crack of Ham's revolver, but it was a futile shot.

"O-oh!" she gasped. "The devils! They got one!" There was no comment at all from the creature before them. "Oscar," she cried, "don't you care? They murdered one of you! Don't you understand?"

"Yes."

"But—doesn't it affect you at all?" The creatures had come, somehow, to hold a sort of human sympathy in Pat's mind. They could talk; they were more than beasts. "Don't you care at all?"

"No."

"But what are those devils to you? What do they do that you let them murder you?"

"They eat us," said Oscar placidly.

"Oh!" gasped Pat in horror. "But—but why don't—"

She broke off; the creature was backing slowly and methodically into its burrow.

"Wait!" she cried. "They can't come here! Our lights—"

The clicking voice drifted out: "It is cold. I go because of the cold."

There was silence.

It was colder. The gusty Underwind moaned more steadily now, and glancing along the ridge, Pat saw that every one of the cave creatures was slipping like Oscar into his burrow. She turned a helpless gaze on Ham.

"Did I—dream this?" she whispered.

"Then both of us dreamed it, Pat." He took her arm and drew her back toward the rocket, whose round ports glowed an invitation through the dusk.

But once in the warm interior, with her clumsy outer garments removed, Pat drew her dainty legs under her, lighted a cigarette, and fell to more rational consideration of the mystery.

"There's something we don't understand about this, Ham. Did you sense anything queer about Oscar's mind?"

"It's a devilishly quick one!"

"Yes; he's intelligent enough. Intelligence of the human level, or even"—she hesitated—"above the human. But it isn't a human mind. It's different, somehow—alien, strange. I can't quite express what I felt, but did you notice Oscar never asked a question? Not one!"

"Why—he didn't, did he? That's queer!"

"It's darn queer. Any human intelligence, meeting another thinking form of life, would ask plenty of questions. We did." She blew a thoughtful puff of smoke. "And that isn't all. That—that indifference of his when the triops attacked his fellow—was that human, or even earthly? I've seen a hunting spider snatch one fly from a swarm of them without disturbing the rest, but could that happen to intelligent creatures? It couldn't; not even to brains as undeveloped as those in a herd of deer, or a flock of sparrows. Kill one and you frighten all."

"That's true, Pat. They're damn queer ducks, these fellow citizens of Oscar's. Queer animals."

"Animals? Don't tell me you didn't notice, Ham!"

"Notice what?"

"Oscar's no animal. He's a plant—a warm-blooded, mobile vegetable! All the time we were talking to him he was rooting around below him with his—well, his root. And those things that looked like legs—they were pods. He didn't walk on them; he dragged himself on his root. And what's more he—"

"What's more?"

"What's more, Ham, those pods were the same sort as the ones that the triops threw at us in the canyon of the Mountains of Eternity, the ones that choked and smothered us so—"

"The ones that laid you out so cold, you mean."

"Anyway, I had wits enough to notice them!" she retorted, flushing. "But there's part of the mystery, Ham. Oscar's mind is a vegetable mind!" She paused, puffing her cigarette as he packed his pipe.

"Do you suppose," she asked suddenly, "that the presence of Oscar and his crew represents a menace to human occupancy of Venus? I know they're darkside creatures, but what if mines are discovered here? What if there turns out to be a field for commercial exploitation? Humans can't live indefinitely away from sunlight, I know, but there might be a need for temporary colonies here, and what then?"

"Well, what then?" rejoined Ham.

"Yes; what then? Is there room on the same planet for two intelligent races? Won't there be a conflict of interests sooner or later?"

"What of it?" he grunted. "Those things are primitive, Pat. They live in caves, without culture, without weapons. They're no danger to man."

"But they're magnificently intelligent. How do you know that these we've seen aren't just a barbaric tribe and that somewhere on the vastness of the dark side there isn't a vegetable civilization? You know civilization isn't the personal prerogative of mankind, because look at the mighty decadent culture on Mars and the dead remnants on Titan. Man has simply happened to have the strangest brand of it, at least so far."

"That's true enough, Pat," he agreed. "But if Oscar's fellows aren't any more pugnacious than they were toward that murderous triops, then they aren't much of a menace."

She shuddered. "I can't understand that at all. I wonder if—" She paused, frowning.

"If what?"

"I—don't know. I had an idea—a rather horrible idea." She looked up suddenly. "Ham, tomorrow I'm going to find out exactly how intelligent Oscar really is. Exactly how intelligent—if I can."

There were certain difficulties, however. When Ham and Pat approached the ice ridge, plodding across the fantastic terrain, they found themselves in utter perplexity as to which of the row of caves was the one before which they had stood in conversation with Oscar. In the glittering reflections from their lamps each opening appeared exactly like every other, and the creatures at their mouths stared at them with lidded eyes in which there was no readable expression.

"Well," said Pat in puzzlement, "we'll just have to try. You there, are you Oscar?"

The clicking voice sounded: "Yes."

"I don't believe it," objected Ham. "He was over more to the right. Hey! Are you Oscar?"

Another voice clicked: "Yes."

"You can't both be Oscar!"

Pat's choice responded: "We are all Oscar."

"Oh, never mind," cut in Pat, forestalling Ham's protests. "Apparently what one knows they all know, so it doesn't make any difference which we choose. Oscar, you said yesterday you were intelligent. Are you more intelligent than I am?"

"Yes. Much more intelligent."

"Hah!" snickered Ham. "Take that, Pat!"

She sniffed. "Well, that puts him miles above you, Yankee! Oscar, do you ever lie?"

Opaque lids dropped over translucent ones. "Lie," repeated the shrill voice. "Lie. No. There is no need."

"Well, do you—" She broke off suddenly at the sound of a dull pop. "What's that? Oh! Look, Ham, one of his pods burst!" She drew back.

A sharply pungent odor assailed them, reminiscent of that dangerous hour in the canyon, but not strong enough this time to set Ham choking or send the girl reeling into unconsciousness. Sharp, acrid, and yet not entirely unpleasant.

"What's that for, Oscar?"

"It is so we—"The voice cut short.

"Reproduce?" suggested Pat.

"Yes. Reproduce. The wind carries our spores to each other. We live where the wind is not steady."

"But yesterday you said fissure was your method."

"Yes. The spores lodge against our bodies and there is a—"Again the voice died.

"A fertilization?" suggested the girl.

"No."

"Well, a—I know! An irritation!"

"Yes."

"That causes a tumorous growth?"

"Yes. When the growth is complete, we split."

"Ugh!" snorted Ham. "A tumor!"

"Shut up!" snapped the girl. "That's all a baby is—a normal tumor."

"A normal—Well, I'm glad I'm not a biologist! Or a woman!"

"So'm I," said Pat demurely. "Oscar, how much do you know?"

"Everything."

"Do you know where my people come from?"

"From beyond the light."

"Yes; but before that?"

"No."

"We come from another planet," said the girl impressively. At Oscar's silence she said: "Do you know what a planet is?"

"Yes."

"But did you know before I said the word?"

"Yes. Long before."

"But how? Do you know what machinery is? Do you know what weapons are? Do you know how to make them?"

"Yes."

"Then-why don't you?"

"There is no need."

"No need!" she gasped. "With light—even with fire—you could keep the triopses—trioptes, I mean—away. You could keep them from eating you!"

"There is no need."

She turned helplessly to Ham.

"The thing's lying," he suggested.

"I—don't think so," she murmured. "It's something else-something we don't understand. Oscar, how do you know all those things?"

"Intelligence."

At the next cave another pod popped sullenly.

"But how? Tell me how you discover facts."

"From any fact," clicked the creature on the ice, "intelligence can build a picture of the—" There was silence.

"Universe?" she suggested.

"Yes. The universe. I start with one fact and I reason from it. I build a picture of the universe. I start with another fact. I reason from it. I find that the universe I picture is the same as the first. I know that the picture is true."

Both listeners stared in awe at the creature. "Say!" gulped Ham. "If that's true we could find out anything from Oscar! Oscar, can you tell us secrets that we don't know?"

"No."

"Why not?"

"You must first have the words to give me. I cannot tell you that for which you have no words."

"It's true!" whispered Pat. "But, Oscar, I have the words time and space and energy and matter and law and cause. Tell me the ultimate law of the universe?"

"It is the law of—" Silence.

"Conservation of energy or matter? Gravitation?"

"No."

"Of—of God?"

"No."

"Of—life?"

"No. Life is of no importance."

"Of—what? I can't think of another word."

"There's a chance," said Ham tensely, "that there is no word!"

"Yes," clicked Oscar. "It is the law of chance. Those other words are different sides of the law of chance."

"Good Heaven!" breathed Pat. "Oscar, do you know what I mean by stars, suns, constellations, planets, nebulae, and atoms, protons, and electrons?"

"Yes."

"But—how? Have you ever seen the stars that are above these eternal clouds? Or the Sun there beyond the barrier?"

"No. Reason is enough, because there is only one possible way in which the universe could exist. Only what is possible is real; what is not real is also not possible."

"That—that seems to mean something," murmured Pat. "I don't see exactly what. But Oscar, why—why don't you use your knowledge to protect yourselves from your enemies?"

"There is no need. There is no need to do anything. In a hundred years we shall be—" Silence.

"Safe?"

"Yes—no."

"What?" A horrible thought struck her. "Do you mean—extinct?"

"Yes."

"But—oh, Oscar! Don't you want to live? Don't your people want to survive?"

"Want," shrilled Oscar. "Want—want—want. That word means nothing."

"It means—it means desire, need."

"Desire means nothing. Need—need. No. My people do not need to survive."

"Oh," said Pat faintly. "Then why do you reproduce?"

As if in answer, a bursting pod sent its pungent dust over them. "Because we must," clicked Oscar. "When the spores strike us, we must."

"I—see," murmured Pat slowly. "Ham, I think I've got it. I think I understand. Let's get back to the ship."

Without farewell she turned away and he followed her thoughtfully. A strange listlessness oppressed him.

They had one slight mishap. A stone flung by some stray trioptes sheltered behind the ridge shattered the left lamp in Pat's helmet. It seemed hardly to disturb the girl; she glanced briefly aside and plodded on. But all the way back, in the gloom to their left now illumined only by his own lamp, hoots and shrieks and mocking laughter pursued them.

Within the rocket Pat swung her specimen bag wearily to the table and sat down without removing her heavy outer garment. Nor did Ham; despite the oppressive warmth of it, he, too, dropped list-lessly to a seat on the bunk.

"I'm tired," said the girl, "but not too tired to realize what that mystery out there means."

"Then let's hear it."

"Ham," she said, "what's the big difference between plant and animal life?"

"Why—plants derive their sustenance directly from soil and air. Animals need plants or other animals as food."

"That isn't entirely true, Ham. Some plants are parasitic, and prey on other life. Think of the Hotlands, or think, even, of some terrestrial plants—the fungi, the pitcher plant, the Dionaea that trap flies."

"Well, animals move, then, and plants don't."

"That's not true, either. Look at microbes; they're plants, but they swim about in search of food."

"Then what is the difference?"

"Sometimes it's hard to say," she murmured, "but I think I see it now. It's this: Animals have desire and plants necessity. Do you understand?"

"Not a damn bit."

"Listen, then. A plant—even a moving one—acts the way it does because it must, because it's made so. An animal acts because it wants to, or because it's made so that it wants to."

"What's the difference?"

"There is a difference. An animal has will, a plant hasn't. Do you see now? Oscar has all the magnificent intelligence of a god, but he hasn't the will of a worm. He has reactions, but no desire. When the wind is warm he comes out and feeds; when it's cold he crawls back into the cave melted by his body heat, but that isn't will, it's just a reaction. He has no desires!"

Ham stared, roused out of his lassitude. "I'll be damned if it isn't true!" he cried. "That's why he—or they—never ask questions. It takes desire or will to ask a question! And that's why they have no civilization and never will have!"

"That and other reasons," said Pat. "Think of this: Oscar has no sex, and in spite of your Yankee pride, sex has been a big factor in building civilization. It's the basis of the family, and among Oscar's people there is no such thing as parent and child. He splits; each half of him is an adult, probably with all the knowledge and memory of the original.

"There's no need for love, no place for it, in fact, and therefore no call to fight for mate and family, and no reason to make life easier than it already is, and no cause to apply his intelligence to develop art or science or—or anything!" She paused. "And did you ever hear of the Malthusian law, Ham?"

"Not that I remember."

"Well, the law of Malthus says that population presses on the food supply. Increase the food and the population increases in proportion. Man evolved under that law; for a century or so it's been suspended, but our race grew to be human under it."

"Suspended! It sounds sort of like repealing the law of gravitation or amending the law of inverse squares."

"No, no," she said. "It was suspended by the development of machinery in the nineteenth and twentieth centuries, which shot the food supply so far ahead, that population hasn't caught up. But it will and the Malthusian law will rule again."

"And what's that got to do with Oscar?"

"This, Ham: He never evolved under that law. Other factors kept his numbers below the limit of the food supply, and so his species developed free of the need to struggle for food. He's so perfectly adapted to his environment that he needs nothing more. To him a civilization would be superfluous!"

"But—then what of the triops?"

"Yes, the triops. You see, Ham, just as I argued days ago, the triops is a newcomer, pushed over from the twilight zone. When those devils arrived, Oscar's people were already evolved, and they couldn't change to meet the new conditions, or couldn't change quickly enough. So—they're doomed.

"As Oscar says, they'll be extinct soon—and—and they don't even care." She shuddered. "All they do, all they can do, is sit before their caves and think. Probably they think godlike thoughts, but they can't summon even a mouse-like will. That's what a vegetable intelligence is; that's what it has to be!"

"I think—I think you're right," he muttered. "In a way it's horrible, isn't it?"

"Yes." Despite her heavy garments she shivered. "Yes; it's horrible.

Those vast, magnificent minds and no way for them to work. It's like a powerful gasoline motor with its drive shaft broken, and no matter how well it runs it can't turn the wheels. Ham, do you know what I'm going to name them? The *Lotophagi Veneris*—the Lotus Eaters! Content to sit and dream away existence while lesser minds—ours and the trioptes'—battle for their planet."

"It's a good name, Pat." As she rose he asked in surprise: "Your specimens? Aren't you going to prepare them?"

"Oh, tomorrow." She flung herself, parka and all, on her bunk.

"But they'll spoil! And your helmet light—I ought to fix it."

"Tomorrow," she repeated wearily, and his own languor kept him from further argument.

When the nauseous odor of decay awakened him some hours later Pat was asleep, still garbed in the heavy suit. He flung bag and specimens from the door, and then slipped the parka from her body. She hardly stirred as he tucked her gently into her bunk.

Pat never missed the specimen bag at all, and, somehow, the next day, if one could call that endless night a day, found them trudging over the bleak plateau with the girl's helmet lamp still unrepaired. Again at their left, the wildly mocking laughter of the night dwellers followed them, drifting eerily down on the Underwind, and twice far-flung stones chipped glittering ice from neighboring spires. They plodded listlessly and silently, as if in a sort of fascination, but their minds seemed strangely clear.

Pat addressed the first Lotus Eater they saw. "We're back, Oscar," she said with a faint rebirth of her usual flippancy. "How'd you spend the night?"

"I thought," clicked the thing.

"What'd you think about?"

"I thought about—" The voice ceased.

A pod popped, and the curiously pleasant pungent odor was in their nostrils.

"About—us?"

"No."

"About—the world?"

"No."

"About—What's the use?" she ended wearily. "We could keep that up forever, and perhaps never hit on the right question."

"If there is a right question," added Ham. "How do you know there are words to fit it? How do you even know that it's the kind of thought our minds are capable of conceiving? There must be thoughts that are beyond our grasp."

Off to their left a pod burst with a dull pop. Ham saw the dust move like a shadow across their beams as the Underwind caught it, and he saw Pat draw a deep draft of the pungent air as it whirled around her. Queer how pleasant the smell was, especially since it was the same stuff which in higher concentration had nearly cost their lives. He felt vaguely worried as that thought struck him, but could assign no reason for worry.

He realized suddenly that both of them were standing in complete silence before the Lotus Eater. They had come to ask questions, hadn't they?

"Oscar," he said, "what's the meaning of life?"

"No meaning. There is no meaning."

"Then why fight for it so?"

"We do not fight for it. Life is unimportant."

"And when you're gone, the world goes on just the same? Is that it?"

"When we are gone it will make no difference to any except the trioptes who eat us."

"Who eat you," echoed Ham.

There was something about that thought that did penetrate the fog of indifference that blanketed his mind. He peered at Pat, who stood passively and silently beside him, and in the glow of her helmet lamp he could see her clear gray eyes behind her goggles, staring straight ahead in what was apparently abstraction or deep thought. And beyond the ridge sounded suddenly the yells and wild laughter of the dwellers in the dark.

"Pat," he said.

There was no answer.

"Pat!" he repeated, raising a listless hand to her arm. "We have to go back." To his right a pod popped. "We have to go back," he repeated.

A sudden shower of stones came glancing over the ridge. One struck his helmet, and his forward lamp burst with a dull explosion. Another struck his arm with a stinging pain, though it seemed surprisingly unimportant.

"We have to go back," he reiterated doggedly.

Pat spoke at last without moving. "What's the use?" she asked dully.

He frowned over that. What was the use? To go back to the twilight zone? A picture of Erotia rose in his mind, and then a vision of that honeymoon they had planned on the Earth, and then a whole series of terrestrial scenes—New York, a tree-girt campus, the sunny farm of his boyhood. But they all seemed very far away and unreal.

A violent blow that stung his shoulder recalled him, and he saw a stone bound from Pat's helmet. Only two of her lamps glowed now, the rear and the right, and he realized vaguely that on his own helmet shone only the rear and the left. Shadowy figures were skittering and gibbering along the crest of the ridge now left dark by the breaking of their lights, and stones were whizzing and spattering around them.

He made a supreme effort and seized her arm. "We've got to go back!" he muttered.

"Why? Why should we?"

"Because we'll be killed if we stay."

"Yes. I know that, but—"

He ceased to listen and jerked savagely at Pat's arm. She spun around and staggered after him as he turned doggedly toward the rocket.

Shrill hoots sounded as their rear lamps swept the ridge, and as he dragged the girl with infinite slowness, the shrieks spread out to the right and left. He knew what that meant; the demons were circling them to get in front of them where their shattered forward lamps cast no protecting light.

Pat followed listlessly, making no effort of her own. It was simply the drag of his arm that impelled her, and it was becoming an intolerable effort to move even himself. And there directly before him, flitting shadows that howled and hooted, were the devils that sought their lives.

Ham twisted his head so that his right lamp swept the area. Shrieks sounded as they found shelter in the shadows of peaks and ridges, but Ham, walking with his head sidewise, tripped and tumbled.

Pat wouldn't rise when he tugged at her. "There's no need of it," she murmured, but made no resistance when he lifted her.

An idea stirred vaguely; he bundled her into his arms so that her right lamp shot its beam forward, and so he staggered at last to the circle of light about the rocket, opened the door, and dumped her on the floor within.

He had one final impression. He saw the laughing shadows that were the trioptes skipping and skittering across the darkness toward the ridge where Oscar and his people waited in placid acceptance of their destiny.

The rocket was roaring along at two hundred thousand feet, because numberless observations and photographs from space had shown that not even the vast peaks of the Mountains of Eternity project forty miles above the planet's surface. Below them the clouds glistened white before and black behind, for they were just entering the twilight zone. At that height one could even see the mighty curvature of the planet.

"Half cue ball, half eight ball," said Ham, staring down. "Hereafter we stick to the cue ball half."

"It was the spores," proceeded Pat, ignoring him. "We knew they were narcotic before, but we couldn't be expected to guess that they'd carry a drug as subtle as that—to steal away your will and undermine your strength. Oscar's people are the Lotus Eaters and the Lotus, all in one. But I'm—somehow—I'm sorry for them. Those colossal, magnificent, useless minds of theirs!" She paused. "Ham, what woke you up to what was happening? What snapped you out of it?"

"Oh, it was a remark of Oscar's, something about his being only a square meal for a triops."

"Well?"

"Well, did you know we've used up all our food? That remark reminded me that I hadn't eaten for two days!"

The Planet of Doubt

Hamilton Hammond started nervously as the voice of Cullen, the expedition's chemist, sounded from his station aft. "I see something!" he called.

Ham bent over the floor port, staring into the eternal green-gray fog that blankets Uranus. He glanced hastily at the dial of the electric plumb; fifty-five feet, it said with an air of positive-ness, but that was a lie, for it had registered that same figure for a hundred and sixty miles of creeping descent. The fog itself reflected the beam.

The barometer showed 86.2 cm. That too was an unreliable guide, but better than the plumb, for the intrepid Young, four decades earlier in 2060, had noted an atmospheric pressure of 86 in his romantic dash from Titan to the cloudy planet's southern pole. But the *Gaea* was dropping now at the opposite pole, forty-five thousand miles from Young's landing, and no one knew what vast hollows or peaks might render his figures utterly useless.

"I see nothing," Ham muttered.

"Nor I," said Patricia Hammond, his wife—or more officially, biologist of the Smithsonian's *Gaea* expedition. "Or—yes! Something moved!" She peered closer. "Up! Up!" she screamed. "Put up!"

Harbord was a good astrogator. He asked no questions, nor even took his glance from his controls. He simply slapped the throttle; the underjets roared in crescendo, and the upward thrust pressed all of them hard against the floor.

Barely in time. A vast gray wave of water rushed smoothly below the port, so close that its crest was carved by the blast, and spray clouded the glass.

"Whew!" whistled Ham. "That was close. Too close. If we'd touched that it would have cracked our jets for sure. They're white-hot."

"Ocean!" said Patricia disgustedly. "Young reported land."

"Yeah, forty-five thousand miles away. For all we know this sea is broader than the whole surface of the Earth."

She considered this, frowning. "Do you suppose," she asked, "that this fog goes right down to the surface everywhere?"

"Young says so."

"But on Venus the clouds form only at the junction of the upper winds and the underwind."

"Yes, but Venus is closer to the Sun. The heat here is evenly distributed, because the Sun accounts for practically none of it. Most of the surface heat seeps through from within, as it does on Saturn and Jupiter, only since Uranus is smaller, it's also cooler. It's cool enough to have a solid crust instead of being molten like the larger planets, but it's considerably colder than the Venusian twilight zone."

"But," she objected, "Titan is as cold as a dozen Nova Zemblas, yet it's one perpetual hurricane."

He grinned. "Trying to trip me? It isn't absolute temperature that causes wind—it's differences in temperature between one place and another. Titan has one side warmed by Saturn, but here the warmth is even or practically even, all around the planet, since it comes from within."

He glanced suddenly at Harbord. "What are we waiting for?" he asked.

"For you," grunted the astrogator. "You're in command now. I command until we sight the surface, and we've just done that."

"By golly, that's right!" exclaimed Ham in a satisfied voice. On his last expedition, that to the night side of Venus, he had been technically under Patricia's orders, and the reversal pleased him. "And now," he said severely, "if the biologist will kindly step aside—"

Patricia sniffed. "So you can pilot us, I suppose. I'll bet you haven't a single idea."

"But I have." He turned to Harbord. "Southeast," he ordered, and the afterjets added their voices to the roar of the others. "Put up to thirty thousand meters," he continued, "we might run into mountains."

The *Gaea*, named for the ancient goddess of Earth, who was wife to the god Uranus, plunged through the infinity of mist away from the planet's pole. In one respect that pole is unique among the Sun's family, for Uranus revolves, not like Jupiter or Saturn or Mars or the Earth, in the manner of a spinning top, but more with the motion of a rolling ball. Its poles are in the plane of its orbit, so that at one point its southern pole faces the Sun, while forty-two years later, halfway around the vast orbit, the opposite pole is Sunward.

Four decades earlier Young had touched at the southern pole; it would be another forty years before that pole again saw noon.

"The trouble with women," grumbled Harbord, "is that they ask too many questions."

Patricia spun on him. "Schopenhauer!" she hissed. "You ought to be grateful that Patrick Burlingame's daughter is lending her aid to a Yankee expedition!"

"Yeah? Why Schopenhauer?"

"He was a woman-hater, wasn't he? Like you!"

"Then he was a greater philosopher than I thought," grunted Harbord.

"Anyway," she retorted acidly, "a couple of million dollars is a lot of money to pay for a square mile of foggy desert. You won't hog this planet the way you tried to hog Venus."

She was referring, of course, to the Council of Berne's decision of 2059, that the simple fact of an explorer's landing on a planet did not give his nation possession of the entire planet, but only of the portion actually explored. On fog-wrapped Uranus that portion would be small indeed.

"Never mind," put in Ham. "No other nation will argue if America claims the whole fog-ball, because no other nation has a base near enough to get here."

That was true. By virtue of its possession of Saturn's only habitable moon, Titan, the United States was the only nation that could send an exploratory rocket to Uranus. A direct flight from the Earth is out of the question, since the nearest approach to the two planets is 1,700,000,000 miles. The flight is made in two jumps; first to Titan, then to Uranus.

But this condition limits the frequency of the visits enormously, for though Saturn and Earth are in conjunction at intervals of a little over a year, Uranus and Saturn are in conjunction only once in about forty years. Only at these times is it possible to reach the vast, mysterious, fog-shrouded planet.

So inconceivably remote is Uranus that the distance to its neighbor, Saturn, is actually greater than the total distance from Saturn to

Jupiter, from Jupiter to the asteroids, from these to Mars, and from Mars to the Earth. It is a wild, alien, mystery-cloaked planet with only icy Neptune and Pluto between it and the interstellar void.

Patricia whirled on Ham. "You!" she snapped. "Southeast, eh! Why southeast? Just a guess, isn't it? Truthfully, isn't it?"

"Nope," he grinned. "I have my reasons. I'm trying to save whatever time I can, because our stay here is limited if we don't want to be marooned for forty years until the next conjunction."

"But why southeast?"

"I'll tell you. Did you ever look at a globe of the Earth, Pat? Then maybe you've noticed that all continents, all large islands, and all important peninsulas are narrowed to points toward the south. In other words, the northern hemisphere is more favorable for land formation, and as a matter of fact, by far the greater part of the Earth's land is north of the equator.

"The Arctic Ocean is nearly surrounded by a ring of land, but the Antarctic's wide open. And that same thing is true of Mars, assuming that the dark, swampy plains are old ocean beds, and also true of the frozen oceans on the night side of Venus.

"So I assume that if all planets had a common origin, and all of them solidified under the same conditions, Uranus must have the same sort of land distribution. What Young found was the land that corresponds to our Antarctica; what I'm looking for is the land that ought to surround this north polar sea."

"Ought to, but maybe doesn't," retorted Pat. "Anyway why southeast instead of due south?"

"Because that direction describes a spiral and lessens the chance of our striking some strait or channel between lands. With a visibility of about fifty feet, it wouldn't take a very wide channel to make us think we were over ocean.

"Even your English Thames would look like the Pacific in this sort of fog, if we happened to come down more than half a hundred feet from either tank."

"And I suppose your American Mississippi would look like Noah's flood," said the girl, and fell to gazing at the gray waste of fog that swirled endlessly past the ports.

Somewhat less than an hour later the *Gaea* was again descending gingerly and hesitatingly. At 85 cm. of air pressure Ham had the

115

rocket slowed almost to a complete stop, and thereafter it dropped on the cushioning blast of the underjets at a speed of inches per minute.

When the barometer read 85.8 cm., Cullen's voice sounded from the stern, where the port was less obscured by the jets themselves. "Something below!" he called.

There was something. The fog seemed definitely darker, and features or markings of some sort were visible. As the ship settled slowly, Ham watched intently, and at last snapped out the order to land. The *Gaea* dropped, with a faint jar, to a resting place on a bare, gray graveled plain domed with a hemisphere of mist that shut off vision as definitely as a wall.

There was something wild and alien about the limited scene before them. As the blast died, all of them stared silently into the leaden-hued vapors and Cullen came wordlessly in to join them. In the sudden silence that followed the cutting of the blast, the utter strangeness of the world outside was thrust upon them.

Venus, where Pat had been born, was a queer enough world with its narrow habitable twilight zone, its life-teeming Hotlands, and its mysterious dark side, but it was twin sister to the Earth.

Mars, the desert planet with its great decadent civilization, was yet stranger, but not utterly alien. Out on the moons of Jupiter were outlandish creatures of bizarre little worlds, and on cold Titan, that circled Saturn, were fantastic beings born to that wild and frigid satellite.

But Uranus was a major planet, no more than half-brother to the little inner worlds, and less than cousin to the tiny satellites. It was mysterious, unrelated, alien; no one had ever set foot on a major planet save the daring Young and his men forty years before.

He had explored, out of all the millions of square miles of surface, just one square kilometer forty-five thousand miles away from where they stood. All the rest was mystery, and the thought was enough to subdue even the irrepressible Patricia.

But not for long. "Well," she observed finally, "it looks just like London to me. Same sort of weather we had last time we were there. I think I'll step outside and look for Piccadilly."

"You won't go out yet," snapped Ham. "I want an atmospheric test first."

"For what? Young and his men breathed this air. I suppose you're going to say that that was forty-five thousand miles away, but even a biologist knows that the law of diffusion of gases would keep a planet from having one sort of air at one pole and another at the opposite. If the air was safe there, it is here."

"Yeah?" asked Ham. "Diffusion's all right, but did it ever occur to you that this fog-ball gets most of its heat from inside? That means high volcanic activity, and it might mean an eruption of poisonous gases somewhere near here. I'm having Cullen make a test."

Patricia subsided, watching the silent and efficient Cullen as he drew a sample of Uranian air into an ampoule. After a moment she flexed her knees and asked. "Why is the gravitation so weak here? Uranus is fifty-four times as large as the Earth and fifteen times as massive, yet I don't feel any heavier here than at home." Home to Pat, of course, was the little frontier town of Venoble, in the Venusian Cool Country.

"That's the answer," said Ham. "Fifty-four times the size of the Earth or Venus, but only fifteen times as heavy. That means its density is much smaller—to be exact .27. Figures out to about nine-tenths the surface gravitation of the Earth, but it feels to me almost equal. We'll check a kilogram weight on the spring balance after a while and get an accurate figure on its mass."

"Safe to breathe?"

"Perfectly. Argon's an inert gas, and a substance can't possibly be poisonous unless it can react chemically in the body."

Pat sniffed. "See? It was safe all the time. I'm going outside."

"You'll wait for me," he growled. "Every time I've indulged that reckless disposition of yours you've got into trouble." He checked the thermometer beyond the port, nine degrees centigrade—the temperature of late autumn back home. "There's the cause of this perpetual fog," he observed. "The surface is always warmer than the air."

Pat was already pulling a jacket over her shoulders. Ham followed suit, and fell to twisting the handle of the air lock. There was a subdued hissing as the slightly denser Uranian air forced its way in, and he turned to speak to Harbord, who was lighting a pipe with great satisfaction—an indulgence strictly forbidden in space, but harmless now that an air supply was assured.

"Keep an eye on us, will you?" Ham said. "Watch us through the port, just in case something happens and we need help."

"We?" grunted Harbord. "Your wife's out of sight already."

With a muttered imprecation, Ham spun around. It was true. The outer door of the air lock was open, and a lazy wisp of fog drifted in, scarcely moving in the utterly stagnant Uranian air.

"The crazy little—Here! Give me that!" He seized a belt with twin holsters, holding a standard automatic as well as a terribly destructive flame pistol. He whipped it around him, seized another bundle, and plunged into the eternal mists of Uranus.

It was exactly as if he stood under an inverted bowl of dull silver. A weird, greenish, half twilight filtered down, but his whole world consisted of the metal ship at his back and a fifty-foot semicircle before him. And Pat—Pat was nowhere visible.

He shouted her name. "Pat!" The sound muffled by the cold dampness of the fog sounded queerly soft to his ears. He bellowed again at the top of his voice, and then swore violently from sheer relief as a thin, hushed reply drifted back out of the grayness.

In a moment she appeared, swinging a zigzag, ropy, greenish-gray organism.

"Look!" she called triumphantly. "Here's the first specimen of Uranian plant life. Loosely organized, reproduces by partition, and—what the devil is the matter?"

"Matter! Don't you know you might have been lost? How did you expect to get back here?"

"Compass," she retorted coolly.

"How do you know it works? We may be right on the magnetic pole, if Uranus has one."

She glanced at her wrist. "Come to think of it, it doesn't work. The needle's swinging free."

"Yes, and you went out unarmed besides. Of all the fool tricks!"

"Young reported no animal life, didn't he? And—wait a minute. I know what you're going to say. 'Forty-five thousand miles away!'"

He glared. "Hereafter," he growled, "you're under orders. You don't go out except in company, and roped together." He drew a length of heavy silken cord from his pocket, and snapped one end to her belt, and the other to his own.

"Oh, don't be so timid! I feel like a puppy on a leash."

"I have to be timid," he responded grimly, "when I'm dealing with a reckless, improvident, careless imp like you."

He disregarded her sniff of disapproval, and set about unwrapping the bundle he had brought. He produced an American flag, and proceeded to dig a depression in the gravel, planted the staff in it and said formally, "I take possession of this land in the name of the United States of America."

"All fifty feet of it?" murmured Patricia, but softly, for, after all, despite her flippant manner, she was loyal to the country of her husband. She fell silent, and the two of them stared at the flag.

It was a strange echo from a pleasant little planet nearly two billion miles away; it meant people and friends and civilization—things remote and almost unreal as they stood here on the soil of this vast, lonely, mysterious planet.

Ham roused from his thoughts. "So!" he said. "Now we'll have a look around."

Young had indicated the technique of exploration on this world where the explorer faced difficulties all but insurmountable.

Ham snapped the end of a fine steel wire to a catch beside the air lock. On a spool at his waist was a thousand foot length of it, to serve as an infallible guide back through the obscurity—the only practical means in a region where sound was muffled and even radio waves were shielded almost as completely as by a grounded metal dome. The wire played the part not only of guide but of messenger, since a tug on it rang a bell within the rocket.

Ham waved at Harbord, visibly puffing his pipe behind the port, and they set out. To the limit of their permitted time, Uranus would have to be explored in thousand-foot circles, moving the rocket each time the details of the area were recorded. A colossal task. It was likely, he remarked to Pat, that the vast planet would never be completely explored, especially with the forty-year interval that must pass between visits.

"And especially," she amended, "if they send timorous little better-be-safe-than-sorry explorers like you."

"At least," he retorted, "I expect to return to tell what I've explored even if it's only a myriare, like Young's achievement."

"But don't you see," she rejoined impatiently, "that wherever we go, just beyond our vision there may be something marvelous? We take little thousand-foot samples of the country, and each time we might be just missing something that may be the whole significance of this planet. What we're doing is like marking off a few hundred-foot circles on the Earth; how much chance is there of finding part of a city, or a house, or even a human being in our circle?"

"Perfectly true, Pat, but what can we do about it?"

"We could at least sacrifice a few precautions and cover a little more territory."

"But we won't. I happen to care about your safety."

"Oh!" she said irritably, turning away. "You're—" Her words were muffled as she ranged out to the full length of the silken cord that bound her to him. She was completely invisible, but occasional jerks and tugs as they tried to move at cross-purposes were evidence enough that they were still joined.

Ham walked slowly forward, examining the pebbled, lifeless terrain where now and then a pool of condensed moisture showed dull, and very occasionally, he came upon one of the zigzag weeds like the one Pat had dropped near the rocket. Apparently rain was unknown on windless Uranus, and the surface moisture followed an endless cycle of condensation in the cool air and evaporation on the warm ground.

Ham came to a spot where boiling mud seemed to be welling up from below, and steamy plumes whirled up to lose themselves in the fog—evidence of the vast internal heat that warmed the planet. He stood staring at it, and suddenly a violent jerk on the cord nearly toppled him backward.

He spun around. Patricia materialized abruptly out of the fog, one hand clutching a ropy plant. She dropped it as she saw him, and suddenly she was clinging frantically to him.

"Ham!" she gasped. "Let's go back! I'm scared!"

"Scared? Of what?" He knew her character; she was valiant to the point of recklessness against any danger she could understand, but let there be a hint of mystery in an occurrence, and her active imagination painted horrors beyond her ability to face.

"I don't know!" she panted. "I—I saw things!"

"Where?"

"In the fog! Everywhere!"

Ham disengaged his arms and dropped his hands to the butts of the weapons in his belt. "What sort of things?" he asked.

"Horrible things! Nightmarish things!"

He shook her gently. "Who's timid now?" he asked, but kindly. The query had the effect he sought; she gripped herself and calmed.

"I'm not frightened!" she snapped. "I was startled. I saw—" She paled again.

"Saw what?"

"I don't know. Shapes in the mist. Great moving things with faces. Gargoyles—devils—nightmares!" She shuddered, then calmed once more.

"I was bending over a little pool out there, examining a bio-pod, and everything was quiet—sort of deadly quiet. And then a shadow passed in the pool—a reflection of something over me—and I looked up and saw nothing. But then I began to hear rustles and murmurs and noises like muffled voices and I began to see the fog shapes—horrible shapes—all around me. And I screamed, and then realized you couldn't hear a scream, so I jerked the rope. And then I guess I just closed my eyes and rushed through them to you." She shivered against him.

"All around you?" he asked sharply. "Do you mean between you and me?"

She nodded. "Everywhere."

Ham laughed shortly. "You've had a day dream, Pat. The rope isn't long enough for anything to pass between us without coming so close to one of us that he could see it clearly, and I saw nothing—absolutely nothing."

"Well, I saw something," she insisted, "and it wasn't imaginary. Do you think I'm just a nervous child afraid of strange places? Why I was born on an alien planet!" At his indulgent grin she flared in indignation. "All right! Let's both of us stand here perfectly quiet; perhaps they'll come back again; then we'll see what you think of them."

He nodded agreement, and they stood silently under the translucent dome of mist. There was nothing, nothing but a deep and endless grayness, and an infinite silence, but a silence not like any Ham had ever experienced in his life. For on Venus—even in the sultriest part of the Hotlands—there is always the rustle of teeming life, and the eternal moaning of the Underwind, while on the Earth no day nor night is ever quite silent.

There is always somewhere the sighing of leaves or the rustle of

121

grass or the murmur of water or the voices of insects, or even in the driest desert, the whisper of sand as it warms or cools. But not here; here was such utter stillness that the girl's breathing beside him was an actual relief; it was a silence utter enough to hear.

He did hear it—or was it simply his own blood pulsing in his ears? A formless throbbing, an infinitely faint rustling, a vague whispering. He frowned in the concentration of listening, and Patricia quivered against him.

"There!" she hissed. "There!"

He peered into the gray dimness. Nothing at all—or was there something? A shadow—but what here could cause a shadow, here in this sunless region of fog? A condensation of mist, that was all. But it moved; mist can't move without the thrust of wind, and here there was no wind.

He strained his eyes in an effort to pierce the obscurity. He saw—or he imagined it—a vast, looming figure, or a dozen figures. They were all around; one passed silently overhead, and numberless others weaved and swayed just beyond the range of vision. There were murmurings and susurrations, sounds like breathing and whispering, patters and rustles. The fog shapes were weirdly unstable, looming from little patches of darkness into towering shadows, dissipating and forming like figures of smoke.

"Good Lord!" gasped Ham. "What can—"

He tried to focus his gaze on one individual in the shadowy throng. It was difficult; they all seemed to shift, to merge, advance, recede, or simply materialize and fade out. But one surprising phenomenon suddenly caught his attention, and for a moment stunned him into rigidity. He saw faces!

Not exactly human faces. They were more such appearances as Patricia had described—the faces of gargoyles or devils, leering, grimacing, grinning in lunatic mirth or seeming to weep in mockery of sorrow. One couldn't see them clearly enough for anything but fleeting impressions—so vague and instantaneous that they had the qualities of an illusion or dream.

They must be illusions, he thought confusedly, if only because their conformation, though not human, imitated the human. It was beyond the bounds of reason to suppose that Uranus harbored a race of humans, or even humanlike beings.

Beside him Patricia whimpered, "Let's go back, Ham. Please let's go back."

"Listen," he said, "those things are illusory, at least in part."

"How do you know?"

"Because they're anthropomorphic. There can't be any creatures here with nearly human faces. Our own minds are adding details that don't exist, just as every time you see a cloud or a crack on the ceiling you try to make a face out of it. All we're seeing is denser spots in the mist."

"I wish I thought you were sure of that," she quavered.

He wasn't at all sure, but he reaffirmed it. "Of course I am. I'll tell you an easy way to prove it, too. We'll turn the infrared camera on them, and that'll bring out enough detail to judge by."

"I'd be afraid to look at the plates," said the girl, shivering as she peered apprehensively at the vague horrors in the fog. "Suppose—suppose they do show those faces. What will you say then?"

"I'll say that it's a queer and unexpected coincidence that Uranian life—if they are forms of life—has developed along somewhat the same lines as terrestrial—at least in outward form."

"And you'll be wrong," she murmured. "A thing like this is beyond coincidence." She trembled against him. "Do you know what I think? Ham, do you suppose it's possible that science has gone all wrong, and that Uranus is Hell? And that those are the damned?"

He laughed, but even his laugh sounded hollow, muffled by the smothering fog. "That's the maddest idea that even your wild imagination has ever produced, Pat. I tell you they're—"

A scream from the girl interrupted him. They had been standing huddled together, staring at divergent angles into the dome of mist, and he spun around now to gaze in the direction she faced.

For a moment his vision was blinded by the shift, and he blinked frantically in an effort to focus his eyes. Then he saw what had startled her. It was a vast, dusky shadow that seemed to originate somewhere near the surface, but was springing upward and curving over them as if it actually climbed a veritable dome of mist, like a dim river of darkness flowing upward.

Despite his derision of Patricia's fear-born imaginings, his nerves were taut. It was a purely automatic gesture that brought his weapon to his hand, and it was pure impulse that sent a bullet flaming into the mist. There was a curiously muffled report from the shot—a single full echo—and then utter silence.

Utter silence. The rustles and murmurings were gone—and so were the fog-shapes. Blinking into the mist, they saw only the sullen grayness of the eternal cloud itself, and they heard no sound but their own tense breathing and the faint after-ring of their eardrums from the concussion.

"They're gone!" the girl gasped.

"Sure. Just what I said. Illusions!"

"Illusions don't run away from gunshots," retorted Patricia, her courage revived instantly with the vanishing of the fog shapes. "They're real. I'm not nearly as afraid of real things as of—well, of things I can't understand."

"Do you understand these?" he rejoined. "And as for illusions not running away from gunshots, I say they might. Suppose these appearances were due to a sort of self-hypnosis, or even merely to the eye strain of staring through this fog. Don't you think a shot would startle us out of the proper mental state, so that we'd no longer see them?"

"Maybe," she said doubtfully. "Anyway, I'm not scared any more. Whatever they are, I guess they're harmless."

She turned her attention to the puddle of mud before them, in which a few curious feathery growths swayed to the bubbling of the surface. "Cryptogamoid," she said, stooping over them. "Probably the only sort of plant that can exist on Uranus, since there's no sign of bees, or other pollen carriers."

Ham grunted, peering into the dismal gray mist. Suddenly both of them were startled into sudden alertness by the sound of the bell on the drum that held the guide wire. One ring; a warning from the *Gaea*!

Pat sprang erect. Ham tugged the wire in instant reply, and muttered, "We'd better go back. Harbord and Cullen must have seen something. It's probably the same sort of things we saw, but we'd better go back."

They began to retrace their steps, the thousand feet of wire humming softly as it wound back on the spring drum at Ham's waist. Other than that and the crunch of their steps on the gravel, there was silence, and the fog was merely a featureless dome of faintly greenish grayness. They had progressed perhaps two hundred yards when it changed.

Patricia saw the fog shapes first. "They're back!" she hissed in his ear, with no sound of fear in her voice now.

He saw them too. Now they were no longer surrounding the two of them, but were rushing past from the direction of the *Gaea* in two parallel streams, or perhaps dividing into two streams just beyond the point of visibility. He and Pat were moving down an alley walled by a continuous double line of rushing shadows.

They huddled closer to each other and bored on through the fog. They were no more than a hundred and fifty feet from the rocket now. And then, with a suddenness that brought them to a sharp halt, something more solid than fog, more solid than fog shapes, loomed darkly straight before them.

It—whatever it was—was approaching. It was visible now as a dark circle at the level of the ground, perhaps six feet in diameter, upright and broadside on. It was moving as fast as a man walks, and it materialized rapidly into a distinct solidity.

Ham and Pat stared fascinated. The thing was featureless—just a dull black circle and a tubular body that stretched off into the fog. Or not quite featureless. Now they could perceive an organ that projected from the center of the circle—a loose, quivering member like a large pancake on a finger-thick stem, whose edges quivered and cupped toward them, as if to catch sounds or scent. The creature was blind.

Yet it possessed some sense that could register distant objects. Thirty feet from them the stalked disc cupped deeply in their direction, the creature swerved slightly, and rushed silently toward the pair!

Ham was ready. His automatic roared its muffled blast, and roared again. The attacker seemed to telescope in upon itself and rolled aside, and behind it appeared a creature identical in all respects—the same featureless black circle, the same quivering disc. But a high, piercing whine of pain slipped like a sharp knife through the fog.

This was a danger Patricia could understand. There was no fear about her now; she had faced too many outlandish creatures on the Hotlands frontiers of Venus, or in the mysterious wilds of the Mountains of Eternity.

She snatched her companion's flame pistol from its holster and stood with the weapon ready to vomit its single blast of destruction. She knew that it represented a last resort, not to be used until other means had failed, so she simply held it, and tugged on the wire to the *Gaea*. Three pulls, and then again three, would summon aid from Cullen and Harbord.

The second creature—or was it another segment of the same animal?—came charging forward. Ham sent two more bullets into the blank, faceless front of it, and again that keening note of pain sounded. The monster swerved and collapsed, and another black circle was rushing toward them. His shot failed to drop this one, but the creature veered.

Suddenly the thing was roaring past them, black and huge as a railroad train. It was a segmented being; it was composed of dozens of eight-foot links, like a train of miniature cars, three pairs of legs to a section.

But it ran like a single creature, with ripples of motion flowing back along its countless legs in exactly the way a centipede runs. Ham had a flashing glimpse of the manner in which the segments were joined by finger-thick ropes of flesh.

He sent three bullets into the middle of a passing section. It was a bad mistake; the segment spouted black liquid and rolled out of line, but the one behind it suddenly turned its stalked member toward the two defenders and came rushing at them. And off in the fog the first section was circling back. They had two to face now instead of one.

Ham had three cartridges left in the clip. He grimly fired one shot full at the quivering disc of flesh that cupped toward him, saw the monster collapse, and sent another bullet into the segment that followed. The thing—or things—seemed to extend indefinitely into the fog.

Beside him he heard the roar of the flame pistol. Pat had waited until the other monster was nearly upon her, so that her single blast might do as much damage as possible.

Ham stole time for a momentary glance at the result; the terrific discharge had simply incinerated a dozen segments, and one solitary survivor was crawling away into the fog.

"Good girl!" he muttered and sent his last bullet into the onrushing monstrosity. It dropped, and behind it, driving inexorably on, came the follower. He flung his empty weapon at the fleshy disc, saw it bound off the black skin, and waited, thrusting Pat behind him.

There was a great, roaring light. A flame pistol! Dim in the fog were the figures of Harbord and Cullen, tracing their way along the wire, and before him were writhing segments of the blasted monster.

What remained of the creature had had enough punishment, apparently, for it veered to the left and went thundering away into the mist, now no more than ten segments long. And all around the group, just beyond visibility, the fog shapes gestured and grimaced and gibbered, and then they too vanished.

Not a word was spoken as the four traced the wire to the door of the *Gaea*. Once within, Patricia let out a low whistle of relief as she pulled off her dripping jacket.

"Well," she breathed. "That was a thrill."

"A thrill!" snorted Ham. "Say, you can have this whole soggy planet for all of me. And I've a mind to limit you to the ship, too. This is no place for a thoughtless imp like you; you draw trouble the way honey draws flies."

"As if I had anything to do with it!" she retorted. "All right; order me to stay aboard if you think it'll do any good."

He grunted and turned to Harbord. "Thanks," he said. "That was close until you two showed up. And by the way, what was the warning for? The fog shapes?"

"Do you mean that Mardi Gras parade that's been going by?" asked Harbord. "Or was it a spiritualist convention? No; we weren't sure they were real. It was for the thing you did get tangled up with; it came humping by here in your direction."

"It or they?" corrected Ham.

"Did you see more'n one of them?"

"I made more than one of them. I cut it in half, and both halves went for us. Pat took care of one with the flame pistol, but all my bullets seemed to do was to knock off pieces." He frowned. "Do you understand the thing, Pat?"

"Better than you do," she retorted sharply. His threat to restrain her to the ship still rankled. "This would be a fine expedition without a biologist, wouldn't it?"

"That's the reason I'm being careful about you," he grinned. "I'm afraid I would be without a biologist. But what's your idea concerning that series of detachable worms out there?"

"Just that. It's a multiple animal. Did you ever hear of Henri Fabre?"

"Not that I remember."

"Well, he was a great French naturalist of about two centuries ago. Among other things, he studied some interesting little insects called processionary caterpillars, who spin themselves a cozy nest of silk and march out of it every night to feed."

"Well?"

"Just listen a moment," said the girl. "They march out single file, every caterpillar touching its head to the tail of the one preceding it. They're blind, you see; so each one trusts the one ahead. The first one's the leader; he picks the route, leads them to the proper tree, and there the column breaks up for feeding. And at sunrise, they form again into little columns, which join again into the big procession, and back they go to their nest."

"I still don't see—"

"You will. Now, whichever caterpillar is in front is the leader. If you take a stick and break the column at any point, the one behind the gap becomes the leader for his followers, and leads them back to the cobweb nest just as efficiently as the original leader. And if you segregate any one caterpillar, he finds his own way, being leader and column in one."

"I begin to see," muttered Ham.

"Yes. That thing—or those things—are something like the processionary caterpillars. They're blind; in fact, eyes would have much less value on Uranus than; on the Earth, and perhaps no Uranian creatures developed eyes—unless the fog shapes possess them. But I think these creatures are a long way ahead of processionaries, because the caterpillars establish their contact along a thread of silk, but these fellows, apparently, do it through actual nerve ganglia."

"Eh?" queried Ham.

"Of course. Didn't you notice how they were joined? That flat organ in front—each one had it slapped like a sucking disc against the one before him—was always placed in identically the same position. And when you shot one out of the middle of the file, I saw the

pulpy lump it had covered on the one it followed. And besides—"
She paused.

"Besides what?"

"Well, didn't it strike you as strange that the whole line cooperated so well? Their legs moved in a sort of rhythm, like the legs of a single creature, like the legs of a myriapod—a centipede.

"I don't think habit or training or discipline could ever account for the way that file of creatures acted, rushing and stopping and veering and circling, all in perfect unison. The whole line must have been under the direct neural control of the leader—hearing and smelling what he heard and smelled, even, perhaps, responding to his desires, hating with him and finally fearing with him!"

"Damned if I don't think you're right!" exclaimed Ham. "The whole bunch of them acted like one animal!"

"Until you carelessly created two by breaking the line," corrected the girl. "You see—"

"I made another leader!" finished Ham excitedly. "The one behind the break in the file became a second leader, able to act independently." He frowned. "Say, do you suppose those things accumulate their intelligence when they join? Does each one add his reasoning power—if any—to the dominating brain of the leader?"

"I doubt it," said the girl. "If that were true, they would be able to build up a colossal intellect just by adding more sections. No matter how stupid each individual might be, they'd only have to click together enough of them to create a godlike intelligence.

"If anything like that existed here, or ever had existed, they wouldn't be rushing around weaponless and savage. There'd be some sort of civilization, wouldn't there? But," she added, "they might pool their experience. The leader might have all the individual memories at his disposal, which wouldn't add a darn thing to his reasoning powers."

"Sounds plausible," agreed Ham. "Now as to the fog shapes. Have you figured out anything about them?"

She shuddered. "Not much," she confessed. "I think there's a relationship between them and these others, though."

"Why?"

"Because they came streaming by us just before the attack. They might simply have been running away from the multiple creature, but in that case they ought to have scattered. They didn't; they came rushing by in two distinct streams, and not only that, but all during the fight they were flickering and shimmering in the background. Didn't you notice that?"

"My attention was occupied," replied Ham dryly. "But what about it?"

"Well, did you ever hear of the indicator albirostris—the honey-guide?"

"It sounds vaguely familiar."

"It's an African bird of the cuckoo family, and it guides human beings to the wild bee colonies. Then the man gets the honey and the bird gets the grubs." She paused. "I think," she concluded, "that the fog shapes played honey-guide to the others. I think they led the creatures to us either because your shot angered them, or because they wanted the leavings after the others were through with us, or because they're just plain destructive. Anyway, that's my guess."

"If they're real," added Ham. "We'll have to turn the infrared camera on the next group or herd or swarm or flock, or whatever you call their gatherings. I still think they're mostly illusory."

She shuddered. "I hope you're right," she murmured.

"Bah!" said Harbord suddenly. "Women don't belong in places like this. Too timid."

"Yeah?" retorted Ham, now fully prepared to defend Patricia. "She was cool enough to notice details during that fracas out there."

"But afraid of shadows!" grumbled Harbord.

However, they weren't shadows. Some hours later Cullen reported that the fog around the *Gaea* was full of shifting, skittering shapes, and he trundled the long-wave camera from port to port.

Handicapped by the argon-laden air with its absorption spectrum that filtered out long rays, the infra-red plates were nevertheless more sensitive than the human eye, though perhaps less responsive to detail. But a photographic plate is not amenable to suggestion; it never colors what it sees by the tint of past experience; it records coldly and unemotionally the exact pattern of the light rays that strike it.

When Cullen was ready to develop his plates, Patricia was still asleep, tired out by the hectic first day on the planet, but Ham came out drowsily to watch the results.

These might have been less than she feared, but they were more than Ham expected. He squinted through a negative toward the light, then took a sheaf of prints from Cullen, frowning down at them.

"Humph!" he muttered. The prints showed something, beyond doubt, but something not much more definite than the unaided eye had seen. Indubitably the fog shapes were real, but it was equally certain that they weren't anthropomorphic.

The demoniac faces, the leering visages, the sardonic countenances, were decidedly absent to the eye of the camera; to that extent the beings they had seen were illusions, whose features had been superimposed by their own minds on the shadows in the fog. But only to that extent, for behind the illusion lay something unmistakably real. Yet what physical forms could achieve that flickering and shifting and change of shape and size that they had observed?

"Don't let Pat see these unless she asks to," he said thoughtfully. "And I think I'll confine her to the ship for the present. Judging from the couple of acres we've seen so far, this place isn't the friendliest sort of locality."

But he figured without the girl on both counts. When, fifteen hours later, he moved the rocket a mile south and prepared for another circuit in the fog, she met his order with a storm of protest.

"What's this expedition for?" she demanded. "The most important thing on a planet is the life it supports, and that's a biologist's business, isn't it?"

She turned indignant eyes on Ham. "Why do you think the Institute chose me for this job? Just to sit idly in the rocket while a couple of incompetents look around—a chemist and an engineer who don't know an epiphyte from a hemipteron?"

"Well, we could bring in specimens," muttered Ham miserably.

That brought a renewed storm. "Listen to me!" she snapped. "If you want the truth, I'm not here because of you. You're here because of me! They could have found a hundred engineers and chemists and astrogators, but how many good extraterrestrial biologists? Darn few!"

Ham had no ready reply, for it was quite true. Despite her youth, Patricia, born on Venus and educated in Paris, was admittedly preeminent in her field. Nor, in all fairness to the backers of the expedition, could he handicap her in her work. After all, not even the government financed Smithsonian could afford to spend somewhat over two million dollars without getting fair return for its money.

Sending a rocket out into the depths where Uranus plowed its lonely orbit was a project so expensive that in simple justice the expedition had to do its utmost, especially since forty long years would elapse before there would be another opportunity to visit the doubtful planet. So he sighed and yielded.

"That shows a faint glimmering of intelligence." said Patricia. "Do you think I'm afraid of some animated links of sausages? I won't make the mistake of cutting them in the middle. And as for those funny-faced shadows, you said yourself that they were illusions, and—by the way, where are the pictures you were going to take of them? Did they show anything?"

Cullen hesitated, then at Ham's resigned nod, he passed her the sheaf of prints. At the first glance she frowned suddenly.

"They're real!" she said, and then bent over them with so intent an expression that Ham wondered what she could read from so vague and shadowy a record. He saw, or fancied he saw, a queer gleam of satisfaction in her eyes, and felt a sensation of relief that at least she wasn't upset by the discovery.

"What d'you make of them?" he asked curiously.

She smiled and made no answer.

Apparently Ham's fears concerning Patricia were ill-founded on all counts. The days passed uneventfully; Cullen analyzed and filed his samples, and took innumerable tests of the greenish Uranian atmosphere; Ham checked and rechecked his standard weights, and in spare moments examined the reaction motor on which the *Gaea* and their lives depended; and Patricia collected and classified her specimens without the least untoward incident.

Harbord, of course, had nothing to do until the rocket plunged once more into the vastness of space, so he served as cook and general utility man—an easy enough task consisting largely of opening cans and disposing of the debris.

Four times the *Gaea* soared aloft, picked her way through the eternal mists to a new station, and settled down while Ham and Patricia explored another thousand-foot circle. And somewhere in the grayness above, forever invisible, Saturn swung into conjunction, passed the slower moving Uranus, and began to recede. Time was growing short; every hour meant additional distance to cover on the return.

On the fifth shift of position, Harbord announced the limit of their stay. "Not more than fifty hours more," he warned, "unless you have an inclination to spend the next forty years here."

"Well, it's not much worse than London," observed Ham, pulling on his outdoor clothing. "Come on, Pat. This'll be our last look at the pleasant Uranian landscape."

She followed him into the gray open, waiting while he clicked his guide wire to the rocket, and the silken rope to her belt. "I'd like to get one more look at our chain-gang friends," she complained. "I have an idea, and I'd like to investigate it."

"And I hope you don't," he grunted. "One look was plenty for me."

The *Gaea* disappeared in the eternal mist. Around them the fog shapes flickered and grimaced as they had done ever since that first appearance, but neither of them paid any attention now. Familiarity had removed any trace of fear.

This was a region of small stony hillocks, and Patricia ranged back and forth at the full length of the rope, culling, examining, discarding, or preserving the rare Uranian flora. Most of the time she was beyond sight or sound, but the cord that joined them gave evidence of her safety.

Ham tugged impatiently. "Like leading a puppy past a row of trees," he growled as she appeared. "Wire's end!" he called. "We'll circle back."

"But there's something beyond!" she cried. By virtue of the rope she could range an additional fifty feet into the obscurity. "There's something growing just out of reach there—something new! I want to see it."

"Hell, you can't. It's out of reach and that's that. We can lengthen the wire a little and come back for it."

"Oh, it's just a few feet." She turned away. "I'll release the rope, take a look, and come back."

"You won't!" he roared. "Pat! Come here!"

He tugged mightily on the rope. A faint exclamation of disgust drifted out of the dimness, and then, suddenly, the rope came free in his hands. She had freed herself!

"Pat!" he bellowed. "Come back! Come back, I say!"

A smothered reply sounded, all but inaudible. Then there was utter silence. He shouted again. The all-enveloping fog muffled his voice in his own ears. He waited a moment, then repeated his call. Nothing; no sound but the rustle of the fog shapes.

He was in a desperate quandary. After another pause he fired his revolver into the air, all ten shots at brief intervals. He waited, then fired another clip without response from the passive, leaden-hued fog. He swore bitterly at the girl's foolhardiness, at his own helplessness, and at the grimacing fog shapes.

He had to do something. Go back to the *Gaea* and set Harbord and Cullen searching. That wasted precious time; every moment Patricia might be wandering blindly away. He muttered a phrase that might have been either an imprecation or a prayer, pulled a pencil and a piece of paper from his pocket, and scrawled a message: "Pat lost. Bring additional spool and attach to wire. Circle for me. Will try to stay within two-thousand-foot radius."

He clipped the paper to the wire's end, weighted it with a stone, and then tugged three times to summon the two from the *Gaea*. Then he deliberately released himself and plunged unguided into the fog.

He never knew how far or how long he walked. The fog shapes gibbered and mocked him, the condensation gathered on his face and dripped from his nose and chin, the fog pressed in about him. He shouted, he fired his automatic, he whistled, hoping that the shriller sounds might carry, he zigzagged back and forth across his route. Surely, he thought, Pat had sense enough not to wander. Surely a girl trained in the Hotlands of Venus knew that the proper procedure when lost was to remain still, lest one stray still farther from safety.

Ham himself was utterly lost now. He had no faintest conception of where the *Gaea* lay, nor in what direction was the guiding wire. Now and again he thought he spied the silver filament of safety, but each time it was only the glint of water or the dull sparkle of stone. He moved under on inverted bowl of fog that blocked off vision on every hand.

In the end it was the very weakness of the lost that saved him. After hours of hopeless plunging through the mist, he tripped—actually tripped—over the wire. He had circled.

Cullen and Harbord loomed suddenly beside him, joined by a silken rope. He gasped. "Have you—have you—"

"No," said Harbord gloomily, his lined visage looking bleak and worn. "But we will. We will."

"Say," said Cullen, "why don't you go aboard and rest up? You look about done in, and we can carry on for you."

"No," said Ham grimly.

Harbord was unexpectedly gentle. "Don't worry," he said. "She's a sensible sort. She'll stay put until we find her. She can't have wandered a full thousand feet beyond the wire's end."

"Unless," responded Ham miserably, "she was driven—or carried."

"We'll find her," repeated Harbord.

But ten hours later, after they had completely circled the *Gaea* at a dozen different distances, it became obvious that Patricia was not within the circumference described by their two-thousand-foot wire. Fifty times during the intolerable circuit Ham had fought against the impulse to free himself of the wire, to probe just a little farther into the tantalizing fog.

She might be sitting despondently just beyond sight and earshot, or she might be lying injured within an easy stone's throw of the circle, and they'd never know it. Yet to release himself from the one guide that marked their base was little better than suicide and somewhat more than sheer insanity.

When they reached the stake that Cullen had driven to mark their starting point, Ham paused. "Back to the ship," he ordered grimly. "We'll move her four thousand feet in this direction and circle again. Pat can't have wandered a mile from the point I lost her."

"We'll find her," reiterated Harbord.

But they didn't find her. After a futile, exhausting search, Ham ordered the *Gaea* to a point at which their wire bound circle was tangent to the two circles already explored, and grimly began again.

Thirty-one hours had passed since the girl had disappeared, and the three were nearing exhaustion. It was Cullen who yielded first, and groped his way wearily back to the ship. When the other two returned to move to a new base, they found him sleeping fully clothed beside a half-drained cup of coffee.

The hours dropped slowly into eternity. Saturn was pulling steadily ahead of the misty planet, bound placidly for their next meeting forty years in the future. Harbord said not a word concerning the passing of time; it was Ham who broached the subject.

"Look here," he said as the *Gaea* slanted down to a new position. "Time's short. I don't want you two marooned here, and if we don't find Pat in this area, I want you and Cullen to leave. Do you understand?"

"I understand English," said Harbord, "but not that sort."

"There's no reason for you two to stay. I'm staying. I'll take our portion of food and all the arms and ammunition, and I'll stay."

"Bah!" growled Harbord. "What's forty years?" He had turned sixty.

"I'm ordering you to leave," said Ham quietly.

"You don't command once we're clear of the surface," grunted the other. "We're staying. We'll find her."

But it began to seem utterly hopeless. Cullen awoke and joined them as they emerged into the infinite fog, and they took their places at six hundred and sixty foot intervals along the wire. Ham took the outermost position and they began their endless plodding through the mists.

He was close to the breaking point. For forty hours he had neither slept nor eaten, save for a hurried gulp of coffee and a bite of chocolate when they moved the *Gaea*. The fog shapes were beginning to take the weirdest conformations in his tired eyes, and they seemed to loom ever closer, and to grin more malevolently.

So it was that he had to blink and squint and peer very closely when, a quarter way around the circuit, he saw something a little denser than the fog shapes in the gloom.

He jerked the wire once to halt Harbord and Cullen, and stared fixedly. There was a sound, too—a faint, steady thrumming quite different from the eerie rustles of the fog shapes. He started sharply as he heard still another sound, indescribable, muffled, but certainly a physical sound. He jerked the wire three times; that would summon his companions.

They came, and he pointed out the dusky mass. "We can reach it," he suggested, "if we tie a couple of our ropes together. Two should be plenty."

They moved cautiously into the mist. Something—something was stirring there. They crept quietly on, fifty feet, sixty. And suddenly Ham realized that he saw a chain of the multiple creatures—a vast chain, apparently, for it was still passing before them. In utter despondency he stopped, staring hopelessly ahead; then, very slowly, he turned back toward the wire.

A sound—a sharp sound—froze him. It sounded like a cough!

He whirled back. Regardless of the dangerous file close before him, he shouted. "Pat! Pat!"

The sublimity of relief! A thin little voice quavered beyond the line. "Ham! Oh, Ham!"

"Are—you—are you safe?"

"Y-yes."

He was at the very side of the passing file. Beyond, pale as the mist itself, was Patricia, no more than ten feet away.

"Thank God!" he muttered. "Pat, when this chain passes, run straight here. Don't move a single step aside—not a single step!"

"Passes?" she quavered. "Oh, it won't pass! It isn't a file. It's a circle!"

"A circle!" Comprehension dawned. "A circle! Then how—how can we get you out? We can't break it or—" He paused. Now the queer parade was leaderless, helpless, but once it were broken at any point, it would turn into a fierce and bloodthirsty thing—and it might attack the girl. "Lord!" he gasped.

Harbord and Cullen were beside him. "Here!" he snapped. He seized the remaining rope. "I'm going across. Stand close."

He crawled to the shoulders of the two. From that height it might be possible to leap the creatures. It had to be possible.

He made it, though it left Cullen and Harbord groaning from the thrust of his hundred and eighty pounds, Uranus weight. He spent only a moment holding Patricia to him; the menace of those circling monsters was too imminent.

He flung an end of the rope to the two beyond the circle. "Can you swing across if we hold it high enough, Pat?" The girl seemed on the verge of exhaustion.

"Of course," she murmured.

He helped her lock elbows and knees around the rope. Slowly, painfully, she inched her way in the manner of a South American tree sloth. Ham had one terrible instant of fear as she wavered directly over the file, but she made it, dropping weakly into Harbord's arms beyond.

Then she cried out, "Ham! How can you get across?"

"Vault 'em!" he flashed.

He spent no time in reflection. He gathered all the strength remaining in his body, drew back for a short run, and actually cleared the six-foot barrier of deadliness, his knuckles just touching a black, blubbery back.

Patricia struggled to her feet, clinging to him. He held her a moment, then said huskily, "Lord! If we hadn't found you—"

"But you did!" she whispered. Suddenly she began to laugh hysterically, the sound broken by choking coughs. "Only what kept you? I expected you sooner!" She stared wildly at the circling file. "I short-circuited them!" she cried. "I—short-circuited—their brains!"

She collapsed against him. Without a word he lifted her and followed Harbord and Cullen back along the wire to the *Gaea*. Behind him, revolving endlessly, was the circle of doomed creatures.

Uranus was a banded green globe behind the flare of the afterjets, and Saturn a brilliant blue star to the left of a tiny, very fierce sun. Patricia, her cough already improved in the conditioned air of the *Gaea*, lay passively in a pivot chair and smiled at Ham.

"You see," she said, "after I cast off the rope—Wait! Don't lecture me again about that!—I stepped just the merest few paces into the fog, and then, after all, the plants I had seen turned out to be the same old zigzag ones I named *Cryptogami Urani*, so I started back and you were gone."

"Gone! I hadn't moved."

"You were gone," she repeated imperturbably. "I walked a short distance and then shouted, but the shouts just sort of muffled out. And then I heard a couple of shots in another direction, and started that way—and suddenly the chain gang came plunging out of the fog!"

"What'd you do?"

"What could I do? They were too close for me to draw my gun, so I ran. They're fast, but so am I, and I kept ahead until I began to lose breath. Then I discovered that by sharp dodging I could keep away—they don't turn very quickly—and I managed for a few minutes, although that blinding fog kept me in danger of tripping. And then I had an inspiration!"

"You needed one!" he muttered.

She ignored him. "Do you remember when I mentioned Fabre and his studies of the pine processionary caterpillars? Well, one of his experiments was to lead the procession around the edge of a big garden vase and close the circle! He did away with the leader, and do you know what happened?"

"I can guess."

"You're right. Lacking leadership, the circle just kept revolving for hours, days, I don't know how long, until at last some caterpillar dropped from exhaustion, and a new leader was created by the gap. And suddenly that experiment occurred to me, and I set about duplicating it. I dodged back toward the rear end of my procession, with the front end following me!"

"I see!" muttered Ham.

"Yes. I intended to close the circle and dodge outside, but something went wrong. I caught up with the rear all right, but I was just about worn out and I stumbled or something, and the next thing I remember was lying on the ground with the feet of the things pounding by my face. And I was inside the circle!"

"You probably fainted from exhaustion."

"I never faint," said Patricia with dignity.

"You did when I got you out."

"That," she retorted, "was simply a case of going to sleep after about forty hours of staying awake without food. Fainting, or syncope, is quite different, being due to an undersupply of blood to the brain—"

"All right," cut in Ham. "If fainting needs a brain, obviously you couldn't faint. Go on."

"Well," she resumed placidly, "there I was. I could have shot a break in the circle, of course, but that would have brought an attack, and besides, I hadn't the least idea where the *Gaea* was. So I sat there, and I sat a week or ten days or a month—"

"Forty hours."

"And the fog shapes kept rustling over the file of sausage creatures, and they kept flickering and rustling and whispering until I thought I'd go mad. It was terrible—even knowing what they were, it was terrible!"

"Knowing what—Do you know what they are?"

"I figured out one good guess. In fact, I had a suspicion as soon as I saw Cullen's infra-red photographs."

"Then what the devil are they?"

"Well, you see I had a good chance to examine the chain things at close range, and they're not perfect creatures."

"I'll say they're not!"

"I mean they're not fully developed. In fact, they're larvae. And I think the fog shapes are what they grow up to be. That's why the fog shapes led the things to us. Don't you see? The chain creatures are their children. It's like caterpillar and moth!"

"Well, that's possible, of course, but what about the weird faces of the fog shapes, and their ability to change size?"

"They don't change size. See here—the light on that part of Uranus comes from directly overhead, doesn't it? Well, any shadows are thrown straight down, then; that's obvious. So what we saw—all that flickering, shifting crew of gargoyles—were just the shadows of floating things, flying things, projected on the fog. That's why the fog shapes grew and shrank and changed shape; they were just shadows following some winged creature that moved up and down and around. Do you see?"

"It sounds plausible. We'll report it that way, and in eighty years, when the north pole part of Uranus gets around to the sunlight again, somebody can run up and check the theory. Maybe Harbord'll pilot them. Eh, Harbord? Think you'd be willing to visit the place again in eighty years?"

"Not with a woman aboard," grunted the astrogator.

Flight on Titan

The gale roared incessantly like all the tormented souls since creation's dawn, driving the two sliding and tumbling into the momentary shelter of a ridge of ice. A cloud of glittering ice needles swept by, rainbow-hued in the brilliant night, and the chill of eighty below zero bit through the sponge rubber of their suits.

The girl placed her visor close against the man's helmet and said steadily: "This is the end, isn't it, Tim? Because I'm glad I came with you, then. I'm glad it's both of us together."

The man groaned despairingly, and the blast tore the sound away. He turned aside, thinking regretfully of the past.

The year 2142, as most people recall, was a disastrous one in the financial world. It was the year of the collapse of the Planetary Trading Corporation and the year that ushered in the resultant depression.

Most of us remember the hysterical two years of speculation that preceded the crash. These followed the final development of the Hocken Rocket in 2030, the annexation of the arid and useless Moon by Russia, and the discovery by the international expeditions of a dead civilization on Mars and a primitive one on Venus. It was the Venus report that led to the formation of the P.T.C. and the debacle that followed.

No one knows now who was to blame. All the members of those intrepid expeditions have suffered under the cloud; two of them were murdered in Paris only a little more than a year ago, presumably by vengeful investors in Planetary. Gold will do such things to men; they will take mad risks with what they have, pursuing a vision of what they hope to have, and, when the crash comes, turn on any scapegoat that's luckless enough to be handy. At any rate, regardless of responsibility, the rumor started that gold was as common on Venus as iron on Earth—and then the damage was done. No one stopped to reflect that the planet's density is less than the Earth's, and that gold, or any heavy metal, should be even rarer there, if not utterly absent, as on the Moon.

The rumors spread like an epidemic, and stories circulated that the expedition members had returned wealthy. All one had to do, it seemed, was to trade beads and jack-knives to the obliging Venusian natives for golden cups, golden axes, golden ornaments.

The shares of the quickly organized Planetary Trading Corporation skyrocketed from a par of fifty to a peak of thirteen hundred. Vast paper fortunes were made; the civilized world went into a frenzy of speculative fervor; prices of everything shot upward in anticipation of a flood of new gold—food, rent, clothing, machinery.

We all remember the outcome. Planetary's first two trading expeditions looked long and arduously for the gold. They found the natives; they found them eager enough for beads and jack knives, but they found them quite destitute of gold. They brought back neat little carvings and a quantity of silver, scientifically valuable records, and a handful of pearlike stones from Venusian seas—but no gold. Nothing to pay dividends to the avid stockholders; nothing to support the rumor-puffed structure of prices, which crashed as quickly as the shares of Planetary, once the truth was out.

The collapse affected investors and non-investors alike, and among them, Timothy Vick and his Canadian wife Diane. The spring of 2142 found them staring at each other in their New York apartment, all but penniless, and in the very depths of despair. Jobs were vanishing, and Tim's training as a salesman of 'vision sets was utterly useless in a world where nobody could afford to buy them. So they sat and stared hopelessly, and said very little.

Tim at last broke the gloomy silence. "Di," he said, "what'll we do when it's all gone?"

"Our money? Tim, something will come before then. It has to!"

"But if it doesn't?" At her silence, he continued: "I'm not going to sit and wait. I'm going to do something."

"What, Tim? What is there to do?"

"I know!" His voice dropped. "Di, do you remember that queer gem the government expedition brought back from Titan? The one Mrs. Advent paid half a million dollars for, just so she could wear it to the opera?"

"I remember the story, Tim. I never heard of Titan."

"One of Saturn's moons. United States possession; there's a confirmatory settlement on it. It's habitable."

"Oh!" she said, puzzled. "But—what about it?"

"Just this: last year half a dozen traders went up there after more. One of 'em returned today with five of the things; I saw it on the news broadcast. He's rich, Di. Those things are almost priceless."

Diane began to see. "Tim!" she said huskily.

"Yes. That's the idea. I'm going to leave you all I can, except what money I must have, and go up there for a year. I've read up on Titan; I know what to take." He paused. "It's coming near Perigee now. There'll be a rocket leaving for Nivia—that's the settlement—in a week."

"Tim!" murmured Diane again. "Titan—oh, I did hear of it! That's—that's the cold one, isn't it?"

"Cold as Dante's hell," replied Tim. He saw her lips form a word of protest and his blue eyes went narrow and stubborn.

She changed her unspoken word. "I'm going with you," she said. Her brown eyes narrowed to meet his.

Diane had won. That was over now—the long hours of argument, the final submission, the months of insufferably stuffy air abroad the rocket, the laborious struggle to erect the tiny hemispherical metal-walled shack that served as living quarters. The rocket had dropped them, cargo and all, at a point determined after a long conference back on Earth with Simonds, the returned trader.

He had been an agreeable sort, but rather discouraging; his description of the Titan climate had sounded rather like a word picture of an Eskimo hell. He hadn't exaggerated, either; Tim realized that now and cursed the weakness that had made him yield to Diane's insistence.

Well, there they were. He was smoking his one permitted daily cigarette, and Diane was reading aloud from a history of the world, taken because it had some thousand pages and would last a long time. Outside was the unbelievable Titanian night with its usual hundred-mile gale screaming against the curved walls, and the glitter of ice mountains showing green under the glare of Saturn with its rings visible edgewise from the satellite since it revolved in the same plane.

Beyond the Mountains of the Damned—so named by Young, the discoverer—a hundred miles away, lay Nivia, the City of Snow. But they might as well have been on a planet of Van Maanen's star so far as human contacts went; surely no one could survive a cross-country journey here through nights that were generally eighty below zero, or even days that sometimes attained the balmy warmth of just above freezing. No; they were marooned here until the rocket returned next year.

Tim shivered as the grinding roar of a shifting mountain sounded above the scream of the wind. That was common enough here; they were always shifting under the enormous tidal pull of the giant Saturn and the thrust of that incredible wind. But it was disquieting, none the less; it was an ever-present danger to their little dwelling.

"Br-r-r!" He shuddered. "Listen to that!"

Diane looked up. "Not used to it yet, after three months?"

"And never will be!" he returned. "What a place!"

She smiled. "I know what'll cheer you," she said, rising. From a tin box she poured a cascade of fire. "Look, Tim! Six of them. Six flame-orchids!"

He gazed at the glowing eggs of light. Like the flush of life itself, rainbow rings rolled in a hundred tints beneath their surfaces. Diane passed her hand above them, and they responded to its warmth with a flame of changing colors that swept the entire keyboard of the spectrum, reds merging into blues, violets, greens, and yellows, then orange and scarlet of blood.

"They're beautiful!" Tim whispered, staring fascinated. "No wonder rich women bleed themselves dry for them. Diane, we'll save one out—the prettiest—for you."

She laughed. "There are things I'd rather have, Tim."

A pounding sounded above the windy bellowing. They knew what it meant; Tim rose and peered through the reinforced window into the brilliant night, and, after a moment of blinking, made out the four-foot-long body of a native sprawled before his door, his curved claws hooked into the ice. On Titan, of course, no creature stood erect against those perpetual howling blasts, no creature, that is, save man, a recent arrival from a gentler world.

Tim opened the door, slipping it wider notch by notch on its retaining chain, since muscular power would have been inadequate to hold it. The wind bellowed gleefully in, sweeping the hanging utensils on the walls into a clanging chorus, spinning a loose garment into a mad dance, chilling the air to bitterness.

The native slithered through like a walrus, his streamlined body seal like and glistening with its two-inch protective layer of blubbery flesh. As Tim cranked the door shut, the creature raised the filmy underlids from its eyes, and they showed large, luminous, and doglike.

This was a Titanian native, not much more intelligent than a St. Bernard dog, perhaps, but peacable and inoffensive, beautifully adapted to its forbidding environment, and the highest form of life yet known on Titan.

He reached into the pouch opening on his rubbery back. *"Uh!"* he said, displaying a white ovoid. As the comparatively warm air of the room struck it, the flame-orchid began to glow in exquisite colors.

Diane took it; against her palms the tints changed more quickly, deepened gloriously. It was a small one, no larger than a robin's egg, but perfect except where it had been attached to some frigid rock.

"Oh!" she exclaimed. "What a beauty, Tim!"

He grinned. "That's no way to bargain."

He pulled out the black case that contained their trade goods, opening it to display the little mirrors, knives, beads, matches, and nondescript trinkets.

The coal-black eyes of the native glittered avidly; he glanced from one article to the next in an agony of longing indecision. He touched them with his clawed, three-fingered hands; he cooed huskily. His eyes wandered over the room.

"Huss!" he said abruptly, pointing. Diane burst into a sudden laugh. He was indicating an old and battered eight-day clock, quite useless to the pair since it lacked the adjustment to permit them to keep other than Earth time. The ticking must have attracted him.

"Oh, no!" She chuckled. "It's no good to you. Here!" She indicated a box of trinkets.

"Ugha! Huss!" The native was insistent.

"Here, then!"

She passed him the clock; he held it close to his skin-shielded ears and listened. He cooed.

Impulsively, Diane picked a pocketknife from the box. "Here," she said, "I won't cheat you. Take this, too."

The native gurgled. He pried open the glittering blade with his hooked claws, closed it and slipped it carefully into his back pouch, stuffing the clock after it. The pouch stood out like a miniature hump as he turned and scuttled toward the door.

"*Uh!*" he said.

Tim let him out, watching through the window as he slipped across the slope, his blunt nose pointed into the wind as he moved sideways.

Tim faced Diane. "Extravagance!" He grinned.

"Oh, a fifty-cent knife for this!" She fondled the gem.

"Fifty cents back home," he reminded her. "Just remember what we paid for freight, and you'll see what I mean. Why, look at Nivia; they mine gold there, pure, virgin gold right out of the rocks, and by the time the cost of shipping it back to Earth is deducted, and the insurance, it barely pays—just barely."

"Gold?"

"Yes. That's simple to understand. You know how little freight a rocket can carry when it has to be fueled and provisioned for a flight from the Earth to Titan, or vice versa. A mere jaunt of seven hundred and eighty million miles and plenty of chance for trouble on the way. I think the insurance on gold is thirty per cent of the value."

"Tim, shall we have to insure these? How shall we ever manage?"

"We won't. We won't insure these because we'll be going with 'em."

"But if they're lost?"

"If they're lost, Diane, insurance wouldn't help us, because, then, we'll be lost, too."

Three more months dragged by. Their little hoard of flame-orchids reached fifteen, then eighteen. They realized, of course, that the gem wouldn't command the fabulous price of that first one, but half that price, even a tenth of it, meant wealth, meant leisure and luxury. It was worth the year of sacrifice.

Titan swung endlessly about its primary. Nine-hour days succeeded nine-hour nights of unbelievable ferocity. The eternal wind howled and bit and tore, and the shifting ice mountains heaved and roared under Saturn's tidal drag.

Sometimes, during the day, the pair ventured into the open, fought the boisterous winds, clung precariously to frigid slopes. Once Diane was swept bodily away, saving herself miraculously on

the verge of one of the deep and mysterious crevasses that bounded their mountain slope, and thereafter they were very cautious.

Once they dared to penetrate the grove of rubbery and elastic whiplash trees that grew in the shelter of the nearest cliff. The things lashed out at them with resounding strokes, not violent enough to fell them, but stinging sharply even through the inch-thick layer of sponge rubber that insulated their bodies from the cold.

And every seven and a half days the wind died to a strange and oddly silent calm, was still for half an hour or so, and then roared with renewed ferocity from the opposite direction. Thus it marked Titan's revolution.

At almost equal intervals, every eight days, the native appeared with the clock. The creature seemed unable to master the intricate problem of winding it and always presented it mournfully, brightening at once as Diane set it ticking again.

There was one impending event that worried Tim at times. Twice in its thirty-year period Saturn eclipses the Sun, and for four Titanian days, seventy-two hours, Titan is in utter darkness. The giant planet was nearing that point now and would reach it long before the rocket ship, speeding from the Earth at perigee, was due.

Human occupation dated back only six years; no one knew what four days of darkness might do to the little world of Titan.

The absolute zero of space? Probably not, because of the dense and xenon-rich atmosphere, but what storms, what titanic upheavals of ice, might accompany that night of eclipse? Glowing Saturn itself supplied a little heat, of course, about a third as much as the distant Sun.

Well, worry was futile. Tim glanced at Diane, mending a rip in the furry face-mask of her outdoor garment, and suggested a stroll. "A stroll in the sunlight," he phrased it sardonically. It was August back on Earth.

Diane agreed. She always agreed, cheerfully and readily. Without her this project would have been utterly unbearable, and he wondered amazedly how Simonds had stood it, how those others scattered around Titan's single little continent were standing it. He sighed, slipped into this thick garment, and opened the door into the roaring hell outside.

That was the time they came near disaster. They crawled, crept, and struggled their way into the lee of an ice hummock, and stood

there panting and gasping for a moment's rest. Tim raised his head to peer over the crest and saw through his visor's protecting goggles something unique in his experience on Titan. He frowned at it through the dense refractive air of the planet; it was hard to judge distances when the atmosphere made everything quiver like heat waves.

"Look, Di!" he exclaimed. "A bird!"

It did look like one, sailing on the wind toward them, wings outspread. It grew larger; it was as large as a pterodactyl, bearing down on them with the force of that hundred-mile wind behind it. Tim could make out a fierce, three-foot beak.

Diane screamed. The thing was headed for them; it was diving now at airplane speed. It was the girl who seized and flung a jagged piece of ice; the thing veered higher, swept like a cloud above them, and was gone. It could not fly upwind.

They looked it up in Young's book at the shack. That intrepid explorer had seen and named the creature; it was a knife-kite, the same sort of beast that had accounted for the death of one of his men. It wasn't a bird; it didn't really fly; it just sailed like a kite before the terrific blasts of Titan, and touched ground only during the weekly calm or when it had succeeded in stabbing some prey.

But life was scarce indeed on the icy little world. Except for the occasional natives, who came and went mysteriously as spirits, and that single knife-kite, and the whiplash trees near the cliff,' they saw nothing living. Of course the crystal bubbles of the ice-ants marked the glacial surface of the hills, but these creatures never emerged, laboring incessantly beneath their little domes that grew like mushrooms as they melted within and received fresh deposits of ice crystals without. A lonely world, a wild, bizarre, forbidding, and unearthly little planet.

It never actually snowed on Titan. The chill air could absorb too little water vapor for condensation as snow, but there was a substitute. During the days, when the temperature often passed the melting point, shallow pools formed on the frozen oceans, augmented sometimes by mighty eruptions of frigid brine from below. The ferocious winds swept these pools into a spindrift that froze and went rushing as clouds of icy needles around the planet.

Often during the darkness Diane had watched from the window

as one of these clouds loomed glittering in the cold-green Saturn-light, sweeping by with a scream and slithering of ice crystals on the walls, and seeming to her mind like a tall, sheeted ghost. At such times, despite the atom-generated warmth of the tiny dwelling, she was apt to shiver and draw her garment closer about her, though she was careful that Tim never observed it.

So time passed in the trading shack, slowly and dismally. The weather, of course, was uniformly, unvaryingly terrible, such weather as only Titan, nearly nine hundred million miles from the moderating Sun, can present. The little world, with its orbital period of fifteen days and twenty-three hours, has no perceptible seasons; only the recurrent shifting of the winds from east to west marks its swing about gigantic Saturn.

The season is always winter—fierce, bitter, unimaginable winter, to which the earthly storms of desolate Antarctica are as April on the Riviera. And little by little, Saturn edged closer to the Sun, until one day the western streak of its rings knifed a dark gash across the reddish disk. The eclipse was at hand.

That night saw the catastrophe. Tim was dozing on the bunk; Diane was dreaming idly of green fields and warm sunlight. Outside roared a gale more than usually vociferous, and a steady parade of ice ghosts streamed past the windows. Low and ominous came the roar of shifting glacial mountains; Saturn and the Sun, now nearly in a direct line, heaved at the planet with a redoubled tidal pull. And then suddenly came the clang of warning; a bell rang ominously.

Diane knew what it meant. Months before, Tim had driven a row of posts into the ice, extending toward the cliff that sheltered the whiplash grove. He had foreseen the danger; he had rigged up an alarm. The bell meant that the cliff had shifted, had rolled upon the first of the stakes. Danger!

Tim was springing frantically from the bunk. "Dress for outside!" he snapped. "Quickly!"

He seized her heavy sponge-rubber parka and tossed it to her. He dragged on his own, cranked the door open to the pandemonium without, and a fierce and bitter blast swept in, upsetting a chair, spinning loose articles around the room.

"Close the emergency pack!" he yelled above the tumult. "I'll take a look."

Diane suppressed her upsurging fear as he vanished. She strapped the pack tightly, then poured the precious eighteen flame-orchids into a little leather pouch, and suspended this about her throat. She forced calmness upon herself; perhaps the ice cliff had stopped, or perhaps only the wind itself had snapped the warning post. She righted the chair and sat with her visor open despite the knife-sharp blasts from the door.

Tim was coming. She saw his gloved hand as he seized the doorframe, then his fur-masked face, eyes grim behind the non-frosting goggles.

"Outside!" he yelled, seizing the pack.

She rose and scrambled after him into the howling inferno just as the second bell clanged.

Barely in time! As the tornado sent her sprawling and clutching, she had a sharply etched glimpse of a mighty pinnacle of glittering ice looming high above the shack; there was a rumble and a roar deeper than the winds, and the shack was gone. One iron wall, caught by the gale, swept like a giant bat above her, and she heard it go clanging and clattering along the slope to the east.

Dazed and horribly frightened, she clawed her way after Tim into the shelter of a ridge, watching him while he wrestled the pack that struggled in the blast like something living. She was calm when at last he got it strapped to his shoulders.

"This is the end, isn't it, Tim?" she said, putting her visor close against his helmet, "Because I'm glad I came with you, then. I'm glad it's both of us together."

Tim groaned despairingly, and the blast tore the sound away. He turned suddenly, slipping his arms around her figure. "I'm sorry, Di," he said huskily.

He wanted to kiss her—an impossibility, of course, in a Titanian night. It would have been a kiss of death; they would have died with lips frozen together. He put away the thought that maybe that might be a pleasanter way, since death was inevitable now, anyway. Better, he decided, to die fighting. He pulled her down into the lee of the ridge and sat thinking.

They couldn't stay here; that was obvious. The rocket wasn't due for three months, and long before then they'd be frozen corpses, rolling away before the hurricane or buried in some crevasse. They couldn't build a habitable shelter without tools, and if they could, their atomic stove was somewhere under the shifting cliff. They couldn't attempt the journey to Nivia, a hundred miles away across the Mountains of the Damned—or could they? That was the only possible alternative.

"Di," Tim said tensely, "we're going to Nivia. Don't be startled. Listen. The wind's just shifted. It's behind us; we have almost eight Earth days before it changes. If we can make it—twelve, thirteen miles a day—if we can make it, we'll be safe. If we don't make it before the wind shifts—" He paused. "Well, it's no worse than dying here."

Diane was silent. Tim frowned thoughtfully behind his goggles. It was a possibility. Pack, parka, and all, he weighed less than Earth weight; not as much less as one would think, of course. Titan, although no larger than Mercury, is a dense little world, and, besides, weight depends not only on a planet's density, but also on distance from its center. But the wind might not hinder them so much, since they were traveling with it, not against it. Its terrible thrust, fiercer than even an equal Earth wind because the air contained thirty per cent of the heavy gas xenon, would be dangerous enough, but—Anyway, they had no choice.

"Come on, Di," Tim said, rising. They had to keep moving now; they could rest later, after sunrise, when the danger of a frozen sleep was less.

Another terrible thought struck Tim—there would be only three more sunrises. Then for four Titanian days, the little satellite would be in the mighty shadow of Saturn, and during that long eclipse, Heaven alone knew what terrific forces might attack the harassed pair crawling painfully toward Nivia, the City of Snow.

But that had to be faced, too. There was no alternative. Tim lifted Diane to her feet, and they crept cautiously out of the shelter of the ridge, bowing as the cruel wind caught them and bruised them, even through their thick suits, by flying ice fragments.

It was a dark night for Titan; Saturn was on the other side of the little world, along with the Sun it was soon to eclipse, but the stars shone brilliant and twinkling through the shallow, but very dense and refractive, atmosphere. The Earth, which had so often lent a green spark of cheer to the lonely couple, was not among them;

from the position of Titan, it was always near the Sun and showed only just before sunrise or just after sunset. Its absence now seemed a desolate omen.

They came to a long, smooth, wind-swept slope. They made the error of trying to cross it erect, trusting to their cleated shoes for secure footing. It was misjudgment; the wind thrust them suddenly into a run, pressed them faster and faster until it was impossible to stop, and they were staggering through the darkness toward unknown terrain ahead.

Tim flung himself recklessly against Diane; they fell in a heap and went sliding and rolling, to crash at last against a low wall of ice a hundred feet beyond.

They struggled up, and Diane moaned inaudibly from the pain of a bruised knee. They crept cautiously on; they circled a bottomless crevasse from the depths of which came strange roarings and shriekings; they slipped miserably past a glittering cliff that shook and shifted above them. And when at last the vast bulk of Saturn rose over the wild land before them, and the tiny reddish Sun followed like a ruby hung on a pendant, they were near exhaustion.

Tim supported Diane to a crevice facing the Sun. For many minutes they were silent, content to rest, and then he took a bar of chocolate from the pack and they ate, slipping the squares hastily through visors opened for each bite.

But under the combined radiance of Saturn and the Sun, the temperature rose rapidly more than a hundred degrees; when Tim glanced at his wrist thermometer it was already nearly thirty-eight, and pools of water were forming in the wind-sheltered spots. He scooped some up with a rubber cup, and they drank. Water at least was no problem.

Food might be, however, if they lived long enough to consume that in the pack. Humans couldn't eat Titanian life because of its arsenical metabolism; they had to exist on food laboriously transported from the Earth, or, as did the Nivian settlers, on Titanian creatures from whose substance the arsenic had first been chemically removed. The Nivians ate the ice-ants, the whiplash trees, and occasionally, it was sometimes whispered, the Titanian natives.

Diane had fallen asleep, lying huddled in a pool of icy water that flowed off into the open and then was whirled into sparkling spray by the wind. He shook her gently; they couldn't afford to lose time now, not with the shadow of the eclipse looming ominously so few hours away. But it tore his heart to see her eyes crinkle in a weary smile as she rose; he damned himself again for ever bringing her to this.

So they plodded on, battered and trampled by the fierce and ruthless gale. He had no idea how far they had traveled during the night; from the crest of a high ridge he looked back, but the shifting hills of ice made localities hard to recognize, and he could not be sure that the grim escarpment far behind was actually the cliff that had crushed their shack.

He let Diane rest again from noon until sunset, nearly five hours. She regained much of the strength spent in the struggle of the night, but when the dropping sun set his wrist thermometer tumbling far toward the hundred-below-zero mark, it seemed to her as if she had not rested at all. Yet they survived another night of inferno, and the gray of dawn found them still staggering and stumbling before the incredible ferocity of that eternal wind.

During the morning a native appeared. They recognized him; in his clawed hands was the battered case of the eight-day clock. He sidled up to them, head toward the wind, and held out his short arms to display the mechanism; he whined plaintively and obviously thought himself cheated.

Tim felt an unreasoning hope at the sight of him, but it vanished immediately. The creature simply couldn't understand their predicament; Titan was the only world he knew, and he couldn't conceive of beings not adapted to its fierce environment. So the man stood silently as Diane wound the clock and responded dully to her smile as she returned it.

"This time, old fellow," she said to the native, "it's ticking away our lives. If we're not in Nivia by the time it stops again—" She patted the blunt head; the creature cooed and sidled away.

They rested and slept again during the afternoon, but it was a weary pair that faced the inferno of night. Diane was nearing exhaustion, not from lack of nourishment, but simply from the incessant battering she had received from the wind, and the terrific struggle that every step required. Tim was stronger, but his body ached, and the cold, striking somehow through the inch-thick parka had left him with a painfully frostbitten shoulder.

By two hours after sunset, he perceived hopelessly that Diane was not going to survive the night. She was struggling bravely, but she was unequal to the effort. She was weakening; the pitiless wind kept lashing her to her knees, and each time she rose more slowly, leaned more heavily on Tim's supporting arm. All too quickly came the moment he had foreseen with despairing heart, when she did not rise at all.

He crouched beside her; tears misted his goggles as he distinguished her words above the screaming of the blast.

"You go on, Tim," she murmured. She gestured toward the bag on her throat. "Take the flame-orchids and leave me."

Tim made no answer, but cradled her tired body in his arms, shielding her as best he could from the furious winds. He thought desperately. To remain here was quick death; at least he might carry Diane to some more sheltered spot, where they could sink more slowly into the fatal sleep of cold. To leave her was unthinkable; she knew that, too, but it had been a brave offer to make.

She clung weakly to him as he lifted her; he staggered a dozen steps before the wind toppled him, and the last struggle brought him to the lee of a low hillock. He dropped behind it and gathered the girl into his arms to wait for the cold to do its work.

He stared hopelessly ahead. The wild splendor of a Titanian night was before him, with the icy stars glittering on cold and glassy peaks. Just beyond their hillock stretched the smooth surface of a wind-swept glacier, and here and there were the crystalline bubbles of the ice-ants.

The ice-ants! Lucky little creatures! He remembered Young's description of them in the book at the shack. Within those domes it was warm; the temperature was above forty. He stared at them, fragile and yet resisting that colossal wind. He knew why; it was their ovoid shape, the same principle that enables an egg to resist the greatest pressure on its two ends. No one can break an egg by squeezing it endways.

Suddenly he started. A hope! He murmured a word to Diane, lifted her, and staggered out on the mirror-surface of the ice. There! There was a dome large enough—fully six feet across. He circled to the lee side and kicked a hole in the glittering roundness.

Diane crawled weakly through. He followed, crouching beside

her in the dusk. Would it work? He gave a long cry of relief as he perceived the scurrying three-inch figures of the ice ants, saw them patching the dome with crystal fragments.

Steam misted his non-frosting goggles. He drew Diane against him and then opened his visor. Warm air! It was like balm after the bitter air without; it was musty, perhaps—but warm! He opened Diane's; she was sleeping in exhaustion and never stirred as he uncovered her pale, drawn features.

His eyes grew accustomed to the gloomy starlight that filtered through the dome. He could see the ice-ants, little three-legged ruddy balls that ran about with a galloping motion. They weren't ants at all, of course, nor even insects in the terrestrial sense; Young had named them ants because they lived in antlike colonies.

Tim saw the two holes that pierced the saucerlike floor; through one, he knew, warm air came up from the mysterious hive below, and the other drained away the melting water of the dome. That dome would grow until it burst, but the ants didn't care; they'd sense the bursting point and have a new dome already started above the holes.

For a time he watched them; they paid no attention at all to the intruders, whose rubber suits offered nothing edible. They were semi-civilized little creatures; he observed them curiously as they scraped a gray mold from the ice, loaded it on tiny sledges that he recognized as leaves of the whiplash tree, and tugged the load to one of the holes, dumping it in, presumably, to a handling crew below. And after a while he fell asleep, and precious time trickled away.

Hours later something awakened him to daylight. He sat up; he had been lying with his head pillowed on his arm to keep his face from the water, and he rubbed the half-paralyzed limb ruefully as he stared about. Diane was still sleeping, but her face was more peaceful, more rested. He smiled gently down on her, and suddenly a flicker of motion caught his eye and, at the same time, a flash of brilliance.

The first was only an ice-ant scurrying across the rubber of her parka. The flash was—he started violently—it was a flame-orchid rolling sluggishly in the stream of water to the vent, and there went another! The ants had cut and carried away for food the little leather bag, exposed on Diane's breast by the opening of her visor.

He snatched the rolling gem of flame from the trickling water and searched desperately for the others. No use. Of their eighteen precious ovoids, he had retrieved exactly one—the small but perfect one for which they had traded the clock. He gazed in utter despondency at the flaming little egg for which they had risked—and probably lost—everything.

Diane stirred, sat up. She saw at once the consternation in his face. "Tim!" she cried. "What's wrong now?"

He told her. "It's my fault," he concluded grimly. "I opened your suit. I should have foreseen this." He slipped the lone gem into his left gauntlet, where it nestled against his palm.

"It's nothing, Tim," said Diane softly. "What use would all eighteen be to us, or a hundred? We might as well die with one as with all of them."

He did not answer directly. He said: "Even one will be enough if we get back. Perhaps eighteen would have glutted the market; perhaps we'll get almost as much for one as we would have for all."

That was a lie, of course; other traders would be increasing the supply, but it served to distract her mind.

Tim noticed then that the ice-ants were busy around the two vents at the center; they were building an inner dome. The crystal egg above them, now eight feet through, was about to crack.

He saw it coming, and they closed their visors. There was a jagged streak of light on the west, and suddenly, with a glistening of fragments, the walls collapsed and went spinning away over the icy floor, and the wind howled down upon them, nearly flattening them to the glacier! It began to thrust them over the ice.

They slid and crawled their way to the jagged crags beyond. Diane was strong again; her young body recovered quickly. In a momentary shelter, he noticed something queer about the light and glanced up to see gigantic Saturn almost half obscuring the Sun. He remembered then. This was the last day; for seventy-two hours there would be night.

And night fell far too quickly. Sunset came with the red disk three quarters obscured, and the bitter cold swept out of the west with a horde of ice ghosts, whose sharp needles clogged the filters of their masks and forced them to shake them out time after time.

The temperature had never been higher than forty below all day, and the night air, coming after that cold day, dropped rapidly to a hundred below, and even the warming filters could not prevent that frigid air from burning in their lungs like searing flame.

Tim sought desperately for an ice-ant bubble. Those large enough were rare, and when at last he found one, it was already too large, and the ice-ants didn't trouble to repair the hole he kicked, but set at once to build a new dome. In half an hour the thing collapsed, and they were driven on.

Somehow, they survived the night, and dawn of the fourth day found them staggering all but helpless into the lee of a cliff. They stared hopelessly at that strange, sunless, Saturn-lighted dawn that brought so little warmth.

An hour after the rising of the eclipsed Sun, Tim glanced at his wrist thermometer to find the temperature risen only to seventy below. They ate some chocolate, but each bite was a burning pain for the moment that their visors were open, and the chocolate itself was numbing cold.

When numbness and drowsiness began to attack his limbs, Tim forced Diane to rise, and they struggled on. Day was no better than night now, except for the cold Saturn light. The wind battered them more fiercely than ever; it was scarcely mid-afternoon, when Diane, with a faintly audible moan, collapsed to her knees and could not rise.

Tim stared frantically about for an ice bubble. At last, far over to the right, he saw a small one, three feet through, perhaps, but big enough for Diane. He could not carry her; he took her shoulders and dragged her painfully to it. She managed to creep wearily in and he warned her to sleep with her visor closed, lest the ants attack her face. A quarter of a mile downwind he found one for himself.

It was the collapse of the bubble that wakened him. It was night again, a horrible, shrieking, howling, blasting night when the temperature on his thermometer showed a hundred and forty below. Stark fear gripped him. If Diane's shelter had fallen! He fought his way madly against the wind to the spot and shouted in relief. The dome had grown, but still stood; he kicked his way in to find Diane trembling and pallid; she had feared him lost or dead. It was almost dawn before the shelter collapsed.

Strangely, that day was easier. It was bitterly cold, but they had reached the foothills of the Mountains of the Damned, and ice-covered crags offered shelter from the winds. Diane's strength held better; they made the best progress they had yet achieved.

But that meant little now, for there before them, white and glittering and cold, loomed the range of mountains, and Tim despaired when he looked at them. Just beyond, perhaps twenty-five miles away, lay Nivia and safety, but how were they ever to cross those needle peaks?

Diane was still on her feet at nightfall. Tim left her standing in the shelter of a bank of ice and set out to find an ant bubble. But this time he failed. He found only a few tiny six-inch domes; there was nothing that offered refuge from a night that promised to be fiercer than any he had seen. He returned at last in despair.

"We'll have to move farther," he told her.

Her grave, weary eyes frightened him.

"No matter," she said quietly. "We'll never cross the Mountains of the Damned, Tim. But I love you."

They moved on. The night dropped quickly to a hundred and forty below, and their limbs turned numb and slow to respond. Ice ghosts whirred past them; cliffs quaked and rumbled. In half an hour they were both nearing exhaustion, and no crystal shelter appeared.

In the lee of a ridge Diane paused, swaying against him, "No use, Tim," she murmured. "I'd rather die here than fight longer. I can't." She let herself sink to the ice, and that action saved their lives.

Tim bent over her, and as he did a black shadow and glistening beak cleaved the air where his head had been. A knife-kite! Its screech of anger drifted faintly back as it whirled away on that hundred-mile wind.

"You see," said the girl, "it's hopeless."

Tim gazed dully around, and it was then that he saw the funnel. Young had mentioned these curious caves in the ice, and sometimes in the rocks, of the Mountains of the Damned. Opening always north or south, he had thought them the homes of the natives, so placed and shaped to prevent their filling with ice needles. But the traders had learned that the natives have no homes.

"We're going in there!" Tim cried.

He helped Diane to her feet and they crept into the opening. The funnel like passage narrowed, then widened suddenly into a chamber, where steam condensed instantly on their goggles. That meant warmth; they opened their visors, and Tim pulled out his electric torch.

"Look!" gasped Diane. In the curious chamber, walled half by ice and half by rock of the mountain, lay what was unmistakably a fallen, carved column.

"Good Heaven!" Tim was startled momentarily from his worries. "This iceberg harbored a native culture once! I'd never have given those primitive devils credit for it."

"Perhaps the natives weren't responsible," said the girl. "Perhaps there was once some higher creature on Titan, hundreds of thousands of years ago, when Saturn was hot enough to warm it. Or perhaps there still is."

Her guess was disastrously right. A voice said, *"Uzza, uzza, uzza,"* and they turned to stare at the creature emerging from a hole in the rock wall. A face—no, not a face, but a proboscis like the head end of a giant earthworm, that kept thrusting itself to a point, then contracting to a horrible, red, ringed disk.

At the point was the hollow fang or sucking tooth, and above it on a quivering stalk, the ice-green, hypnotic eye of a Titanian threadworm, the first ever to be faced by man. They gazed in horrified fascination as the tubular body slid into the chamber, its ropelike form diminishing at the end to the thickness of a hair.

"Uzza, uzza, uzza," it said, and strangely, their minds translated the sounds. The thing was saying "Sleep, sleep, sleep," over and over.

Tim snatched for his revolver—or intended to. The snatch turned into a gentle, almost imperceptible movement, and then died to immobility. He was held utterly helpless under the glare of the worm's eye.

"Uzza, uzza, uzza," thrummed the thing in a soothing, slumberous buzz. *"Uzza, uzza, uzza."* The sound drummed sleepily in his ears. He was sleepy anyway, worn to exhaustion by the hell without. *"Uzza, uzza, uzza."* Why not sleep?

It was the quick-witted Diane who saved them. Her voice snapped him to wakefulness. "We are sleeping," she said. "We're both asleep. This is the way we sleep. Don't you see? We're both fast asleep."

The thing said *"Uzza, uzza,"* and paused as if perplexed.

"I tell you we're sleeping!" insisted Diane.

"Uzza!" buzzed the worm.

It was silent, stretching its terrible face toward Diane. Suddenly Tim's arm snapped in sharp continuation of his interrupted movement, the gun burned cold through his glove, and then spat blue flame.

A shriek answered. The worm, coiled like a spring, shot its bloody face toward the girl. Unthinking, Tim leaped upon it; his legs tangled in its ropy length and he crashed on his hands against the rocky wall. But the worm was fragile; it was dead and in several pieces when he rose.

"Oh!" gasped Diane, her face white. "How—how horrible! Let's get away—quickly!" she swayed and sat weakly on the floor.

"It's death outside," said Tim grimly.

He gathered the ropy worm in his hands, stuffed it back into the hole whence it had emerged. Then, very cautiously, he flashed his beam into the opening, peered through. He drew back quickly.

"Ugh!" he said, shuddering.

"What, Tim? What's there?"

"A—a brood of 'em." He raised the broken end of the column in his arms; the shaft fitted the hole. "At least that will fall if another comes," he muttered. "We'll be warned. Di, we've got to rest here a while. Neither of us could last an hour out there."

She smiled wanly. "What's the difference, Tim? I'd rather die in clean cold than by—by those things." But in five minutes she was sleeping.

As soon as she slept, Tim slipped the glove from his left hand and stared gloomily at their lone flame-orchid. He had felt it shatter when he struck the wall, and there it lay, colorless, broken, worthless. They had nothing left now, nothing but life, and probably little more of that.

He cast the pieces to the rock-dusty floor and then seized a fragment of stone and viciously pounded the jewel into dull powder and tiny splinters. It vented his feelings.

Despite his determination, he must have dozed. He woke with a start, glanced fearfully at the plugged hole, and then noticed that dim green light filtered through the ice wall. Dawn. At least, as much dawn as they'd get during the eclipse. They'd have to leave at once, for today they must cross the peaks. They must, for tonight would see the shifting of the wind, and when that occurred, hope would vanish.

He woke Diane, who sat up so wearily that his eyes felt tears of pity. She made no comment when he suggested leaving, but there was no hope in her obedience. He rose to creep through the funnel, to be there to help her when the wind struck her.

"Tim!" she shrieked. "Tim! What's that?

He spun around. She was pointing at the floor where he had slept and where now flashed a thousand changing colors like rainbow fire. Flame-orchids! Each splinter he had cracked from the ruined one was now a fiery gem; each tiny grain was sprouting from the rock dust of the floor.

Some were as large as the original, some were tiny flames no bigger than peas, but all glowed perfect and priceless. Fifty of them—a hundred, if one counted the tiny ones.

They gathered them. Tim told her of their origin, and carefully wrapped a few grains of the rock dust in tinfoil from their chocolate.

"Have it analyzed," he explained. "Perhaps we can raise 'em back on Earth."

"If we ever—" began Diane, and then was silent. Let Tim find what pleasure he could in the discovery.

She followed him through the passage into the howling inferno of Titanian eclipse weather.

That day gave both of them all the experience of souls condemned to hell. They struggled hour after hour up the ice-coated slopes of the Mountains of the Damned. The air thinned and turned so cold that the hundred and fifty below which was the minimum on Tim's thermometer dial was insufficient and the needle rested full against the stop.

The wind kept flinging them flat against the slopes, and a dozen times the very mountains heaved beneath them. And this was day; what, he wondered fearfully, would night be like, here among the peaks of the Mountains of the Damned?

Diane drove herself to the limit, and even beyond. This was their last chance; at least they must surmount the crest before the wind shifted. Again and again she fell, but each time she rose and clambered on. And for a time, just before evening, it seemed that they might make it.

A mile from the summit the wind died to that weird, unnatural calm that marked, if you care to call it so, the half-hour Titanian summer season. They burst into a final effort; they rushed up the rugged slope until their blood pounded in their ears. And a thousand feet short of the summit, while they clung helplessly to a steep icy incline, they heard far off the rising whine that meant failure.

Tim paused; effort was useless now. He cast one final glance over the wild magnificence of the Titanian landscape, then leaned close to Diane.

"Goodby, ever valiant," he murmured. "I think you loved me more than I deserved."

Then, with a bellow of triumph, the wind howled down from the peaks, sending them sliding along the crag into darkness.

It was night when Tim recovered. He was stiff, numb, battered, but living. Diane was close beside him; they had been caught in a cupped hollow full of ice crystals.

He bent over the girl. In that roaring wind he couldn't tell if she lived; at least her body was limp, not yet frozen or set in the rigor of death. He did the only thing possible to him; he clutched her wrist and started clawing his way against that impossible gale, dragging her behind him.

A quarter mile away showed the summit. He ascended a dozen feet; the wind hurled him back. He gained fifty feet; the wind smashed him back into the hollow. Yet, somehow, dazed, all but unconscious, he managed to drag, push, roll Diane's body along with him.

He never knew how long it took, but he made it. While the wind bellowed in colossal anger, somehow, by some miracle of doggedness, he thrust Diane across the ridge of the summit, dragged himself after, and gazed without comprehension on the valley beyond, where glowed the lights of Nivia, the City of Snow.

For a while he could only cling there, then some ghost of reason returned. Diane, loyal, courageous Diane, was here dying, perhaps dead. Doggedly, persistently, he pushed and rolled her down the slope against a wind that sometimes lifted her into mid-air and flung her back against his face. For a long time he remembered nothing at all, and then suddenly he was pounding on a metal door, and it was opening.

Tim couldn't sleep yet. He had to find out about Diane, so he followed the government man back through the sunken passage to the building that served Nivia as hospital. The flame-orchids were checked, safe; theft was impossible in Nivia, with only fifty inhabitants and no way for the thief to escape.

The doctor was bending over Diane; he had stripped off her parka and was flexing her arms, then her bared legs.

"Nothing broken," he said to Tim. "Just shock, exposure, exhaustion, half a dozen frostbites, and a terrific mauling from the wind. Oh, yes—and a minor concussion. And a hundred bruises, more or less."

"Is that all?" breathed Tim. "Are you sure that's all?"

"Isn't that enough?" snapped the doctor.

"But she'll—live?"

"She'll tell you so herself in half an hour." His tone changed to admiration. "I don't see how you did it! This'll be a legend, I tell you. And I hear you're rich, too," he added enviously. "Well, I've a feeling you deserve it."

The Red Peri

The Dutch rocket *Aardkin*—out of Middleburg, passengers and freight—dropped gingerly toward the mist and cloud-girt Earth some twelve thousand miles below, underjets cushioning the fall. This last leg of the journey from Venus was the ticklish part of the trip; for the great cigar-shaped rockets, beautifully swift in space, were anything but maneuverable in a strong gravitational field; and Captain Peter Ten Eyck had no particular desire to descend in either central Europe or mid-Atlantic, to the resultant disgust of the home office. He wanted to hit Middleburg in Zeeland.

Off to the right appeared a very curious shape, visible no more than a quarter of a mile away through the bridge room port. *"Donder!"* said Captain Ten Eyck feelingly.

At the same moment the annunciator beside him remarked, "Cut your jets!"

"Aasvogel!" rejoined the captain. *"Vaarken!"* His other epithets were somewhat too expressive for permanent record.

The apparition against the black sky was swiftly drifting closer. It was distinguishable now as a glittering, metal rocket, but in no way like the tapering, cylindrical *Aardkin*, nor like any other rocket—save one.

It was a tubular triangle, from each corner of which rose a strong girder to meet an apex above. In effect, its sides and girders outlined a skeleton tetrahedron, and from the apex of the girders, the blue atomic blast flared down to spread fanlike into the space below. As it approached, the strange vessel was dwarfed by the giant freighter; it was no more than a hundred feet on a side, not an eighth the length of the *Aardkin*.

Again the annunciator uttered its metallic tones. It was responding, apparently, to a beam from the stranger. "Cut your jets!" it repeated. "Cut your jets, or we'll top you!"

Captain Ten Eyck ended his mutterings in a heavy sigh. He had no wish to have his vessel exposed to the withering blast of the pirate. He grumbled an order into the box beside him, and the roar of the jets ceased. Whatever maneuverability the lumbering freighter possessed was gone now; there was no longer any chance of ramming the agile attacker.

With the cessation of the jets came also complete weightlessness, since they were in a free fall; but a twelve-thousand-mile fall takes considerable time to become serious. Ten Eyck sighed again, ordered the floor magnets on, and waited phlegmatically for further directions. After all, he reflected, his cargo was insured, and Boyd's Marine could afford the indemnity. Besides, Boyd's was an English concern, and he had no mind to risk a good Netherlands ship and—if he did say it himself—a good Netherlands captain to save an English insurance company from loss.

The door to the bridge room opened. Hawkins, the first officer, clattered in. "What's here?" he shrilled. "The jets are off—" He caught sight of the glistening shape beyond the port. "The *Red Peri*! The blasted pirate!"

Captain Ten Eyck said nothing, but his pale blue eyes stared moodily at the painted figure plainly visible on the attacker's hull— the figure of a crimson, winged imp. He needed no sign to identify the pirate; the queer construction of the vessel was proof enough, for there wasn't another such ship in the sky. The voice sounded again. "Open your air lock." Ten Eyck gave the order and stalked grimly out to receive the boarding party. He heard the thud of the extending gangway as it struck, and the faint grind as the magnet bit to the freighter's hull. There came a brisk pounding on the inner door of the lock. The captain gave the order to open, his voice curiously equable. He was thinking again of the insurance company.

Most of the *Aardkin*'s score of passengers were crowded along the passage. The cutting of the jets, and perhaps the sound of Hawkins' voice from the beam room as he called hopefully for assistance, had apprised all of them of the events, and the glittering triangle of the *Red Peri* indicated their nature.

The lock swung inward, opening upon the steel-ribbed, rubber-sheathed tunnel of the gangway. Figures in space suits, worn either for disguise or simply as precaution against the possible need of cutting their way in, filed through the circular doorway, automatics and gas guns menacingly visible.

There were no words spoken; a dozen buccaneers clanked methodically away toward the aft hold, and one, a slighter figure, stood grimly guarding the lock. In five minutes they were filing back, dragging whatever loot they had found, with the queer movement of inertia without weight—much as if they floated the objects through water.

Ten Eyck saw the cases of xixtchil pods, valuable as so many diamonds, disappear into the lock; and the seventeen crated ingots of Venusian silver followed. He swore under his breath as he recognized the casket of emeralds from the mines in the Dutch Alps of Venus, and wondered blasphemously how they had managed to crack the *Aardkin's* safe with neither torch nor explosive.

Glancing into the purser's office, he saw a queer, jagged hole in the big steel box, that looked more as if it had rusted or simply broken away than as if it had been cut. Then the freebooters were silently passing back to their vessel, having neither addressed nor molested officers, crew, or passengers.

Except, perhaps, for one: among the group of watchers was young Frank Keene, American radiologist and physicist returning from the solar-analysis station of Patrick's Peak in the Mountains of Eternity. He had edged close to the air lock, and now, as the departing marauders passed through, he suddenly leaned forward with narrowed eyes, and peered boldly into the cloudy visor of the guard.

"Hah!" he said. "A redhead, eh?"

The guard said nothing, but raised a steel-gauntleted hand. The metal thumb and forefinger bit viciously into Keene's suntanned nose, and he was thrust violently back into the crowd, with two spots of blood welling from the abused organ.

Keen grunted in pain. "O.K., fellow," he said stolidly. "I'll see you again some day."

The guard spoke at last in a voice that clinked out metallically from the helmet's diaphragm. "When you do, there'd better be two of you." Then this figure followed the rest; the outer lock clanged shut; the magnets released the gangway's grip; and the *Red Peri*, agile as a swallow and swift as a comet at perihelion, flared into the black void.

Beside Keene sounded the voice of Captain Ten Eyck. "What a ship! Mynheer Keene, is that not a ship—that *Red Peri*?"

He was still exclaiming over it at intervals during the laborious task of laying a new landing course; and when, an hour later, a blunt little League rocket appeared in answer to Hawkin's call, he informed its officers flatly that the pirate was hopelessly beyond reach. "Even if your fat *beeste* of a boat could match its acceleration, which it couldn't."

A year later Frank Keene had almost completely forgotten the *Red Peri* and the red-headed pirate, though occasionally, during the interval, mention of the famous marauder had brought his experience to mind. After all, when a freebooter has scoured the skyways for nearly fifteen years without capture, he becomes something of a legend, a figure of heroic proportions. Papers and broadcasts give daily references to him, and he is blamed for, or perhaps credited with, many a feat performed by some less-celebrated desperado.

The lair of the *Red Peri* remained a mystery, though League ships scoured asteroids, the far side of the desolate Moon, and even the diminutive satellites of Mars. The swift pirate, striking invariably as his victim inched gingerly through some planet's gravitational field, came and went untouched.

But Frank Keene had little time at the moment for consideration of the famous freebooter. He and his companion, fifty-five year old Solomon Nestor of the Smithsonian, were out where few men had ever been, and in a predicament that was perhaps unique. They were dropping their rocket *Limbo* toward the rugged, black disc of Pluto, two billion miles from home, and they were not happy about it.

"I tell you," growled Keene, "we've got to land. Do you think I'm settling on this chunk of coal from choice? We've got to make repairs. We can't navigate with one stern jet gone, unless you have a notion to fly in circles."

Old Solomon was a marvel on hard radiations, stellar chemistry, and astrophysics, but hardly an engineer. He said plaintively, "I don't see why we can't zigzag."

"Bah! I told you why. Didn't I spend five hours figuring out the time it'd take to reach the nearest inhabited place? That's Titan near Saturn, just one billion—one billion, I said—miles from here. And at the speed we could make zigzagging, because we couldn't keep a constant acceleration, it would take us just exactly four years and three months. We've got food enough for three months, but what would we live on during the four years? Atomic energy?"

"But what can we do on Pluto?" queried old Nestor. "And why didn't we carry a spare jet?"

"Jets aren't supposed to melt off," muttered Keene disgustedly. "As for what we can do, maybe we can find a virgin deposit of some refractory metal—platinum or iridium or tungsten, or any other with a high melting point—and build up a jet long enough to keep the blast from melting our stern away. Because that's what it'll do if we try running it this way."

"There's tungsten here," observed the older man hopefully, gazing down at the black expanse. "Hervey reported it, and so did Caspari. But there isn't any atmosphere, or rather, what there is, is liquid or solid, except about half a centimeter's pressure of helium. Pluto has a diameter of about ten thousand miles, a surface gravity of about 1.2, and an albedo—"

"Not interested," grunted Keene, and then, relenting, "Listen, Solomon, I'm sorry. I guess I'm taking it out on you because we had a defective jet. But it's a hell of a mess all the same, and somebody's going to suffer for it when we get back. With all the money the institute has, you'd think they'd be able to afford respectable equipment." He glared down through the floor port. "There she comes!"

With a rasp and a jar, the *Limbo* came to rest. Outside, a mixed column of dust and smoke billowed around the glasses, rose and then settled as quickly as a burst of sand, in the near vacuum that surrounded the ship.

Keene cut the blast. "Come on," he said, turning to a space suit swaying on its hook. "No use wasting time. We'll take a look around." He clambered into the heavy garment, noting irritably its greater weight on the surface of the black planet. The Plutonian gravitation added thirty-six pounds to his Terrestrial hundred and eighty.

"No gun?" asked Nestor.

"Gun? For what? This planet's dead as the brain of whoever tested that jet. How can there be organic life in no air and ten degrees absolute?" He pulled open the inner door of the air lock. "Well," he said, his voice sharply metallic through his helmet's diaphragm, "here goes the Smithsonian Expedition for the Determination of the Intensity of Cosmic Radiation in Extra-planetary Space. We determined it all right; now the only problem of the expedition is to get home with our statistics." He flung open the outer door and stepped out on the black surface of Pluto.

So far as Keene knew, he was the fourth man and Nestor the fifth to set foot on the black planet. Atsuki, of course, was the first, if one credits his figures and photographs, the intrepid Hervey the second, and Caspari the third. Here on this lonely outpost of the solar system, high noon was hardly brighter than full moonlight on Earth, and the queer, black surface that gives Pluto its low albedo made it seem still darker.

But Keene could distinguish the outlines of fantastic mountains beyond the hollow where the Limbo rested, and innumerable mysterious crags and hillocks, unweathered by wind or water, loomed closer. Directly to his right lay a patch of glistening, snow-like white; but he knew it wasn't snow, but frozen air. One dared not step in such a drift; for the cold would bite through his insulated space suit, since frozen air was a far better conductor of heat than the rocky ground.

Overhead glittered all the stars of the galaxy, as changeless as though he stood on a pleasant green planet two billion miles sunward, for what was two billion miles to the infinite remoteness of the stars? The landscape was bleak, black, desolate and cold. This was Pluto, the planet that circled at the very edge of the System.

The two started heavily toward a ridge where something glowed faintly, something that might be virgin metal. Strangely, their own footsteps were audible, for the substance of their space suits conducted the sound; but all else was a vast and ominous silence. They did not speak, for their suits, designed only for emergency repairs in space, had no radio; and to communicate it was necessary to touch hand or arm to one's companion; over such a material bridge, sound traveled easily enough.

At the ridge Keene paused, glowering down at a vein of bright, starlighted fragments. He placed a hand against Nestor's shoulder, "Pyritic," he grunted. "We'll have to look farther."

He turned right, treading heavily under nearly sixty pounds more than his Earth weight. Surely, he mused, old Solomon Nester wouldn't be capable of an extended search in such circumstances. He frowned; Caspari had reported great quantities of heavy metals here, and they shouldn't need such a lengthy search. He stopped sharply; a stone came sliding past him on the rocky surface. A signal.

Off in the dusk Nestor was gesturing. Keene turned and hurried back, clambering along the uneven terrain with such haste that his breath shortened and his visor began to cloud. He clapped his hand on the old man's arm. "What is it?" he asked. "Metal?"

"Metal? Oh, no." Nestor's voice was triumphant. "What did you say about no organic life on Pluto, eh? Well, what about inorganic life? Look there!"

Keene looked. Out of a narrow chasm or cleft in the ridge something moved. For a moment Keene thought he saw a brook flowing, but a brook—liquid water—was an impossibility on Pluto. He squinted sharply. Crystals! Masses of crystals, gray-white in the dusk, crawling in a slow parade.

"I'll be damned!" he said. "Caspari didn't say anything about this."

"Don't forget," said Nestor, "that Pluto has thirty-six per cent more surface than the whole Earth. Not a ten-thousandth part of it has been explored—probably never will be, because it's such a task to get a rocket here. If Atsuki—"

"I know. I know," interrupted Keene impatiently. "But these things aren't tungsten or platinum. Let's move on." But he still stared at the crawling, faintly radiant mass. In the silence he heard infinitely faint rustlings, cracklings, and susurrations, transmitted through the ground to his feet, and thence to his helmet. What makes them move?" he asked. "Are they alive?"

"Alive? I don't know. Crystals are as close as inorganic matter comes to life. They feed; they grow."

"But they don't live!"

Old Solomon Nestor was in his element now. "Well," he proceeded in professorial tones, "what is the criterion of life? Is it movement? No; for wind, water, and fire move, while many living forms do not. Is it growth? No; for fire grows, and so do crystals. Is it reproduction? Again no; for again fire and crystals reproduce themselves, if their proper food supply is present. Then just what differentiates dead matter from living?"

"That's what I'm asking you!" snapped Keene.

"And I'm telling you. There's just one, or perhaps two criteria.

170

First, living things show irritation. And second, and more important, they show adaptation."

"Eh?"

"Listen," continued Nestor. "Fire moves, grows, feeds, and reproduces, doesn't it? But it doesn't run away from water. It doesn't betray the irritation life shows in the presence of a poison, though water's poison to it. Any living thing that encounters poison makes an attempt to throw it off; it develops antibodies or fever, or it ejects the poisonous matter. Sometimes it dies, of course, but it tries to survive. Fire doesn't.

"As for adaptation, does fire ever make a voluntary attempt to reach its food? Does it deliberately flee from its enemies? Even the lowest form of life known does that; even the miserable amoeba makes positive gestures of adaptation to its environment."

Keene stared more closely at the sluggish crystalline stream, which was now impinging on the black plain at his feet. He bent over it, and suddenly perceived a fact that had hitherto escaped him.

"Look here," he said, touching old Solomon's arm. "These things are organisms. They're not loose crystals, but masses of them."

It was true. The rustling crystals moved in glittering chunks from thumbnail size to aggregations as large as dogs. They crackled and rustled along, apparently moving by a slow shifting of the lower crystals, much as a snake moves on its scaly belly, but far stiffer and slower. Abruptly Keene sent his metal boot crashing into one. It shattered with a blue flash of released static electricity, and the pieces passively resumed their progress.

"They certainly don't show irritation," he remarked.

"But look!" shrilled Nestor. "They do show adaptation. There's one feeding!"

He pulled Keene a few feet down the ridge. There was a small bluish deposit of something that looked like frozen clay, a product, perhaps, of the infinitely remote past when Pluto's own heat had maintained liquid water and gaseous air to grind its rocks to powder. A crystalline mass had paused at the edge, and before their gaze it was growing, gray-white crystals springing out of it as frost spreads over a winter-chilled windowpane.

"It's an aluminum-eater!" shrieked Nestor. "The crystals are alums; it's eating the clay!"

Keene was far less excited than old Solomon, perhaps because he was considerably more practical.

"Well," he said decisively, "we can't waste any more time here. We need refractory metal, and we need it bad. You try along the ridge, and I'll cross over."

He broke off suddenly, staring appalled at the foot with which he had shattered the moving crystals. On its surface glittered a spreading mass of tiny, sparkling points!

A break in the surface of his space suit meant death, for the oxygen generator could certainly never maintain its pressure against any appreciable leakage. He bent over, scraping desperately at the aluminum feeders, and then realized that the infection would spread—had spread to his gauntlets. While Nestor babbled futilely and inaudibly behind his visor, Keene rubbed his hands in the gritty, pyritic soil on which he stood.

That seemed to work. The rough substance scoured away the growing crystals, and with frantic vigor he rasped a handful along his shoe. If only no hole, no tiniest pin prick had opened! He scoured furiously, and at last the metal surface showed scratched and pitted, but free of the growths.

He stood up unsteadily, and placed his hand against the gesturing Nestor's side.

"Keep away from them!" he gasped. "They eat—"

Keene never finished his sentence. Something hard jarred against the back of his armor. A metallic voice clicked, "Stand still-both of you!"

2

"What the devil!" gulped Keene. He twisted his head within his immovable helmet, peering through the rear visor glasses. Five—no, six figures in blue metal space suits were ranged behind him; they must have approached in the inaudibility of a vacuum while he had been scouring his suit free of the crystals. For a moment he had an eerie sensation of wonder, fearful that he faced some grotesque denizens of the mysterious black planet, but a glance revealed that the forms were human. So were the faces dim in the dusk behind the visors; so had been the voice he had heard.

Keene hesitated. "Listen," he said. "We're not interfering with you. All we want is some tungsten in order to fix our—"

"Move!" snapped the voice, whose tones traveled through the weapon hard against Keene's back. "And remember that I'm two thirds inclined to kill you anyway. Now move!"

Keene moved. There was little else he could do, considering the appearance of the threatening automatics in the hands of their captors. He tramped heavily along, feeling the thrust of the muzzle against his back, and beside him Solomon Nestor trudged with pace already showing the drag of weariness. The old man touched his arm.

"What's this about?" he quavered.

"How do I know?" snorted Keene.

"Shut up!" admonished the voice behind him.

They walked past the looming shape of the *Limbo*—five hundred feet past it, a thousand. Directly ahead was the other rim of the cup-shaped depression in which they had landed, high, black cliffs in fantastic shapes. Suddenly Keene started; what had seemed but a smaller cliff showed now as a skeleton, tetrahedral frame of metal, three webbed shafts rising to a point from a tubular triangle below.

"The *Red Peri*!" he gasped. "The *Red Peri*!"

"Yeah. Why the surprise?" queried the sardonic voice. "You found what you were looking for, didn't you?"

Keene said nothing. The appearance of the pirate ship had amazed him. No one had ever dreamed that the swift marauder could operate from a base as infinitely remote as the black planet. How could even the agile vessel scour the traffic lanes of the minor planets from dusky Pluto, two billion miles out in the empty cosmos?

To his knowledge only two ships—three, if Atsuki hadn't lied---had ever reached those vast depths before their own *Limbo*, and he knew what endless travail and painful labor each of those journeys had cost. In his mind echoed Captain Ten Eyck's words of a year and a half before. "What a ship!" he muttered. "Lord, what a ship!"

There was an opening in the cliff wall as they rounded the bulk of the *Red Peri*. Yellow light streamed out, and he glimpsed an ordinary fluorolux bulb in the roof of the cavern. He was shoved forward into the opening, and suddenly his visor was clouded with moisture. That meant air and warmth, though he had seen no air lock, nor heard one operate. He suppressed the impulse to brush a metal-sheathed hand across the glass, knowing that he couldn't wipe the condensation away in that fashion.

The voice again, still queerly sardonic, yet somehow soft. "You can open your helmets. There's air."

Keene did so. He stared at the figures surrounding himself and Nestor, some still helmeted, others already removing the uncomfortable space suits. Before him stood a figure shorter than the rest, and he recalled the red-haired pirate on the *Aardkin*. The short one was twisting the cumbersome helmet.

It came off. Keene gulped again at the face revealed, for it was that of a woman. A woman? A girl, rather, for she seemed no more than seventeen. But Keene's gasp was not entirely surprise; mostly, it was sheer admiration.

Her hair was red, true enough, if one could call red a lovely and subtle shade between copper and mahogany. Her eyes were bright green, and her skin was the silken, soft, and pale skin of one whose flesh is but seldom exposed to the sunlight, yet gently tanned by the violet-rich rays of the fluorolux.

She let the cumbrous metal suit clank away from her, and stepped out in the quite civilized garb of shirt, shorts, and dainty, laced buskins, such as one had to wear in a space suit. Her figure—well, Keene was only twenty-six, but even old Nestor's pallid eyes were fixed on her as she turned toward them. She was slim, curved, firm; despite her slimness, there was a litheness and sturdiness to her limbs, the result, perhaps, of a lifetime under the supernormal gravitation of Pluto.

"Take off your suits," she ordered coldly, and as they complied, "Marco, lock these up with the rest."

A tall, dark individual gathered up the clanking garments. "Yes, commander," he said, taking a key she held out and moving away into the cavern.

"Commander, eh?" said Keene. "So you're the Red Peri!"

Her green eyes flickered over him. She surveyed his own figure, which was still hard and brown and powerful from his swimming days at the university. "You," she said impassively. "I've seen you before."

"You have a good memory," he grunted. "I was on the *Aardkin*."

She gave him a momentary smile of amused remembrance. "Yes. Did your nose scar?" She glanced at the organ. "I'm afraid not."

People—two or three of them—came hurrying up the long corridor of the cave to stand staring curiously at Keene and Nestor. Two were men; the third was a pale, pretty, flaxen-haired girl. The Red Peri glanced briefly at them and seated herself on a boulder against the rocky wall.

"Cigarette, Elza," she said, and took one from the pale girl.

The scent of tobacco tantalized Keene, for such indulgences were impossible in the precious air of a space ship. It had been four months since he had smoked, in the frigid little town of Nivia, the city of snow on Titan.

"May I have one?" he asked.

The green eyes turned an icy glance on him. "No," said the Red Peri briefly.

"Well, I'll be—Why not?" He was angered.

"I don't think you'll live long enough to finish it," responded the girl coolly, "and our supply is limited here."

"Yeah, limited to what you find on looted freighters!" he snapped.

"Yes," she agreed. She blew a tormenting plume of smoke toward him. "I'll tell you what I'll do. I'll trade you a cigarette for the information as to how you managed to trace us here."

"Trace you?" he echoed, puzzled.

"That's what I said. It's a generous offer, too, because I'm quite capable of torturing the knowledge out of you."

Staring into her lovely, glittering green eyes, Keene was not disposed to doubt her capability. He said mildly, "But we didn't trace you here."

"I suppose," she retorted, "that you came to Pluto looking for a good business corner. Or perhaps on a little camping trip. Is that your story?"

He flushed under her cool insolence. "We came here by accident," he growled. "One of our afterjets melted off, and if you don't believe it, go look at it."

"Jets don't melt unless they're planned to," said the Red Peri coldly. "And what were you doing in the neighborhood of Pluto anyway? And I suppose that out of all the millions of square miles of surface, you just accidentally picked this valley as a landing place. Well, it won't do you any good to lie, because you're going to die regardless, but you might die a little less painfully if you tell the truth."

"It just happens that I'm telling the truth!" he blazed. "Whether you believe it or not, we landed in this valley by pure chance. We're the Smithsonian's expedition to study cosmic rays in outer space, and you can verify that by our clearance papers from Nivia."

"A good disguise for the secret service," she sneered. "You could get any sort of government papers you want, couldn't you?"

"Disguise! Listen, if we were hunting the *Red Peri*, do you think we'd come armed with cameras, interferometers, electroscopes, polariscopes, and fly-wing bolometers? Search our ship; you'll find one gun in it—one measly automatic. I'll tell you where it is. It's in the upper right-hand drawer of the navigation table. And we landed here because Pluto was the nearest solid place to where we burned off our jet—and that's the truth!"

The Red Peri's glance was faintly speculative. "I don't see," she said thoughtfully, "that it makes much difference. If you're telling the truth, it simply means that you're a very unlucky expedition, because I certainly can't let you go, and I haven't any particular desire to keep you here. In other words, it still looks very much as if you were destined to die." She paused. "What are your names?"

"This is Smithsonian's Professor Solomon Nestor," he said, "and I'm Frank Keene, radiation engineer."

Her green eyes shifted to the old man. "I've heard of Solomon Nestor," she observed slowly. "I really shouldn't like to kill him, but I don't see exactly what other course is open." She flashed her gaze back to Keene. "Do you?" she asked coolly.

"You could take our words not to give out any information," he grunted.

She laughed. "The Red Peri trusts very little to promises," she retorted. "Anyway, would you give your word to that?"

For a full half minute he stared into her mocking eyes. "I wouldn't," he said at last. "When I entered the Smithsonian's service I took their usual oath to uphold the law in the far places. Maybe many of their explorers consider that oath just so many words; I know some of them have found wealth at the expense of the institute. But I keep my oaths."

The Red Peri laughed again. "No matter," she said indifferently. "I wouldn't trust my safety to any one's word. But the question of your disposal still remains." She smiled with a faint hint of malice. "Would you prefer to die instantly, or do you think you can stand the torture of suspense while I check your story and think it over? Because frankly, I think it will be necessary to kill you anyway. I see no alternative."

"We'll wait," said Keene stolidly.

"Very well." She flipped away the stub of her cigarette, crossed her dainty legs, and said, "Another, Elza."

Keene looked sharply at the yellow-haired girl as she held a light to the cigarette. There was something dimly inimical in her manner, as if she were struggling to suppress a hatred, a hidden enmity. She withdrew the flame with an abrupt, irritable gesture.

"That's all," said the green-eyed leader. "I'll lock you up somewhere until I'm ready."

"Wait a minute," said Keene. "Now will you answer a few of my questions?"

She shrugged. "Perhaps."

"Are you the only Red Peri?"

"The one and only," she smiled. "Why?"

"Because you must have been born like Lao-tse at the age of eighty, then. These raids have been going on for fifteen years, and you're not a day over seventeen. Or did you start your career of piracy at the age of two?

"I'm nineteen," she said coolly.

"Oh. You began at four, I suppose."

"Never mind. Any further questions?"

"Yes. Who designed your ship, the *Red Peri*?"

"A very clever designer," she said, and then murmured softly, "a very clever one."

"He must have been!" snapped Keene angrily.

"He was. Have you anything else to ask?"

"You haven't answered one question so far," he growled. "But here's another. What do you think will happen when the *Limbo* doesn't arrive in Nivia when due? Don't you know that the next

government rocket will be out to look for us? And don't you realize that they'll look for us first on Pluto? Your base here is bound
to be discovered, and if you murder us it'll go just that much
harder with you."

The Red Peri laughed. "That isn't even a good bluff," she said.
"Titan isn't a quarter of the way between the Earth and Pluto, and
it's getting farther from us every day. The next conjunction of Saturn and Pluto is fifty years in the future, and about the only time
your clumsy rockets can make the jump is at conjunction. You
ought to know that.

"And what's more, by the time you're missed, there won't be
a thing to do but give you up as lost, and you'll not be the first
Smithsonian expedition to be lost. And finally, if they did send out
a searching party, how would they expect to find you? By blind
reckoning?"

"By radio!" grunted Keene.

"Oh. And have you a radio on the *Limbo*?" she asked gently.

He groaned and subsided. Of course there was no radio on the
little expeditionary rocket; all its precious space was occupied by
fuel, food, and necessary equipment, and besides, what possible use
could a radio be to explorers out in the lonely vastness of extraplan-
etary space? The nearest settlement, Nivia on Titan, was hundreds
of millions of miles beyond range of the most powerful beam yet
developed.

The Red Peri knew as well as he how utterly hopeless was the
expectation of any search for himself and Nestor. They'd simply
be given up, called martyrs to science, regretted by the few experi-
menters who were interested in their results, and then forgotten,

"Any more questions?" asked the flaming-haired one mockingly.

Keene shrugged, but suddenly and unexpectedly old Solomon
Nestor spoke. "That entrance," he squeaked irrelevantly, pointing to the arch of the cave. "How do you keep the air here from
rushing out?"

Keene whirled and stared in amazement. It was true; the cave
was open to the frigid, airless outdoors; he could see the dusky Plutonian twilight through an unglassed, unblocked archway.

"At least that question is sensible," said the Red Peri. "We do it
with a field."

"A field!" echoed Keene. "What sort—"

"You've asked enough questions," she cut in tartly. "I answer no more." She turned. "Elza, take these two into any unoccupied room with a metal door. If they're hungry, send them food. That's all."

She rose without a glance at the prisoners. Keene's eyes followed the exquisitely graceful figure as she trod as lightly as if she walked an Earthly corridor, followed by the five men who remained. Her radiant hair glowed far down the length of the passage until she turned aside and vanished.

He and Nestor followed the flaxen-haired Elza, and behind them, grimly silent, came the two men who had first appeared with her. She led them past a number of niches, side aisles, and several obviously artificial chambers. The cavern seemed to stretch indefinitely into the depths of the Plutonian mountain, and was undubitably a natural cave, though here and there the floor or walls showed signs of human workmanship. At last the girl indicated a chamber to the right, and they entered a small room, furnished comfortably enough with an aluminum chair, a table, and two couches. These last were covered with deep and gloriously beautiful brocades, beyond doubt plunder from some freighter's cargo.

"This is yours," said Elza, and turned toward the door. She paused. "Are you hungry?" she asked.

"No," said Keene. He saw the two men standing in the corridor, and lowered his voice. "But will you talk to us a while, Elza? Alone?"

"Why?"

"I'd like to ask you something."

"What is it?"

He dropped his voice to a whisper. "You hate the Red Peri, don't you, Eliza? As much as we do?"

She turned abruptly to the door. "Father," she said evenly, "will you and Basil bring something to eat? I'll stay here; you can bolt the door on us."

There was a murmur without.

"Hush!" she said. "You heard. These two are gentlemen." The door closed and she faced them. "Well?"

"Can we be heard here?" asked Keene, glancing around the rock-walled chamber.

"Of course not. The Peri has no need to spy on her followers. She's clever enough to read men's feelings in their glances and the tone of their voices."

"Then she must know you hate her, Elza."

"I haven't said that I hate her."

"But you do. Does she know it?"

"I hope not."

"But you just said that she could read—"

"I said men," cut in the flaxen-haired girl.

Keene chuckled. "Why do you hate her, Elza?"

Her blue eyes hardened. "I will not say."

"Well, it doesn't matter, I suppose." He shrugged. "Elza, is there any chance of our escaping? Would you help us to—say, to steal the *Red Peri*? Our own ship's useless."

"They've gone to repair it. As for the *Red Peri*, I don't think you could operate it. It doesn't control like your rocket. I don't know how to run it."

"I could make a good try at it," said Keene grimly. "It would have to be the *Red Peri* anyway. They could run the *Limbo* down in three hours and blast it." A thought struck him. "Unless we could cripple the *Red Peri* first."

"I don't see how you could," said Elza. "She has the key to it hidden somewhere. And how could you even reach it? The space suits are locked up, too. You can't even step beyond the entrance."

That brought a new thought. "How do they seal the air at the entrance, Elza?"

"I don't understand how."

Solomon Nestor spoke. "I know that. She said they used a field. She meant—"

"Never mind now," said Keene. "Elza, are there any others here that might—well, side with us against the Peri?"

"No men. All of them worship her and"—her face darkened— "half of them love her."

"For which you can hardly blame them," muttered Keene. "She's about as lovely a female devil as you'd find this side of hell. Still, one would think she'd have some enemies, if only because of her cruel nature."

"She isn't cruel," said Elza reluctantly. "She's ruthless and arrogant and proud, but she isn't cruel—not exactly. I don't think she really enjoys torture."

"Well, her green eyes look cruel enough. Say, Elza, that dark fellow she called Marco. What of him?"

The girl flushed. "He's Marco Grandi. Why do you ask me about him?"

"Because he looks like a sly, calculating, shrewd customer, and there's a big reward for the Peri. I thought we might work on him."

Elza's flush darkened to anger. "He's—he's wonderful!" she blazed. "And if you think money would tempt him—or any of us—you're wrong. Each of us has a dozen times the amount of the reward."

Keene saw his error. "I'm sorry," he said hastily. "After all, I just caught a glimpse of him." He paused. "Does he, by any chance, love the Red Peri?"

She winced. "He's no different in that way than the rest."

"I see. But you—perhaps—wish that he were different—in that way?"

Elza brushed a white hand across her face. "All right," she said sullenly. "I love him. I admit it. That's why I hate her. He's dazzled; he thinks she'll learn to care for him; he can't see how utterly heartless and indifferent she is. That's why I'll do whatever I can to hurt her, but nothing to endanger him. If I help you, you must swear to protect him. If you escape, you must swear to that."

"I'll swear to it, but—can you help us?"

"I don't know. I'll try. I don't think she really wants to kill you, or she'd have blasted you there in the corridor. It isn't her way to hesitate and temporize and think things over. But you are a problem to her."

"That's good news," said Keene. "Say, how many residents are there in this pirate's paradise?"

"A hundred and five, including the children."

"A hundred and—Lord! This must be a pretty well established colony. How old is it?"

"Sixteen years. Her father built it, and it's almost self-supporting. There are gardens off in the side passages." She frowned. "I've lived here since I was four. I'm twenty now."

"And have you never seen the Earth?" Keene saw a chance now

to offer more tangible inducement for aid. "Elza, you've missed the most glorious planet in the system—green fields and white snow, great cities and rolling, blue oceans, life, people, gaiety—"

"I went to school there for five years, at Gratia," she interposed coolly. "Don't you suppose we all visit there? Only of late the Peri has refused to let me go. I—I suppose she suspects."

"If we escape," said Keene softly, "you'll be free to live there forever. There will be life and happiness for you, Elza, once this pirate queen is taken and her band destroyed."

"Destroyed?" Her face paled again. "Not Marco. Not my father and my brother Basil. You promise me that. Promise it!"

"I'll promise. All I want is to bring the Red Peri to justice. I don't care about the rest, but"—he rubbed his nose—"I've a little score to settle with her. Just the Red Peri herself."

A knock sounded. "Elza!" came a voice.

"Yes, father. Unlock the door and I'll take the tray." She turned.

"But you'll help?" whispered Keene. "With the Red Peri gone, you and Marco—do you understand, Elza? Will you help—just against her?"

"To my last breath!" she whispered.

3

Keene woke with a sense of unaccustomed luxury, and for a moment was at a loss to account for it. Then he realized that it was the sweetness of the air, strange to his nostrils after so many months of an atmosphere that, despite the hard-working rectifiers of the *Limbo*, was anything but sweet. He wondered casually where the Red Peri secured her colony's supply of oxygen.

The Red Peri! He sat up sharply at the memory of the fantastically lovely pirate princess, for despite the reassurance of the girl Elza, he mistrusted the intentions behind the Peri's mocking green eyes. He rose, fumbled for the light switch, and glanced at his wrist watch. Though night and day were one in the cavern, he perceived that Pluto's ten-hour night was past, and that whatever daylight the black planet enjoyed was trickling over it.

Old Nestor still slept. Keene pulled a hanging aside and found water in a tiny pool; he bathed and pulled on the shirt, shorts, and shoes that were the only clothing he possessed. He ran his hand over his sandy, one-day beard, but his razor was inaccessably remote on the *Limbo*. Then he turned to see old Solomon's pale-blue eyes blinking at him.

"Morning," he grunted. "Glad to see we weren't murdered in our sleep by our pleasant hostess."

Solomon Nestor nodded. "I haven't slept so well since we left Nivia," he quavered. "Fresh air is a blessing."

"Yes. Wonder where she gets it."

"Mines it, I don't doubt," said Nestor. "There are millions of tons of it frozen out on the surface."

"That's true."

"And," continued the old man, "did you notice anything queer about it?"

"No, except that it smells good and fresh."

"I did. When that yellow-haired girl—Elza—lighted the Peri's cigarettes, did you notice the cast of the flame? Purple, distinctly purple."

"So what?"

"Why, it means neon. Nitrogen is scarce here; Hervey and Caspari both said that, and so they use neon as their filler. No one can breathe pure oxygen, and neon is a good substitute for nitrogen, nearly the same density, and absolutely inert and non-poisonous. That's important to remember. It may help us."

"Help us?'"

The old man waggled his head. "You'll see."

"Say," asked Keene suddenly, "what is the explanation of the cave entrance? We walked right through it—vacuum on one side, air on the other. She said they did it with a field—remember?"

"I remember. She meant an electrostatic field. You know that like charges repel, and the molecules of air, battering against the field, acquire the same charge. They're repelled; they can't cross the field. It's like the electric wind from a static discharge, but here the wind that tries to blow in just balances the wind that tries to go out. Result, no wind either way."

"But we walked through it. Motion through a field produces a current. I didn't feel any."

"Of course not. You didn't walk through at a mile per second like a gas molecule, did you? Whatever current your motion produced was instantly grounded through your body and space suit, which are conductors. Air at normal pressure is a very poor conductor, so it retains its charge. Gases do retain static charges, as witness ball lightning."

"I see," muttered Keene. "Clever. Better than an air lock as far as convenience goes, though heat must radiate away through the field. But if they use atomic heat, they can afford a little waste."

"There'd be less loss there," said Nestor, "than to the rock walls. Heat could radiate, true enough, but it couldn't escape by conduction. A vacuum is the best heat insulator there is; look at our thermos containers on the *Limbo*. Radiation at temperatures below red heat is a very slow process. And remember that, too."

"I will," grunted Keene, "but right now I'm remembering that we have had no breakfast. Do you suppose her method of execution is slow starvation?" He strode over to the door and pounded vigorously on it. "Hey! Hey, out there!"

There was no response. Irritably, he seized the knob and rattled it, and almost fell backward as the door swung smoothly open. It was unbarred!

"I'll be hanged!" he exploded. He peered into the deserted corridor. "Do you suppose this is Elza's doing—"

"If it is, it's not much help," said old Solomon.

"No. All the same, I'm going to take a look around. Come on; perhaps we can find some space suits."

"You'd need the key to the *Red Peri*, too, or at least the key to the *Limbo*, if they've locked it. I think"—old Nestor's brow wrinkled—"I'll sit right here and figure out something I've been thinking of. Even old heads sometimes get ideas."

"Suit yourself," grunted Keene, with very little faith in the potential ideas of the impractical old scientist. He strode boldly into the passageway.

There was no one visible. He turned left and proceeded toward the entrance of the cavern. Ahead of him a figure came suddenly out of an aisle—a feminine figure. He recognized the girl Elza, carrying a bright aluminum spade, and called her name softly.

She turned. "Hello," she said briefly, as he fell into step beside her.

"Been burying some pirate treasure, Elza?"

"No. Just some seeds in the garden."

"Did you unlock our door?" he asked.

"I? Yes. The Peri ordered it unlocked."

"Ordered it! Why?"

"Why not? Can you escape from here?" She gestured at a massive metal door as they passed. "Behind that is her room, and behind another within it are the space suits and the keys to both ships. You're as much a prisoner as ever."

"I know, but isn't she afraid of violence? We could kill her."

"She isn't afraid of anything," said Elza. "Anyway, what good would killing her do? It would be simply committing suicide."

"That's true," said Keene. They were approaching the entrance with its invisible electrostatic seal; now they stood staring out over the dismal, black, airless, Plutonian valley, where a thousand feet away was the dark cylinder of the *Limbo*. Suddenly a flare of light appeared beside it, flashed a moment, then vanished.

"What's that?" he asked sharply.

"Father's out there welding your jet. She thinks she may have a use for your ship."

"For what?"

"I don't know. It has exactly the lines of a League guard rocket. Perhaps she plans to use it as a decoy."

"And perhaps," said a cool voice behind them, "as a flying mausoleum with you two among the occupants."

They whirled. The Red Peri was approaching with her steps muffled by the soft buskins on her feet; besides her stalked Marco Grandi. Keene did not fail to note Elza's flush as she met the gaze of the dark man, but he felt a surge of anger at himself as he realized that his own face was reddening under the green eyes and mocking smile of the red-haired girl. He spat angrily, "You're a pleasant player when you hold all the cards!"

She said only, "Have you eaten breakfast?"

"No!"

"Well, perhaps that explains your ill temper. Elza, go order a tray for two sent to my room, and one to Professor Nestor. And you, Marco—suppose you leave me."

"Here with him?"

She laughed and tapped an automatic at her belt. "I can take care of myself. Do you doubt it? You can go, Marco."

He muttered, "Yes, commander," and backed reluctantly away. The Red Peri turned her glorious, taunting eyes on Keene, smiled again, and said, "I've checked over your ship. Your story's straight enough."

"Well? What about us, then?"

"Oh, I haven't decided. You may have to die; it's more than likely that you will, but with no malice on my part. Purely as a matter of convenience, you understand."

He grunted. "Why'd you have our door unlocked?"

"Why not? I'm sure you can't escape. Look here." She took the bright aluminum spade Elza had placed against the wall, and thrust it half through the field into the airless outdoors beyond. We stared at it; except for a slight change in color as its crystals rearranged under the slow radiation of its heat, it seemed unaltered. When the knuckles of her dainty hand began to whiten with the cold of the metal, she tossed the implement on the floor at her feet.

Now it changed. Instantly white frost formed on the part that had been exposed; glittering crystals grew an inch thick, fuzzy covering, and began to spread along the handle. They sprang out as swift as the second hand on a watch, an inch—two inches deep.

The Peri laughed. "Would you like to stroll outside?" she gibed. "It's not cold—just ten above zero. Above absolute zero, I mean. Cold enough to liquefy and freeze all gases but hydrogen and helium. How long do you think it would take to freeze that hot blood and hotter head of yours?"

"Bah!" he said. "What's to keep me now from overpowering you, dragging you into some room, and using you as hostage to bargain for our safety?"

"If you could," she retorted coolly. "Even then it would be a poor idea; if you killed me your own death would follow very soon and very painfully; if you didn't, I'd never be bound to any promises you wrung from the others. Your wisest course is to leave things as they are until I decide what to do with you. And incidentally," she added, with a narrowing of her green eyes, "don't pin your faith on Elza."

"On—Elza?" He was startled. "What do you mean?"

"Oh, I know she hates me. She's in love with Marco, or fancies so. I amuse myself by tormenting her, and I suspect that she'd go to some lengths for revenge, but she's quite as helpless as you. As a matter of fact, I'm doing her a good turn, for Marco is not particularly honorable. So I save her and insure his loyalty to me, all with one stroke."

"You—devil!" Keene gasped. "If there's one thing I'd like above all else, it's to drag you to justice. Ever since that day on the *Aardkin*—"

"When I pinched your nose?" she queried sweetly. "Here, then." With a rapid snap of her hand she twisted the same member with painful violence, laughed into his exasperated face, and turned away. "Come on," she ordered. "Here's breakfast."

"I'll be damned if I'll eat with you!" he snarled.

She shrugged. "As you like. This is all the breakfast you'll get, I promise you."

After all, breakfast was breakfast—he growled and followed her to the massive metal door; as it swung open he forgot a part of his anger in sheer amazement at the luxury of her chamber

She had, apparently, culled the prize plunder of a score of raids to furnish this room. There were deep, silken rugs on the floor, rich tapestries, paintings from the salon of some luxurious Venusian liner, delicately worked aluminum furniture, even a carved mirror whose utter perfection must have originated in the incomparable lost art of Mars.

The man who bore the breakfast tray placed it silently on a table and withdrew. Here was another surprise. Eggs! And fresh ones, too, judging by the smell.

"Oh, we have a few chickens," said the Red Peri, reading his glance. "Enough to supply me, at least. Feeding them is rather a-problem, you see."

Keene remembered his anger in time to reply with an irritable "humph!" For a moment he wondered why the exquisite presence of the Peri should affect him so violently, for he realized that much of his irritation was directed at himself. But of one thing he was certain, and that was that his most ardent desire was to humble the arrogant, self-sufficient, proud, and mocking pirate princess, to see her pay the assigned penalty for her crimes.

Then he frowned. Was he anxious to see her punished? What he really wanted was simply to see her arrogance and insolence humbled, to see her—well, frightened, or pleading with him, as a sort of recompense for the contemptuous way in which she treated him.

She spoke. "You're a silent table partner," she observed, "and yet

I'm rather glad you two blundered in. I was getting frightfully tired and bored; I was considering paying a little visit to civilization."

"I suppose you realize," he growled, "that if we ever get back to Earth, your little visits are over. I'd be very glad to furnish a full description of the Red Peri."

"And do you think I'm the only redhead alive?"

"You're probably the most beautiful, and you know it."

She laughed contemptuously. "Keene, if you think you can play the sophisticated giver of compliments to my innocence, think again. I've been around. I've spent enough time in London, Paris and New York to know the social game. In fact, I have a carefully built-up identity there; my terrestrial friends think I live On Venus. So don't try what they call a fish net on me."

Her words gave him an idea. "Fish net?" he echoed with a deliberate air of sadness. "No. It's just that I have the misfortune to be about half in love with you, while the other half is pure hatred." Suddenly he wondered how much of a lie that really was.

She laughed again. "I half believe you."

"Which half?"

"Never mind. But," she added derisively, "whichever half it is, remember that it takes a better man than you to win the Red Peri's love."

"I didn't say I wanted it!" he snapped. "All you are to me is a vicious law breaker, and all I want is the chance to see you taken."

"Which you'll never have," she returned coolly. She leaned back in her chair and slipped a cigarette from a box. "Smoke?" she asked.

It was in the nature of a peace offering. He accepted both the truce and the cigarette, and puffed with thorough enjoyment.

"Keene," said the Peri, "would you like to see our establishment?"

He nodded. If the girl were proffering friendship, or at least tolerance, he was in no position to refuse it while she held the upper hand. But he would not accept it under false colors.

"Listen," he said, "there are lots of things I like about you. You've plenty of courage, and you've the devil's own beauty. But get this. If I see any chance of escape or any chance to capture you, I'm taking it. Is that plain?"

She nodded. "Keene, if you ever outwit the Red Peri, you're welcome to your winnings. But you never will."

She rose, and he followed her into the stone-walled corridor, glancing briefly at the mysterious archway with its invisible electrostatic seal.

"If your power ever failed," he said, "what would happen to your air here?"

"It won't fail. It's generated directly from disintegration. No moving parts at all. But if it should—" she gestured to the cavern roof—"there's an emergency air door. It will close instantly if there's any appreciable outward current. There's plenty of power to retain our atmosphere; we only keep a pressure of eleven to twelve pounds."

"About the same as the altitude of Denver," he muttered as he followed her. "Prepared for anything, aren't you?"

He was really impressed by the neat little gardens in the side aisles, raised on Plutonian soil carefully selected for the proper elements. "But nitrogen is a troublesome job," she explained. "There's little of it to be had, and what there is, is all mixed with frozen argon. We fractionate it, and then form ammonia, and so finally get it into usable form."

"I know the process," he said.

They penetrated deeper into the series of caverns that pierced the black Plutonian mountain. The fluorolux lights were fewer now, and there were long stretches of dim side passages with no lights at all.

"They're sealed off," said the Peri. "We're approaching the seal of the main cavern now. Do you see where it narrows ahead there? That's an electrostatic seal, but the side passages are blocked with concrete to keep out the crystal crawlers."

"The crystal crawlers!" echoed Keene. He had almost forgotten those curious creatures of the plutonian valley. "Why don't they come through the electrostatic seal?"

"They do, but they seldom get far. You'll see why."

"What are the things?" he asked. "Are they alive? No one—Atsuki or Hervey or Caspari—ever reported them."

"I think they originated in these caverns. This whole region is honey-combed, and those in the valley are just strays. Explorers wouldn't be apt to encounter them."

"But are they alive?" he persisted.

"No-o-o," said the Red Peri slowly. "Not exactly alive. They're—well—on the borderline. They're chemical-crystalline growths, and their movement is purely mechanical. There are half a dozen varieties—aluminum feeders and iron and silicon and sulphur feeders, and others." She smiled impishly. "I have a use for at least one sort. Do you remember, or did you notice, the safe of the *Aardkin*? An iron feeder comes in very handy at times."

He grunted; somehow it pained him to hear the girl refer to piratical activities. Before he could make any other reply they came suddenly into a large natural cavern beyond which showed the narrow opening which the Peri had indicated as the place of the electrostatic seal. A single light shed a dim radiance from far above, and in the faint luminosity he perceived a narrow, deep gash, a gorge or pit, that crossed the chamber from wall to wall and even split the walls in dark tunnels to right and left.

"Here is our crawler trap," said the girl. She indicated a curious span across the chasm, a single heavy girder of metal that bridged the twenty-foot gap in four sharp zigzags. A precariously narrow bridge; the girder was no more than twelve inches in width.

"Copper!" he said.

"Yes. Apparently there are no such things as copper feeders to destroy our bridge. Do you see how the trap works? The crystal crawlers have no eyes nor sense of touch; they just crawl. The chances are infinitely against any of them moving at the proper angles to cross the gap. They go crashing down and crawl away below; although one blundered across once.

"Most of them aren't dangerous except to whatever they feed on." She gestured. "Beyond the seal is our air supply. There's a regular frozen subterranean sea of neon, argon, and oxygen, and we can draw on it almost forever. Don't you want to cross over and look at it?"

Keene stepped to the brink of the chasm and peered down. It was deep; the light from above trickled away into a mysterious darkness where only a few faint sparkles responded—crystals, doubtless, for a slow flicker of movement showed. He scowled at the precarious slenderness of the copper zigzag, and then, cautiously, he abandoned dignity, dropped to his knees, and crept slowly across on all fours.

It was only when he reached the far side and stood erect that he became conscious of the Peri's contemptuous sniff of laughter, and turned to see her walk casually and steadily across the angling span, balancing as easily as if she trod a wide roadway. He flushed a slow red; the girl had nerves of steel, true enough but he realized she had done this as a deliberate taunt.

She strode to the narrow opening, where he now perceived the ring of copper points whence issued the electrostatic field, and above, on the roof, a suspended emergency lock like that at the outer arch.

"There," she said, pointing. "You can see it."

He squinted into the darkness. A dozen feet away, the passage seemed to widen again, but into such a vast hollow that the light from behind him failed utterly to show its bounds. But dimly and faintly as a sea of ectoplasm, he made out a shimmering, illimitable expanse of white, a vast subterranean drift of Pluto's fossil air.

"There goes the pipe to it," said the Peri. "We can get all we need by the simple process of heat, but now and then we have to lengthen the pipe. That's why this end of our colony is sealed by electrostatic. Oh! O-o-oh!"

She broke off in a startled scream. Keene whirled; the cave floor between the two of them and the bridge was covered with a rustling, irregular parade of blackish crystals!

"What's the matter!" he gasped. "We can kick them aside." He moved as if to do so.

"No!" cried the Peri. She seized his arm, dragging him back. "They're carbon feeders! Don't you understand? They're carbon feeders! Your body has carbon. They're—*look out!*"

4

Keene started back, realizing that a gray-black, flat-crystalled, dully shining lump was almost at his feet. He stared at the crawling masses; they had come, apparently, from beyond a jutting wall of rock to his right. The floor was speckled everywhere with them, and now and again one slipped with a faint tinkle over the edge of the central pit. But there were hundreds more; one couldn't wait here until the floor had cleared. He skipped aside; another had silently approached almost to his feet.

He acted. Suddenly he seized the Peri, raised her bodily in his arms, and dashed in an angling, irregular course for the bridge.

The girl squirmed and said, "Put me—" Then she lay very still as he picked his way as delicately as a dancer, sidestepping, skipping, twisting, to the copper span—and over it. Half running, he took the four sharp angles, and at last, breathless, he set the Peri on the rock on the far side.

She looked coolly up at him. "Well!" she said calmly. "Why did you do that?"

"That's pretty thanks for it!" he snapped.

"Don't you think I could have done as well?" she retorted. "I asked you why you did it."

"Because—" He paused. Why had he done it? He suddenly realized that he had no desire to see the exquisite Peri die. To see her humbled, yes. Even to see her punished—but not to see her die. "It was pure impulse," he finished grimly. "If I had thought a second or two, I'd have left you to die."

"Liar!" she said, but smiled. "Well, I thank you for your intentions, though I could have done quite as well alone. But you're very strong, and—Frank!" Her voice rose. "Your foot! Your shoe! Quickly!"

He blinked down. Scarcely visible on the leather, a grayish-black coating of crystals was spreading, and almost immediately came a prickling pain in his toe. With a growling oath he kicked violently. The skin buskin went sailing in an arc over the pit, to fall squarely among the crawlers. Instantly it was a fuzzy mass of needlelike crystals.

The Peri was on her knees. "Your toe!" she wailed. Swift as a serpent she planted her own dainty foot firmly upon the arch of his. From somewhere she snatched a tiny, jeweled penknife, its blade flashing sharp as a razor. Still resting her full weight on his foot, she cut.

Despite his bellow of pain and surprise, she sliced away half his toenail and a goodly strip of skin beneath, kicked the bloody strip into the pit, examined her own pink toes for a moment, and faced Keene. For the first time in their acquaintance she seemed shaken; her wild, green eyes were wide with concern.

But it passed instantly. "Fool!" she snapped. "Fool!"

He was staring aghast at his bleeding toe. "Good Lord!" he muttered. "That was a narrow escape. Well—I'm not so sparing in my thanks as you. I say thanks for it."

"Bah! Do you think I want carbon feeders on this side of the pit? That's why I did it!"

"You could have pushed me into the pit, then," he retorted.

"And I wish I had!" she snapped. She turned abruptly, and padded, barefooted, up the cavern toward the colony.

Keene shifted his remaining buskin to his injured foot and limped after. He was in a turmoil of emotions. There was something splendid about this pirate princess, something more than the simple fact of her exquisite and fantastic beauty. He swore angrily to himself for even admitting it, but limped hastily until he caught her.

"What's your name?" he asked abruptly.

"If you need a name to address me," she said coldly, "let it be commander."

"The only person I'll call commander is one I'm willing to serve, and that'll never be the Red Peri."

She glanced sidewise at him. "What's a name, anyway?" she asked in altered tones. "See here. You're Frank Keene, but you're neither keen enough to outwit me nor frank enough to admit you love me."

"Love you!" he snorted. "Love you! Why—" He broke off suddenly. "Even if it were true," he went on, "do you think I'd have anything to do with a pirate, a murderess? However I felt, I'd still exert every effort to bring you to justice. How many deaths have you caused? How much suffering?"

"I don't know," she said. "But murder? I never killed anybody except in sheer self-defense."

"So you say. What about the atrocities on the *Hermes?*"

She looked up at him. "Frank," she said softly, "I had nothing to do with the *Hermes*. Don't you realize that people blame everything on the *Red Peri*? Every captain who suffers from some sneaking little freebooter blames me for it. Why, I'd need a hundred ships to commit all the crimes they've pinned on me."

"But you're a pirate, nevertheless."

"Yes, but I have my reasons. I have, Frank. And—oh, why should I justify myself to you, anyway? I don't care what you think of me."

"All the same," he growled, "I'll tell you what I think. I think your parents should have given you a series of good spankings. You're nothing but a spoiled, reckless, dangerous child."

"My parents," she echoed.

"Yes. Do you think they'd be proud of you now?"

'I hope," she said slowly, "that one of them would be." She Paused at the door of her chamber, unlocking it. "Come in here," she ordered sharply.

He followed her into the lavish interior. She disappeared into an adjacent room, returning in a moment with a bottle and a strip of gauze. "Here," she said. "Dress your toe."

"It's nothing. It needs no dressing."

"Dress it!" she snapped. "I want no cases of infection here."

"I might"—he observed as he took the bottle—"die of the infection and thus save you a murder."

Her green eyes seemed to soften. "Remember this, Frank," she said in a low voice. "I could have let you die back there at the edge of the pit. I could have, but I didn't."

He had no answer. For a moment he gazed thoughtfully at the exquisite delicacy of her face, and then, irrelevantly, he asked again, "What is your name?"

She smiled. "Peri," she said.

"Really? Peri what? That's a strange name."

"Yes. It's the Persian word for imp or elf."

"I know. I've worked in Iraq. But it means more than just that; it's the name given to the child of a disobedient angel, waiting to be admitted into paradise."

Her features grew suddenly wistful. "Yes," she murmured. "Waiting to be admitted into paradise."

"But Peri what?" he repeated.

She hesitated. "If I told you," she said slowly, "you might understand. I think I will tell you, Frank. Did you ever hear of Perry Maclane?"

He frowned. "Perry Maclane," he muttered. "I—think so. Wait a minute. Do you mean Red Perry Maclane, the inventor who had the famous legal battle with Interplanetary? But that was years ago, years and years. I was a child of seven or eight; you must scarcely have been born."

"I was just born. Perry Maclane was my father."

"Red Perry your father? And—the ship! I see—*Red Peri*, named after him."

"Named by him, after me. He built it. He built it purposely to be a pirate craft, and you can't blame him!"

"Can't blame him! Why not?"

"Listen to me, Frank." Her glorious eyes were intense and serious. "Perry Maclane was robbed by Interplanetary and their associates. Do you know how dangerous space travel used to be, twenty-five or thirty years ago? Even fifty years after the first colonies were founded on Venus, it was a gamble with death to travel there.

"Trade was all but impossible; because the rocket blasts kept failing, and ships kept crashing in trying to land, or even plunged into the Sun. And then the thermoid expansion chamber was developed; the blasts became steady, safe, usable. Trade was possible, and Interplanetary became an enormous, wealthy corporation. But do you know who invented the expansion chamber? Do you?"

"Why-----"

"Perry Maclane did! He invented it and patented it. But Interplanetary wouldn't let a little thing like honor stand in their way. They copied the patent; they claimed one of their engineers had developed the chamber first; they fought the case through every court, and at last they fought Perry Maclane out of money, and won. It took four years to do it; and in the last year I was born and my mother died; and Perry Maclane was ruined.

"But he didn't give up. He worked at anything he could find—he, the greatest rocket engineer in the world! He dug sewers and planned drainage systems; he did any sort of work, but meanwhile, all the time, he was carrying the idea of revenge.

"Evenings he worked on the plans of such a ship as no one had dreamed of, a rocket with inherent stability, one that could flash through gravitational fields as easily as through interplanetary space, instead of teetering down on its jets, wabbling and compensating and inching lower. And when he had it—I was three then—he found those who supplied money to build it.

"He wasn't the only man Interplanetary had ruined; others hated the corporation, too. So he built the *Red Peri*, and began raiding corporation ships. He had no trouble manning his ship; he could have had a thousand men; but he picked and chose among the best for his crew.

"At first he worked out of the Australian desert as a base, but that became dangerous. He thought of the Moon, and of an asteroid; but at last, because he had a ship to which planetary distances meant nothing, he came here to build his colony. Save for the years I spent at school, I've lived here ever since."

"But what of Red Perry Maclane?" asked Keene.

"He was killed three years ago. Do you remember when Interplanetary's Captain Thorsen of the *Lucrece* shot one of the pirates? That was my father; he died and was buried as he wanted to be—in space. It was I who killed Thorsen, with my own hand as he shot at me."

He stared at her. Those were certainly tears in the glorious, emerald eyes. "Peri," he said softly, "but what will be the end of it? Are you going on all your life pursuing revenge for your father? You're not really hurting Interplanetary, you know; they carry insurance. But you are slowing down the development of the planets. It's come to a point where people are actually afraid to travel."

"Good!" she flashed. "Then it's less trade and fewer fares to swell the coffers of Interplanetary."

"But—good heavens, Peri! With a design like that of your ship you could make millions legitimately!"

"Oh, of course!" she retorted sarcastically. "Just as my father did from the thermoid expansion chamber."

There was no answer to that. He shook his head sadly. "Then do you intend to live out your life as a pirate until you're finally captured, or until you die out here on this miserable black planet?"

"I do not. I intend to carry out the plans of Red Perry Maclane. He wasn't fighting out of blind passion, you know. He built up his organization, here and on Earth, for a single purpose. Little by little, the plunder we take from Interplanetary goes back to Earth, to be turned into cash and securities, in banks in New York, London, Berlin, Paris, Tokyo. When I have enough—and a hundred million dollars will be enough—do you know what I'll do?"

"I don't, Peri." His eyes were glued to her tense, lovely face.

"Then listen!" she said fiercely. "I'll open a line competing with Interplanetary. I'll build ships like the *Red Peri*, and I'll drive their corporation to ruin! I'll have them groveling and begging, but this time I'll have money enough so they can't fight with crooked lawyers and bribed judges. I'll annihilate them!"

The Red Peri

For a long time he stared at her strange loveliness, her wild, green eyes and flaming hair. "Oh, Peri!" he said at last, in tones of sadness. "Don't you see how insane such a plan is? Don't you know that once you produce the design of this ship, you'll be known as the pirate? No one else knows of it."

"I don't care!" she blazed. "The law can't touch anyone with a hundred million dollars. My father learned that from Interplanetary." And at his continued silence, she snapped, "Your advice would be to take it lying down, I suppose. I prefer to fight."

"But you don't have to declare war on the whole Earth on account of an injury done your father."

"War on the Earth? I haven't. But—" her green eyes glowed fiercely—"if I ever should, I could give them such a war as they never dreamed of!"

"What do you mean, Peri?"

"I'll tell you! Suppose I were to take one of those carbon feeders, like the ones that nipped your toe. Suppose I took just one tiny Crystal and dropped it in the jungles of Africa or in Middle Europe or in the wheat belt of America. All life has carbon in it. What would happen to the pretty, green Earth Frank? What would happen to the crooked lawyers and the bribed judges, and all the rest, honest and dishonest, right up to the heads of Interplanetary itself?"

"My Lord!" he said.

"Can't you see the crystal crawlers rustling their way along?" she cried. "Wheat fields, houses, horses, humans!"

"Listen!" he said huskily. "Do you know what I ought to do? I know what my duty is. It's to kill you, right now and here, while I've got you alone. Otherwise that mad and reckless spirit of yours may some day drive you to do just that. I ought to strangle you now, but—by heavens—I can't!"

All the passion drained suddenly from her face, leaving it alluringly wistful. "I'm glad you said those last two words, Frank," she murmured. "Look." She raised her arms; he saw her hand resting firmly on the butt of her revolver. "Would it please you," she asked softly, "if I promised you never to think again of that Particular revenge?"

"You know it would!"

"Then I promise. And now, tell me if you still blame me for being—the Red Peri. Do you?"

197

"I don't know. I think—perhaps—you are justified for feeling as you do, but, Peri, it's madness."

"What would you want me to do?"

"Why—the sane course, the honorable course, would be to make restitution, to return everything you've stolen; and then to give yourself up, to expiate the wrongs you've done, and so be free to live without the need of burying yourself out here at the edge of nothingness. I don't say you could do all of that, but at least you could return what you've taken and live as you were meant to live—honorably and happily."

"Honorably and happily!" she echoed bitterly. "Yes, except for the realization that I had failed my father."

"Your father was wrong, Peri."

She blazed in sudden anger. "Oh, you're too smug and self-righteous to live. I was going to offer you your freedom; I thought you'd understand and protect me, but now do you think I dare trust you to return to Earth? Now you'll stay as my prisoner!"

"Some day," he said evenly, "I'll drag you back to justice, Peri, and after you're free you'll thank me for it."

"Get out!" she cried. "You're stupid! I hate stupidity!"

He looked quietly at her angry, exquisite face, rose, and stalked out of the door. For a moment he stood irresolute in the corridor; then he strode toward the room he shared with Solomon Nestor, ignoring the glances of a number of residents as he went. And as he opened the door, the first person he saw was the girl Elza, in close conversation with the old man.

They looked up as he entered, and the flaxen-haired girl drew away, staring at him with a curious expression in her blue eyes.

"Oh, bosh!" said the old man. "Elza, you're simply letting your imagination make you nervous. Listen, Frank—this girl came running here to tell me that you've been spending hours in the Red Peri's company, and that you were probably falling under her magic charms; and now Elza's afraid you're going to betray her to the Peri. Ridiculous, isn't it?"

"Utterly!" snapped Keene, wondering how much of it was ridiculous. He felt himself reddening, and repeated hastily, "Utterly ridiculous!"

"You see?" said old Nestor triumphantly. "All right, Elza, let's get on with this. You say you're sure you can't smuggle space suits to us?"

"I'm sure I can't. They're kept locked up by the Red Peri, and I can't get to them."

"But your father and brother wear them when they go to either ship, don't they?"

"Yes, but I wouldn't dare ask them. They'd tell the Peri. I know that."

"Well," said old Solomon thoughtfully, "if we can't get space suits, we'll have to do without. But you can get the key to one of the ships, can't you?"

"Not to the *Red Peri*," said Elza. "To your ship, perhaps, because my father has that while he's working on it. I could steal it away from him, I think. He just keeps it in a desk."

"What good would the *Limbo* do us?" grunted Keene. "They could run us down with the other. They could blast us to bits."

"They could, but they won't," retorted the old man. "You leave this to old Solomon. Now Elza when will your father have the jet repaired?"

"I think he's finishing it now."

"And could you smuggle the key to us tonight?"

"I think so. I'll try. Tonight or tomorrow."

"Good!" said Solomon Nestor. "You run along now, Elza. You'll have your revenge on the Red Peri—if you're a good girl."

The yellow-haired girl vanished. Old Nestor turned quizzical eyes on Keene and said mockingly, "Ridiculous, eh! Utterly ridiculous!"

"What?"

"That you should be impressed by the Red Peri. How could so unattractive a being effect the redoubtable Frank Keene? Very ridiculous!"

"Oh, shut up!" growled Keene. "I admit she's beautiful, and I admit that what she told me has changed my opinion of her. All the same, I think she's arrogant and overbearing. I'm just as anxious as ever to see her take a fall, and if I can trip her, that's fine. But I don't see how the key to the *Limbo* helps."

"You will. Tell me what the Peri said to you."

Keene recounted the story of "Red" Perry Maclane. Despite

himself, he told it with a tinge of sympathy, and when, after concluding it, he described the events at the copper bridge, he was uncomfortable aware of old Nestor's steady gaze. He finished his tale and stared defiantly back.

"Well!" said the old man. "I suppose you realize that she risked her life for you—or at least the chance of having to cut off a finger or two. What if she'd touched the carbon feeders on your toe?"

"I—I hadn't thought of it."

"And now that you do think of it, are you still so bitterly determined to humble her?"

Keene considered. "Yes!" he snapped. "I am. I don't want to hurt her, but I do want to get back at her for the way she's insulted, browbeaten, and mocked me. I want to see her take a fall."

"Even though it means capture for her?"

Keene groaned. "Listen, Solomon. Right now I'm so puzzled that I'm not sure. But I do know that I want to see the Red Peri paid back for the way she's acted toward me."

"All right. I think you're in love with her, Frank, though it's none of my business."

"Damn' right it isn't!"

"But," proceeded Nestor, "just how badly do you want to do this?"

"With all my heart!"

"Would you risk your life and hers to do it?"

"My life," said Keene grimly, "but not hers."

"Good enough. Now the first thing to do is talk you out of a few superstitions."

"I haven't any."

"You have, but you don't know it. Listen, now." The old man bent closer and began to talk in a low, earnest voice. At his first words Keene paled and started; then he sat very still and very intent. After five minutes of listening, he drew a deep breath, expanding his mighty chest to the full.

"I used to plunge at the university," he said exultantly. "I could hold my breath for four minutes. I can still do three and a half!"

"That's plenty," said Nestor.

"Yes, if it works. If it works!"

"If I were you," said the old man, "I'd find out—now!"

For a full minute Keene stared at him. Suddenly he nodded, turned swiftly away, and darted out into the corridor. In five minutes he was back again, but sadly changed, for his lips were swollen, his eyes red, and his breath a rasping gurgle. But he was smiling—

"It works!" he gasped triumphantly. "It's unadulterated hell—but it works!"

5

Elza did not appear that night, although Keene tossed and twisted wakefully for miserable hours. In the darkness the thing he had to do appeared grotesque, fantastic, impossible; and this despite the fact that he had already tested the truth of old Solomon Nestor's reasoning. His toe ached and his lips and eyes burned, but more painful than all else was the idea of inflicting harm on the courageous and proud Red Peri.

When, well toward the end of the ten-hour Plutonian night, he finally fell into troubled slumber, it was but for a brief while, and he rose sullen and morose to pace the floor of the chamber.

The fluorolux light awakened old Nestor. For a few moments he watched the pacing Keene, and then asked, "Did Elza come?"

"No, and I hope she doesn't," snarled Keene. "I hope she couldn't get the key—and if she does get it, I'm not going through with this!"

"It's your business," said Nestor indifferently. "It doesn't mean anything to me, because I'd never live through it, not at my age. I have to stay here anyway, and I don't mind, because Elza said they'd moved my instruments into the cave; and I can work here almost as well as farther out in space. But if you love the girl so intently, why don't you act like a human being and tell her so?"

"Love her!" yelled Keene. "Just because I feel like a dirty dog at the thought of this, doesn't mean I love her! She's a girl, isn't she?"

"And a very beautiful one."

"Bah! She's a girl, and I hate to fight women!"

"Well, don't then," suggested old Solomon.

"Yet I want like the very devil to get back at her."

"Then do."

"And yet, in a way I can't blame her."

"Then don't."

Keene resuming his pacing. In another minute he stopped, faced the old man, and said defiantly, "Solomon, I can't do it. I know she's a pirate and a menace to trade and civilization, but I can't do it."

Before the other could reply, a knock sounded on the door. Keene whirled. "I hope," he muttered, "that it's breakfast—just breakfast."

It was. Elza brought it in silently, placed it on the table, and retired; and Keene felt a vast surge of relief. She hadn't managed to get the key! He was almost ready to sing until he picked up his cup of coffee and there it was—the familiar key to the outer door of the *Limbo's* air lock.

He met old Nestor's amused, blue eyes with a cold glare, and it was hardly softened by the other's murmur: "After all, Frank, you don't have to use it."

"I know I don't!" he snarled. "I have a fine choice, haven't I? I can stay here the rest of my life, if our hostess doesn't take a notion to kill me, or I can escape by following your scatterbrained plan of doing a thing I hate. I can't escape alone, for they'd simply run me down with their pirate ship."

"Or you could turn pirate," suggested Solomon Nestor.

"Gr-r-r!" said Keene amiably.

He was unaccustomed to this sort of agonized indecision. He had never encountered a situation that pulled so many ways at once; for in all his experience right had been right and wrong had been wrong—yet now he was not at all sure but that the laws of relativity operated in the moral field as well as in the physical. Certainly the Red Peri was not entirely in the wrong, yet equally certainly she was a pirate, a menace to progress, an antisocial being, and therefore a criminal. If she would only give up this mad purpose of hers; if she would make restitution; if she—He swore bitterly and strode out of the door, scarcely realizing that the Limbo's key was in his pocket.

He turned at random toward the outer arch of the cave. Figures in space suits were passing in and out through the electrostatic seal, and he noticed that the outgoing men were laden with cases, boxes, cans, and bundles. He stood at the very edge of the seal and stared out into the dim, nightlike morning of the black planet. Beside him a row of metal-clad figures clanked outward, their footsteps dropping to sudden silence the instant they trod into the airless outdoors.

He watched them carry their burdens to the *Red Peri*, where an air lock swung open to admit them. They were loading the ship.

Keene stared disinterestedly, without comprehension. Then, abruptly, the meaning dawned on him. He stiffened, peered closely through narrowed eyes, and spun to accost a metal-sheathed figure that approached, Marco Grandi, for he could see the dark, aquiline features behind the visor.

"What's this?" Keene snapped. "You're cargoing the *Peri*. For what?"

Grandi made no answer, and Keene planted himself squarely in the other's way. "For what?" he blazed.

The metallic voice of the diaphragm clicked. "Stand aside. We're busy."

"I'll keep you busy!" he roared. "I'll—I'll—"

"You'll what?" queried the cool tones of the Peri.

Keene whirled. The girl stood at his side, clad in an all-enveloping, clinging robe of bright green that echoed the infinitely more brilliant emerald of her eyes.

"They're stocking the *Red Peri*!" he shouted.

"I know it."

"Why? For what purpose?"

"For purposes of business."

"Business! You mean for purposes of piracy!"

"Piracy," she said coldly, "is my business."

"It was your business, you mean!" With a great effort he controlled himself and faced the mocking green eyes. "Peri," he said more calmly, "I want to talk to you."

"It isn't mutual."

"I want to talk to you," he repeated stubbornly, "alone." He glanced at the hostile eyes of Marco Grandi.

The Peri shrugged. "Go on out, Marco," she ordered, and then to Keene, "Well? What is it?"

"Listen," he said. "I want you to quit this business. I want you to be fair to yourself. You're capable of infinitely greater things than piracy."

"I know it. When I'm ready, I'll achieve those greater things."

"Oh, revenge!" he snapped. "Suppose you succeed. Do you think you'll be any happier?"

"And if I'm not," she countered, "what is it to you?"

He drew a deep breath. "It's a lot to me," he said soberly, "because you see, Peri, I happen to love you."

Her green eyes did not change. "What you call love," she said contemptuously, "isn't my conception. If you loved me you'd take me exactly as I am."

"I was brought up to believe in honesty, Peri."

"And I," she retorted, "was brought up to believe in honor. Red Perry Maclane's honor needs avenging, and there's none but his daughter to see to it."

Keene pounded his fist impatiently against the wall. "Peri," he said at last, "do you love me?"

She made no immediate reply. From somewhere in her heavy silken gown she produced a cigarette, lighted it, and blew a gray plume of smoke toward the seal. "No," she said.

"Why did you risk your life for me back there at the pit? What if you had touched the carbon feeders?"

She glanced out into the cold, black valley. "I may have thought I loved you then," she murmured, eyes still averted. "That was before I knew how little you could understand my feelings. We're just—not the same sort."

"I think we are," said Keene. "We've simply learned different moral codes, but—Peri—my code's the right one. Even you can see that."

"It's not for me. What my father wanted is the thing I want and the thing I'm going to do."

He groaned and abandoned that line of attack. "What do you expect to do with Solomon Nestor and me?"

She made a helpless little gesture. "What can I do? I have to leave you here." She turned her green eyes back to him. "Frank, if you'd promise to keep this place and my identity a secret, I think I'd be willing to release you."

"I can't promise that."

Her voice hardened. "Then here you stay."

"So you've given up the idea of killing us?"

"Oh," she said indifferently, "I'm always indulgent to those who claim to be in love with me."

Her attitude angered him. "You're pretty confident, aren't you?

If you leave us here while you're off pirating, you know damn well we'll be doing our best to overcome you."

"And I know damn well that you'll never outwit me," she retorted.

Keene's hand suddenly encountered the *Limbo's* key in his pocket. "I won't, eh?" he muttered. "See here, Peri. Are you determined once and for all to stick to this scheme of yours?"

"Once and for all, I am."

"And it makes no difference that I tell you I love you?"

She turned abruptly and faced the grim outdoors, staring over the dead, cold, black Plutonian landscape. "It makes no difference, Frank."

"And nothing I can say will make a difference?"

She gestured impatiently, still staring far away. "Oh, what's the use of arguing? No, Frank."

He looked silently at her, seeing her, seeing her glorious hair flaming against the cold background of black mountains. He peered thoughtfully down the deserted corridor, and then at the Red Peri. The valley was lifeless; the men were within the vessel and the air lock was closed. Dim across the plain was the dull bulk of the *Limbo*, whose key was clutched in his hand.

"Well," he muttered sadly, "you've asked for it, Peri."

She did not turn. "For what, Frank?"

"For this!" he cried, and with a sudden lunge he sent her and himself staggering, unarmored, into the airless Plutonian plain, and into a temperature of ten degrees above absolute zero!

6

Instantly he was in hell. The breath rushed out of his lungs in a faint expansion mist that dissipated at once, the blood pounded in his aching ear drums, his eyes seemed to bulge, and a thin stream of blood squirted darkly from his nose. His whole body felt terribly, painfully bloated as he passed from a pressure of twelve pounds per square inch to one of nearly zero. He fought his agony grimly; he had to hold consciousness as long as he could. But old Nestor had been right; he was living.

He had a momentary impression of the Peri's green gown billowing up from her glorious body like a balloon, to settle back instantly as the bound air escaped. Then she whirled, eyes wide, mouth open and straining for air that simply was not there, hands clutching frantically at her gasping throat. She was in full command of her own agile mind, and she sprang convulsively for the archway and the seal. Grimly he thrust her back.

She was trying to scream. Her breast rose and fell in futile, soundless, panting gasps; moisture formed on her forehead and vanished instantly. Swift as a deer she darted again for the archway; and again he controlled his agony to smash her back.

For once in her life the Peri knew sheer panic. No longer had she the coordination of mind and muscle that might yet have encompassed escape. Fierce pain and utter fright had robbed her of it; and for a few seconds she could only thrust aimlessly against Keene's braced body, her hands fluttering frantically, her legs pushing convulsively, her lovely, pain-racked, wild, green eyes but inches from his own.

He had a double task now; he had to hold her back from the entrance and at the same time keep any part of her twisting body save her shod feet from contact with the searing cold of the rocky ground. He clutched her violently against him. Suddenly her struggles grew weaker, her hands went vainly to her tortured throat, her hands closed, and she collapsed.

They were almost at the air lock of the *Red Peri*. He saw it fly open, he glimpsed Marco Grandi's appalled face behind his visor, but he had no fraction of a second to lose. He swung the Peri across his shoulder and set off on a staggering run for the *Limbo*, more than nine hundred feet away across a vacuum and a cold only less than those of space itself. Grandi could never catch him; no one could run in a space suit.

The Peri was not light; on Earth she might have weighed a hundred and fifteen pounds, but here it was more like a hundred and forty. His own weight was greater too, but he felt none of that; the excruciating torment that racked his body erased all lesser tortures.

He crashed unseeing through a parade of aluminum feeders, and blood spurted wildly from a tiny scratch on his ankle, and then—then he was fumbling at the *Limbo's* lock.

The door flew open from its inner pressure; he bundled himself and the Peri within, pulled it to, and collapsed as the hissing of the automatic valve sent a heavenly stream of air against his face. He had crossed a thousand feet of vacuum and still lived!

The air pressure reached normal. He fought to his knees, opened the inner door, and dragged the girl through it. She lay with her magnificent hair streaming on the steel floor; blood trickled from her nose—but she breathed.

Keene had work to do. He thrust wide the feed to the underjets, and the ship roared, rising shakily as he peered through the floor port at Marco Grandi plodding desperately across the plain. He let the *Limbo* rise aimlessly; later he could set a course.

He dragged the limp Peri to a chair. About her slim waist he twisted the iron chain from the aft ventilator, and locked it with the padlock of Nestor's empty bolometer case. The other end he locked carefully to a hand hold on the wall, and only then, laboring and gasping, did he turn his attention to the medicine kit.

He poured a half tumbler of whiskey and forced a good portion of it between the Peri's lips. Still pain-tortured, it was yet agony to him to see the lines of anguish on her unconscious face, and to hear the choking of her breath. She coughed weakly from the liquor, and moved convulsively as he sprang back to the controls and set the *Limbo* nosing Sunward. That was close enough for the present; later he could lay a course for Titan.

The Peri stirred. Her uncomprehending green eyes looked vaguely toward him, and then about the chamber. She spoke, "Frank! Frank! Where am I?"

"On the *Limbo*."

"On the—" She glanced down; her hand had encountered the chain about her waist. "Oh!" she murmured, and stared at it a full half minute. When she looked up again her eyes were quite clear and conscious. "You—you've got me, Frank, haven't you?"

"Right where I want you," he said grimly. Strangely, there was no satisfaction in it. He had wanted to see her humbled, but now it was pure pain.

"Why—aren't we dead, Frank?" she asked slowly. "We were— in the airless valley, weren't we? How is it that we still live?"

"I'll tell you, Peri. It was old Solomon's idea. Everybody's been believing a lot of superstitions about space, but he figured out the truth. It isn't the vacuum that's dangerous, and it isn't the cold; it's the lack of air. We couldn't freeze, because a vacuum is the best insulator there is; we aren't like that aluminum spade of yours, because our bodies actually produced heat faster than we radiate it away. In fact, it really felt warm to me—as far as I could be conscious of any feeling in that hell.

"And as for all the gruesome stories of lungs collapsing and all that, every high school physics student sees the experiment of the mouse under the bell jar. An air pump exhausts the jar to the highest vacuum it can attain, the mouse loses consciousness—just as you did, Peri—but when the air returns, it recovers.

"Its lungs don't collapse because there's no outer pressure to crush them, and its body doesn't burst because the tissues are strong enough to maintain that much internal pressure. And if a mouse can stand it, why not a human being? And I knew I could stand lack of air longer than you."

"It seems you could," she admitted ruefully. "But still, Frank, that terrible drop in pressure! I see that we didn't explode from it, though it felt as though we should; but I still don't see why."

"I tell you because our tissues are too tough. Look here, Peri. The pressure at sea level on Earth is 14.7 pounds per square inch. The pressure on top of Mount Everest is four pounds per square inch. That's about six miles above sea level.

"A hundred and fifty years ago, way back in 1930, open airplanes flew over Mount Everest. The pilots didn't suffer much from lack of pressure; just as long as they had oxygen to breathe, they could live. Yet from sea level to 29,000 feet altitude is a drop of eleven pounds per square inch—almost exactly the drop from the pressure in your cave to the pressure outside.

"The human body can stand that much of a drop; all it really does is cause altitude sickness. As a matter of fact, a pearl diver going down in four or five fathoms of water meets a greater variation than that. Plenty of South Sea skin divers work in that depth, utterly unprotected. What might have happened to us is the bends, but your own air system thoughtfully prevented that danger."

"M–my own air system?"

"Yes, Peri. The bends are the result of decreasing pressure, which ordinarily causes the blood to give up its dissolved nitrogen as bubbles. It's the bubbles that cause the disease. But your air doesn't contain nitrogen; it's made of oxygen and neon, and neon doesn't dissolve! So—no dissolved gases, no bubbles, and no bends."

"But—it's fantastic! It's impossible!"

"We did it. What do you think of that?"

"Why"—her voice was meek—"I think you're very courageous, Frank. You're the only man ever to see the Red Peri frightened, and you've seen that—twice."

"Twice? When was the other time?"

"When—when I saw the carbon feeders on your foot."

"Peri!" he groaned. "This whole thing has hurt me enough, but now if you mean—"

"Of course I mean it," she said, looking steadily at him. "I love you, Frank."

"If I dared believe you, Peri—you know I love you, don't you?"

A faint trace of her old mockery glistened green in her eyes. "Oh, of course," she said. "I could tell it because you've been so kind to me."

Her sarcasm tortured him. "I had to do it. I have to bring you over to my side of the fence, Peri—the honest side."

"And you think you can?"

"I can try."

"Really?" she taunted. "Frank, don't you know my ship will be alongside in a matter of minutes? You can't outrun the *Red Peri* in this tub. You have me helpless now, but I won't be so for long!'

"Indeed? Well, tub or not, the *Limbo's* solid. They don't dare blast the ship with you aboard, and if they try to tie up and cut their way in"—he turned narrowed eyes on her—"I'll ram the *Peri*. As I said, this ship is solid, far more solid than your triangular speedster. I'll smash it!"

The faint color that had returned to the Peri's face drained out of it. After a moment she said in very low tones, "What are you going to do with me, Frank?"

"Peri, I'm going to take you back to trial. After you've expiated your crimes—and with your beauty in an American court the sentence will be light—I'm going to marry you."

"Marry? Yes, I'd marry you, Frank, but don't you realize piracy is tried under maritime law? The penalty is—death!"

"Not for such a woman as you. Three years—no more."

"But I'm wanted in every country on Earth, Frank. They'll extradite me. What if I'm tried for murder in an English court?"

"Murder?" he echoed blankly. "I—I hadn't thought of that. My Lord, Peri! What can we do?"

"What we do is in your hands," she said dully. He saw tears in her green eyes.

"I—don't know. I swore a solemn oath to uphold the law, I—can't break an oath. Peri," he cried fiercely, "I have money. I'll fight through every court in the country to prevent your extradition. You'll return all you've taken. They'll be lenient; they have to be!"

"Perhaps," she said tonelessly, "Well, I don't care. You've won, Frank. I love you for it."

Impulsively he dropped the controls, strode over to the chained girl, and kissed her. He had to make it brief, for his own eyes were suddenly misty. At the controls again, he swore bitterly to himself, for he realized now that he could never risk bringing the Red Peri to trial. He thought somberly of his broken oath; that meant nothing if keeping it endangered the girl he loved.

He formed a plan. At Nivia on Titan there'd be an inspection of the ship. He'd hide the Peri—in a cool jet, perhaps—and tell his story without mention of her capture. He'd disclose the location of the pirate base and let the government rockets rescue old Solomon and destroy the colony. And then he—

Then? Well, he'd land the *Limbo* in Iraq. He had friends there who'd keep the Peri safe. He'd fly home and resign his damned official position, and so be free to marry pirate or murderess or any one he chose—and no one would ever know that the lovely Mrs. Keene had once been the dreaded Red Peri.

For the present he'd let the girl believe he was taking her back to punishment; at least that might frighten her into a respectable life. He smiled, and looked up to find the luminous green eyes fixed steadily and unhappily on his face.

Before he could speak the buzzer of the static field sounded the signal that warned of meteors. But meteors were rare indeed out here beyond the orbit of Jupiter. He stared back at the vast black disc of Pluto, and true enough, there was a little flare of light against the blackness that could mean only a rocket blast. Second by second the flame approached, and the *Red Peri* rushed toward him as if his own blast were silent.

The pirate ship paralleled his course. Suddenly the annunciator above him spoke; they had trained an inductive beam on it. "Cut your jets!" came the words in a cold metallic voice that was still recognizable as Marco Grandi's.

He had no means of reply, so he bored grimly on. The *Red Peri* slipped close beside him. "Cut your jets," came the order, "or we'll blast you!"

Keene thought suddenly of the communication system from the pilot room to the stern. If he spoke into that, and if their tubes were sensitive enough, it was possible that their receiver might pick up the induced current. He switched it on full.

"*Red Peri!*" he called. "Can you hear me? Can you hear me?"

Reply was immediate. "We hear you. Cut your jets!"

"I won't," said Keene. "If you come a single yard closer I'll ram you. The Peri's aboard, and if you blast this ship you'll kill her as well as me."

There was a silence. "How do we know she's alive?" asked Grandi's voice.

"Watch the forward port," said Keene. He unlocked the chain at the hand hold. The girl made no resistance as he led her to the port, following as meekly as a puppy on a leash.

"I'll have to make this look serious," he said. "I'm sorry, Peri." He twisted his hand roughly in her glorious hair and thrust her close against the port. After a moment he released her, led her back to her chair, and relocked the chain.

"*Red Peri*," he called, "move away or I'll ram you. Keep a quarter mile distance."

There was no reply, but the pirate ship slanted silently away. Like a child's model it hung in the void, tenaciously paralleling his course. But he knew it was helpless; Grandi dared not risk the Peri's safety.

Nearly an hour passed before the Peri spoke. "I don't understand you, Frank," she said miserably. "When your life was in danger I risked mine to save you, but you risk your life to destroy me. Is that what you mean by love?"

"I risked mine, not to destroy you, but to save you," he muttered. "Peri, I couldn't bear the thought of your living such a life as you have been living. I want you to be happy."

"Happy," she echoed mournfully. "If this is your idea of happiness—" She left the sentence unfinished.

Hour after hour the pirate clung grimly beside them. After a long time Keene slept, trusting to the buzzer to rouse him if Grandi should attempt to cut through. The last thing he saw was the luminescent eyes of the Peri, and they were the first thing he saw on awakening. She sat as if she had not moved.

Another day passed. Pluto was a pallid, tiny disk far behind them, Neptune and Uranus were beyond the Sun; but Saturn gleamed brightly. All day the Peri was mournfully silent, and when he kissed her before sleeping, she clung to him almost as if in panic. He remembered that later, for when he awoke she was—gone.

Gone! The chain was missing, and only a square of paper—a star chart—lay on her chair. She wasn't on the *Limbo*, and the *Red Peri* no longer hung silent on the left. He seized the note in a frantic clutch. He read.

> *Frank—dearest Frank—this is farewell. I love you; and the proof of it is that I could have escaped before this while you slept; but I wanted to stay. I was all but willing to suffer before the law if it meant having you—but I can't. Not even three years, because I'd die without freedom.*
>
> *I had an iron feeder in my pocket, for I always carry them on raids, as you remember from the* Aardkin. *It's eating the chain now, but it won't attack chrome steel; your floors and walls are safe.*
>
> *Frank, if you had weakened, if you had promised me safety, I think I should have stayed, but—perhaps—then I should have loved you less than I do now.*
>
> *Goodbye.*

The note was unsigned. She had taken a red chart pencil and drawn a creditable picture of a tiny, winged elf—a red peri.

Keene knew what she had done. There were no space suits on the Limbo, for he and Solomon had worn them to the pirate cave. She had signaled her ship, opened the air lock, and braved once more the vacuum of space to fling herself across.

When he had finally exhausted his vocabulary of expletives and blasphemies, when he had at last called himself all the varieties of fool he knew, Keene realized what he had to do. He couldn't find her on Pluto, since the Peri would certainly move her base elsewhere for fear he'd direct a government rocket there. But what he could do, what he had to do, was to get a job on an interplanetary freighter, and then wait. Sooner or later—sooner or later, he repeated grimly—he'd meet the Red Peri again.

The Mad Moon

"Idiots!" howled Grant Calthorpe. "Fools—nitwits—imbeciles!" He sought wildly for some more expressive terms, failed and vented his exasperation in a vicious kick at the pile of rubbish on the ground.

Too vicious a kick, in fact; he had again forgotten the one third normal gravitation of Io, and his whole body followed his kick in a long, twelve-foot arc.

As he struck the ground the four loonies giggled. Their great, idiotic heads, looking like nothing so much as the comic faces painted on Sunday balloons for children, swayed in unison on their five-foot necks, as thin as Grant's wrist.

"Get out!" he blazed, scrambling erect. "Beat it, skiddoo, scram! No chocolate. No candy. Not until you learn that I want ferva leaves, and not any junk you happen to grab. Clear out!"

The loonies—*Lunae Jovis Magnicapites*, or literally, Big-heads of Jupiter's Moon—backed away, giggling plaintively. Beyond doubt, they considered Grant fully as idiotic as he considered them, and were quite unable to understand the reasons for his anger. But they certainly realized that no candy was to be forthcoming, and their giggles took on a note of keen disappointment.

So keen, indeed, that the leader, after twisting his ridiculous blue face in an imbecilic grin at Grant, voiced a last wild giggle and dashed his head against a glittering stone-bark tree. His companions casually picked up his body and moved off, with his head dragging behind them on its neck like a prisoner's ball on a chain.

Grant brushed his hand across his forehead and turned wearily toward his stone-bark log shack. A pair of tiny, glittering red eyes caught his attention, and a slinker—*Mus Sapiens*—skipped his six-inch form across the threshold, bearing under his tiny, skinny arm what looked very much like Grant's clinical thermometer.

Grant yelled angrily at the creature, seized a stone, and flung it vainly. At the edge of the brush, the slinker turned its ratlike, semi-human face toward him, squeaked its thin gibberish, shook a microscopic fist in manlike wrath, and vanished, its batlike cowl of skin fluttering like a cloak. It looked, indeed, very much like a black rat wearing a cape.

It had been a mistake, Grant knew, to throw the stone at it. Now the tiny fiends would never permit him any peace, and their diminutive size and pseudo-human intelligence made them infernally troublesome as enemies. Yet, neither that reflection nor the loony's suicide troubled him particularly; he had witnessed instances like the latter too often, and besides, his head felt as if he were in for another siege of white fever.

He entered the shack, closed the door, and stared down at his pet parcat. "Oliver," he growled, "You're a fine one. Why the devil don't you watch out for slinkers? What are you here for?"

The parcat rose on its single, powerful hind leg, clawing at his knees with its two forelegs. "The red jack on the black queen," it observed placidly. "Ten loonies make one half-wit."

Grant placed both statements easily. The first was, of course, an echo of his preceding evening's solitaire game, and the second of yesterday's session with the loonies. He grunted abstractedly and rubbed his aching head. White fever again, beyond doubt.

He swallowed two ferverin tablets, and sank listlessly to the edge of his bunk, wondering whether this attack of *blancha* would culminate in delirium.

He cursed himself for a fool for ever taking this job on Jupiter's third habitable moon, Io. The tiny world was a planet of madness, good for nothing except the production of ferva leaves, out of which Earthly chemists made as many potent alkaloids as they once made from opium.

Invaluable to medical science, of course, but what difference did that make to him? What difference, even, did the munificent salary make, if he got back to Earth a raving maniac after a year in the equatorial regions of Io? He swore bitterly that when the plane from Junopolis landed next month for his ferva, he'd go back to the polar city with it, even though his contract with Neilan Drug called for a full year, and he'd get no pay if he broke it. What good was money to a lunatic?

The whole little planet was mad—loonies, parcats, slinkers and

215

Grant Calthorpe—all crazy. At least, anybody who ever ventured outside either of the two polar cities, Junopolis on the north and Herapolis on the south, was crazy. One could live there in safety from white fever, but anywhere below the twentieth parallel it was worse than the Cambodian jungles on Earth.

He amused himself by dreaming of Earth. Just two years ago he had been happy there, known as a wealthy, popular sportsman. He had been just that too; before he was twenty-one he had hunted knife-kite and threadworm on Titan, and triops and uniped on Venus.

That had been before the gold crisis of 2110 had wiped out his fortune. And—well, if he had to work, it had seemed logical to use his interplanetary experience as a means of livelihood. He had really been enthusiastic at the chance to associate himself with Neilan Drug.

He had never been on Io before. This wild little world was no sportsman's paradise, with its idiotic loonies and wicked, intelligent, tiny slinkers. There wasn't anything worth hunting on the feverish little moon, bathed in warmth by the giant Jupiter only a quarter million miles away.

If he had happened to visit it, he told himself ruefully, he'd never have taken the job; he had visualized Io as something like Titan, cold but clean.

Instead it was as hot as the Venus Hotlands because of its glowing primary, and subject to half a dozen different forms of steamy daylight—sun day, Jovian day, Jovian and sun day, Europa light, and occasionally actual and dismal night. And most of these came in the course of Io's forty-two-hour revolution, too—a mad succession of changing lights. He hated the dizzy days, the jungle, and Idiots' Hills stretching behind his shack.

It was Jovian and solar day at the present moment, and that was the worst of all, because the distant sun added its modicum of heat to that of Jupiter. And to complete Grant's discomfort now was the prospect of a white fever attack. He swore as his head gave an additional twinge, and then swallowed another ferverin tablet. His supply of these was diminishing, he noticed; he'd have to remember to ask for some when the plane called—no, he was going back with it.

Oliver rubbed against his leg. "Idiots, fools, nitwits, imbeciles," remarked the parcat affectionately. "Why did I have to go to that damn dance?"

"Huh?" said Grant. He couldn't remember having said anything about a dance. It must, he decided, have been said during his last fever madness.

Oliver creaked like the door, then giggled like a loony. "It'll be all right," he assured Grant. "Father is bound to come soon."

"Father!" echoed the man. His father had died fifteen years before. "Where'd you get that from, Oliver?"

"It must be the fever," observed Oliver placidly. "You're a nice kitty, but I wish you had sense enough to know what you're saying. And I wish father would come." He finished with a suppressed gurgle that might have been a sob.

Grant stared dizzily at him. He hadn't said any of those things; he was positive. The parcat must have heard them from somebody else—Somebody else? Where within five hundred miles was there anybody else?

"Oliver!" he bellowed. "Where'd you hear that? Where'd you hear it?"

The parcat backed away, startled. "Father is idiots, fools, nitwits, imbeciles," he said anxiously. "The red jack on the nice kitty."

"Come here!" roared Grant. "Whose father? Where have you— Come here, you imp!"

He lunged at the creature. Oliver flexed his single hind leg and flung himself frantically to the cowl of the wood stove. "It must be the fever!" he squalled. "No chocolate!"

He leaped like a three-legged flash for the flue opening. There came a sound of claws grating on metal, and then he had scrambled through.

Grant followed him. His head ached from the effort, and with the still sane part of his mind he knew that the whole episode was doubtless white fever delirium, but he plowed on.

His progress was a nightmare. Loonies kept bobbing their long necks above the tall bleeding-grass, their idiotic giggles and imbecilic faces adding to the general atmosphere of madness.

Wisps of fetid, fever-bearing vapors spouted up at every step on the spongy soil. Somewhere to his right a slinker squeaked and gibbered; he knew that a tiny slinker village was over in that direction, for once he had glimpsed the neat little buildings, constructed of small, perfectly fitted stones like a miniature medieval town, complete to towers and battlements. It was said that there were even slinker wars.

His head buzzed and whirled from the combined effects of ferverin and fever. It was an attack of *blancha*, right enough, and he realized that he was an imbecile, a loony, to wander thus away from his shack. He should be lying on his bunk; the fever was not serious, but more than one man had died on Io, in the delirium, with its attendant hallucinations.

He was delirious now. He knew it as soon as he saw Oliver, for Oliver was placidly regarding an attractive young lady in perfect evening dress of the style of the second decade of the twenty-second century. Very obviously that was a hallucination, since girls had no business in the Ionian tropics, and if by some wild chance one should appear there, she would certainly not choose formal garb.

The hallucination had fever, apparently, for her face was pale with the whiteness that gave *blancha* its name. Her gray eyes regarded him without surprise as he wound his way through the bleeding-grass to her.

"Good afternoon, evening, or morning," he remarked, giving a puzzled glance at Jupiter, which was rising, and the sun, which was setting. "Or perhaps merely good day, Miss Lee Neilan."

She gazed seriously at him. "Do you know," she said, "you're the first one of the illusions that I haven't recognized? All my friends have been around, but you're the first stranger. Or are you a stranger? You know my name—but you ought to, of course, being my own hallucination."

"We won't argue about which of us is the hallucination," he suggested. "Let's do it this way. The one of us that disappears first is the illusion. Bet you five dollars you do."

"How could I collect?" she said. "I can't very well collect from my own dream."

"That is a problem." He frowned. "My problem, of course, not yours. I know I'm real."

"How do you know my name?" she demanded.

"Ah!" he said. "From intensive reading of the society sections of

218

the newspapers brought by my supply plane. As a matter of fact, I have one of your pictures cut out and pasted next to my bunk. That probably accounts for my seeing you now. I'd like to really meet you some time."

"What a gallant remark for an apparition!" she exclaimed. "And who are you supposed to be?"

"Why, I'm Grant Calthorpe. In fact, I work for your father, trading with the loonies for ferva."

"Grant Calthorpe," she echoed. She narrowed her fever-dulled eyes as if to bring him into better focus. "Why, you are!"

Her voice wavered for a moment, and she brushed her hand across her pale brow. "Why should you pop out of my memories? It's strange. Three or four years ago, when I was a romantic schoolgirl and you the famous sportsman, I was madly in love with you. I had a whole book filled with your pictures—Grant Calthorpe dressed in parka for hunting threadworms on Titan—Grant Calthorpe beside the giant uniped he killed near the Mountains of Eternity. You're—you're really the pleasantest hallucination I've had so far. Delirium would be—fun"—she pressed her hand to her brow again—"if one's head—didn't ache so!"

"Gee!" thought Grant, "I wish that were true, that about the book. This is what psychology calls a wish-fulfillment dream." A drop of warm rain plopped on his neck. "Got to get to bed," he said aloud. "Rain's bad for *blancha.* Hope to see you next time I'm feverish."

"Thank you," said Lee Neilan with dignity. "It's quite mutual."

He nodded, sending a twinge through his head. "Here, Oliver," he said to the drowsing parcat. "Come on."

"That isn't Oliver," said Lee. "It's Polly. It's kept me company for two days, and I've named it Polly."

"Wrong gender," muttered Grant. "Anyway, it's my parcat, Oliver. Aren't you Oliver?"

"Hope to see you," said Oliver sleepily.

"It's Polly. Aren't you, Polly?"

"Bet you five dollars," said the parcat. He rose, stretched and loped off into the underbrush. "It must be the fever," he observed as he vanished.

"It must be," agreed Grant. He turned away. "Goodby, Miss—or I might as well call you Lee, since you're not real. Goodby, Lee."

"Goodby, Grant. But don't go that way. There's a slinker village over in the grass."

"No. It's over there."

"It's there," she insisted. "I've been watching them build it. But they can't hurt you anyway, can they? Not even a slinker could hurt an apparition. Goodby, Grant." She closed her eyes wearily.

It was raining harder now. Grant pushed his way through the bleeding-grass, whose red sap collected in bloody drops on his boots. He had to get back to his shack quickly, before the white fever and its attendant delirium set him wandering utterly astray. He needed ferverin.

Suddenly he stopped short. Directly before him the grass had been cleared away, and in the little clearing were the shoulder-high towers and battlements of a slinker village—a new one, for half-finished houses stood among the others, and hooded six-inch forms toiled over the stones.

There was an outcry of squeaks and gibberish. He backed away, but a dozen tiny darts whizzed about him. One stuck like a tooth-pick in his boot, but none, luckily, scratched his skin, for they were undoubtedly poisoned. He moved more quickly, but all around in the thick, fleshy grasses were rustlings, squeakings, and incomprehensible imprecations.

He circled away. Loonies kept popping their balloon heads over the vegetation, and now and again one giggled in pain as a slinker bit or stabbed it. Grant cut toward a group of the creatures, hoping to distract the tiny fiends in the grass, and a tall, purple-faced loony curved its long neck above him, giggling and gesturing with its skinny fingers at a bundle under its arm.

He ignored the thing, and veered toward his shack. He seemed to have eluded the slinkers, so he trudged doggedly on, for he need-ed a ferverin tablet badly. Yet, suddenly he came to a frowning halt, turned, and began to retrace his steps.

"It can't be so," he muttered. "But she told me the truth about the slinker village. I didn't know it was there. Yet how could a hal-lucination tell me something I didn't know?"

Lee Neilan was sitting on the stonebark log exactly as he had left her with Oliver again at her side. Her eyes were closed, and two slinkers were cutting at the long skirt of her gown with tiny, glittering knives.

Grant knew that they were always attracted by Terrestrial textiles; apparently they were unable to duplicate the fascinating sheen of satin, though the fiends were infernally clever with their tiny hands. As he approached, they tore a strip from thigh to ankle, but the girl made no move. Grant shouted, and the vicious little creatures mouthed unutterable curses at him, as they skittered away with their silken plunder.

Lee Neilan opened her eyes. "You again," she murmured vaguely. "A moment ago it was father. Now it's you." Her pallor had increased; the white fever was running its course in her body.

"Your father! Then that's where Oliver heard—Listen, Lee. I found the slinker village. I didn't know it was there, but I found it just as you said. Do you see what that means? We're both real!"

"Real?" she said dully. "There's a purple loony grinning over your shoulder. Make him go away. He makes me feel—sick."

He glanced around; true enough, the purple-faced loony was behind him. "Look here," he said, seizing her arm. The feel of her smooth skin was added proof. "You're coming to the shack for ferverin." He pulled her to her feet. "Don't you understand? I'm real!"

"No, you're not," she said dazedly.

"Listen, Lee. I don't know how in the devil you got here or why, but I know Io hasn't driven me that crazy yet. You're real and I'm real." He shook her violently. "I'm real!" he shouted.

Faint comprehension showed in her dazed eyes. "Real?" she whispered. "Real! Oh, Lord! Then take me out of this mad place!" She swayed, made a stubborn effort to control herself, then pitched forward against him.

Of course on Io her weight was negligible, less than a third Earth normal. He swung her into his arms and set off toward the shack, keeping well away from both slinker settlements. Around him bobbed excited loonies, and now and again the purple-faced one, or another exactly like him, giggled and pointed and gestured.

The rain had increased, and warm rivulets flowed down his neck, and to add to the madness, he blundered near a copse of stinging palms, and their barbed lashes stung painfully through his shirt. Those stings were virulent too, if one failed to disinfect them; indeed, it was largely the stinging palms that kept traders from gathering their own ferva instead of depending on the loonies.

Behind the low rain clouds, the sun had set and it was ruddy Jupiter daylight, which lent a false flush to the cheeks of the unconscious Lee Neilan, making her still features very lovely.

Perhaps he kept his eyes too steadily on her face, for suddenly Grant was among slinkers again; they were squeaking and sputtering, and the purple loony leaped in pain as teeth and darts pricked his legs. But, of course, loonies were immune to the poison.

The tiny devils were around his feet now. He swore in a low voice and kicked vigorously, sending a ratlike form spinning fifty feet in the air. He had both automatic and flame pistol at his hip, but he could not use them for several reasons.

First, using an automatic against the tiny hordes was much like firing into a swarm of mosquitoes; if the bullet killed one or two or a dozen, it made no appreciable impression on the remaining thousands. And as for the flame pistol, that was like using a Big Bertha to swat a fly. Its vast belch of fire would certainly incinerate all the slinkers in its immediate path, along with grass, trees, and loonies, but that again would make but little impress on the surviving hordes, and it meant laboriously recharging the pistol with another black diamond and another barrel.

He had gas bulbs in the shack, but they were not available at the moment, and besides, he had no spare mask, and no chemist has yet succeeded in devising a gas that would kill slinkers without being also deadly to humans. And, finally, he couldn't use any weapon whatsoever right now, because he dared not drop Lee Neilan to free his hands.

Ahead was the clearing around the shack. The space was full of slinkers, but the shack itself was supposed to be slinker-proof, at least for reasonable lengths of time, since stone-bark logs were very resistant to their tiny tools.

But Grant perceived that a group of the diminutive devils were around the door, and suddenly he realized their intent. They had looped a cord of some sort over the knob, and were engaged now in twisting it!

Grant yelled and broke into a run. While he was yet half a hundred feet distant, the door swung inward and the rabble of slinkers flowed into the shack.

He dashed through the entrance. Within was turmoil. Little

hooded shapes were cutting at the blankets on his bunk, his extra clothing, the sacks he hoped to fill with ferva leaves, and were pulling at the cooking utensils, or at any and all loose objects.

He bellowed and kicked at the swarm. A wild chorus of squeaks and gibberish arose as the creatures skipped and dodged about him. The fiends were intelligent enough to realize that he could do nothing with his arms occupied by Lee Neilan. They skittered out of the way of his kicks, and while he threatened a group at the stove, another rabble tore at his blankets.

In desperation he charged at the bunk. He swept the girl's body across it to clear it, dropped her on it, and seized a grass broom he had made to facilitate his housekeeping. With wide strokes of its handle he attacked the slinkers, and the squeals were checkered by cries and whimpers of pain.

A few broke for the door, dragging whatever loot they had. He spun around in time to see half a dozen swarming around Lee Neilan, tearing at her clothing, at the wrist watch on her arm, at the satin evening pumps on her small feet. He roared a curse at them and battered them away, hoping that none had pricked her skin with virulent dagger or poisonous tooth.

He began to win the skirmish. More of the creatures drew their black capes close about them and scurried over the threshold with their plunder. At last, with a burst of squeaks, the remainder, laden and empty-handed alike, broke and ran for safety, leaving a dozen furry, impish bodies slain or wounded.

Grant swept these after the others with his erstwhile weapon, closed the door in the face of a loony that bobbed in the opening, latched it against any repetition of the slinker's trick, and stared in dismay about the plundered dwelling.

Cans had been rolled or dragged away. Every loose object had been pawed by the slinkers' foul little hands, and Grant's clothes hung in ruins on their hooks against the wall. But the tiny robbers had not succeeded in opening the cabinet nor the table drawer, and there was food left.

Six months of Ionian life had left him philosophical; he swore heartily, shrugged resignedly, and pulled his bottle of ferverin from the cabinet.

His own spell of fever had vanished as suddenly and completely as *blancha* always does when treated, but the girl, lacking ferverin, was paper-white and still. Grant glanced at the bottle; eight tablets remained.

"Well, I can always chew ferva leaves," he muttered. That was less effective than the alkaloid itself, but it would serve, and Lee Neilan needed the tablets. He dissolved two of them in a glass of water, and lifted her head.

She was not too inert to swallow, and he poured the solution between her pale lips, then arranged her as comfortably as he could. Her dress was a tattered silken ruin, and he covered her with a blanket that was no less a ruin. Then he disinfected his palm stings, pulled two chairs together, and sprawled across them to sleep.

He started up at the sound of claws on the roof, but it was only Oliver, gingerly testing the flue to see if it were hot. In a moment the parcat scrambled through, stretched himself, and remarked, "I'm real and you're real."

"Imagine that!" grunted Grant sleepily.

When he awoke it was Jupiter and Europa light, which meant he had slept about seven hours, since the brilliant little third moon was just rising. He rose and gazed at Lee Neilan, who was sleeping soundly with a tinge of color in her face that was not entirely due to the ruddy daylight. The blancha was passing.

He dissolved two more tablets in water, then shook the girl's shoulder. Instantly her gray eyes opened, quite clear now, and she looked up at him without surprise.

"Hello, Grant," she murmured. "So it's you again. Fever isn't so bad, after all."

"Maybe I ought to let you stay feverish," he grinned. "You say such nice things. Wake up and drink this, Lee."

She became suddenly aware of the shack's interior. "Why— Where is this? It looks—real!"

"It is. Drink this ferverin."

She obeyed, then lay back and stared at him perplexedly. "Real?" she said. "And you're real?"

"I think I am."

A rush of tears clouded her eyes. "Then—I'm out of that place? That horrible place?"

"You certainly are." He saw signs of her relief becoming hysteria, and hastened to distract her. "Would you mind telling me how you happened to be there—and dressed for a party too?"

She controlled herself. "I was dressed for a party. A party. A party in Herapolis. But I was in Junopolis, you see."

"I don't see. In the first place, what are you doing on Io, anyway? Every time I ever heard of you, it was in connection with New York or Paris society."

She smiled. "Then it wasn't all delirium, was it? You did say that you had one of my pictures—Oh, that one!" She frowned at the print on the wall. "Next time a news photographer wants to snap my picture, I'll remember not to grin like—like a loony. But as to how I happen to be on Io, I came with father, who's looking over the possibilities of raising ferva on plantations instead of having to depend on traders and loonies. We've been here three months, and I've been terribly bored. I thought Io would be exciting, but it wasn't—until recently."

"But what about that dance? How'd you manage to get here, a thousand miles from Junopolis?"

"Well," she said slowly, "It was terribly tiresome in Junopolis. No shows, no sport, nothing but an occasional dance. I got restless. When there were dances in Herapolis, I formed the habit of flying over there. It's only four or five hours in a fast plane, you know. And last week—or whatever it was—I'd planned on flying down, and Harvey—that's father's secretary—was to take me. But at the last minute father needed him and forbade my flying alone."

Grant felt a strong dislike for Harvey. "Well?" he asked.

"So I flew alone," she finished demurely.

"And cracked up, eh?"

"I can fly as well as anybody," she retorted. "It was just that I followed a different route, and suddenly there were mountains ahead."

He nodded. "The Idiots' Hills," he said. "My supply plane detours five hundred miles to avoid them. They're not high, but they stick right out above the atmosphere of this crazy planet. The air here is dense but shallow."

"I know that. I knew I couldn't fly above them, but I thought I could hurdle them. Work up full speed, you know, and then throw the plane upward. I had a closed plane, and gravitation is so weak here. And besides, I've seen it done several times, especially with a rocket-driven craft. The jets help to support the plane even after the wings are useless for lack of air."

"What a damn fool stunt!" exclaimed Grant. "Sure it can be done, but you have to be an expert to pull out of it when you hit the air on the other side. You hit fast, and there isn't much falling room."

"So I found out," said Lee ruefully, "I almost pulled out, but not quite, and I hit in the middle of some stinging palms. I guess the crash dazed them, because I managed to get out before they started lashing around. But I couldn't reach my plane again, and it was—I only remember two days of it—but it was horrible!"

"It must have been," he said gently.

"I knew that if I didn't eat or drink, I had a chance of avoiding white fever. The not eating wasn't so bad, but the not drinking—well, I finally gave up and drank out of a brook. I didn't care what happened if I could have a few moments that weren't thirst-tortured. And after that it's all confused and vague."

"You should have chewed ferva leaves."

"I didn't know that. I wouldn't have even known what they looked like, and besides, I kept expecting father to appear. He must be having a search made by now."

"He probably is," rejoined Grant ironically. "Has it occurred to you that there are thirteen million square miles of surface on little Io? And that for all he knows, you might have crashed on any square mile of it? When you're flying from north pole to south pole, there isn't any shortest route. You can cross any point on the planet."

Her gray eyes started wide. "But I—"

"Furthermore," said Grant, "this is probably the last place a searching party would look. They wouldn't think any one but a loony would try to hurdle Idiots' Hills, in which thesis I quite agree. So it looks very much, Lee Neilan, as if you're marooned here until my supply plane gets here next month!"

"But father will be crazy! He'll think I'm dead!"

"He thinks that now, no doubt."

"But we can't—" She broke off, staring around the tiny shack's single room. After a moment she sighed resignedly, smiled, and said softly, "Well, it might have been worse, Grant. I'll try to earn my keep."

"Good. How do you feel, Lee?"

"Quite normal. I'll start right to work." She flung off the tattered blanket, sat up, and dropped her feet to the floor. "I'll fix dinn—Goodness! My dress!" She snatched the blanket about her again.

He grinned. "We had a little run-in with the slinkers after you had passed out. They did for my spare wardrobe too."

"It's ruined!" she wailed.

"Would needle and thread help? They left that, at least, because it was in the table drawer."

"Why, I couldn't make a good swimming suit out of this!" she retorted. "Let me try one of yours."

By dint of cutting, patching, and mending, she at last managed to piece one of Grant's suits to respectable proportions. She looked very lovely in shirt and trousers, but he was troubled to note that a sudden pallor had overtaken her.

It was the *riblancha*, the second spell of fever that usually followed a severe or prolonged attack. His face was serious as he cupped two of his last four ferverin tablets in his hand.

"Take these," he ordered. "And we've got to get some ferva leaves somewhere. The plane took my supply away last week, and I've had bad luck with my loonies ever since. They haven't brought me anything but weeds and rubbish."

Lee puckered her lips at the bitterness of the drug, then closed her eyes against its momentary dizziness and nausea. "Where can you find ferva?" she asked.

He shook his head perplexedly, glancing out at the setting mass of Jupiter, with its bands glowing creamy and brown, and the Red Spot boiling near the western edge. Close above it was the brilliant little disk of Europa. He frowned suddenly, glanced at his watch and then at the almanac on the inside of the cabinet door.

"It'll be Europa light in fifteen minutes," he muttered, "and true night in twenty-five—the first true night in half a month. I wonder—"

He gazed thoughtfully at Lee's face. He knew where ferva grew. One dared not penetrate the jungle itself, where stinging palms and arrow vines and the deadly worms called toothers made such a venture sheer suicide for any creatures but loonies and slinkers. But he knew where ferva grew—

In Io's rare true night even the clearing might be dangerous.

227

Not merely from slinkers, either; he knew well enough that in the darkness creatures crept out of the jungle who otherwise remained in the eternal shadows of its depths—toothers, bullet-head frogs, and doubtless many unknown slimy, venomous, mysterious beings never seen by man. One heard stories in Herapolis and—

But he had to get ferva, and he knew where it grew. Not even a loony would try to gather it there, but in the little gardens or farms around the tiny slinker towns, there was ferva growing.

He switched on a light in the gathering dusk. "I'm going outside a moment," he told Lee Neilan. "If the *blancha* starts coming back, take the other two tablets. Wouldn't hurt you to take 'em anyway. The slinkers got away with my thermometer, but if you get dizzy again, you take 'em."

"Grant! Where—"

"I'll be back," he called, closing the door behind him.

A loony, purple in the bluish Europa light, bobbed up with a long giggle. He waved the creature aside and set off on a cautious approach to the neighborhood of the slinker village—the old one, for the other could hardly have had time to cultivate its surrounding ground. He crept warily through the bleeding-grass, but he knew his stealth was pure optimism. He was in exactly the position of a hundred-foot giant trying to approach a human city in secrecy—a difficult matter even in the utter darkness of night.

He reached the edge of the slinker clearing. Behind him, Europa, moving as fast as the second hand on his watch, plummeted toward the horizon. He paused in momentary surprise at the sight of the exquisite little town, a hundred feet away across the tiny square fields, with lights flickering in its hand-wide windows. He had not known that slinker culture included the use of lights, but there they were, tiny candles or perhaps diminutive oil lamps.

He blinked in the darkness. The second of the ten-foot fields looked like—it was—ferva. He stooped low, crept out, and reached his hand for the fleshy, white leaves. And at that moment came a shrill giggle and the crackle of grass behind him. The loony! The idiotic purple loony!

Squeaking shrieks sounded. He snatched a double handful of ferva, rose, and dashed toward the lighted window of his shack. He had no wish to face poisoned barbs or disease-bearing teeth, and the slinkers were certainly aroused. Their gibbering sounded in chorus; the ground looked black with them.

He reached the shack, burst in, slammed and latched the door. "Got it!" He grinned. "Let 'em rave outside now."

They were raving. Their gibberish sounded like the creaking of worn machinery. Even Oliver opened his drowsy eyes to listen. "It must be the fever," observed the parcat placidly. Lee was certainly no paler; the *riblancha* was passing safely. "Ugh!" she said, listening to the tumult without. "I've always hated rats, but slinkers are worse. All the shrewdness and viciousness of rats plus the intelligence of devils."

"Well," said Grant thoughtfully, "I don't see what they can do. They've had it in for me anyway."

"It sounds as if they're going off," said the girl, listening. "The noise is fading."

Grant peered out of the window. "They're still around. They've just passed from swearing to planning, and I wish I knew what. Some day, if this crazy little planet ever becomes worth human occupation, there's going to be a showdown between humans and slinkers."

"Well? They're not civilized enough to be really a serious obstacle, and they're so small, besides."

"But they learn," he said. "They learn so quickly, and they breed like flies. Suppose they pick up the use of gas, or suppose they develop little rifles for their poisonous darts. That's possible, because they work in metals right now, and they know fire. That would put them practically on a par with man as far as offense goes, for what good are our giant cannons and rocket planes against six-inch slinkers? And to be just on even terms would be fatal; one slinker for one man would be a hell of a trade."

Lee yawned. "Well, it's not our problem. I'm hungry, Grant."

"Good. That's a sign the *blancha's* through with you. We'll eat and then sleep a while, for there's five hours of darkness."

"But the slinkers?"

"I don't see what they can do. They couldn't cut through stonebark walls in five hours, and anyway, Oliver would warn us if one managed to slip in somewhere."

It was light when Grant awoke, and he stretched his cramped limbs painfully across his two chairs. Something had wakened him, but he didn't know just what. Oliver was pacing nervously beside him, and now looked anxiously up at him.

"I've had bad luck with my loonies," announced the parcat plaintively.

"You're a nice kitty."

"So are you," said Grant. Something had wakened him, but what? Then he knew, for it came again—the merest trembling of the stone-bark floor. He frowned in puzzlement. Earthquakes? Not on Io, for the tiny sphere had lost its internal heat untold ages ago. Then what?

Comprehension dawned suddenly. He sprang to his feet with so wild a yell that Oliver scrambled sideways with an infernal babble. The startled parcat leaped to the stove and vanished up the flue. His squall drifted faintly back.

"It must be the fever!"

Lee had started to a sitting position on the bunk, her gray eyes blinking sleepily.

"Outside!" he roared, pulling her to her feet. "Get out! Quickly!"

"Wh-what—why—"

"Get out!" He thrust her through the door, then spun to seize his belt and weapons, the bag of ferva leaves, a package of chocolate. The floor trembled again, and he burst out of the door with a frantic leap to the side of the dazed girl.

"They've undermined it!" he choked. "The devils undermined the—"

He had no time to say more. A corner of the shack suddenly subsided; the stone-bark logs grated, and the whole structure collapsed like a child's house of blocks. The crash died into silence, and there was no motion save a lazy wisp of vapor, a few black, ratlike forms scurrying toward the grass, and a purple loony bobbing beyond the ruins.

"The dirty devils!" he swore bitterly. "The damn little black rats! The—"

A dart whistled so close that it grazed his ear and then twitched a lock of Lee's tousled brown hair. A chorus of squeaking sounded in the bleeding-grass.

"Come on!" he cried. "They're out to exterminate us this time. No—this way. Toward the hills. There's less jungle this way."

They could outrun the tiny slinkers easily enough. In a few moments they had lost the sound of squeaking voices, and they stopped to gaze ruefully back on the fallen dwelling.

"Now," he said miserably, "we're both where you were to start with."

"Oh, no." Lee looked up at him. "We're together now, Grant. I'm not afraid."

"We'll manage," he said with a show of assurance. "We'll put up a temporary shack somehow. We'll—"

A dart struck his boot with a sharp blup. The slinkers had caught up to them.

Again they ran toward Idiots' Hills. When at last they stopped, they could look down a long slope and far over the Ionian jungles. There was the ruined shack, and there, neatly checkered, the fields and towers of the nearer slinker town. But they had scarcely caught their breath when gibbering and squeaking came out of the brush.

They were being driven into Idiots' Hills, a region as unknown to man as the icy wastes of Pluto. It was as if the tiny fiends behind them had determined that this time their enemy, the giant trampler and despoiler of their fields, should be pursued to extinction.

Weapons were useless. Grant could not even glimpse their pursuers, slipping like hooded rats through the vegetation. A bullet, even if chance sped it through a slinker's body, was futile, and his flame pistol, though its lightning stroke should incinerate tons of brush and bleeding-grass, could no more than cut a narrow path through the horde of tormentors. The only weapons that might have availed, the gas bulbs, were lost in the ruins of the shack.

Grant and Lee were forced upward. They had risen a thousand feet above the plain, and the air was thinning. There was no jungle here, but only great stretches of bleeding-grass, across which a few loonies were visible, bobbing their heads on their long necks.

"Toward—the peaks!" gasped Grant, now painfully short of breath. "Perhaps we can stand rarer air than they."

Lee was beyond answer. She panted doggedly along beside him as they plodded now over patches of bare rock. Before them were two low peaks, like the pillars of a gate. Glancing back, Grant caught a glimpse of tiny black forms on a clear area, and in sheer anger he fired a shot. A single slinker leaped convulsively, its cape flapping, but the rest flowed on. There must have been thousands of them.

The peaks were closer, no more than a few hundred yards away. They were sheer, smooth, unscalable.

"Between them," muttered Grant.

The passage that separated them was bare and narrow. The twin peaks had been one in ages past; some forgotten volcanic convulsion had split them, leaving this slender canyon between.

He slipped an arm about Lee, whose breath, from effort and altitude, was a series of rasping gasps. A bright dart tinkled on the rocks as they reached the opening, but looking back, Grant could see only a purple loony plodding upward, and a few more to his right. They raced down a straight fifty-foot passage that debouched suddenly into a sizeable valley—and there, thunderstruck for a moment, they paused.

A city lay there. For a brief instant Grant thought they had burst upon a vast slinker metropolis, but the merest glance showed otherwise. This was no city of medieval blocks, but a poem in marble, classical in beauty, and of human or near-human proportions. White columns, glorious arches, pure curving domes, an architectural loveliness that might have been born on the Acropolis. It took a second look to discern that the city was dead, deserted, in ruins.

Even in her exhaustion, Lee felt its beauty. "How—how exquisite!" she panted. "One could almost forgive them—for being—slinkers!"

"They won't forgive us for being human," he muttered. "We'll have to make a stand somewhere. We'd better pick a building."

But before they could move more than a few feet from the canyon mouth, a wild disturbance halted them. Grant whirled, and for a moment found himself actually paralyzed by amazement. The narrow canyon was filled with a gibbering horde of slinkers, like a nauseous, heaving black carpet. But they came no further than the valley end, for grinning, giggling, and bobbing, blocking the opening with tramping three-toed feet, were four loonies!

It was a battle. The slinkers were biting and stabbing at the miserable defenders, whose shrill keenings of pain were less giggles than shrieks. But with a determination and purpose utterly foreign to loonies, their clawed feet tramped methodically up and down, up and down.

Grant exploded, "I'll be damned!" Then an idea struck him. "Lee! They're packed in the canyon, the whole devil's brood of 'em!"

He rushed toward the opening. He thrust his flame pistol between the skinny legs of a loony, aimed it straight along the canyon, and fired.

Inferno burst. The tiny diamond, giving up all its energy in one terrific blast, shot a jagged stream of fire that filled the canyon from wall to wall and vomited out beyond to cut a fan of fire through the bleeding-grass of the slope.

Idiot's Hills reverberated to the roar, and when the rain of debris settled, there was nothing in the canyon save a few bits of flesh and the head of an unfortunate loony, still bouncing and rolling.

Three of the loonies survived. A purple-faced one was pulling his arm, grinning and giggling in imbecile glee. He waved the thing aside and returned to the girl.

"Thank goodness!" he said. "We're out of that, anyway."

"I wasn't afraid, Grant. Not with you."

He smiled. "Perhaps we can find a place here," he suggested. "The fever ought to be less troublesome at this altitude. But—say, this must have been the capital city of the whole slinker race in ancient times. I can scarcely imagine those fiends creating an architecture as beautiful as this—or as large. Why, these buildings are as colossal in proportion to slinker size as the skyscrapers of New York to us!"

"But so beautiful," said Lee softly, sweeping her eyes over the glory of the ruins. "One might almost forgive—Grant! Look at those!"

He followed the gesture. On the inner side of the canyon's portals were gigantic carvings. But the thing that set him staring in amazement was the subject of the portrayal. There, towering far up the cliff sides, were the figures, not of slinkers, but of—loonies! Exquisitely carved, smiling rather than grinning, and smiling somehow sadly, regretfully, pityingly—yet beyond doubt, loonies!

"Goodness!" he whispered. "Do you see, Lee? This must once have been a loony city. The steps, the doors, the buildings, all are on their scale of size. Somehow, some time, they must have achieved civilization, and the loonies we know are the degenerate residue of a great race."

"And," put in Lee, "the reason those four blocked the way when the slinkers tried to come through is that they still remember. Or probably they don't actually remember, but they have a tradition of past glories, or more likely still, just a superstitious feeling that this place is in some way sacred. They let us pass because, after all, we look more like loonies than like slinkers. But the amazing thing is that they still possess even that dim memory, because this city must have been in ruins for centuries. Or perhaps even for thousands of years."

"But to think that loonies could ever have had the intelligence to create a culture of their own," said Grant, waving away the purple one bobbing and giggling at his side. Suddenly he paused, turning a gaze of new respect on the creature. "This one's been following me for days. All right, old chap, what is it?"

The purple one extended a sorely bedraggled bundle of bleeding-grass and twigs, giggling idiotically. His ridiculous mouth twisted; his eyes popped in an agony of effort at mental concentration.

"Canny!" he giggled triumphantly.

"The imbecile!" flared Grant. "Nitwit! Idiot!" He broke off, then laughed. "Never mind. I guess you deserve it." He tossed his package of chocolate to the three delighted loonies. "Here's your candy."

A scream from Lee startled him. She was waving her arms wildly, and over the crest of Idiots' Hills a rocket plane roared, circled, and nosed its way into the valley.

The door opened. Oliver stalked gravely out, remarking casually. "I'm real and you're real." A man followed the parcat—two men.

"Father!" screamed Lee.

It was some time later that Gustavus Neilan turned to Grant. "I can't thank you," he said. "If there's ever any way I can show my appreciation for—"

"There is. You can cancel my contract."

"Oh, you work for me?"

"I'm Grant Calthorpe, one of your traders, and I'm about sick of this crazy planet."

"Of course, if you wish," said Neilan. "If it's a question of pay—"

"You can pay me for the six months I've worked."

"If you'd care to stay," said the older man, "there won't be trading much longer. We've been able to grow ferva near the polar cities, and I prefer plantations to the uncertainties of relying on loonies. If you'd work out your year, we might be able to put you in charge of a plantation by the end of that time."

Grant met Lee Neilan's gray eyes, and hesitated. "Thanks," he said slowly, "but I'm sick of it." He smiled at the girl, then turned back to her father. "Would you mind telling me how you happened to find us? This is the most unlikely place on the planet."

"That's just the reason," said Neilan. "When Lee didn't get back, I thought things over pretty carefully. At last I decided, knowing her as I did, to search the least likely places first. We tried the shores of the Fever Sea, and then the White Desert, and finally Idiots' Hills. We spotted the ruins of a shack, and on the debris was this chap"—he indicated Oliver—"remarking that 'Ten loonies make one half-wit.' Well, the half-wit part sounded very much like a reference to my daughter, and we cruised about until the roar of your flame pistol attracted our attention."

Lee pouted, then turned her serious gray eyes on Grant. "Do you remember," she said softly, "what I told you there in the jungle?"

"I wouldn't even have mentioned that," he replied. "I knew you were delirious."

"But—perhaps I wasn't. Would companionship make it any easier to work out your year? I mean if—for instance—you were to fly back with us to Junapolis and return with a wife?"

"Lee," he said huskily, "you know what a difference that would make, though I can't understand why you'd ever dream of it."

"It must," suggested Oliver, "be the fever."

235

Redemption Cairn

Have you ever been flat broke, hungry as the very devil, and yet so down and out that you didn't even care? Looking back now, after a couple of months, it's hard to put it into words, but I think the low point was the evening old Captain Harris Henshaw dropped into my room—my room, that is, until the twenty-four-hour notice to move or pay up expired.

There I sat, Jack Sands, ex-rocket pilot. Yeah, the same Jack Sands you're thinking of, the one who cracked up the Gunderson Europa expedition trying to land at Young's Field, Long Island, in March, 2110. Just a year and a half ago! It seemed like ten and a half. Five hundred idle days. Eighteen months of having your friends look the other way when you happened to pass on the street, partly because they're ashamed to nod to a pilot that's been tagged yellow, and partly because they feel maybe it's kinder to just let you drop out of sight peacefully.

I didn't even look up when a knock sounded on my door, because I knew it could only be the landlady. "Haven't got it," I growled. "I've got a right to stay out my notice."

"You got a right to make a damn fool of yourself," said Henshaw's voice. "Why don't you tell your friends your address?"

"Harris!" I yelled. It was "Captain" only aboard ship. Then I caught myself. "What's the matter?" I asked, grinning bitterly. "Did you crack up, too? Coming to join me on the dust heap, eh?"

"Coming to offer you a job," he growled.

"Yeah? It must be a swell one, then. Carting sand to fill up the blast pits on a field, huh? And I'm damn near hungry enough to take it—but not quite."

"It's a piloting job," said Henshaw quietly.

"Who wants a pilot who's been smeared with yellow paint? What outfit will trust its ships to a coward? Don't you know that Jack Sands is tagged forever?"

"Shut up, Jack," he said briefly. "I'm offering you the job as pilot under me on Interplanetary's new Europa expedition."

236

I started to bum up then. You see, it was returning from Jupiter's third moon, Europa, that I'd smashed up the Gunderson outfit, and now I got a wild idea that Henshaw was taunting me about that. "By Heaven!" I screeched. "If you're trying to be funny—"

But he wasn't. I quieted down when I saw he was serious, and he went on slowly, "I want a pilot I can trust, Jack. I don't know anything about your cracking up the *Hera*; I was on the Venus run when it happened. All I know is that I can depend on you."

After a while I began to believe him. When I got over the shock a little, I figured Henshaw was friend enough to be entitled to the facts.

"Listen, Harris," I said. "You're taking me on, reputation and all, and it looks to me as if you deserve an explanation. I haven't been whining about the bump I got, and I'm not now. I cracked up Gunderson and his outfit all right, only"—I hesitated; it's kind of tough to feel that maybe you're squirming in the pinch—"only my co-pilot, that fellow Kratska, forgot to mention a few things, and mentioned a few others that weren't true. Oh, it was my shift, right enough, but he neglected to tell the investigating committee that I'd stood his shift and my own before it. I'd been on for two long shifts, and this was my short one."

"Two long ones!" echoed Henshaw. "You mean you were on sixteen hours before the landing shift?"

"That's what I mean. I'll tell you just what I told the committee, and maybe you'll believe me. They didn't. But when Kratska showed up to relieve me he was hopped. He had a regular hexy-lamine jag, and he couldn't have piloted a tricycle. So I did the only possible thing to do; I sent him back to sleep it off, and I reported it to Gunderson, but that still left me the job of getting us down.

"It wouldn't have been so bad if it had happened in space, because there isn't much for a pilot to do out there except follow the course laid out by the captain, and maybe dodge a meteor if the alarm buzzes. But I had sixteen solid hours of teetering down through a gravitational field, and by the time my four-hour spell came around I was bleary."

"I don't wonder," said the captain. "Two long shifts!"

Maybe I'd better explain a rocket's pilot system. On short runs like Venus or Mars, a vessel could carry three pilots, and then it's a simple matter of three eight-hour shifts. But on any longer run, because air and weight and fuel and food are all precious, no rocket ever carries more than two pilots.

So a day's run is divided into four shifts, and each pilot has one long spell of eight hours, then four hours off, then four hours on again for his short shift, and then eight hours to sleep. He eats two of his meals right at the control desk, and the third during his short free period. It's a queer life, and sometimes men have been co-pilots for years without really seeing each other except at the beginning and the end of their run.

I went on with my story, still wondering whether Henshaw would feel as if I were whining. "I was bleary," I repeated, "but Kratska showed up still foggy, and I didn't dare trust a hexylamine dope with the job of landing. Anyway, I'd reported to Gunderson, and that seemed to shift some of the responsibility to him. So I let Kratska sit in the control cabin, and I began to put down."

Telling the story made me mad all over. "Those lousy reporters!" I blazed. "All of them seemed to think landing a rocket is like settling down in bed; you just cushion down on your underblast. Yeah; they don't realize that you have to land blind, because three hundred feet down from the ground the blast begins to splash against it.

"You watch the leveling poles at the edge of the field and try to judge your altitude from them, but you don't see the ground; what you see under you are the flames of Hell. And another thing they don't realize: lowering a ship is like bringing down a dinner plate balanced on a fishing rod. If she starts to roll sideways—blooey! The underjets only hold you up when they're pointing down, you know."

Henshaw let me vent my temper without interruption, and I returned to my story. "Well, I was getting down as well as could be expected. The *Hera* always did have a tendency to roll a little, but she wasn't the worst ship I've put to ground.

"But every time she slid over a little, Kratska let out a yell—he was nervous from his dope jag, and he knew he was due to lose' his license, and on top of that he was just plain scared by the side roll. We got to seventy feet on the leveling poles when she gave a pretty sharp roll, and Kratska went plain daffy."

I hesitated. "I don't know exactly how to tell what happened. It went quick, and I didn't see all of it, of course. But suddenly Kratska, who had been fumbling with the air lock for ten minutes, shrieked something like 'She's going over!' and grabbed the throttle. He shut off the blast before I could lift an eyelash, shut it off and flung himself out. Yeah; he'd opened the air lock.

"Well, we were only seventy feet—less than that—above the field. We dropped like an overripe apple off a tree. I didn't have time even to move before we hit, and when we hit, all the fuel in all the jets must have let go. And for what happened after that you'd better read the newspapers."

"Not me," said Henshaw. "You spill it."

"I can't, not all of it, because I was laid out. But I can guess, all right. It seems that when the jets blew off, Kratska was just picked up in a couple of cubic yards of the soft sand he had landed in, and tossed clear. He had nothing but a broken wrist. And as for me, apparently I was shot out of the control room, and banged up considerably. And as for Gunderson, his professors, and every one else on the *Hera*—well, they were just stains on the pool of molten ferralumin that was left."

"Then how," asked Henshaw, "did they hang it on you?"

I tried to control my voice. "Kratska," I said grimly. "The field was clear for landing; nobody can stand in close with the blast splashing in a six-hundred-foot circle. Of course, they saw someone jump from the nose of the ship after the jets cut off, but how could they tell which of us? And the explosion shuffled the whole field around, and nobody knew which was what."

"Then it should have been his word against yours."

"Yeah; it should have been. But the field knew it was my shift because I'd been talking over the landing beam, and besides, Kratska got to the reporters first. I never even knew of the mess until I woke up at Grand Mercy Hospital thirteen days later. By that time Kratska had talked and I was the goat."

"But the investigating committee?"

I grunted. "Sure, the investigating committee. I'd reported to Gunderson, but he made a swell witness, being just an impurity in a mass of ferralumin alloy. And Kratska had disappeared anyway."

"Couldn't they find him?"

"Not on what I knew about him. We picked him up at Junopolis on Io, because Briggs was down with white fever. I didn't see him at all except when we were relieving each other, and you know what that's like, seeing somebody in a control cabin with the sun shields up. And on Europa we kept to space routine, so I couldn't even give you a good description of him. He had a beard, but so have ninety per cent of us after a long hop, and he said when we took him on that he'd just come over from the Earth." I paused. "I'll find him some day."

"Hope you do," said Henshaw briskly. "About this present run, now. There'll be you and me, and then there'll be Stefan Coretti, a physical chemist, and an Ivor Gogrol, a biologist. That's the scientific personnel of the expedition."

"Yeah, but who's my co-pilot? That's what interests me."

"Oh, sure," said Henshaw, and coughed. "Your co-pilot. Well, I've been meaning to tell you. It's Claire Avery."

"Claire Avery!"

"That's right," agreed the captain gloomily. "The Golden Flash herself. The only woman pilot to have her name on the Curry cup, winner of this year's Apogee race."

"She's no pilot!" I snapped. "She's a rich publicity hound with brass nerves. I was just curious enough to blow ten bucks rental on a 'scope to watch that race. She was ninth rounding the Moon. Ninth! Do you know how she won? She gunned her rocket under full acceleration practically all the way back, and then fell into a braking orbit.

"Any sophomore in Astronautics II knows that you can't calculate a braking orbit without knowing the density of the stratosphere and ionosphere, and even then its a gamble. That's what she did—simply gambled, and happened to be lucky. Why do you pick a rich moron with a taste for thrills on a job like this?"

"I didn't pick her, Jack. Interplanetary picked her for publicity purposes. To tell the truth, I think this whole expedition is an attempt to get a little favorable advertising to offset that shady stock investigation this spring. Interplanetary wants to show itself as the noble patron of exploration. So Claire Avery will take off for the television and papers, and you'll be politely ignored."

"And that suits me! I wouldn't even take the job if things were a little different, and—" I broke off suddenly, frozen. "Say," I said weakly, "did you know they'd revoked my license?"

"You don't say," said Henshaw. "And after all the trouble I had talking Interplanetary into permission to take you on, too." Then he grinned. "Here," he said, tossing me an envelope. "See how long it'll take you to lose this one."

But the very sight of the familiar blue paper was enough to make me forget a lot of things—Kratska, Claire Avery, even hunger.

The take-off was worse than I had expected. I had sense enough to wear my pilot's goggles to the field, but of course I was recognized as soon as I joined the group at the rocket. They'd given us the *Minos*, an old ship, but she looked as if she'd handle well.

The newsmen must have had orders to ignore me, but I could hear plenty of comments from the crowd. And to finish things up, there was Claire Avery, a lot prettier than she looked on the television screens, but with the same unmistakable cobalt-blue eyes, and hair closer to the actual shade of metallic gold than any I'd ever seen. The "Golden Flash," the newsmen called her. Blah!

She accepted her introduction to me with the coolest possible nod, as if to say to the scanners and cameras that it wasn't her choice she was teamed with yellow Jack Sands. But for that matter, Coretti's black Latin eyes were not especially cordial either, nor were Gogrol's broad features. I'd met Gogrol somewhere before, but couldn't place him at the moment.

Well, at last the speeches were over, and the photographers and broadcast men let the Golden Flash stop posing, and she and I got into the control cabin for the take-off. I still wore my goggles, and huddled down low besides, because there were a dozen telescopic cameras and scanners recording us from the field's edge.

Claire Avery simply ate it up, though, smiling and waving before she cut in the underblast. But finally we were rising over the flame. She was worse than I'd dreamed. The Minos was a sweetly balanced ship, but she rolled it like a baby's cradle. She had the radio on the field broadcast, and I could hear the description of the take-off: "—heavily laden. There—she rolls again. But she's making altitude. The blast has stopped splashing now, and is coming down in a beautiful fan of fire. A difficult take-off, even for the Golden Flash." A difficult take-off! Bunk!

I was watching the red bubble in the level, but I stole a glance to Claire Avery's face, and it wasn't so cool and standoffish now. And just then the bubble in the level bobbed way over, and I heard the girl at my side give a frightened little gasp. This wasn't cradle rocking any more—we were in a real roll!

I slapped her hands hard and grabbed the U-bar. I cut the underjets completely off, letting the ship fall free, then shot the full blast through the right laterals. It was damn close, I'm ready to swear, but we leveled, and I snapped on the underblast before we lost a hundred feet of altitude. And there was that inane radio still talking: "They're over! No—they've leveled again, but what a roll! She's a real pilot, this Golden Flash—"

I looked at her; she was pale and shaken, but her eyes were angry. "Golden Flash, eh?" I jeered. "The gold must refer to your money, but what's the flash? It can't have much to do with your ability as a pilot." But at that time I had no idea how pitifully little she really knew about rocketry.

She flared. "Anyway," she hissed, her lips actually quivering with rage, "the gold doesn't refer to color, Mr. Malaria Sands!" She knew that would hurt; the "Malaria" was some bright columnist's idea of a pun on my name. You see, malaria's popularly called Yellow Jack. "Besides," she went on defiantly, "I could have pulled out of that roll myself, and you know it."

"Sure," I said with the meanest possible sarcasm. We had considerable upward velocity now, and plenty of altitude, both of which tend toward safety because they give one more time to pull out of a roll. "You can take over again now. The hard part's over."

She gave me a look from those electric blue eyes, and I began to realize just what sort of trip I was in for. Coretti and Gogrol had indicated their unfriendliness plainly enough, and heaven knows I couldn't mistake the hatred in Claire Avery's eyes, so that left just Captain Henshaw. But the captain of the ship dare not show favoritism, so all in all I saw myself doomed to a lonely trip.

Lonely isn't the word for it. Henshaw was decent enough, but since Claire Avery had started with a long shift and so had the captain, they were having their free spells and meals on the same schedule, along with Gogrol, and that left me with Coretti. He was pretty cool, and I had pride enough left not to make any unwanted advances.

Gogrol was worse; I saw him seldom enough, but he never addressed a word to me except on routine. Yet there was something familiar about him—As for Claire Avery, I simply wasn't in her scheme of things at all; she even relieved me in silence.

Offhand, I'd have said it was the wildest sort of stupidity to send a girl with four men on a trip like this. Well, I had to hand it to Claire Avery; in that way she was a splendid rocketrix. She took the inconveniences of space routine without a murmur, and she was so companionable—that is, with the others—that it was like having a young and unusually entertaining man aboard.

And, after all, Gogrol was twice her age and Henshaw almost three times; Coretti was younger, but I was the only one who was really of her generation. But as I say, she hated me; Coretti seemed to stand best with her.

So the weary weeks of the journey dragged along. The Sun shrunk up to a disk only a fifth the diameter of the terrestrial Sun, but Jupiter grew to an enormous moon-like orb with its bands and spots gloriously tinted. It was an exquisite sight, and sometimes, since eight hours' sleep is more than I can use, I used to slip into the control room while Claire Avery was on duty, just to watch the giant planet and its moons. The girl and I never said a word to each other.

We weren't to stop at Io, but were landing directly on Europa, our destination, the third moon outward from the vast molten globe of Jupiter. In some ways Europa is the queerest little sphere in the Solar System, and for many years it was believed to be quite uninhabitable. It is, too, as far as seventy per cent of its surface goes, but the remaining area is a wild and weird region.

This is the mountainous hollow in the face toward Jupiter, for Europa, like the Moon, keeps one face always toward its primary. Here in this vast depression, all of the tiny world's scanty atmosphere is collected, gathered like little lakes and puddles into the valleys between mountain ranges that often pierce through the low-lying air into the emptiness of space.

Often enough a single valley forms a microcosm sundered by nothingness from the rest of the planet, generating its own little rainstorms under pygmy cloud banks, inhabited by its indigenous life, untouched by, and unaware, of all else.

In the ephemeris, Europa is dismissed prosaically with a string of figures: diameter, 2099 M.—period, 3 days, 13 hours, 14 seconds—distance from primary, 425,160 M. For an astronomical ephemeris isn't concerned with the thin film of life that occasionally blurs a planet's surface; it has nothing to say of the slow libration of Europa that sends intermittent tides of air washing against the mountain slopes under the tidal drag of Jupiter, nor of the waves that sometimes spill air from valley to valley, and sometimes spill alien life as well.

Least of all is the ephemeris concerned with the queer forms that crawl now and then right up out of the air pools, to lie on the vacuum-bathed peaks exactly as strange fishes flopped their way out of the Earthly seas to bask on the sands at the close of the Devonian age.

Of the five of us, I was the only one who had ever visited Europa—or so I thought at the time. Indeed, there were few men in the world who had actually set foot on the inhospitable little planet; Gunderson and his men were dead, save me and perhaps Kratska, and we had been the first organized expedition.

Only a few stray adventurers from Io had preceded us. So it was to me that Captain Henshaw directed his orders when he said, "Take us as close as possible to Gunderson's landing."

It began to be evident that we'd make ground toward the end of Claire's long shift, so I crawled out of the coffinlike niche I called my cabin an hour early, and went up to the control room to guide her down. We were seventy or eighty miles up, but there were no clouds or air distortion here, and the valleys crisscrossed under us like a relief map.

It was infernally hard to pick Gunderson's valley; the burned spot from the blast was long since grown over, and I had only memory to rely on, for, of course, all charts were lost with the *Hera*. But I knew the general region, and it really made less difference than it might have, for practically all the valleys in that vicinity were connected by passes; one could walk between them in breathable air.

After a while I picked one of a series of narrow parallel valleys, one with what I knew was a salt pool in the center—though most of them had that; they'd be desert without it—and pointed it out to Claire. "That one," I said, adding maliciously, "and I'd better warn you that it's narrow and deep—a ticklish landing place."

She flashed me an unfriendly glance from sapphire eyes, but said nothing. But a voice behind me sounded unexpectedly: "To the left! The one to the left. It—it looks easier."

Gogrol! I was startled for a moment, then turned coldly on him. "Keep out of the control room during landings," I snapped.

He glared, muttered something, and retired. But he left me a trifle worried; not that his valley to the left was any easier to land in—that was pure bunk—but it looked a little familar! Actually, I wasn't sure but that Gogrol had pointed out Gunderson's valley.

But I stuck to my first guess. The irritation I felt I took out on Claire. "Take it slow!" I said gruffly. "This isn't a landing field. Nobody's put up leveling poles in these valleys. You're going to have to land completely blind from about four hundred feet, because the blast begins to splash sooner in this thin air. You go down by level and guess, and Heaven help us if you roll her! There's no room for rolling between those cliffs."

She bit her lip nervously. The *Minos* was already rolling under the girl's inexpert hand, though that wasn't dangerous while we still had ten or twelve miles of altitude. But the ground was coming up steadily.

I was in a cruel mood. I watched the strain grow in her lovely features, and if I felt any pity, I lost it when I thought of the way she had treated me. So I taunted her.

"This shouldn't be a hard landing for the Golden Flash. Or maybe you'd rather be landing at full speed, so you could fall into a braking ellipse—only that wouldn't work here, because the air doesn't stick up high enough to act as a brake."

And a few minutes later, when her lips were quivering with tension, I said, "It takes more than publicity and gambler's luck to make a pilot, doesn't it?"

She broke. She screamed suddenly, "Oh, take it! Take it, then!" and slammed the U-bar into my hands. Then she huddled back in her corner sobbing, with her golden hair streaming over her face.

I took over; I had no choice. I pulled the Minos out of the roll Claire's gesture had put her in, and then started teetering down on the under jets. It was pitifully easy because of Europa's low gravitation and the resulting low falling acceleration; it gave the pilot so much time to compensate for side sway.

I began to realize how miserable little the Golden Flash really knew about rocketry, and, despite myself, I felt a surge of pity for her. But why pity her? Everyone knew that Claire Avery was simply a wealthy, thrill-intoxicated daredevil, with more than her share of money, of beauty, of adulation. The despised Jack Sands pitying her? That's a laugh!

The underblast hit and splashed, turning the brown-clad valley into black ashes and flame. I inched down very slowly now, for there was nothing to see below save the fiery sheet of the blast, and I watched the bubble on the level as if my life depended on it—which it did.

I knew the splash began at about four hundred feet in this density of air, but from then on it was guesswork, and a question of settling down so slowly that when we hit we wouldn't damage the underjets. And if I do say it, we grounded so gently that I don't think Claire Avery knew it until I cut off the bast.

She rubbed the tears away with her sleeve and glared blue-eyed defiance at me, but before she could speak, Henshaw opened the door. "Nice landing, Miss Avery," he said.

"Wasn't it?" I echoed with a grin at the girl.

She stood up. She was trembling and I think that under Earthly gravitation she would have fallen back into the pilot's seat, for I saw her knees shaking below her trim, black shorts.

"I didn't land us," she said grimly. "Mr. Sands put us to ground."

Somehow my pity got the best of me then. "Sure," I said. "It's into my shift. Look." It was; the chronometer showed three minutes in. "Miss Avery had all the hard part—"

But she was gone. And try as I would, I could not bring myself to see her as the hard, brilliant thrill seeker which the papers and broadcasts portrayed her. Instead, she left me with a strange and by no means logical impression of—wistfulness.

Life on Europa began uneventfully. Little by little we reduced the atmospheric pressure in the *Minos* to conform to that outside. First Coretti and then Claire Avery had a spell of altitude sickness, but by the end of twenty hours we were all acclimated enough to be comfortable outside.

Henshaw and I were first to venture into the open. I scanned the valley carefully for familiar landmarks, but it was hard to be sure; all these canyonlike ditches were much alike. I know that a copse of songbushes had grown high on the cliff when the *Hera* had landed, but our blast had splashed higher, and if the bushes had been there, they were only a patch of ashes now.

At the far end of the valley there should have been a cleft in the hills, a pass leading to the right into the next valley. That wasn't there; all I could distinguish was a narrow ravine cutting the hills to the left.

"I'm afraid I've missed Gunderson's valley," I told Henshaw. "I think it's the next one to our left; it's connected to this one by a pass, if I'm right, and this is one I came in several times to hunt." It recurred to me suddenly that Gogrol had said the left one.

"You say there's a pass?" mused Henshaw. "Then we'll stay here rather than chance another take-off and another landing. We can work in Gunderson's valley through the pass. You're sure it's low enough so we won't have to use oxygen helmets?"

"If it's the right pass, I am. But work at what in Gunderson's valley? I thought this was an exploring expedition."

Henshaw gave me a queer, sharp look, and turned away. Right then I saw Gogrol standing in the port of the *Minos*, and I didn't know whether Henshaw's reticence was due to his presence or mine. I moved a step to follow him, but at that moment the outer door of the air lock opened and Claire Avery came out.

It was the first time I had seen her in a fair light since the take-off at Young's Field, and I had rather forgotten the loveliness of her coloring. Of course, her skin had paled from the weeks in semidarkness, but her cadmium-yellow hair and sapphire-blue eyes were really startling, especially when she moved into the sun shadow of the cliff and stood bathed only in the golden Jupiter light.

Like Henshaw and myself, she had slipped on the all-enveloping ski suit one wore on chilly little Europa. The small world received only a fourth as much heat as steamy Io, and would not have been habitable at all, except for the fact that it kept its face always toward its primary, and therefore received heat intermittently from the Sun, but eternally from Jupiter.

The girl cast an eager look over the valley; I knew this was her first experience on an uninhabited world, and there is always a sense of strangeness and the fascination of the unknown in one's first step on an alien planet.

She looked at Henshaw, who was methodically examining the scorched soil on which the *Minos* rested, and then her glance crossed mine. There was an electric moment of tension, but then the anger in her blue eyes—if it had been anger—died away, and she strode deliberately to my side.

She faced me squarely. "Jack Sands," she said with an undertone of defiance, "I owe you an apology. Don't think I'm apologizing for my opinion of you, but only for the way I've been acting toward you. In a small company like this there isn't room for enmity, and as far as I'm concerned, your past is yours from now on. What's more, I want to thank you for helping me during the take-off, and"—her defiance was cracking a bit—"d-during the—the landing."

I stared at her. That apology must have cost her an effort, for the Golden Flash was a proud young lady, and I saw her wink back her tears. I choked back the vicious reply I had been about to make, and said only, "O.K. You keep your opinion of me to yourself and I'll do the same with my opinion of you."

She flushed, then smiled. "I guess I'm a rotten pilot," she admitted ruefully. "I hate take-offs and landings. To tell the truth, I'm simply scared green of the *Minos*. Up to the time we left Young's Field, I'd never handled anything larger than my little racing rocket, the *Golden Flash*."

I gasped. That wouldn't have been credible if I hadn't seen with my own eyes how utterly unpracticed she was. "But why?" I asked in perplexity. "If you hate piloting so, why do it? Just for publicity? With your money you don't have to, you know."

"Oh, my money!" she echoed irritably. She stared away over the narrow valley, and started suddenly. "Look!" she cried. "There's something moving on the peaks—like a big ball. And way up where there's no air at all!"

I glanced over. "It's just a bladder bird," I said indifferently. I'd seen plenty of them; they were the commonest mobile form of life on Europa. But of course Claire hadn't, and she was eagerly curious.

I explained. I threw stones into a tinkling grove of song-bushes until I flushed up another, and it went gliding over our heads with its membrane stretched taut.

I told her that the three-foot creature that had sailed like a flying squirrel was the same sort as the giant ball she had glimpsed among the airless peaks, only the one on the peaks had inflated its bladder. The creatures were able to cross from valley to valley by carrying their air with them in their big, balloonlike bladders. And, of course, bladder birds weren't really birds at all; they didn't fly, but glided like the lemurs and flying squirrels of Earth, and naturally, couldn't even do that when they were up on the airless heights.

Claire was so eager and interested and wide-eyed that I quite forgot my grudge. I started to show her my knowledge of things Europan; I led her close to the copse of song-bushes so that she could listen to the sweet and plaintive melody of their breathing leaves, and I took her down to the salt pool in the center of the valley to find some of the primitive creatures which Gunderson's men had called "nutsies," because they looked very much like walnuts with the hulls on. But within was a small mouthful of delicious meat, neither animal nor vegetable, which was quite safe to eat raw, since bacterial life did not exist on Europa.

I guess I was pretty exuberant, for after all, this was the first chance at companionship I'd had for many weeks. We wandered down the valley and I talked, talked about anything. I told her of the various forms life assumed on the planets, how on Mars and Titan and Europa sex was unknown, though Venus and Earth and Io all possessed it; and how on Mars and Europa vegetable and animal life had never differentiated, so that even the vastly intelligent beaked Martians had a tinge of vegetable nature, while conversely the song-bushes on the hills of Europa had a vaguely animal content. And meanwhile we wandered aimlessly along until we stood below the narrow pass or ravine that led presumably into Gunderson's valley to our left.

Far up the slope a movement caught my eye. A bladder bird, I thought idly, though it was a low altitude for one to inflate; they usually expanded their bladders just below the point where breathing became impossible. Then I saw that it wasn't a bladder bird; it was a man. In fact, it was Gogrol.

He was emerging from the pass, and his collar was turned up about his throat against the cold of the altitude. He hadn't seen us, apparently, as he angled down what mountaineers call a col, a ledge or neck of rock that slanted from the mouth of the ravine along the hillside toward the *Minos*. But Claire, following the direction of my gaze, saw him in the moment before brush hid him from view.

"Gogrol!" she exclaimed. "He must have been in the next valley. Stefan will want—" She caught herself sharply.

"Why," I asked grimly, "should your friend Coretti be interested in Gogrol's actions? After all, Gogrol's supposed to be a biologist, isn't he? Why shouldn't he take a look in the next valley?"

Her lips tightened. "Why shouldn't he?" she echoed. "I didn't say he shouldn't. I didn't say anything like that."

And thenceforward she maintained a stubborn silence. Indeed, something of the old enmity and coolness seemed to have settled between us as we walked back through the valley toward the *Minos*.

That night Henshaw rearranged our schedule to a more convenient plan than the requirements of space. We divided our time into days and nights, or rather into sleeping and waking periods, for, of course, there is no true night on Europa. The shifts of light are almost as puzzling as those on its neighbor Io, but not quite, because Io has its own rotation to complicate matters.

On Europa, the nearest approach to true night is during the eclipse that occurs every three days or so, when the landscape is illumined only by the golden twilight of Jupiter, or at the most, only by Jupiter and Io light. So we set our own night time by arbitrary Earth reckoning, so that we might all work and sleep during the same periods.

There was no need for any sort of watch to be kept; no one had ever reported life dangerous to man on little Europa. The only danger came from the meteors that swarm about the giant Jupiter's orbit, and sometimes came crashing down through the shallow air of his satellites; we couldn't dodge them here as we could in space. But that was a danger against which a guard was unavailing.

It was the next morning that I cornered Henshaw and forced him to listen to my questions.

"Listen to me, Harris," I said determinedly. "What is there about this expedition that everybody knows but me? If this is an exploring party, I'm the Ameer of Yarkand. Now I want to know what it's all about."

Henshaw looked miserably embarrassed. He kept his eyes away from mine, and muttered unhappily, "I can't tell you, Jack. I'm damned sorry, but I can't tell you."

"Why not?"

He hesitated. "Because I'm under orders not to, Jack."

"Whose orders?"

Henshaw shook his head. "Damn it!" he said vehemently. "I trust you. If it were my choice, you'd be the one I'd pick for honesty. But it isn't my choice." He paused. "Do you understand that? All right"—he stiffened into his captain's manner—"no more questions, then. I'll ask the questions and give the orders."

Well, put on that basis, I couldn't argue. I'm a pilot, first, last, and always, and I don't disobey my superior's orders even when he happens to be as close a friend as Henshaw. But I began to kick myself for not seeing something queer in the business as soon as Henshaw offered me the job.

If Interplanetary was looking for favorable publicity, they wouldn't get it by signing me on. Moreover, the government wasn't in the habit of reissuing a revoked pilot's license without good and sufficient reason, and I knew I hadn't supplied any such reason by loafing around brooding over my troubles. That alone should have tipped me off that something was screwy.

And there were plenty of hints during the voyage itself. True, Gogrol seemed to talk the language of biology, but I'll be dogged if Coretti talked like a chemist. And there was that haunting sense of familiarity about Gogrol, too. And to cap the climax was the incongruity of calling this jaunt an exploring expedition; for all the exploring we were doing we might as well have landed on Staten Island or Buffalo. Better, as far as I was concerned, because I'd seen Europa but had never been to Buffalo.

Well, there was nothing to be done about it now. I suppressed my disgust and tried as hard as I could to cooperate with the others in whatever project we were supposed to be pursuing. That was rather difficult, too, because suspicious-appearing incidents kept cropping up to make me feel like a stranger or an outcast.

There was, for instance, the time Henshow decided that a change in diet would be welcome. The native life of Europa was perfectly edible, though not all as tasty as the tiny shell creatures of the salt pools. However, I knew of one variety that had served the men of the *Hera*, a plantlike growth consisting of a single fleshy hand-sized member, that we had called liver-leaf because of its taste.

The captain detailed Coretti and myself to gather a supply of this delicacy, and I found a specimen, showed it to him, and then set off dutifully along the north—that is, the left—wall of the valley.

Coretti appeared to take the opposite side, but I had not gone far before I glimpsed him skirting my edge of the salt pool. That meant nothing; he was free to search anywhere for liver-leaf, but it was soon evident to me that he was not searching. He was following me; he was shadowing my movements.

I was thoroughly irritated, but determined not to show it. I plodded methodically along, gathering the fat leaves in my basket, until I reached the valley's far end and the slopes back and succeeded in running square into Coretti before he could maneuver himself out of a copse of song-bushes.

He grinned at me. "Any luck?" he asked.

"More than you, it seems," I retorted, with a contemptuous look at his all but empty basket.

"I had no luck at all. I thought maybe in the next valley, through the pass there, we might find some."

"I've found my share," I grunted.

I thought I noticed a flicker of surprise in his black eyes. "You're not going over?" he asked sharply. "You're going back?"

"You guessed it," I said sharply. "My basket's full and I'm going back."

I knew that he watched me most of the way back, because halfway to the *Minos* I turned around, and I could see him standing there on the slope below the pass.

Along toward what we called evening the sun went into our first eclipse. The landscape was bathed in the aureate light of Jupiter alone, and I realized that I'd forgotten how beautiful that golden twilight could be.

I was feeling particularly lonesome, too, so I wandered out to stare at the glowing peaks against the black sky, and the immense, bulging sphere of Jupiter with Ganymede swinging like a luminous pearl close beside it. The scene was so lovely that I forgot my loneliness, until I was suddenly reminded of it.

A glint of more brilliant gold caught my eye, up near the grove of song-bushes. It was Claire's head; she was standing there watching the display, and beside her was Coretti. While I looked, he suddenly turned and drew her into his arms; she put her hands against his chest, but she wasn't struggling; she was perfectly passive and content. It was none of my business, of course, but—well, if I'd disliked Coretti before, I hated him now, because I was lonely again.

I think it was the next day that things came to a head, and trouble really began. Henshaw had been pleased with our meal of indigenous life, and decided to try it again. This time Claire was assigned to accompany me, and we set off in silence. A sort of echo of the coolness that had attended our last parting survived, and besides, what I had seen last night in the eclipse light seemed to make a difference to me. So I simply stalked along at her side, wondering what to choose for the day's menu.

We didn't want liver-leaves again. The little nutsies from the salt pool were all right, but it was a half day's job to gather enough, and besides, they were almost too salty to be pleasant fare for a whole meal. Bladder birds were hopeless; they consisted of practically nothing except thin skin stretched over a framework of bones. I remembered that once we had tried a brown, fungoid lump that grew in the shade under the song-bushes; some of Gunderson's men had liked it.

Claire finally broke the silence. "If I'm going to help you look," she suggested, "I ought to know what we're looking for."

I described the lumpy growths. "I'm not so sure all of us will like them. Near as I can remember, they tasted something like truffles, with a faint flavor of meat added. We tried them both raw and cooked, and cooked was best."

"I like truffles," said the girl. "They're—"

A shot! There was no mistaking the sharp crack of a .38, though it sounded queerly thin in the rare atmosphere. But it sounded again, and a third time, and then a regular fusillade!

"Keep back of me!" I snapped as we turned and raced for the *Minos*. The warning was needless; Claire was unaccustomed to the difficulties of running on a small planet. Her weight on Europa must have been no more than twelve or fifteen pounds, one eighth Earth normal, and though she had learned to walk easily enough—one learned that on any space journey—she had had no opportunity to learn to run. Her first step sent her half a dozen feet in the air; I sped away from her with the long, sliding stride one had to use on such planets as Europa.

253

I burst out of the brush into the area cleared by the blast, where already growth had begun. For a moment I saw only the *Minos* resting peacefully in the clearing, then I reeled with shock. At the air lock lay a man—Henshaw—with his face a bloody pulp, his head split by two bullets.

There was a burst of sound, voices, another shot. Out of the open air lock reeled Coretti; he staggered backward for ten steps, then dropped on his side, while blood welled up out of the collar of his suit. And standing grimly in the opening, an automatic smoking in his right hand, a charged flame pistol in his left, was Gogrol!

I had no weapon; why should one carry arms on airless Europa? For an instant I stood frozen, appalled, uncomprehending, and in that moment Gogrol glimpsed me. I saw his hand tighten on his automatic, then he shrugged and strode toward me.

"Well," he said with a snarl in his voice, "I had to do it. They went crazy. Anerosis. It struck both of them at once, and they went clean mad. Self-defense, it was."

I didn't believe him, of course. People don't get anerosis in air no rarer than Europa's; one could live his whole life out there without ever suffering from air starvation. But I couldn't argue those points with a panting murderer armed with the most deadly weapon ever devised, and with a girl coming up behind me. So I said nothing at all.

Claire came up; I heard her shocked intake of breath, and her almost inaudible wail, "Stefan!" Then she saw Gogrol holding his guns, and she flared out, "So you did it! I knew they suspected you! But you'll never get away with it, you—"

She broke off under the sudden menace of Gogrol's eyes, and I stepped in front of her as he raised the automatic. For an instant death looked squarely at both of us, then the man shrugged and the evil light in his eyes dimmed.

"A while yet," he muttered. "If Coretti dies—" He backed to the air lock and pulled a helmet from within the *Minos*, an air helmet that we had thought might serve should we ever need to cross the heights about a blind valley.

Then Gogrol advanced toward us, and I felt Claire quiver against my shoulder. But the man only glared at us and spat out a single word. "Back!" he rasped. "Back!"

We backed. Under the menace of that deadly flame pistol he herded us along the narrow valley, eastward to the slope whence angled the ravine that led toward Gunderson's valley. And up the slope, into the dim shadows of the pass itself, so narrow in places that my outstretched hands could have spanned the gap between the walls. A grim, dark, echo-haunted, and forbidding place; I did not wonder that the girl shrank against me. The air was thin to the point of insufficiency, and all three of us were gasping for breath.

There was nothing I could do, for Gogrol's weapons bore too steadily on Claire Avery. So I slipped my arm about her to hearten her and inched warily along that shadowy canyon, until at last it widened, and a thousand feet below stretched a valley—Gunderson's valley, I knew at once. Far away was the slope where the *Hera*, had rested, and down in the lower end was the heart-shaped pool of brine.

Gogrol had slipped on the helmet, leaving the visor open, and his flat features peered out at us like a gargoyle's. On he drove us, and down into the valley. But as he passed the mouth of the ravine, which by now was no more than a narrow gorge between colossal escarpments that loomed heavenward like the battlements of Atlantis, he stooped momentarily into the shadows, and when he rose again I fancied that a small sound like the singing of a tea kettle followed us down the slope. It meant nothing to me then.

He waved the automatic. "Faster!" he ordered threateningly. We were down in the talus now, and we scrambled doggedly among the rocks and fallen debris. On he drove us, until we stumbled among the boulders around the central pond. Then, suddenly, he halted.

"If you follow," he said with a cold intensity, "I shoot!" He strode away not toward the pass, but toward the ridge itself, back along the slopes that lay nearest the *Minos*, hidden from view in the other valley. Of course, Gogrol could cross those airless heights, secure in this helmet, carrying his air supply like the bladder birds.

He seemed to seek the shelter of an ascending ridge. As the jutting rock concealed him, I leaped to a boulder.

"Come on!" I said. "Perhaps we can beat him through the pass to the ship!"

"No!" screamed Claire, so frantically that I halted. "My Lord, no! Didn't you see the blaster he left?"

The singing tea kettle noise! I had barely time to throw myself beside the girl crouching behind a rock when the little atomic bomb let go.

I suppose everybody has seen, either by eye or television, the effect of atomic explosions. All of us, by one means or the other, have watched old buildings demolished, road grades or canals blasted, and those over forty may even remember the havoc-spreading bombs of the Pacific War. But none of you could have seen anything like this, for this explosion had a low air pressure and a gravitation only one eighth normal as the sole checks to its fury.

It seemed to me that the whole mountain lifted. Vast masses of crumbling rock hurtled toward the black sky. Bits of stone, whistling like bullets and incandescent like meteors, shot past us, and the very ground we clung to heaved like the deck of a rolling rocket.

When the wild turmoil had subsided, when the debris no longer sang about us, when the upheaved masses had either fallen again or had spun beyond Europa's gravitation to crash on indifferent Jupiter, the pass had vanished. Mountain and vacuum hemmed us into a prison.

Both of us were slightly stunned by the concussion, although the thin atmosphere transmitted a strangely high pitched sound instead of the resounding b-o-o-m one would have heard on the Earth. When my head stopped ringing, I looked around for Gogrol, and saw him at last seven or eight hundred feet up the slope of the mountain. Anger surged in me; I seized a stone from the margin of the pool, and flung it viciously at him. One can throw amazing distances on small worlds like Europa; I watched the missile raise dust at his very feet.

He turned; very deliberately he raised the automatic, and stone splinters from the boulder beside me stung my face. I dragged Claire down behind the shelter, knowing beyond doubt that he had meant that bullet to kill. In silence we watched him climb until he was but a tiny black speck, nearing the crest.

He approached a bladder bird crawling its slow way along the airless heights. Up there the creatures were slow as snails, for their flight membranes were useless in the near vacuum. But they had normally no enemies on the peaks.

I saw Gogrol change his course purposely to intercept the thing. Intentionally, maliciously, he kicked a hole in the inflated bladder, collapsing it like a child's balloon. He stood watching while the miserable creature flopped in the agonies of suffocation, then moved methodically on. It was the coldest exhibition of wanton cruelty I had ever witnessed.

Claire shuddered; still in silence we watched the man's leisurely progress along the ridge. There was something in his attitude that suggested searching, seeking, hunting. Suddenly he quickened his pace, and then halted abruptly, stooping over what looked to me like a waist-high heap of stones, or perhaps merely a hummock on the ridge.

But he was burrowing in it, digging, flinging stones and dirt aside. And at last he stood up; if he held anything, distance hid it, but he seemed to wave some small object at us in derisive triumph. Then he moved over the crest of the hills and disappeared.

Claire sighed despondently; she seemed very little like the proud and rather arrogant Golden Flash. "That settles it," she murmured disconsolately. "He's got it, and he's got us trapped so we're quite helpless."

"Got what?" I asked. "What was he digging for up there?"

Her blue eyes widened in amazement. "Don't you know?"

"I certainly don't. I seem to know less about this damn trip than anybody else on it."

She gazed steadily at me. "I knew Stefan was wrong," she said softly. "I don't care what you were when you wrecked the *Hera*, Jack Sands; on this trip you've been decent and brave and a gentleman."

"Thanks," I said dryly, but I was a little touched for all that, because, after all, the Golden Flash was a very beautiful girl. "Then suppose you let me in on a few of the secrets. For instance, what was Coretti wrong about? And what did Gogrol dig for?"

"Gogrol," she said, watching me, "was digging in Gunderson's cairn."

I looked blank. "Gunderson's what? This is news to me."

She was silent for a moment. "Jack Sands," she said at last, "I don't care what Stefan or the government or anybody thinks of you. I think you're honest, and I think you've had an injustice done you somehow, and I don't believe you were to blame in the *Hera* crash. And I'm going to tell you all I know about this matter. But first, do you know the object of Gunderson's expedition to Europa?"

"I never knew it. I'm a pilot; I took no interest in their scientific gibberish."

She nodded. "Well, you know how a rocket motor works, of course. How they use a minute amount of uranium or radium as catalyst to release the energy in the fuel. Uranium has low activity; it will set off only metals like the alkalis, and ships using uranium motors burn salt. And radium, being more active, will set off the metals from iron to copper, so ships using a radium initiator usually burn one of the commoner iron or copper ores."

"I know all that," I grunted. "And the heavier the metal, the greater the power from its disintegration."

"Exactly." She paused a moment. "Well, Gunderson wanted to use still heavier elements. That required a source of rays more penetrating than those from radium, and he knew of only one available source—Element 91, protactinium. And it happens that the richest deposits of protactinium so far discovered are those in the rocks of Europa, so to Europa he came for his experiments."

"Well?" I asked. "Where do I fit in this mess?"

"I don't quite know, Jack. Let me finish what I know, which is all Stefan would tell me. Gunderson succeeded, they think; he's supposed to have worked out the formula by which protactinium could be made to set off lead, which would give much more power than any present type of initiator. But if he did succeed, his formula and notes were destroyed when the *Hera* crashed!"

I began to see. "But what—what about that cairn?"

"You really don't know?"

"I'll be double damned if I do! If Gunderson built a cairn, it must have been that last day. I had the take-off, so I slept through most of it. But—why, they did have some sort of ceremony!"

"Yes. Gunderson mentioned something about it when your ship touched at Junopolis on Io. What the government hopes is that he buried a copy of his formula in that cairn. They do, you know. Well, nobody could possibly know of the location except you and a man named Kratska, who had disappeared.

"So Interplanetary, which is in bad shape anyway because of some stock transactions, was ordered to back this expedition with you as pilot—or at least, that's what Stefan told me. I guess I was taken along just to give the corporation a little more publicity, and, of course, Stefan was sent to watch you, in hopes you'd give away the location. The formula's immensely valuable, you see."

"Yeah, I see. And how about Gogrol?"

She frowned. "I don't know. Stefan hinted that he had some connections with Harrick of Interplanetary, or perhaps some hold over him. Harrick insisted on his being a member."

"The devil!" I exploded suddenly. "He knew about the cairn! He knew where to look!"

Her eyes grew wide. "Why, he did! He's—could he be the representative of some foreign government? If we could stop him! But he's left us absolutely helpless here. Why didn't he kill us?"

"I can guess that," I said grimly. "He can't fly the *Minos* alone. Henshaw's dead, and if Coretti dies—well, one of us is due for the job of pilot."

A tremor shook her. "I'd rather be dead, too," she murmured, "than to travel with him alone."

"And I'd rather see you so," I agreed glumly. "I wish to heaven you had stayed out of this. You could be home enjoying your money."

"My money!" she flashed. "I haven't any money. Do you think I take these chances for publicity or thrills or admiration?"

I gaped; of course, I'd thought exactly that.

She was literally blazing. "Listen to me, Jack Sands. There's just one reason for the fool things I do—money! There isn't any Avery fortune, and hasn't been since my father died. I've needed money desperately these last two years, to keep the Connecticut place for my mother, because she'd die if she had to leave it. It's been our family home for two hundred years, since 1910, and I won't be the one to lose it!"

It took a moment to adjust myself to what she was saying. "But a racing rocket isn't a poor man's toy," I said feebly. "And surely a girl like you could find—"

"A girl like me!" she cut in bitterly. "Oh, I know I have a good figure and a passable voice, and perhaps I could have found work in a television chorus, but I needed real money. I had my choice of two ways to get it: I could marry it, or I could gamble my neck against it. You see which way I chose. As the Golden Flash, I can get big prices for endorsing breakfast foods and beauty preparations.

That's why I gambled in that race; my racing rocket was all I had left to gamble with. And it worked, only"—her voice broke a little—"I wish I could stop gambling. I—I hate it!"

It wasn't only pity I felt for her then. Her confession of poverty had changed things; she was no longer the wealthy, unattainable being I had always imagined the Golden Flash to be. She was simply a forlorn and unhappy girl; one who needed to be loved and comforted. And then I remembered the evening of the eclipse, and Coretti's arms about her. So I gazed for an instant at the sunlight on her hair, and then turned slowly away.

After a while we gathered some liver-leaves and cooked them, and I tried to tell Claire that we were certain to be rescued. Neither of us believed it; we knew very well that Gogrol would carry no living companion to Io; whoever helped him run the *Minos* would certainly be dead and cast into space before landing. And we knew that Gogrol's story, whatever it might be, would not be one likely to encourage a rescue party. He'd simply report us all dead somehow or other.

"I don't care," said Claire. "I'm glad I'm with you."

I thought of Coretti and said nothing. We were just sitting in glum silence near the fire when Gogrol came over the hills again.

Claire saw him first and cried out. Despite his helmet, neither of us could mistake his broad, squat figure. But there was nothing we could do except wait, though we did draw closer to the area of wild and tumbled boulders about the central pool.

"What do you suppose—" asked Claire nervously.

"Coretti may have died, or may be too injured to help."

Pain twisted her features. "Yes, or—Oh, I know, Jack! It's that Gogrol can't plot a course. He can pilot; he can follow a course already laid out, but he can't plot one—and neither can Stefan!"

Instantly I knew she must be right. Piloting a ship is just a question of following directions, but plotting a course involves the calculus of function, and that, let me tell you, takes a mathematician. I could do it, and Claire handled a simple route well enough—one had to in rocket racing—but astrogators were not common even among pilots.

You see, the difficulty is that you don't just point the ship at your destination, because that destination is moving; you head for where the planet will be when you arrive. And in this case, assuming Gogrol meant to make for Io, a journey from Europa to that world meant speeding in the direction of the colossal mass of Jupiter, and if a rocket once passed the critical velocity in that direction—good night!

A hundred feet away Gogrol halted. "Listen, you two," he yelled, "I'm offering Miss Avery the chance to join the crew of the *Minos*."

"You're the crew," I retorted. "She's not taking your offer."

Without warning he leveled his revolver and fired, and a shock numbed my left leg. I fell within the shelter of a boulder, thrusting Claire before me, while Gogrol's bellow followed the crash of his shot: "I'll shut your mouth for you!"

There began the weirdest game of hide and seek I've ever played, with Claire and me crawling among the tumbled boulders, scarcely daring to breathe. Gogrol had all the advantage, and he used it. I couldn't stand upright, and my legs began to hurt so excruciatingly that I was afraid each minute of an involuntary groan forcing its way through my lips. Claire suffered with me; her eyes were agonized blue pools of torment, but she dared not even whisper to me.

Gogrol took to leaping atop the boulders. He glimpsed me, and a second bullet struck that same burning leg. He was deliberately hunting me down, and I saw it was the end.

We had a momentary shelter. Claire whispered to me, "I'm going to him. He'll kill you otherwise, and take me anyway."

"No!" I croaked. "No!"

Gogrol heard, and was coming. Claire said hastily, "He's—bestial. At least I can plot a course that will—kill us!" Then she called, "Gogrol! I'll surrender."

I snatched at her ankle—too late. I went crawling after her as she strode into the open, but her steps were too rapid. I heard her say, "I give up, if you won't—shoot him again."

Gogrol mumbled, and then Claire's voice again, "Yes. I'll plot your course, but how can I cross the peaks?"

"Walk," he said, and laughed.

"I can't breathe up there."

"Walk as far as you can. You won't die while I take you the rest of the way."

There was no reply. When I finally crept into the open, they were a hundred feet up the slope.

Helpless, raging, pain-maddened, I seized a stone and flung it. It struck Gogrol in the back, but it struck with no more force than if I'd tossed it a dozen feet on Earth. He spun in fury, thrust the screaming Claire aside, and sent another bullet at me. Missed me, I thought, though I wasn't sure for pain had numbed me. I couldn't be sure of anything.

Claire saw that I still retained some semblance of consciousness. "Goodby!" she called, and added something that I could not hear because of the red waves of pain, but I knew Gogrol laughed at it. Thereafter, for what seemed like a long time, I knew only that I was crawling doggedly through an inferno of torture.

When the red mist lifted, I was only at the base of the rise. Far above I could see the figures of Claire and Gogrol, and I perceived that though he strode with easy steps, protected by his helmet, the girl was already staggering from breathlessness. While I watched, she stumbled, and then began to struggle frantically and spasmodically to jerk away from him. It wasn't that she meant to break her promise, but merely that the agonies of suffocation drove her to attempt any means of regaining breathable air.

But the struggle was brief. It was less than a minute before she fainted, passed out from air starvation, and Gogrol slung her carelessly under one arm—as I said, she weighed, about twelve pounds on Europa—and pressed on. At the very crest he paused and looked back, and in that thin, clear air I could see every detail with telescopic distinctness, even to the shadow he cast across Claire's drooping golden head.

He raised the revolver to his temple waved it at me with a derisive gesture and then flung it far down the mountainside toward me. His meaning was unmistakable; he was advising me to commit suicide. When I reached the revolver, there was a single unused cartridge in the clip; I looked up, tempted to try it on Gogrol himself, but he was gone across the ridge.

Now I knew all hope was gone. Perhaps I was dying from that last bullet anyway, but whether I were or not, Claire was lost, and all that remained for me was the madness of solitude, forever imprisoned by empty space in this valley. That or—suicide.

I don't know how many times I thought of that single cartridge, but I know the thought grew very tempting after a few more hours

of pain. By that time, for all I knew, the *Minos* might have taken off
on its dash to death, for the roar of its blast could not carry over the
airless heights, and it would be so high and small by the time I could
see it above the hills that I might have missed it.

If only I could cross those hills! I began to realize that more important than my own life was Claire's safety, even if it meant saving
her for Coretti. But I couldn't save her; I couldn't even get to her
unless I could walk along the hills like a bladder bird.

Like a bladder bird! I was sure that it was only the delirium of
fever that suggested that wild thought. Would it work? I answered
myself that whether it worked or failed it was better than dying here
without ever trying.

I stalked that bladder bird like a cat. Time after time I spent long
minutes creeping toward a copse of song-bushes only to have the
creature sail blithely over my head and across the valley. But at last I
saw the thing crouched for flight above me; I dared not delay longer
lest my wounds weaken me too much for the trial of my plan, and
I fired. There went my single cartridge.

The bladder bird dropped! But that was only the beginning of
my task. Carefully—so very carefully—I removed the creature's
bladder, leaving the vent tube intact. Then, through the opening
that connects to the bird's single lung, I slipped my head, letting the
bloody rim contract about my throat.

I knew that wouldn't be air-tight, so I bound it with strips torn
from my clothing, so closely that it all but choked me. Then I took
the slimy vent tube in my mouth and began an endless routine.
Breathe in through the vent tube, pinch it shut, breathe out into
the bladder—over and over and over. But gradually the bladder
expanded with filthy, vitiated, stinking, and once breathed air.

I had it half filled when I saw that I was going to have to start if
I were to have a chance of living long enough for a test. Breathing
through the vent tube as long as there was air enough, peering dully
through the semitransparent walls of the bladder, I started crawling
up the hill.

I won't describe that incredible journey. On Earth it would have
been utterly impossible; here, since I weighed but eighteen pounds,
it was barely within the bounds of possibility. As I ascended, the
bladder swelled against the reduced pressure; by the time I had to

start breathing the fearful stuff, I could feel it escaping and bubbling through the blood around my neck.

Somehow I made the crest, almost directly above the *Minos*. It was still there, anyway. Gogrol hadn't come this way, and now I saw why. There was a sheer drop here of four hundred feet. Well, that only equaled fifty on Earth, but even fifty—But I had to try it, because I was dying here on the peaks. I jumped.

I landed with a wrench of pain on my wounded leg, but much more lightly than I had feared. Of course! Jumping down into denser air, the great bladder had acted like a parachute, and, after all, my weight here was but eighteen pounds. I crawled onward, in agony for the moment when I could cast off the stinking, choking bladder.

That moment came. I had crossed the peaks, and before me lay the *Minos*. I crawled on, around to the side where the air lock was. It was open, and a voice bellowed out of it. Gogrol!

"You'll trick me, eh!" he screeched. "You'll lay a course that will crash us! We'll see! We'll see!" There came the unmistakable sound of a blow, and a faint whimper of pain.

Somewhere I found the strength to stand up. Brandishing the empty automatic, I swayed into the air lock, sliding along the walls to the control room.

There was something about the figure that bent in the dusk above a sobbing girl that aroused a flash of recognition. Seeing him thus in a shadowed control room with the sun shields up—I knew what I should have known weeks ago. Gogrol was—Kratska!

"Kratska!" I croaked, and he whirled. Both he and Claire were frozen into utter rigidity by surprise and disbelief. I really think they were both convinced that I was a ghost.

"How—how—" squeaked Gogrol, or rather Kratska.

"I walked across. I'd walk across hell to find you, Kratska." I brandished the gun. "Get outside. Get out and get away quick, if you expect to escape the blast. We're leaving you here until police from Io can pick you up—on that *Hera* matter among others." I spoke to the dazed Claire. "Close the air lock after him. We're taking off."

"Jack!" she cried, comprehending at last. "But Stefan's wired to a tree out there. The blast will incinerate him!"

"Then loose him, and for Heaven's sake, quickly!"

But no sooner had she vanished than Kratska took his chance. He saw how weak I was, and he gambled on the one shot he thought remained in the magazine of my weapon. He rushed me.

I think he was mad. He was screaming curses. "Damn you!" he screeched. "You can't beat me! I made you the goat on the *Hera*, and I can do it here."

And I knew he could, too, if he could overcome me before Claire released Coretti. She couldn't handle him, and we'd all be at his mercy. So I fought with all the life I had left, and felt it draining out of me like acid out of burette. And after a while it was all drained, and darkness filled up the emptiness.

I heard curious sounds. Someone was saying, "No, I'll take off first and lay out the course after we reach escape velocity. Saves time. We've got to get him to Io." And a little later, "Oh, Lord, Stefan! If I roll her now—Why am I such a rotten pilot?" And then there was the roar of the blast for hours upon hours.

A long time later I realized that I was lying on the chart room table, and Coretti was looking down at me. He said, "How you feel, Jack?" It was the first time he had used my name.

"O.K.," I said, and then memory came back. "Gogrol! He's Kratska!"

"He was," said Coretti. "He's dead."

"Dead!" There went any chance of squaring that *Hera* mess.

"Yep. You killed him, smashed in his head with that automatic before we could pull you off. But he had it coming."

"Yeah, maybe, but the *Hera*—"

"Never mind the *Hera*, Jack. Both Claire and I heard Kratska admit his responsibility. We'll clear you of that, all right." He paused. "And it might make you feel a little more chipper if I tell you that we got the formula, too, and that there's a reward for it that will leave us sitting in the clover field, even split three ways. That is, Claire keeps insisting on three ways; I know I don't deserve a split."

"Three ways is right," I said. "It'll give you and Claire a good send-off."

"Me and Claire?"

"Listen, Coretti. I didn't mean to, but I saw you the evening of the eclipse. Claire didn't look as if she was fighting you."

He smiled. "So you saw that," he said slowly. "Then you listen. A fellow who's asking a girl to marry him is apt to hold the girl a little close. And if she's got any heart, she doesn't push him away. She just says no as gently as possible."

"She says no?"

"She did that time. I'd bet different with you."

"She—she—" Something about the familiar sound of the blast caught my attention. "We're landing!"

"Yeah, on Io. We've been landing for two hours."

"Who took off?"

"Claire did. She took off and kept going. She's been sitting there fifty hours. She thinks you need a doctor, and I don't know a damn thing about running a rocket. She's taken it clear from Europa."

I sat up. "Take me in there," I said grimly. "Don't argue. Take me in there!"

Claire barely raised her eyes when Coretti slid me down beside her. She was all but exhausted, sitting there all those weary hours, and now up against her old terror of landing. "Jack, Jack!" she whispered as if to herself. "I'm glad you're better."

"Honey," I said—her hair did look like honey—"I'm taking half the U-bar. Just let me guide you."

We came down without a roll, and landed like a canary feather. But I hadn't a thing to do with it; I was so weak I couldn't even move the U-bar, but she didn't know that. Confidence was all she needed; she had the makings of a damn good pilot. Yeah; I've proved that. She is a damn good pilot. But all the same, she went to sleep in the middle of our first kiss.

Tidal Moon*

Bob Amherst shivered a little despite the heated interior of the autobus, but grinned none the less as he made out the frosty towers of Hydropole. He was always glad to return to the polar city, if only for the pleasure of staring up at buildings piled story upon story like those of his native Syracuse on a gray planet some half a billion miles sunward.

Hydropole, south polar city of Jupiter's third major moon, Ganymede, was a chilly town at all seasons with its thirty degree Fahrenheit mean, and its variation of only ten degrees. But it was certainly the only settlement on the satellite that was worthy of the title of city.

Amherst had served four terrestrial years on the watery planet as collector for Cree, Inc., moving from town to town gathering the precious medicinal moss, to take it finally to Hydropole, the rocket port, for transhipment to Earth.

He was one of the hundreds of such collectors for the giant company, each with his own route, each picking his own way from town to town, riding his hipp (the sea-horse of Ganymede, *Hippocampus Catamiti*) through the wild torrents of the afterfloods, past mountains whose locked valleys were apt to spill countless millions of tons of water upon him with no warning save the crash of the bursting mountain walls.

Only in Hydropole was there safety. Situated on the south pole, it escaped the great wash of water which, due to the strong gravitational pull of Jupiter, every three months encircled the tiny moon.

As a result, only in, and for a few miles around Hydropole, was there vegetation. Save for the strange moss, *cree*, which clung so close to the rocky crevices of the mountain that even the raging tides could not pry it loose, not a living plant broke the great, gray expanse of rock.

So, on Ganymede, all life revolved about the blue moss, cree.

---

*Story completed by Helen Weinbaum after her husband's death.

267

Ages back, the Nympus, natives of Ganymede, had carried it deep
underground where, piled layer after layer on the solid rock around
the doomed villages, it served as earth. There, with seeds garnered
from the small area about Hydropole, they grew the small variety of
food on which they lived.

Above ground the moss had a deep, blue color. As litmus paper,
colored by the Earth lichen, *rocella tinctoria* shows the presence of
acid or alkali by its color change, so Ganymedian cree reacted to the
ammoniated atmosphere of the planet. The air underground, however, artificially produced, had little ammonia content, and there the
moss was red. Indeed, even the mountain cree, after being washed
by the hydrogen containing waters of the flood, for a short time
showed red.

Up to a short time ago, the gatherers had had only a limited time
in which to pick the moss. Red cree lacked the medicinal quality
of the blue in which, partly because of its chemical reaction to the
ammoniated air and partly due to the latent eggs it harbored, lay
the curative power so much in demand on Earth. Now, however,
Carl Kent had evolved a formula by which cree picked red might
be endowed with the healing power of the blue. So, in the area
around his small trading station in Aquia, red as well as blue cree
was gathered.

The autobus turned silently down the wide street of Hydropole.
Robot-guided, insulated from noise and cold, it was certainly preferable to traveling by hipp. But hipp travel was unavoidable from
here on. The trip to Aquia verged on the wet side of the planet—the
side from which burst the mighty floods. So, added to steep, rocky
drops, impassable by autobus, were the dank, muddy flats which
only the hipp could traverse.

Amherst zipped the parka-like garment closed about his long,
muscular body, pulling the sillicell visor before his rugged features
before he stepped from the autobus. The cold was penetrating. Even
vacuum suits—misnamed, for they did not work on the principle of
the thermos bottle but had the inner layer held from the outer by
thin, radium-warmed wires—were scant enough protection.

Turning, he watched the Nympus unload the autobus. There
was something revolting about them as they waddled about on
their short legs, jointed only at hip and ankle; their heads, flaring

into strange mushroom tops almost hiding their noseless faces; their arms, long and webbed to their bodies.

"Umhurr." He turned to the queer, throaty croak. It was the Nympus' version of his name.

"Yes?"

"Go see." One long, webbed arm pointed in the direction of the rocket port office.

"Oh, thanks." He walked toward the circular glass dome, under which MacGowan sat looking, for all the world, like some giant god's experiment under a bell jar.

"Hello, Bob. How goes it?" MacGowan's round, smooth-cheeked face was sharp contrast to Amherst's rather angular, wind-beaten features.

"As always. What's new here?"

"Nothing. Except there's a rumor that they've discovered red cree on Io."

"Io? That's Jupiter's first major moon."

"Right. And a skin exporting company called Ionian Products has it tied up as tightly as Cree, Inc., has Ganymede."

"Well, red cree is no good, Mac. There's no curative power in it." MacGowan leaned back in his chair.

"You forget," he answered, "that since Carl Kent's discovery we pick red cree on Ganymede."

"Yes. I did forget." Amherst stretched his long legs before him. "I haven't been to Aquia since the formula's been in use there." For a moment his thoughts dwelt on the small domed settlement, on the young girl, Carol Kent, with her pixie face and laughing eyes. "Say," he sat up suddenly as the full implication of MacGowan's words penetrated his mind, "that's bad. Those birds will glut the market!"

"Well, so far it's only a rumor. And Carl Kent is the only one who knows his formula anyway. Still, you'd better tell him when you get to Aquia. I got the dope two months ago."

Amherst shook his head.

"That's ironic. In 2083, two months' old news has to be carried by hipp. It's like going back to post medievalism."

"It is. But you know radio is useless on the flood belt of Ganymede. The atmosphere's too disturbed. It's only at Hydropole that we can get reception." MacGowan's eyes caught a notation on his desk. "Oh, I almost forgot. I've got company for you to Aquia."

"Who?"

"Kirt Scaler." He spoke into his desk transmitter. "Ask Mr. Scaler to come in."

"I don't know what he's here for," he continued, turning back to Amherst, "but his papers are in order and I don't think he'll cause you much trouble."

Yes, Amherst agreed, as Kirt Scaler entered, this man certainly looked as if he could take the hazardous journey to Aquia in his stride. His red-brown eyes, on a level with Amherst's own, had the serene out-flowing look of the hardened adventurer. One saw him gazing long distances, accepting danger, meeting and conquering it. His teeth flashed white against tawny skin, and the steely grip of his hand did not belie the reckless strength of his appearance.

"Business trip?" Amherst asked.

"No, just touring."

Amherst smiled at the idea of anyone's taking a pleasure trip on Ganymede.

"You've traveled by hipp, I suppose."

"No. This is the first time I've left earth."

Strange how mistaken one can be, Amherst reflected. He could have sworn this man had been hardened by such adventure as existed, nowadays, only on the planets.

"In that case," he smiled, "you've got something interesting in store for you tomorrow."

Flood time was coming near. Seasickness and Amity, the two hipps, were restless. Always, at flood time, the instinct to be free rose in them, filling them with a wild yearning to buck the mountainous tide of water, to swim fiercely to the top, there to sport with the large Gamma Rorqual, that ferocious whale-like mammal with the long spiked tooth from which only the hipps, because of their hard, outer shell, were safe.

Even when the flood was not imminent, hipps were not the easiest riding. They walked with a queer, undulating motion: the two feet forward first while the body rested on the tail, then the tail brought to meet the feet. On their twenty-foot long body, the rider had to pick his seat carefully. If he sat too near the head, the animal would not move: too near the tail meant that he would be jarred at every step. A little behind the legs was best. There he could ride with a minimum of jolting.

Night was coming on. Though the men had been out only a few hours, the sky was already darkening. Days were short in Ganymede. Thus far, they had spoken intermittently; the discomforts of travel occupied much of their attention. Scaler, it turned out, was a rather taciturn man, revealing little of his past and nothing of his reasons for touring Ganymede. He rode silently, looking neither right nor left, keeping his eyes fastened on the green-scaled back of Amity, his hipp.

There was, however, not much to look at. If one excepted the scattered stilt houses in the flats, nothing broke the monotony of mountains, rocks and mudholes. Still, Amherst reflected, stilt houses ought to be interesting to a man from Earth. He remembered the first time he had seen the square boxlike hives made of compressed cree, standing on twenty-foot poles—how he had wondered if, indeed, they could survive the flood. No one had stayed above ground long enough to find out.

Carl Kent, however, with his inquiring mind, had found out how they worked. At the first ten feet of water, the Nympus drew the stilts up through the sides of the house, allowing it to float. But no one, save the Nympus who lived inside one, could say for sure whether it survived the flood, for the water carried it so far from the original starting point that there was no way of checking.

Suddenly a scream broke the air—a raucous, harsh scream, but, unmistakably, a scream of pain. They were rounding down a mountain and, as they covered the next turn, they came upon a hideous struggling mass of flesh. While from a slimy, flat body long tentacles gripped the rock, others clung to the writhing form of a Nympus. Creeping, in the manner of a snake, they encircled his flailing arms, drawing the heavy body with its long center spear greedily toward the native.

Scaler stared horrified, his face paling behind the visor. The animal looked like some grotesque nightmare. Amherst drew his gun and fired. There was a soft hiss, before the thing collapsed, spilling its yellowish blood on the rock.

The Nympus sprang to his feet, chattering wildly, then, rushing to a crevice in the mountain where the cree showed blue, placed a handful of the wet moss on his wounds.

For a moment the tentacles waved feebly; then, falling into the sticky mess which had once been a body, lay still. Only the long spear retained definite shape.

"There," Amherst said, "is evolution in a nutshell."

"It hadn't evolved very far," Scaler breathed deeply. "It looked like a jelly fish with a horn."

"Perhaps it was once jellyfish," Amherst returned. "It's hard to tell now. It has metamorphosed too often from its original form. Like the butterfly which goes through successive stages from egg to larva, larva to chrysalis, chrysalis to butterfly, this, starting out as an amoeba-like protoplasm and, like the amoeba, absorbing food at every part of its body, changes form each time it surrounds its prey."

"You mean it doesn't absorb, it becomes what it eats?"

"Exactly. This amoeba attaches itself to a higher form of life and becomes that form, always, however, retaining its original power of becoming its next prey. But, here's the strange thing: certain characteristics of its previous meal may remain even after it has adopted another form. This one, for example, was part Gamma Rorqual, as you can see from the spike, part land leet—it had land leet tentacles—and if we hadn't come along, it would have been part Nympus as well."

"Funny planet," Scaler remarked.

Slowly, they continued down the mountain, reaching now and then a bleak plateau which wind and water had swept to glassy smoothness. The flying mammals, which always heralded the flood, swooped overhead.

As they crossed one of the plateaus, above the roar of the wind they heard a loud beating. A mammoth bird, jet black against the mountain, its two sets of wings flapping alternately at a spread of thirty feet, came toward them. Flying the gale, it neared them quickly. For a second, the men sat transfixed; then, wrenching themselves from the coma of fear, drew guns. Seasickness beat her tail frantically, jolting Amherst's gun from his hand.

"Don't shoot, Scaler," he yelled, diving after the spinning weapon. "You'll never kill it."

Before Amherst could reach his gun, Scaler fired. His shot, far to the right, missed the body. Yet the bird dropped, thrashing, to the ground. Again he fired and, with a scream so shrill it hurt their eardrums, it lay still.

"Whew! That was close," Amherst said. "Say, how did you know?"

"Know what?"

"Know enough to break the wing muscle."

"It's a Blanket Bat," Scaler answered. "It doesn't kill, but it draws electrical energy from its prey and leaves it weak to the point of helplessness. That's the only way you can ground them too. There's a similar species on Io."

"Right." Amherst looked speculatively at his companion. "But I was sure a man with no planetary experience would have aimed left, at the heart. That would have been unfortunate. For, as you undoubtedly know inasmuch as you hit it squarely on your second shot, the heart of the Blanket Bat is in the center."

Scaler shrugged.

"Even on Earth," he answered, "those things get around."

When they reached the bottom of the mountain, it was too dark to go further. Jupiter shone pale and ghostlike in the night sky and far off, a tiny pinprick in the black, was Earth. The wind had risen, so they tethered Seasickness and Amity to a rock and took shelter in the lee of the mountain. A few land leets, disturbed by their presence, dragged themselves slowly from the rock. Amherst, who always preferred fresh food to the concentrates of his kit, caught and cooked them in the ray stove for dinner. The octopus-like animals were good eating, so afterward the two men settled down contentedly for the night.

The next morning, as soon as the sun had risen, they started on their way. Today their travel was over the flats where, every now and then, a stilt house stood high on the bleak landscape. Once in awhile they found a Nympus lying lazily before one, but they did not stop. In the outlying sections, Nympus spoke a Ganymedian patois which few Earthmen understood.

As they splashed along, Scaler broke a long silence to ask, "By the way, Amherst, just what is cree?"

"Cree is the source of the drug *crephine* used in the treatment of all the malignant diseases. It not only deadens pain, but heals."

"But there's so much of it on Ganymede," Scaler objected, "it doesn't seem as if there'd be use for all of it."

"It takes over a bale of cree to produce one ounce of crephine," Amherst answered, "And in the past ten years the demand for it has increased enormously. Besides, on most of Ganymede the time for picking is short."

"You mean on account of the floods? But why most of Ganymede then? Why isn't gathering time short on the whole planet?"

"Because," Amherst started—then, "I was thinking of Hydropole," he amended. "The floods don't cover that but, of course, there's little cree there. Yes, the time for gathering is short on account of the floods."

"And on account of the color change after the floods?" Scaler asked slyly.

"Yes, that's true. How did you know?"

"I guess I read it somewhere. By the way," he asked casually, "what's the trader at Aquia like?"

"Carl Kent? He's a nice fellow. Lives there with his daughter, Carol."

"Is that where we stay out the flood?"

"Yes. They're glad enough to see a new face."

"There's no way of leaving the village during flood time, I suppose."

"None whatever. You couldn't open a door against the pressure of the water even if you wanted to, which no one does. Once underground, you've got to stay there!"

Scaler hummed to himself a few minutes before he spoke again.

"When does this next flood pass?" he asked finally.

"Let's see." Amherst shifted his position on Seasickness' back. "It's due in two days now. You can probably leave Aquia about May twelfth, terrestrial date. By the way," he faced Scaler squarely, "how do you expect to get back to Hydropole? You'd never find your way alone."

"Oh, I figured that out with MacGowan. I'll wait there until you make the trip to Dripwater and Weepy Hills. You always stop at Aquia on your way back, don't you?"

"Yes. But I can't see what you expect to do for two months in the settlement at Aquia."

"More sightseeing, perhaps," Scaler smiled.

When night came on, they did not stop. Flood time was too close to waste time in rest. Now, near the wet side of the planet, mudholes occurred frequently; though the hipps braved them valiantly, progress was slow. The wind had increased and, riding against it, they were forced to hold their seats tightly.

After a few hours, they came to a mountain. Knowing the dark, rocky climb would slow them still more, Amherst decided to cut around on the flats. Riding the uncharted ground, half asleep, suddenly he felt a bright light shining on him. In the mountain's shadow, the night was black and the unexpected glare shocked him awake. From the side a huge, black bulk, that blinding light in its center, moved toward him. A grinding sound, as of rocks rubbed one on the other, deadened his ears, above everything, he was conscious of the light.

Scaler, riding nearest the mountain, continued forward, but Seasickness suddenly switched her course, heading straight for the glare. Amherst jerked the guiding rein, but she did not turn. Then, as the beam fell full on him, he felt himself being drawn. Ahead was the light, bright, warm, hypnotizing—at either side was nothing.

He felt his mind sinking, felt his body go lax, lean forward. Then something flew before his eyes. For a second, the light was blocked off, and in that second his strength flowed back. At once, he realized the thing ahead had been drawing his will from him— that if he were ever to get away, he must shield Seasickness' eyes and pull the rein hard. Now the bulk was so close that he could make out a great, yawning hole, inside which a piston-like rod moved up and down.

As he stared, a rock rolled into the hole and, on the descent of the piston, was ground to bits. With a mighty effort, he shut his eyes. Then, raising his visor to the freezing air, he gripped Seasickness' reins in his teeth and, blindfolding her with his hands, pulled with all the strength he had in him. She swerved.

Now—if the thing didn't change direction, they were safe. Otherwise they were sunk. Without looking full into the light, Amherst watched breathing deeply to still the pounding of his heart. Safe! The thing moved steadily forward, unaware that its prey had escaped.

Scaler, outside the hypnotic power of the light, asked what the trouble was.

"We couldn't change direction while the light shone on us," Amherst told him, "But that wasn't the strangest thing. That beacon or animal or whatever it was, ate rocks! Outside of the Pyramid Builder of Mars, I've never heard of that before."

"Evidently it wanted to add you to its mineral diet," Scaler observed.

"And it almost did." Amherst laughed in relief. "So it must be the extreme of omnivorous, needing life as well as minerals to keep it going."

"Just another verse in the saga of evolution." Scaler shifted his position on Amity's back and closed his eyes for a few minute's rest.

***

Two terrestrial days later they sighted the domes of Aquia which, huddled on the Ganymedian waste, resembled the half-buried eggs of some giant bird, left ages back to turn the same slate gray as the rest of the landscape. Faint on each dome were the outlines of a door, sole evidence of human habitation in the clustered mounds. Still, to the two men, stiff and tired after days and nights of riding, the sight of the small, domed village was cheering.

"So this is Aquia," Scaler sighed. "Aquia of Ganymede. It sounds almost Biblical."

From far away came a dull roar. "Just to make it more so," Amherst answered, "here's the flood."

Bob Amherst looked admiringly at the slim girl in the trading station.

"Is it you, Carol, or is it what you're going to be ten years hence?" he said lightly, his eyes twinkling. Last time he had seen the girl, she had been a gangling child of sixteen or so; now she was a blonde goddess, rounded, appealing, vital. Her golden hair and blue eyes were in sharp contrast to the drabness of the trading station. She seemed to have grown up all at once.

"I hope it's both." She shut the door against the freezing air.

"Why, you're beautiful." To hide his astonishment, he spoke to her as a child. "Your hair is combed, and your face is clean, and—"

"And you're too fresh." Her eyes turned to Scaler.

"Oh, I forgot. This is Mr. Scaler, Carol."

276

Scaler's brown eyes swept over her appreciatively.

"Where's your father?" Amherst asked.

Carol's face sobered.

"Father didn't come back last flood time. I'm carrying on."

Didn't come back! There was no need to say more. Everyone knew what it meant to be caught away from the domed village when the torrents of water came thundering down. It was tough! Carl Kent could be spared least of the traders on Ganymede. And it was a pity that he had to go so soon after his precious formula had been completed. It was too bad for Carol, too. She was all alone now.

They followed her through the underground passage which led from the trading station to her living quarters. Under the domes, so exact in their engineering that they could withstand the terrific pressure of water during the flood, the air was warm. They removed their vacuum suits.

Outside Carol's door which, like all the rest opened onto a central square, Nympus and Earthmen scurried about to make ready for the deluge. Like a huge ant hill, the village teemed with activity. Tanks had to be made ready to store the water from which their oxygen came. The nitrogen mixers had to be checked so that they would be prepared to blend perfectly the two gases and insure the air supply for the duration of the flood.

While Amherst went about his business, looking over the cree, tethering the hipps in their floating cages anchored to the village, seeing that all was ready for the tidal rush, Scaler and Carol sat together in the warm, Earth like room that Carl Kent had furnished.

"When you said you were carrying on here, the most important trading station on Ganymede, I could hardly believe it." Scaler's warm, brown eyes rested admiringly on the girl's face.

"I have to. I'm the only one who could. Father was caught in the flood before he had a chance to set up laboratories in the other stations."

"Was he planning to? I should think it would be dangerous to let too many people learn his secret."

"Not at all," Carol answered. "There's no cree anywhere but Ganymede, and Cree, Inc., covers the entire planet."

"Oh, I didn't know." He moved over to sit next to her. "It's too bad for you to bury yourself here," he said abruptly. "You don't belong. You should be living on Earth—seeing, doing and, most important, being seen."

Carol smiled. She had never visited the small pinprick in the black called Earth, but she had read of it, read of its cities built into the air, its underground highways, its beautiful women. "Tell me about the World," she said softly. "Is it so different from Ganymede?"

"So very different, I don't know where to begin."

"I've always wanted to see New York." She looked enviously at Scaler.

Amherst entered the room in time to hear her last words.

"It's nothing but froth, Carol," he broke in. "There are many things on Earth we wouldn't want on Ganymede."

Scaler smiled.

"Gangsters and greed," he said, "went out long ago."

"Gangsters did," Amherst answered shortly. Suddenly the thought of Scaler's presence during the long flood period annoyed him. Perhaps, without knowing, he had been looking forward to being alone with Carol. Now, he realized that Scaler, shut in the underground village with nothing to occupy his time, would make that impossible.

At that moment, deep underground as they were, they heard the crash of mountain walls as the flood came pouring down. As always, in the village of the cree-gatherers, it was quiet, almost menacingly quiet, as if everyone stood impassive, waiting to see whether or not this time the domes would hold. For a few hours, until the air tanks were working efficiently, they would have this strange, dead sensation in their heads.

As Amherst had foreseen, Carol and Kirt Scaler spent much time together. Often they walked the narrow tunnels leading to the farms and there stood on the flat-covered expanse, like some tremendous basement, the water valves overhead dripping flood water brought from the surface to the crop below. And sometimes they stood by the nitrogen mixers, deafened by the mighty roar as the artificial air came pouring out.

Indeed, Scaler seemed to have perpetual interest where life at Aquia was concerned. Often Amherst entered a room to hear him questioning Carol about various technicalities. But at other times, he fought clear of anything to do with Ganymede and, instead, talked at length about the world Carol had never seen. At such times, she listened fascinated, a faraway look in her blue eyes as if they saw, through Scaler's, the things he was describing.

As the days passed, Amherst became more and more aware of Scaler's attraction for the girl though, as yet, he was not sure whether it was the man himself who charmed her or the world he came from. Thinking to find out, he waited for one of the few times that he and Carol were alone together. Then, walking over and taking her chin in his hand, he asked, "Just how much do you know about Kirt Scaler, Carol?"

"Not very much. What difference does it make?"

"It might make a lot. It might be a revival of the old, old stories of the city slicker and the farmer's daughter."

She jerked away angrily.

"Mind your own business, Bob Amherst."

He put his arm around her.

"You're my business."

"Since when."

Lacking an answer, he pulled her to him and kissed her roughly. She jerked away, flouncing angrily from the room.

He watched her go absentmindedly, not so much concerned with her anger as with trying to decide what it would mean to him if she were indeed serious where Kirt Scaler were concerned.

Since Carl's death, he had felt an increasing sense of responsibility for Carol—and something more too. For Carol, even as a young girl, had aroused in him a more than friendly interest. So the thought of her falling in love and, perhaps, marrying someone else was painful. Besides, the more he saw of Scaler, the more he realized how uncommunicative the man really was. He had not yet given reason for his trip to Aquia other than the obviously ridiculous one of *touring*.

And surely, attractive as Carol was, tales of her charm had not drawn him almost four hundred million miles through space. Still, aside from Scaler's interest in the life at Aquia, so far Carol seemed his only excuse for coming.

★★★

For the next few days, Carol treated Amherst coolly, never giving

279

him a chance to speak to her alone and continuing to spend much time in Scaler's company. Amherst seldom entered a room but that he saw the golden head in close proximity to the brown, and heard, with a twinge at his heart, the soft note in Scaler's voice.

As the days passed, however, Scaler seemed to become restless. Often he wandered the village alone, not waiting for Carol. Once Amherst found him scanning a terrestrial calendar and figuring on a small pad he carried. Consequently, Amherst's heart lightened a bit, though, as yet, he could not break through Carol's reserve.

Just a day and a half before complete ebb, he was sitting alone in the trading station when the girl entered.

"It's funny," she said abruptly, "I can't find the formula. I know it by heart, of course, but the paper is gone."

"Gone!" Amherst jumped to his feet, recalling, for the first time in weeks, the rumor that red cree had been found on Io.

"Don't get excited, Bob," she said coldly, seating herself leisurely. "What would anyone want it for?"

"They've discovered red cree on Io." Amherst was halfway out the door. What a fool he had been not to tell Carol, especially after he had been told to bring the news to Carl. She hurried to follow him.

Inside the laboratory, he turned to face her.

"It's my fault," he groaned. "I should have told you. News of your father's death must have knocked it from my mind. Are you sure it's gone? Nothing seems to have been disturbed."

"Yes. I kept it here." She opened a drawer.

"Who has been in this room, Carol? Who, besides yourself, has ever been here?"

"Some Nympus gatherers, when Father was alive."

"Who else?" Amherst paced the floor impatiently. "They haven't the intelligence to steal it." He paused for a moment. "Did you ever bring Scaler in?" He asked.

"Yes, once. He wanted to see red cree under treatment."

"Of course he did." Amherst turned abruptly. "Stupid of me not to have suspected it. He was undoubtedly sent here by Ionian Products just to get the formula. Touring, indeed! No wonder he recognized the Blanket Bat!"

"What shall we do?" Carol rummaged helplessly through the papers in the drawer.

"Search the village. He can't possibly leave until the water ebbs and that's at least a day and a half away. He must be here somewhere. There's no place else to go."

They hunted the village for Scaler, but the search was fruitless. It seemed impossible for a man to disappear in the small underground village, and yet five precious hours had gone and they had found no trace of him. It was incredible.

"Bob, what will it mean to Cree, Inc., if Ionian Products exports blue cree to Earth?" Carol asked anxiously after a while.

"Severe competition, a glutted market, shrinkage in sales, eventual bankruptcy, perhaps. You know there's an enormous expenditure required to keep the company going on Ganymede."

"Then we've got to find Kirt Scaler. Father would—would have hated that!"

"I know." Amherst stood undecided for a moment. "There's only one thing left for us to do though: we must start over. Somewhere, we have missed him."

Three hours later, footsore and weary, they returned again to the farms, their second quest as unproductive as the first.

Far in the distance a lone Nympus worked the field, at the entrance to the tunnel.

"You know strange Earthman?" Amherst spoke wearily to the toiling Nympus.

"Yeh." The crusty, mushroom head nodded rapidly.

"Have you seen him today?"

"Yeh." The head nodded again.

"Where!" Amherst grasped the green, scaled shoulder. The Nympus waved an arm vaguely toward the outskirts of the farm, to the bare rock wall where the farm ended.

"Where?" Amherst shook the native's shoulder excitedly.

"In Iticht phulph."

"In locked valve," Amherst shouted. "Of course. It's the only place he could be."

At that moment, far down the farm, almost where the rock wall began, a stream of water shot heavily to the earth. "That's the one," Amherst cried. "That valve was just opened to the outside. Carol," he cried as he started running toward the water, "get me a vacuum suit and bring it here—quickly!"

When he reached the spot, the water had thinned to a narrow stream. Evidently ebb was over. A mound of cree earth beneath the pipe opening showed how Scaler had managed to reach his hiding place. Through the slanting man-sized aqueduct, Amherst could see light from above. Undoubtedly Scaler had just escaped. Probably knowledge that the Nympus farmer had seen him, had made him aware of the danger of hiding there longer.

However, it was impossible to follow until Carol returned with the vacuum suit. He waited impatiently, comforting himself with the thought that Scaler could not get very far in the torrents of the afterflood on foot, and that, as no one had been above ground since the flood started, there was no hipp tethered outside to carry him. As relief for his impatience, Amherst piled more cree on the mound Scaler had left. It would save time when Carol arrived with the suit if he could raise himself easily to the opening in the rock ceiling.

At last Carol, clad in a vacuum suit herself, came running across the field.

"You can't come," Amherst told her. Hurriedly he stepped into the garment she handed him. Without replying she stood watching him draw his long body through the pipe opening.

Creeping up the slanting hundred yard aqueduct as quickly as possible, Amherst emerged dripping to the wet Ganymedian surface. A few seconds later, Carol appeared.

"Go back." He was trying to free his sillicell visor of the mud it had gathered on the ascent through the wet pipe. Scaler was not in sight.

A rocket ship, however, was visible in the sky. He started walking, Carol beside him. Scaler might easily be in the valley on the other side of the hill.

"What's that ship doing?" Carol asked. "It can't land here."

"It looks as if it's going to."

True, the ship was coming lower. A mile or so in front of them, it lost altitude rapidly. Wonderingly, they watched it, knowing no rocket ship had ever landed in the muddy areas of Ganymede until, straining their eyes, they saw a ladder unfurling from its fuselage. So that was going to be the manner of Scaler's escape!

Amherst started to run, splashing through the water and mudholes which slowed his progress. Carol followed, gaping with the exertion of pulling herself in the heavy suit through the sticky mud.

Hopelessly, they saw the ship dip behind the brow of the hill, to rise a second later with a black dot clinging to its downflung ladder. As they watched disconsolately, the red speck soared high in the sky. Red! The color of the space ships of Io! For, since the signing of the Interplanetary Peace Treaty, each planet colored its space ships differently. There was no doubt now where their formula was going.

Carol sat down despondently. For a few moments neither spoke. At last they rose and, silently, started to walk toward the village of the cree gatherers.

"What was the formula, Carol?" Amherst asked finally. "As long as Scaler is taking it to Ionian Products, I might as well know."

"It was simple," the girl said. "It merely duplicated the chemical changes taking place in the moss after the passing of the flood. The color change in cree is due to ammonia in the air, as you know. Well, part of the medicinal value lies there and part in latent eggs deposited in the moss. Father's formula was exactly that: an equal mix of blue gallnuts and ammonia."

Bob Amherst stopped abruptly. "Gallnuts, did you say? Blue gallnuts?"

Yes. It's the name given the vegetable excrescence which forms around the egg of the gall-ant. We breed gall-ants, pulverize their eggs and—"

"Carol!" Amherst pounded his knee in delight. "We're saved! Much good our formula will do them," He waved toward Io, ghostlike in the pale sky.

"Why? They've got the cree on Io."

"They've got the cree all right, and they've got the formula—but they haven't got the ants! And they'll never get them either. Gall-ants can't live in methane—I remember that from Biology—and the air on Io is mostly methane!"

"Why can't they?"

"Because their systems are geared to breathing ammoniated air—exactly the opposite of methanated air. Don't you see? Ammonia is a base: methane is a hydrocarbon, an acid."

"Well, can't they make ammonia?"

"Of course. But where will they get the ants? Gall-ants breed only on Ganymede, in Ganymedian cree. To get the ants they'd have to buy our cree and, inasmuch as they'd have to use the ant eggs to get the gallnuts to make the formula to turn their cree blue," Amherst drew a long breath, "the ants couldn't reproduce. So they'd have to continue buying our cree to get the ants to get the nuts to get—"

"I see," Carol interrupted. "Never mind the rest."

"Besides which," Amherst continued, "even after they succeeded in turning the cree blue—if they succeeded, which they wouldn't, inasmuch as we wouldn't sell them the cree to get the ants to get the nuts and so forth—they'd have to keep the methanated air of Io away from it. Otherwise it would turn red again. Think what that means: hundreds of bales of cree vacuum-packed to shield them from contact with the outside air. It would raise the cost of production so enormously, they couldn't compete with us anyway."

"I guess you're trying to say they can't use the formula. Anyway, I'm relieved." Carol sighed.

"So am I—for another reason, though."

"What other reason is there?"

"That it was only the formula Scaler wanted after all."

"What do you mean, only?" She turned to face him before the smooth, round dome of the trading station.

"For awhile I thought it was you."

"Oh that." Carol scuffed one foot on the ground. "Yes, he wanted me too. I refused him."

"But why? You seemed to like him well enough at first."

"I did," she said slowly, "at first. It was that kiss changed my mind—that rough one."

CLASSIC SF FROM LEONAUR
AVAILABLE IN SOFTCOVER OR HARDCOVER WITH DUST JACKET

Lightning Source UK Ltd.
Milton Keynes UK
UKOW02f1807260716

279295UK00001B/42/P